AF446577

Praise for **THE INDEPENDENT**

"*The Independent* is a fresh take on the age-old concerns around the two-party political system in the United States. A pulse-pounding, ripped from the headlines political thriller sure to entertain and entice readers on both sides of the aisle."
—Eric Bishop, author of *The Body Man* and *Breach of Trust*

"Brad Goodwin's tale of Beltway power-struggles is a gripping, fast-paced ride! With many twists and turns, a leading man you can't help rooting for, and a cast of villains to boot, this page turner will keep you at the edge of your seat. Could Mr. Goodwin have found the answer to the current quagmire that is Washington? This is political intrigue at its best!"
—L.D. Beyer, author of *In Sheep's Clothing*

"A protest-inspired candidate becomes something more in Goodwin's debut political novel. The plot is propelled by intriguing ideas, and political junkies of all stripes will likely get swept up in Jack's revolutionary journey."
—*Kirkus Reviews*

"A thrilling page turner of a novel by a highly imaginative and talented first-time author. The premise is original and the character development shows the talent of a seasoned writer."
—Jonathan Harries, chairman emeritus of Foote, Cone & Belding (FCB) and author of *The Tailor of Riga*

"Embedded with the fire of promise, the passion of purpose, and a moral and ethical compass, *The Independent* is highly recommended reading for fans of political thrillers who will find it thought-provoking and surprising. There is little predictable here—Brad Goodwin's debut thriller is full of eminently satisfying twists and turns."

—D. Donovan, Senior Reviewer, *Midwest Book Review*

"Brad Goodwin's debut novel is a tightly woven glimpse of a future where party politics have rendered the U. S. government nonfunctional. As the populace revolts, a long shot independent candidate comes from nowhere. When his momentum builds, those in power will stop at nothing to shut him down. Packed with subplots, twists, and diverse characters, *The Independent* builds to a full-out sprint that will leave readers inspired and trying to catch their breath."

— Mark Anthony Powers, MD, author of
the Phineas Mann medical thriller series

"Jack, a disgraced prosecutor turned professor, gets caught on camera when his 'what if' political musings go unexpectedly viral. *The Independent* will wake up the disenchanted hearts of a broken nation, but not before transporting readers into a maze of plot twists."

—Paula Erskine, author

"Brad Goodwin channels simmering discontent with politics as usual, adds relatable characters and believable situations, then spins them into a masterful and very relevant political thriller. *The Independent* is a slow burn with twists and turns marching to a heart-pounding climax that will leave readers begging for a sequel."

—Mikael Carlson, political thriller novelist

THE
INDEPENDENT

THE
INDEPENDENT

BRAD
GOODWIN

A POLITICAL THRILLER

Copyright © 2024 by Brad Goodwin

All rights reserved. No part of this publication may be reproduced, stored, or transmitted in any form or by any means without written permission of the publisher or author, except in the case of brief quotations embodied in critical articles and reviews.

The Independent is a work of fiction. Other than any actual historical events, people, and places referred to, all names, characters, and incidents are from the author's imagination. Any resemblances to persons, living or dead, are coincidental, and no reference to any real person is intended.

Published by
Sweet Briar Press

To contact the author or order books in bulk, visit www.bradgoodwinauthor.com

Editor: John Robert Marlow
Book cover design: Adrijus Guscia, Rocking Book Covers
Book interior design: Christy Day, Constellation Book Services
Author photo credit: Marea Kavanagh

ISBN (paperback): 979-8-9910315-0-9
ISBN (ebook): 979-8-9910315-1-6

Library of Congress Control Number: 2024917142

Printed in the United States of America

For Marea,
Because there is no dress rehearsal.

PROLOGUE

July, 2040

ASSISTANT DISTRICT ATTORNEY Jack Sanborn checked his watch for the third time in as many minutes. The dark-paneled Manhattan courtroom was filled to capacity but strangely quiet, with only the occasional whisper to break the silence.

Jack sat at the prosecutor's table, thinking, *She shouldn't have to do this twice.* Putting young victims on the stand was an unfortunate necessity in most assault cases, but putting them there twice meant the prosecution had screwed up. Jack had fumbled at the worst possible moment in the highest-profile case of his career, and the whole courtroom knew it. As did the larger audience that had been following the case for weeks on LiveCourtTV.

Jack cursed his mistake. Answering questions about the circumstances surrounding her sexual assault had been hard enough on seventeen-year-old Gracie the first time. Now, because of him—she had to do it again. A sense of shame settled over him like a damp fog. The sense of subdued excitement at the defense table made it worse. They couldn't wait for a second chance to discredit the victim, or try to. *It was your job to protect her,* he thought, *not give those bastards another shot at her.*

Jack glanced over at the jury: six women, six men. He could see that seven were disappointed in him, three had moved past that to anger, and the other two just wanted the damned trial over with so they could go home.

He checked his watch again. Gracie should have been brought back in by now. She must be stalling, and who could blame her. The lead counsel for the defense cleared his throat and pulled himself up from his chair, smoothing his silk tie as he stood. He looked to Jack. "Mr. Assistant District Attorney," he said, "will the *alleged* victim be joining us at any point this morning?" Jack wanted to ask the man whether his conscience may too be joining them, but he already knew the answer.

He heard the doors at the back of the courtroom open. He would have turned around, but that would have meant looking into the eyes of Gracie's parents, who were seated behind him. A moment later, a police officer walked quickly past and approached the bench. Jack heard more movement behind him and turned around. A second officer was quietly escorting Gracie's parents toward the big double doors as a murmur rose in the courtroom. Where the hell was Gracie?

The first officer whispered something to the judge, who glared at Jack for a moment before declaring a recess, thumping his gavel and storming from the room.

CHAPTER 1

Four Years Later: July 2044

JACK RUBBED HIS EYES, taking in the pale morning light that seeped through the bedroom blinds. "Main bedroom, light level one," he said and sat up. The bedside lamps brightened, giving the room a soft glow. Jack swung his legs off the bed and glanced over his shoulder. The covers on the other side of the mattress looked undisturbed. The pillows were missing.

He pushed his lean, six-foot frame upright and padded to the bathroom. He gazed into the mirror for a moment, wondering if the lines around his green eyes had deepened in the past week alone. *Forty-five seems a bit early for wrinkles*, he thought, though the face staring back at him was still boyish. Jack brushed aside the thick brown bangs that kept his appearance somewhere between handsome and nerdish. Flecks of grey had begun to appear but were not yet obvious to anyone but him.

He showered and dressed quickly, liberated his phone from the bathroom charger and made his way down the hall. He paused, drawn to the first door on the left, and went inside. The smell of the new carpet was still invigorating. Until seven weeks ago, it had been a sign of new things to come.

He looked at the crib, still home to the small collection of tissue-filled gift bags from the baby shower two months ago. Above them, a dangling mobile kept watch. Jack cocked his head and reached out to adjust the angle of the mobile, which seemed a little crooked. He stood there watching until the dangling figures ceased to move. He knew he'd have to deal with the baby's room, but today was not the day. He stepped out and quietly closed the door behind him.

Jack descended the wooden steps of the small North Carolina Colonial that had been the perfect home for the past four years. It didn't hurt that the place was far removed from his former life in Manhattan. He paused in the living room doorway. The missing pillows and a blanket were neatly bundled at the end of the couch. His wife Sarah sat cross-legged on the floor in pale blue pajamas, her long blonde hair failing to conceal the redness under her eyes. The floor around her was a disaster area in soft pastels, littered with infant clothes and toys. Jack recognized the clothing: Sarah's own baby clothes, discovered in an overlooked trunk of her mother's belongings back in Minnesota. The items had taken on new meaning for Sarah, as if the opportunity to put them to use brought back a small piece of the mother she'd lost as a teenager.

"Hey," Jack said softly, "I missed you last night."

Sarah didn't look up. "Mmm."

"What are you doing, Babe?"

"I'm packing it all away," Sarah said, folding a tiny sleeve. "Like you said, I need to get over it."

Jack bit down on his lip. "That's not at all what I said, Sarah, and you know that."

Sarah's gaze drifted upward, and Jack could see the naked grief in her eyes, still as raw as before. "I figure this is a step in the right direction," she said. "What more do you want?"

The words landed like a blow. Jack wished he could stay home from work. "I said we might need to see someone to help us get through it," he said. "That's not the same as saying you need to get over it. I know it takes time."

"Then maybe you can give me some tips, Jack. Because you seem to be moving on without a hitch."

Jack flinched inwardly. "That's not true. I just don't have the lux . . . I just don't process things the same way you do."

Sarah's eyes darkened. "You were going to say you don't have the luxury. Weren't you?"

Jack exhaled and wiped a hand across his mouth, as if the motion might somehow erase his clumsy choice of words. "Sarah, please . . . "

His wife's eyes were suddenly brimming with tears. "There's no coffee," she blurted, dropping the onesie she'd been holding. "I forgot to order more."

"It's fine," Jack stumbled, unsure whether to be grateful for the *non sequitur.* "I'll get some on campus." He watched as Sarah retrieved the tiny garment and began to fold it again. "Will you text me later?" he asked.

"Sure . . . If I can think of something to say, I'll text you."

Jack watched as she finished with the onesie and placed it in the worn cardboard box that had resided first in her mother's attic, and then in a storage locker. He had no idea what the right words for such a moment might be and settled uselessly on "I need to go." He scooped up his well-worn messenger bag from the sofa table. "I'll bring Thai food tonight."

Sarah nodded absently and pressed a baby blanket to her cheek.

Jack headed for the door.

Once outside, he paused on the front steps, trying to summon the right words so he could go back inside and say something that would matter. The right words at the right time had always been a gift of his, first as a lawyer in New York, and now as a law professor at the University of North Carolina. But in the aftermath of a stillborn child and a wife's near-death from a ruptured placenta, there probably were no right words. He knew he should feel grateful that Sarah was still alive, but he mostly felt useless and unable to help the woman he loved, as she spiraled toward he-didn't-know-what.

He looked around, seeking a target for his frustration. He settled on a knee-high weed in the flowerbed and jerked it from the ground. "Damn weeds."

The car door slid open at his approach, welcoming him into the vehicle's first class-like interior. "Destination: work," Jack said. The engine whispered to life, and the car hummed down the tree-lined street.

Jack pulled a tablet from his messenger bag. With no steering wheel in front of him, he crossed his legs and leaned back, going over the notes he'd prepared for his second-year Constitutional Law class. He had everything committed to memory by the time the car reached the freeway and set the tablet aside. "News," he said. "Big screen." He felt his body pressed back into the seat as the car accelerated onto the freeway. The windows tinted nearly black, Jack's view of the traffic ahead replaced by the latest newscast. It was better than watching hundreds of vehicles speeding along mere inches apart. He'd grown up before that advancement and had never quite gotten used to it. In fact, the sight made him nauseous.

On the windshield-screen before him, a newscaster with piercing blue eyes droned on as images played beside her. *"—as the federal government shutdown approaches month seven with no end in sight. Despite growing unrest, both parties still appear unable or unwilling to compromise on the budget or any other topic, and President Perez's latest effort to broker an agreement between Democrats and Republicans has reportedly failed . . . "*

Jesus, Jack thought. He was beginning to think both parties were actually insane, preferring economic collapse to compromise.

"—unemployment reached another high this month as collateral impacts of the shutdown have spiked widespread job cuts and business closures. Crime rates are rising almost as fast as interest rates, and federal low-income assistance programs—including food and health care assistance—remain unfunded . . . "

The bad news just kept coming. Jack's mind flashed briefly to an article he'd penned for the *UNC Law Review* during the previous record shutdown, three years earlier. He'd called for antitrust laws to be applied to the two-party system, which had long ago written its own rules aimed at preventing any form of political competition. Reaction to the premise had been mixed, and when the three-month shutdown ended a week after publication, the article was forgotten.

"*—the SoMAD rally scheduled to take place later today in Washington DC is expected to be the largest DC protest in history. Local police have called on agencies from surrounding areas to help maintain order during the event . . .*"

The car slowed for the off-ramp. Jack cleared the side windows, and the outside world returned. SoMAD. *Somebody Make A Decision.* SoMAD protests had been held in every state, but it seemed to make no difference. The people in charge—assuming anyone actually *was* in charge—simply ignored them, along with everyone else. Jack felt sure that wouldn't be the case had their own livelihoods been threatened.

Jack gazed out the window as the car rolled down historic Franklin Street in the heart of Chapel Hill. The once bustling thoroughfare was now home to more closed shops than open ones. Their boarded-up facades were a depressing reminder of better times behind. SoMAD graffiti was scrawled across most of the buildings, the letters jagged and angry. The place bore little resemblance to the picturesque campus town Jack had come to know four years before.

"*—Republican presidential nominee and House Speaker Clay Overton had more harsh words for the President this morning,*" the newscaster continued.

Jack looked back at the windshield-screen, and the image of Speaker of the House Clay Overton, who had somehow maneuvered to repeatedly block budget settlement attempts while convincing much of the public that the President was to blame. "The American people have suffered long enough," said Overton, "and can hardly expect solutions from President Perez, whose own party backed a rival for the nomination. When I am elected President, I will put an end to this shutdown. Without delay."

Jack watched Overton's face. Having spent years reading witnesses and juries, Jack's assessments of people were remarkably accurate.

Overton was a tough read, but Jack knew he couldn't be trusted to babysit a cockroach.

A window popped up on screen, with Sarah's picture and the words INCOMING CALL. "News off," Jack said. "Answer on screen." Sarah's face appeared, larger than life, her vulnerability still raw as an open wound.

"I'm sorry," she began, her eyes dry but still red.

"Me too," Jack said, a sense of relief washing over him.

"I know you're just trying to help," Sarah added, "and it's hard to know what to do."

"It's okay."

"You still getting Thai food tonight?" Sarah asked.

"You bet. With your extra lime and cilantro."

Sarah smiled a little. "Thanks. I'll get some wine for us. Might as well focus on the positives . . . I can drink wine again."

"See you tonight," Jack said, and pressed two fingers to his lips, their long-distance shorthand for a kiss. Sarah did the same and signed off.

Jack exhaled deeply and reveled in the moment; that was the first time Sarah had smiled since the hospital. It made him think back to the first time she'd ever smiled at him, nine years before. That time, she was just smiling to be polite, but it was still the most beautiful thing he had ever seen. He'd been wheeling his bicycle out the front door of his East Side Manhattan apartment building, and found Sarah cursing a flat front tire on the sidewalk. They talked a little, and he asked if she wanted to borrow his wheel, which was the same size as hers. That was when she smiled. "I'm okay, thanks," she said.

But Jack's prosecutor-gaze caught the slight flutter of her lids as her eyes flicked up and to the right; two pretty good tells that she was not as okay as she claimed. He unclipped his quick release front tire. "Just take it," he said.

"I can't take your tire," she protested.

"It's more of a trade, really," Jack said. "You'd have to leave yours here."

Sarah shook her head. "You were about to ride. That's not fair."

"Yeah, but I'm ten steps from home, and presumably you're not. Besides, I just joined the New York chapter of the Pop-A-Wheelie Club, so I don't really need two wheels to ride, you know?"

Sarah looked at Jack and did her best to suppress a genuine smile. The first of many to come.

The car slowed again for the UNC staff entrance. Jack waved at the burly guard who stepped from the gatehouse and scanned the car for weapons. He gave Jack a thumbs-up and opened the gate.

The lush greenery of the historic campus was a welcome contrast to the city around it. The car parked and Jack got out, grabbing a coffee from a stand and heading towards the columned entrance of the Van Hecke-Wettach law school building. The well-traveled route was presided over by stately hemlock trees that towered over passersby. Students spoke or waved greetings as they passed, which Jack returned. He remembered every student he'd ever taught, their faces recorded in his mind.

When the Dean added second-year Constitutional Law to Jack's course load four years before, his only advance briefing comment was, "See what you can do with it." Before Jack's arrival, the most common word used in on-line student reviews of Con Law II was "dry," with many opinions expressed in more colorful language. Attendance had been declining, prompting calls from Administration to cancel the course outright. Jack had changed that.

He figured the surprising enrollment numbers during his first year of teaching had been boosted by the curiosity factor—a desire to study under a prosecutor who'd spent time on the national stage, even if his departure from that stage had been less than graceful. But by Jack's second year of teaching, word of his passion for constitutional law had spread, and enrollment went up even as the novelty-prosecutor effect waned. By his third year teaching Con Law, students knew they had to register early because the class would fill up quickly. Now, in his fourth year, Jack had been asked to add a summer semester to handle the overflow and been granted a full professorship—a rate of progression much faster than most could hope for. Despite Jack's New York and Philadelphia roots, North Carolina had come to feel like home.

"Wait up, Professor!" a familiar voice called from behind.

Jack turned to greet Max Peller with a smile. "Hi, Max." Jack checked his watch. "Looks like you'll actually be on time for my afternoon class . . . six hours from now."

Max was a mix of idealism and insatiable curiosity, with a personality that even the most cynical fail to dislike for long. Max turned up in Jack's class twice a week and usually late, but eager to learn. His wavy black hair was always a mess, and was currently tucked under a black ballcap with a SoMAD logo on the front. He wore khakis, bright white trainers and a UNC Tar Heels t-shirt. "How can you drink the stuff they sell here?" he asked, glancing at Jack's coffee cup. "It tastes like acid, only worse."

Jack laughed. "Caffeine emergency. Had to lower my standards. What's up?"

"Two things . . . I'm toying with the idea of becoming a prosecutor, and I won't be in class this afternoon."

"Cool on the first count," Jack replied, ignoring the fact that Max had cleverly placed the noble-calling before the skipping-class note. Jack cleared his throat. "Though I have to say I saw you as more the private practice type, so color me surprised."

"I have a question though, if you don't mind."

"Fire away," Jack replied.

"Do you think I'd make it as a prosecutor?"

Jack appraised his favorite student for a long moment before answering. He'd spent a decade building a reputation as a fearless criminal prosecutor who could snatch victory from the jaws of defeat, but it had been a tumultuous journey. He lasted much longer and achieved far more than most who subjected themselves to the rigors of the Manhattan District Attorney's office, but in the end, the high stakes had taken their toll. "Well," he said, "for starters, it's not for everyone, and it's definitely not like what you see on TV."

"For sure, Professor, but what advice would you give if I was seriously considering it?"

"I'd tell you two things," Jack said. "First, you need to be able to keep your feet on the ground. Despite the lousy pay, it can be a high-visibility job if you do it well. You need to be able to deal with the spotlight, which can really mess with your head if you let it."

Jack had learned that the hard way. Riding high on a nine-verdict winning streak in high-profile capital cases, he'd drawn headlines and a growing national audience on LiveCourtTV. His name had even been whispered in the halls of power in Albany, as a potential choice for an open Senate seat. And then one day, also thanks to LiveCourtTV, all that disappeared. And his final case lived on in his haunted dreams.

"The second thing," he said to Max, "is you need to have the stomach for it. You're dealing with real victims, real families, trying to do what's right for them—and you have to be ready when things don't go your way, and the bad guy gets away. Because that'll happen."

Max's face flushed when he realized his question had dredged up painful memories. "Absolutely, Professor," he said. "Thank you. I need to think about that for sure."

"So, what's this about cutting class?" Jack asked.

Max pointed to his ballcap and grinned. "SoMAD protest in DC. I'm leaving in a few minutes. It's gonna be huge, bigger than anything. I'm one of the speakers. Politics is wrecking the country and people are pissed."

"Are you sure going to the biggest-ever protest is a good idea?" Jack asked. Just last week, some lunatic in Sacramento had managed to override his car's safety features and run down three protestors.

"Change is messy, Professor. Didn't you teach us that?"

"Sounds like me," Jack said. "Just be careful."

"You could come along," Max pressed, "I'd hand you the mic in a heartbeat; you're a great speaker. You could tell the crowd that every 1% rise in unemployment means 37,000 more deaths."

"Is that an accurate figure?" Jack asked.

"Absolutely. Every one percent increase means 22,000 more heart attacks, 970 more suicides, 688 more homicides, 4,011 more mental hospital admissions and—"

"I get the idea," Jack said. "But I'll be here, teaching the class you're missing."

"Oh, right," Max said. "Well, I'll be wearing a bodycam. Maybe you can tune in before class. Hashtag UNCSoMAD on Twitter-X!"

"Sounds good," Jack replied. They bumped fists. "And I think you'd make a great prosecutor."

"Thanks, Professor!" Max beamed and hurried off toward a line of waiting buses.

CHAPTER 2

JADE XU STOOD MOTIONLESS in the gym. Sizing up her target, her gloved hands at her side.

Useless piece of shit.

She blinked, banishing the images that pinwheeled through her head. She glanced around. The gym in the basement of Alibaba Global News was largely empty in the late afternoon. A couple of Peloton bikes were occupied, the two pedaling women more intent on chatting than riding. She saw them look her way and mutter something.

She tore into the heavy bag, which jumped on its chain, despite weighing twice as much as she did.

Lying, groping, stinking piece of shit.

Her fists of fury thundered into the bag in a series of jabs and uppercuts, a sharp grunt accompanying every blow, and each hit coming faster than the last. Soon her skin glistened with sweat and she labored for air. Her dark brown eyes blazed, never leaving the bag as she unleashed repeated combinations that echoed through the gym.

Piece . . . of . . . fucking . . . dogshit.

She stepped back from the target and circled, chest heaving as her dark ponytail swayed behind her. She stepped forward, launching into a series of front and side kicks that rattled the heavy bag's chain in its ceiling bracket. The grunts grew louder, prompting another look from the Peloton Sisters.

The sweat began to sting Jade's eyes, which only made her kick harder. If the bag had fallen from the ceiling at that moment, she would have kept on kicking it. *She* would decide when it was time to stop. No one else. Certainly not the Peloton Sisters. She stepped close enough to catch a whiff of the bag's fake leather, and unleashed several uppercuts, using every ounce of strength she had. Her classically beautiful face twisted with a rage that no amount of past teen therapy had managed to dampen.

She stepped back, sucking in air as she peeled the Velcro glove straps open with her teeth. She tossed the gloves in her bag and wiped her face with a towel, feeling her pulse begin to slow. The moments following her heavy bag workouts were the closest Jade ever felt to inner peace . . . if there was such a thing.

She stuffed the sweaty towel in her bag and headed for the locker room, passing the Peloton Sisters on the way. She could feel their eyes on her, but couldn't make out their whispered words. "What are you bitches looking at?" she said, and stalked into the locker room.

Ten minutes later, Jade found herself at her home-away-from-home; her nine-by-nine cubicle on the AGN Building's sixteenth floor. She was one of a hundred reporters in the DC newsroom. Not a bad place to be, considering that AGN had recently been crowned the world leader in 24-hour news. The people around her cluttered their cubicles with family photos, plants, or mugs with stupid phrases on them, but Jade's workspace was as bare as the day she'd arrived eight years before. Jade was, like her employer, an unsentimental news machine.

"Glad to see you made it back," said a voice Jade preferred to hear as seldom as possible. She swiveled her chair around to face Hal Green, a bulging, tobacco-stained newsman who had at some point realized he couldn't write and opted to become an editor instead. He seemed to take extra satisfaction in criticizing Jade at every opportunity, so she readied herself for another volley.

"Did you have a good time?" Hal asked.

Jade shrugged. "Ask the bag."

"Jade, maybe you've forgotten why you're here." He stepped closer, bringing the smell of stale tobacco with him. "You haven't done a piece in weeks. Actually, make that a month."

"You count real good, Hal." She knew her tone was pushing it but didn't much care; he shouldn't be criticizing her out in the open like this.

"You know I could fire your ass and claw back your last four years of 401k match if I wanted to?"

Jade returned her boss' stare. Despite being only five-foot-two, her constant simmer and natural glare somehow made others feel they were looking up at her, even when she was sitting down. The thought of the recent Employer's Rights Bill being used to savage her savings made her teeth grind. Jade looked around for support, but her cubicle-mates seemed suddenly engrossed in their work, which had been considerably less fascinating a moment before. Then again, Jade wasn't exactly Miss Congeniality.

"Eyeballs!" Hal said loudly, the familiar ratings mantra yanking Jade back into the unwanted conversation. Hal had an annoying way of speaking in sentence fragments, like someone who'd only recently learned English. But she was pretty sure he was from Maryland. "No eyeballs, no AGN!" Always the audience metrics. Eyeballs meant audience. Audience meant revenue. Revenue meant less shit coming down from the suits on high and—not coincidentally—less shit passed on to her.

Despite her prickliness, Jade had managed to earn some real stripes in her eight years at Alibaba Global News. She fed the daily news beast better than most. With eighteen separate channels each broadcasting 24/7, any viewer of any political disposition could find a slant to match, no matter the topic. With 18,000-plus reporters worldwide, many equipped with drone cameras and 30G live uplink capability, AGN kept the daily eyeball magnet machine rolling along at a smooth clip.

Jade had chosen to start her journalistic climb as most did, doing local freelance work that paid—up to a modest ceiling—by the number of webpage views. She wasn't charismatic. More like a bloodhound; sniffing out hidden things and digging until she found them. The last few years had seen her break away from the pack with a few big corruption stories that helped AGN resemble an actual check on those in power. And that was something the suits in Shanghai smiled upon.

She still remembered the day four years ago, when she broke the story on five Congressmen, a Congresswoman and two federal judges—all implicated in a human trafficking ring. She wasn't proud of the tactics she used to get that story, but every time she took down someone in authority, it felt like throwing another shovel of dirt onto the memory of a stepfather she wanted to bury.

"Hal," she said, as coolly as she could manage. "You're not going to touch my 401k, and do you know why? Because you know when I deliver, it's big. And that makes your bosses very happy."

Hal shifted in place. "Why don't you at least go cover the protests at the Capitol? Do something."

"What am I gonna do at a protest? It's covered to death already and you can't see shit from the ground. Send a drone."

"It's DC," Hal said. "No drones."

"Then send someone with a ladder. Someone who isn't me."

Hal reached into his pocket, unwrapped a Tums and popped it in his mouth. The act gave Jade a small measure of satisfaction. "Jade," he said, his tone shifting toward pleading, "we need more content. Way more than once a month. You gotta deliver more often. I'm under a lot of pressure here."

"As a matter of fact," Jade told him, "I'm working several sources right now. Something's bound to break soon." It was a lie she told often. But it turned out to be true often enough to be believable.

"Well, it better, because—"

Jade shot a hand up to silence him, her other hand brushing the arm of her smart glasses. The incoming message popped up on the lenses, where only she could see it. "It's my source," she announced. This was another useful lie when she needed an exit strategy, but this time it happened to be true. She closed her laptop and tucked it in her bag.

"What source? Who?" Hal asked. "I don't believe that for a minute."

Jade slipped past him. "Gotta work, Hal."

"Hey," he called after her. "I was still talking. Where the fuck are you going?"

Jade waved a hand without looking back. "You can thank me later." Her mind was already on the upcoming meeting with her source. She could feel the muscles in her chest tightening. She always worked alone, but at times like this, she often wished she didn't.

CHAPTER 3

BY THE TIME JADE'S SELF-DRIVING CAR made it out of DC's rush-hour traffic, it was dark. The location specified for the meeting was an old truck stop thirty miles out of town, abandoned now that trucks didn't need to stop for gas, and there were no drivers in need of food, sleep, or sex workers.

It had been years since Jade had been to a truck stop, but she remembered the last time well. Being fondled at the age of fifteen and kissed roughly on the mouth by her sour-breathed stepfather on a cross-country trip in the family van, was not easily forgotten. Her mother had flown east from California to start her new job, and her stepfather followed with Jade, towing a small, rented trailer crammed with those few possessions that would fit. Jade had asked to fly with her mother, but the cost of another ticket had been out of the question.

The abuse that came later had largely blurred together over time, but the shock of that first mauling never quite went away. Nor, despite much therapy, did her deep regret that the terror of the moment had prevented her from fighting back and smashing her stepfather in his leering, pockmarked face.

Jade backed her car into one of about a hundred empty parking spaces, facing what was left of the old truck stop. There were only two other vehicles in the lot, the most attractive features of which were burned-out lampposts and foot-high weeds growing through random cracks in the asphalt. The place looked like something from a post-apocalyptic movie. Jade waited and watched. That was the agreement: *Wait for the signal, do not initiate.* She'd made the first move at one of their earlier meetings, and the source had simply left.

The other two vehicles were dark. There was no moon, and the only light was a sputtering lamp on the side of a service building. One of the other vehicles, a dark sedan, flashed its lights twice. Jade opened her door and stepped from the car, filling her lungs with the cool night air to calm her nerves. Or try to. She was eager to learn what her source had to share, but being near him made her skin crawl. Especially in the middle of nowhere.

She walked toward the sedan, trying to find a pace that would conceal her nerves, because she knew he would be watching closely. There was a van parked two spaces over from the sedan. That wasn't creepy at all. It was sleek, with tinted windows, and closer to the size of a food truck than a work van. She kept an eye on it as she approached. A brief light caught her eye inside the sedan. She was glad her source was there, and not in the van.

She expected the sedan's door or window to open when she arrived, but neither did. She leaned down to look in the tinted passenger window, but it was impossible to see inside. She tried the door handle. It was locked.

A hollow *clunk* came from behind her, followed by the sound of a sliding door being opened. She whirled to face the van, her hands up and ready to hit whatever was there. Instead, she heard the familiar wet-gravel voice of her source, House Speaker Clay Overton. "Good evening, Jade. Do come in." His face appeared in the doorway, lips stretched wide in a syrupy smile that looked like he'd read about it in a manual and practiced in front of a mirror. It was the identical smile Jade had seen many times before, occasionally up close, but more often on TV.

"Jesus," she said. "What is this now, your mobile lair? This cloak-and-dagger stuff is getting a bit over the top, don't you think?"

"Just being cautious, my dear."

"Really. So, another precaution is scaring the shit out of me?"

"A byproduct of the sad times in which we live, I'm afraid."

With the presidential election only thirteen weeks off, Overton had sewn up the Republican nomination with commanding style; not a single prominent Republican stepped forth to oppose him. It was, by all accounts, a historic campaign, but for Overton it was the anticipated outcome of a meticulously executed, thirty-year plan.

The fact that the number of Americans who actually participated in primaries or voted in elections was at an all-time low did nothing to dampen the Speaker's enthusiasm for a goal that was now within reach. Despite the lack of drama during the Republican primary season, the conservative media were in a frenzy, hailing the Republican Party's singular convergence on Clay Overton as a sign of great things to come.

The truth was it had all been perfectly orchestrated. A masterful mix of persuasion, coercion and, in the final hours leading up to the first primary in Iowa, a bit of blackmail—had ensured the Speaker's unchallenged ascendance.

Currently polling fifteen points ahead of incumbent Democratic President Michael Perez, Overton had reason to wear a smile, even if it was a highly practiced one.

Another *clunk* sounded behind Jade. This time it was Overton's blonde-haired, totem-pole-sized bodyguard unfolding himself from the sedan. "What the fuck?" Jade said.

Overton stopped smiling. "You've met my associate, Anton Reverdy," he said. The bodyguard gave Jade a soulless nod, his pale-eyed gaze seeming to graze her skin. "He means you no harm, I assure you."

Tell that to my racing heart, Jade thought.

"Come in, Jade," Overton said warmly, extending his large hand to assist her. Everything about him was large, including his ego.

"I'm not getting in there with you and Lurch," Jade said, jerking a thumb toward Anton, who leaned against the sedan.

"You are going to want what I've got," said Overton. "Believe me." His hooded grey eyes bore into hers in a way that made it feel like he was taking something from her. "Anton will remain outside." Overton withdrew and sat down, patting the seat beside him.

Jade stepped inside and settled in the seat across from him. The van's interior looked more like a private jet than a car, filled with dark screens and fancy leather seats. "What's all this?" she asked, looking around.

"Let's just say this little investment affords me the ultimate in mobile privacy, when and where I need it." He tapped a button, and the door slid shut behind her. "I could almost start a war from here."

"Why don't you start with some lights instead?" Jade looked toward the back of the van and realized she was looking at some kind of sofa bed. She decided to keep her eyes on the Speaker and her fists ready in case they were needed. *This story better be fucking worth it.*

A dim light suffused the interior. Very dim. "Do you know why you're here with me, Jade?" Overton asked.

"Because you said you have something for me."

"No. You're here because I chose you." An uncomfortable pause followed. Then Overton reached into his suit pocket and pulled out a thin black memory card. "This is a Pulitzer, right here in my hand."

"What's on that?"

"Certainly, a great deal more than you're entitled to," he said, his gaze flicking down along Jade's body.

Creep. She imagined blood pouring from his nose after she punched him in the face. She let her eyes convey her revulsion.

"But I'm willing to give you the benefit of the doubt." He held out the black card.

"I asked you what's on that." She knew that once she took it—whatever it was—there would be no turning back.

"Something sure to cleanse the highest office in the land."

Jade tried to show no reaction. "You mean the Oval Office?"

"Yes, although I suppose in the most practical sense I should have said the second-highest office in the land—after my own." The edges of his mouth curled upwards as if tugged by tiny strings.

"So," Jade said, "I guess the rumor of another round of shutdown settlement talks between you and the president is just that—a rumor?"

Overton pursed his lips in disapproval. "You're losing focus already, my dear. Don't make me regret bringing you here. Many others would eagerly take your place."

Don't fucking call me dear. "You mean losing focus on the fact that the shutdown is sabotaging the whole country and ruining lives? Is that what you mean, Mr. Speaker?"

Overton's eyes flashed. "Jade," he replied, "you shouldn't get distracted by morality when we are thirteen weeks from the most important election in a lifetime. A few more months of sacrifice doesn't compare to the generational benefits to come from a sweeping victory in November."

Jade could feel her temperature rising. "I wasn't thinking so much about morality. More about the fact that a third of Americans can't afford *milk* right now, Mr. Speaker. And that for them, November is a long ways off."

The Speaker ignored the comment and held the card up between the two of them, his eyes locked on hers. "Want it?"

Jade extended her hand, her eyes simmering as Overton placed it in her palm. "You'd best run along now, darling." He tapped the button that opened the door. "So much to do. For both of us."

Dismissive prick. Jade's teeth clenched as she stepped from the van. Anton was just where they'd left him, leaning against the sedan. She headed for her car, feeling their eyes on her as she walked.

"We'll see you soon, Ms. Xu," Anton called after her.

Jade wasn't sure which thought disturbed her more: being beholden to a man like Clay Overton, or that he might become president.

CHAPTER 4

PRESIDENT MICHAEL PEREZ SAT ALONE in the Oval Office, a situation that seemed increasingly common in recent months. He rapped a thick pen on the legal pad before him. He'd intended to fill the page with options, but that meant accepting his predicament, which he was not yet ready to do. He tapped the intercom, connecting him to one of his assistants. "Is Angela in the building?" he asked.

"Yes, Mr. President. She's almost here."

"Thank you." *Chingada madre . . . This job.* Perez shook his head and spread his hands across the massive Resolute Desk where he'd made so many decisions over the past three and a half years. He'd vowed to shrink the partisan divide in Washington, and had tried each day to live up to that promise. The futile effort had aged him a decade; his once-thick hair now thinner and greyer, his complexion veering toward pallor.

He reached for the lowball of twenty-year-old añejo tequila he'd poured earlier, and took a long pull of the salty amber liquid. It was the only real vice he had left, and even that used to taste a hell of a lot better than it did now. It used to be the taste of home in San Joaquin, California. On good days, it reminded him of the reckless desires of a turbulent youth he'd somehow survived. Many friends from *el barrio* had not been so fortunate. On the not-so-good days, which lately had become more plentiful, it reminded him of the twists of fate that had catapulted him here after an impulsive choice—at the age of twenty-six—to run for mayor of San Joaquin. Twenty-seven years later, as governor, he'd posted the largest state budget surplus in California's history. Some said the hand of God had guided his improbable path from the pistachio orchards of Fresno County to the White House. And there were times—had been, times—when he could persuade himself that was true. But not lately. Because he didn't believe God was that cruel. He took another long pull of tequila, nearly emptying the glass. *Puta madre.* The liquid seemed vile, unrecognizable.

During his first weeks in office, it became apparent to Perez that Clay Overton and the Republicans would not be his only adversaries. The emboldened leftist faction of the Democratic party was equally problematic, decrying all attempts at compromise with the hated Republicans. The ultimate humiliation came later, as a sitting president having to face a challenger within his own party for the re-nomination.

That drawn out battle allowed Overton to paint the warring Democrats as the problem; they couldn't even agree with each other, much less work with the dedicated Republicans working to end the shutdown. Leading to the present debacle, where Perez trailed Overton by fifteen points.

The door clicked open, admitting Perez' chief of staff, Angela Dembe. "Good evening, Mr. President." She cut a striking image with her six-foot frame, dark skin, and tailored cream pantsuit. She stopped before the desk, her hands folded at the waist.

"What did you find out?" Perez asked. "Is it going to leak?"

"I'm afraid so, sir. Containment is no longer an option."

"How long?"

"A day. Maybe two."

Perez leaned back in his chair.

"And, I'm fairly certain Secretary Holmes is the source." Alan Holmes was Perez' secretary of defense.

"I should have fired him two years ago when I had the chance." The fact that Angela had advised him to do so was left unsaid. Perez was the bridge-builder, amassing and guiding his own 'team of rivals' to pursue the greater good; repeating a strategy that had worked in California. Angela was the mercenary, mistrusting everyone; repeating the strategy that had worked for her growing up in Nigeria, and throughout her long, strange path to the halls of American power.

"What's our best response?" Perez asked.

"The story gives us another chance to reinforce the benefits of the TAP deal," said Angela. "It was a very presidential decision, made in America's best economic interests."

They both knew, though, how incredibly difficult any positive spin on the situation would be, regardless of the number of jobs created by the Technology Asset Pact with China. Perez rubbed his temples. While they could trot out the statistics again, and talk about the end of China's decades-long theft of U.S. intellectual property, he knew the reality: simple headlines about secret deals just worked better for the media.

He felt another headache coming on as he imagined the headlines. Governing a vast country in complex and unpredictable times meant making decisions that were not always easy—or even possible—to explain. And on the surface, this one looked pretty bad. "Overton has probably been sitting on this," he said. "The timing is just too perfect. He's been holding it until just before the election." He let out a long sigh. *Fifteen points down will feel like a wild fantasy after this.*

"How do you want to proceed, Mr. President?"

The fact that the forever hard-charging Angela Dembe wasn't recommending a plan of attack was telling in itself. Perez wondered if she might be planning to resign, as many others already had. He tapped his pen on the desk again, then tossed it aside. "Get Holmes on *Meet the Press* tomorrow. Call his bluff. He won't publicly admit he wasn't for it—that would make him look weak—and his ego is way too damned big for that."

Angela hesitated. "Sir, I'm not sure that will work. Air too much of that publicly and the Chinese may try to walk back on TAP. But more than that, I don't think you can bank on what he will or won't say. I'd keep him as far away from this as possible."

"Well, what about Palmer then? The VP is supposed to be my attack dog at times like this."

Angela was silent. They both knew Perez' relationship with the vice president had ceased to be an asset some time ago.

Perez felt his face start to flush. No one had come out and said it, but he could read the signs well enough. People were distancing themselves from what they perceived as a doomed candidate. Sitting president or not, business was business, and elections were the biggest business of all. The DNC and its largest donors had apparently concluded that Americans would –rightly or wrongly—hold their president accountable for the ongoing shutdown. Or, at least, for failing to end it. Rumor had it even Vice President Palmer had been in earlier talks to run against him for the nomination. Humiliating didn't quite cover it.

Perez glanced down at his pad again. It was still blank.

CHAPTER 5

IT WAS JUST PAST MIDNIGHT when the guard at AGN snorted awake at the *beep* from Jade's iris scan as she passed through the security turnstile. His look was a mix of embarrassment at having nodded off, and confusion upon waking. Jade seldom went to the office so late, but she wanted to be in a secure place when she looked at whatever it was Overton had given her. And her dingy Brentwood DC apartment was anything but secure.

Moments later she was back in the newsroom, relieved to find herself alone in the cavernous space. The Washington Bureau was mainly a political hub, with a smattering of international and business reporters for good measure. Most of Jade's political colleagues had precious little faith left in government, and treated their work like what it was—a job. Get eyeballs, move up the ladder, get more eyeballs, get paid a little more, move a little higher. You might get a quick rush from taking down one of the sociopaths walking the halls of Congress—but if you did, your access to that political party would get shut down. For a while at least. It was a thankless job.

She moved to her desk in the first row of cubicles, just outside the glass-walled editorial offices. AGN treated cubicle position and even desk size as status symbols. But sometimes Jade found herself longing for a tiny cubicle at the back, closer to the exits, and to anonymity. And if she didn't file a story soon, she might wind up right there. Rankings and cubical positions were fluid, and dependent upon results.

Jade took a seat and pulled Overton's black card from her purse, turning it over in her fingers. It seemed somehow heavier than before.

She knew the point of no return had already been passed, yet couldn't help but pause before taking the final step toward whatever-this-was. She looked around the newsroom. Still empty.

Jade took a deep breath and switched her computer to dark mode, isolating it from the internet, the company network and anything or anyone else that might pry. She tapped the card to the reader. The monitor came to life, casting its eerie light across her features. She scrolled through the document. *"Holy shit . . . "*

After several moments she realized she'd been holding her breath, and exhaled. The pages were untitled, but it soon became clear she was looking at a transcript of the 2041 US/China summit. It was the only such meeting in President Perez' term, but other than a few brief statements and photo-ops, the summit's meetings had been closed-door only, with the TAP deal announced months later.

Jade found an audio file. She plugged in a headset and hit PLAY. The file had multiple voices, including translators, and was muffled in parts but one voice was unmistakable: President Michael Perez. She leaned forward as she listened, then rocked back in her chair like she'd been slapped. *Did he just offer classified U.S. military radar technology to the Chinese?* She skipped the recording back a few seconds and listened again to make sure she'd heard it right. *Oh my God. He did. Why would he do that?*

Her mind drifted back to the details of the TAP agreement. It was one of Perez' most notable achievements, though largely forgotten in the wake of the shutdown. At the time, it was all the Perez administration had talked about. Jobs, jobs, jobs—kept right here in America because China would finally stop pirating intellectual property and undercutting American businesses. Jade chewed a nail and listened again, as the President of the United States overtly traded military secrets for jobs.

Her mind began to whirl. *Why would Perez make such a trade, even in secret?* She thought about calling an AGN colleague on the White House Desk and asking them to seek an official comment, but rejected the notion before it was fully formed. That particular reporter was a sycophantic imbecile who could be trusted only to get it wrong, giving the White House too much time to pre-empt the story.

There must have been a reason to make a trade like that.

Too, the fact that Overton had furnished Jade with the evidence gave her reason to pause. *There's no making up the polling gap after this.* Overton was right; this was political dynamite.

She sat there for a few moments in silence, mulling over the obvious but undesirable consequence of her next actions:

President-elect Clay Overton.

She bounced it back and forth in her mind until one thought rose to prominence and drowned out the others. The thought had been deeply ingrained in a fifteen-year-old girl who still regretted her silence: *Stop thinking —throw the punch —right where it hurts the most.* She found her phone and tapped in a number she seldom used. This story needed to go much higher than her editor Hal.

CHAPTER 6

JACK SLEPT FITFULLY, TWISTING AGAINST the fabric of the same dream that always waited in the darkness. For him and him alone. There were too many cameras in the packed courtroom, Cyclopean eyes moving nearer. Accusing. He tried to speak, but no words came forth. The only sound was the pounding of his heart. Like a drum in an echo chamber. Beating faster with each torturous moment.

The faces in the gallery drifted toward him. He looked away but could still feel their hollow eyes upon him. He waited for defense counsel's voice, asking where his witness was. As it had asked a thousand times before. The voice spoke, as he'd known it would. But he had no answer—because he never did.

The police officer walked past him, grinning at Jack as he passed. Whispering to the judge, who glared at Jack and *thumped* his gavel on the bench like Thor's hammer. Shattering the scene—walls, people, furniture—into tumbling glass shards.

Another voice called from far away. Frantic. *"Jack! Jack!"* And then suddenly it was closer, and his whole body was shaking. *"Wake up, Jack!"*

He woke with Sarah shaking him by the shoulders. "It's okay, Jack. You're here now. We're both here." He sat up and felt his heart begin to slow. He took a long, shuddering breath. "Sorry."

"You have to stop blaming yourself," Sarah said, not having to ask him what the dream was about. "It wasn't your fault."

Jack's limbs felt damp and heavy. He focused on slowing his heart a bit more. Deep breaths.

"You did more good there in ten years than most do in a career," Sarah said. "You need to remember that."

"I do," Jack said. "But the dream just never goes away."

Sarah ran her fingers over his sweaty hair. "It will. One day. And it's probably done for tonight, so . . . Try to get some sleep?"

Jack leaned back into the mattress, Sarah's arm across his chest. He stayed awake for a while, listening to a screen door thudding somewhere in the night wind. As he drifted off, the gentle knocking felt like a faint reminder from the darker corners of his mind, letting him know that the dream would never stop coming.

CHAPTER 7

MAX'S UNTAMED HAIR AND GENERALLY disheveled appearance conveyed a laid-back impression, though Max himself was anything but. He cursed under his breath while making his way through the mass of tightly-packed protesters still gathering on the National Mall that ran between the Capitol Building and the Lincoln Memorial. Under normal circumstances, the walk from The Lincoln Memorial to the U.S. Capitol might take forty minutes; now, with nearly a million people jockeying for space, it seemed like a journey of a thousand miles.

With most events, Max didn't mind being late; in fact, lateness was a deliberate choice meant to spare him the unimportant preliminaries that inevitably accompanied most gatherings. But he had a speaking slot at the biggest SoMAD protest in history—and he absolutely could not be late for that.

He'd planned ahead, and his group had arrived early, but Max had seriously miscalculated the time required to cross the Mall to the Capitol Building, where speeches would be given. He'd been walking for two hours, and was finally nearing the stage at the edge of Union Square. He was directly in front of the Capitol, but separated from it by the concrete barricades and fifteen-foot iron fence that had become permanent byproducts of the Capitol riots of '21.

"Sorry!" Max shouted over the din of the gathered protesters. "Gotta get to the stage, please!" His voice was already hoarse. He hoped he'd still be able to speak when he got to the microphone. A hundred handheld signs blocked his view of the stage, but for an instant, he glimpsed someone fiddling with the mic. Damn. They were about to start. He pressed forward, the volume of the alternating chants around him almost deafening.

SoooMAD . . . Make a Decision!

Clean the House . . . Vote Them Out!

It was supposed to be a student protest, at least initially, the permit applications filled out by students and submitted to the National Park Service, which oversaw the Mall and twelve other sites in the nation's Capitol. But it was much more than that now. People from all walks of life had descended on the Mall in unexpected numbers. And this crowd felt angry. SoMAD. Hundreds of Capitol Police lined the edges of the Mall, decked out in riot gear.

Finally, Max reached the side of the stage, where a guy with a SoMAD cap and a tablet seemed to be directing things. Max thought about his omnipresent father for the first time in a few days, thinking *He's not going to like it when he sees me here . . . way too many unforeseeable variables.* Which was why Max hadn't told him about coming here. He'd find out soon enough, because his father was as close to all-seeing as any human being could be. But for the moment at least, Max was here, and his father wasn't.

"Hey!" Max shouted to tablet-holder. "I'm Max Peller . . . Finally made it!"

"Jesus, Dude! From UNC, right? We were about to drop you from the list!" He tapped his tablet display. "You're third up! Stay right here!"

Max looked back at the Mall; it was a sea of humanity that stretched almost two miles. It looked like someone could crowd-surf the whole distance and never touch the ground. He flinched as a booming male voice exploded from the big speakers that faced the crowd.

"Look at all these beautiful people who are *SOOOOOO MAAAAAD!!!!!*"

The crowd cheered wildly, thrusting their signs in the air. Max turned to look up at the first speaker, a large black man with dreadlocks.

"ARE YOU PEOPLE AS MAD AS I AM??? LEMME HEAR IT!!! WHAT ARE YOU???"

The crowd thundered back, SO *MAD!!!*

"WHAT ARE YOU???"

"SO MAD!!!

Max's heart began to pound. How was he supposed to follow that? He'd been planning an emotional-but-factual appeal that he hoped might be heard on the news by the Powers That Be. But on seeing the protestors whipped into a frenzy by the first speaker, Max feared his own speech would land like a book reading at a wrestling match. A nearby argument drew his attention; the guy with the tablet was waving a piece of paper and yelling at a police officer.

"That's bullshit, Man, it's *right here*!"

The cop, who was flanked by several other officers, shook his head. "That's an assembly permit only!" he shouted over the noise around them. "You need different permits for stage and electrical!"

"You can't pull that on me now! What am I supposed to do?!"

"I'm sorry," the officer told him. "But the organizers were informed about this weeks ago. You need to kill the generators and lose the stage."

Tablet Guy held up his hands. "It's too late. I can't do that!"

"If you don't kill the generators," the cop said, "we will." More police arrived.

The student organizer was doing his best to remain calm as more officers arrived beside the stage. "Please, Officer, don't—"

"You don't have to, you just fucking WANT TO!" yelled a burly bandana-wearing protestor, glaring at the cops. "You won't silence us!!" He pushed closer, his bulbous red face inches from the lead police officer, who stood his ground.

A bottle came flying over the crowd and shattered on the back of the cop's helmet. When he whirled around to see where it came from, the shield on his arm clipped a teenage girl in the face. Blood streamed from her nose. The burly protestor grabbed the cop's shield and jerked him off his feet. Another cop tackled the protester, and the crowd closed in.

The escalation happened fast, but to Max, it seemed like slow motion.

More cops piled on the burly man. Protesters piled on the cops, and the whole thing spun out of control with Max three feet away. The only way out was up, so he clambered onto the stage to escape the melee. The first speaker helped him up, then pointed down at the fracas and yelled into the mic. "RIGHT IN FRONT OF OUR EYES!!! THE MAN IS BEATING US DOWN, RIGHT HERE!!!"

The crowd surged forward. Police at the edge of the crowd fired 40mm CS tear gas grenades, aiming for the fight at the base of the stage. Max turned, intercepting an errant gas canister—which traveled at 540 feet per second—with his head. It felt like his skull exploded. He let out a half-scream and his legs buckled beneath him. He dimly felt his face smack the edge of the wooden stage a half-second later. Tear gas poured from the canister beside him as the sound of the angry crowd faded away.

CHAPTER 8

AS USUAL, JACK ARRIVED EARLY FOR CLASS, and made his way to the front of the room, which was shaped like an orchestra pit. Instead of reviewing his lecture notes before class, he tuned into Max's livestream on Twitter-X, but saw nothing but white static. The UNCSoMAD hashtag was down too. He checked an AGN news feed, and the first thing he saw was: *Violence Erupts at SoMAD DC Rally.* Jack felt his stomach tighten. He tapped into the video and saw chaos: tear gas, protesters fighting with police, people trying to climb the fifteen-foot fence around the Capitol Building.

One of Jack's students, Keya Jameson, came into the room. "Are you watching the news?" she asked.

Jack nodded. More students streamed in and took their seats. Jack asked if anyone had heard from Max. Most of the students shook their heads. "I texted him about an hour ago," someone said. "No answer yet." Jack tried to dismiss the sense of dread stirring inside him.

"It's a friggin' shit show up there," said Derek Matthews, the too-loud class jock in the front row. "Cops and people pummeling each other."

"Well, let's not panic," Jack said, "I'm sure Max will turn up soon." The truth was, Jack wasn't sure at all.

Derek shook his head. "I told him DC was a bad idea."

"Aren't you the smart one," Keya snapped back. "It's just a pity all those brain cells are busy playing football. At least Max is trying to do something useful."

"Look," Derek said, "I'm just saying you go up against the system, you're gonna get crushed, that's all."

"That's pretty fatalistic," Jack put in as the whole class began following the conversation. "I thought the Alpha generation was supposed to be about questioning authority and making change."

"Not when the system's totally broken," said another student.

"But that's when we need change the most," Jack said, studying the group for a few seconds. "Though I suppose in some ways, I can understand your view."

"Really?"

"Sure," Jack said. "Your entire life so far, actually, most of mine too, all the two parties do is oppose one another. Every day, with every breath. It's what we know because it's all they ever do."

"That's just politics," another student added. "It's why nobody with real talent wants to be a politician anymore . . . They'd be wasting their time."

Jack paused for a moment. "Tell you what guys . . . Let's forget the regular class today."

"But I stayed up late finishing my classwork!" someone called out. Others laughed.

"Preparation noted," Jack said. "And we'll get to that. But right now, I think we need to have a conversation about how we got here. Politically." He didn't know exactly where that would go, but many of his best summations for juries came when he went off-script and followed his gut. It had terrified the DA when Jack improvised, but it worked. "Why has the government been shut down for seven months?" he asked the class.

"Because the system is broken," someone answered.

"Not nearly specific enough. Come on. *Why* has it been shut down *that long.*"

"Because they can't agree on a budget, and nobody wants to compromise."

"A bit closer," Jack said, and started pacing. Now, *why* can't they agree on a budget? Why won't they compromise, even when they know it is overwhelmingly in the public interest to do so?"

Another student piped up. "They hate each other?"

"Way too simple," Jack replied. "And by the way I don't think they all hate each other either. They oppose each other daily but they don't all hate each other."

The students kept it coming. "The media?"

Jack cracked a slight smile. "A bit warmer still; that plays a role, but it doesn't get to the core of why there's no compromise."

The room grew suddenly quiet, the students looking at each other blankly.

"It's actually quite simple," Jack said. "People react to incentives. We naturally do what rewards us. And today's politicians have absolutely no incentive to reach a compromise."

"How so?"

"What's in it for them?" Jack asked. "Nothing. In fact, they actually stand to *lose* if they compromise."

"Lose by doing what most people want them to do?"

Jack nodded, reading the intrigue on the faces before him. Like the juries of his past life, he knew he had the class primed to truly listen. That had always been Jack's greatest strength as a prosecutor; being able to read the jury and tailor his message to suit the moment, and the jurors. That was the superpower that fueled his lengthy string of convictions.

Jack cleared his throat. "John Adams was the second president of the United States, and in 1789, he pretty much nailed what's happening today. He recited the quote from memory as he searched the Web and put it up on the screen:

"There is nothing which I dread so much as a division of the republic into two great parties, each arranged under its leader, and concerting measures in opposition to each other. This, in my humble apprehension, is to be dreaded as the greatest political evil under our Constitution."

Jack let the words sink in for a moment before continuing. "*The greatest political evil,*" he said. "Pretty strong words." Students nodded their agreement. "But the forefathers feared this day would come.

It took over two hundred years, but here we are, in a place where the machinery of government matters more than the purpose it was created to serve. The government's overriding priority has become . . . the perpetuation of government."

"Say more about that," one of the students called out, prompting Jack to smile because that was the common phrase he used to nudge his students to dive deeper when their comments were not specific enough.

"Some of you may have heard the phrase *indispensable enemies*, and that's what we're looking at here: a two-party system that's really a shared monopoly that writes its own rules. Somewhere along the way they discovered that getting elected has nothing to do with making progress, and everything to do with appearing to stand against the despicable opposing party that will surely wreck the country if not stopped. It's always those fascist Republicans or those socialist Democrats, dead set on destroying everything we believe in."

A few students chuckled. He knew he had the more emotional half of the room, and that the more analytical half was still sitting on the fence. "This . . . political drift, let's call it, happened over decades. Slowly at first. And now it's moving at warp speed. The place we're in now should scare the hell out of everyone in the country—Democrat, Republican or independent. It scares the hell out of me . . .

"Once every ten years, Princeton runs a massive statistical analysis of every piece of federal legislation passed over a decade—so, roughly 3,000 data points." He scribbled the number on his tablet, and it appeared on the screen at the front of the room. "They compare the new laws with data on public opinion about the issues addressed, to determine how often legislation that gets passed aligns with the interests of the masses. Would anyone care to guess what the correlation is? Anyone?'"

A few students threw out numbers. "Fifty percent?"

"No," Jack said.

"Eighty percent?"

"No."

"Ten percent?"

"The correlation," Jack said, drawing a large circle on the screen, "is basically zero."

"Seriously?"

Jack nodded. "Seriously. Zero correlation between what the public wants, and what actually gets passed into law. A similar study tracked every legislative topic that was of interest to at least half the country and found that, thirty years ago, about twenty-five percent of those issues were permanently gridlocked in Congress. Today *ninety percent* of those issues are in permanent gridlock . . .

"Jesus," muttered Derek as he shook his head.

Jack continued on. "One reason for that gridlock? Forty years ago, two-thirds of politicians in Congress could be classified as moderates—basically these were the people willing to accept reasonable compromise in order to get things done. Today, moderates are nearly extinct, down to two percent . . ."

"If politicians don't serve the public interest," Keya said, "they should be voted out of office."

"That's their usual response in self-defense," Jack replied. "But here's the clever part if you're them—who else are you going to vote for—that Nazi, Commie, gun-loving, Godless-tax-raiser or whatever label you want to assign to the other side of the aisle? Your own party's *indispensable enemy?* You wouldn't dare, and they know it."

This was greeted with a flurry of nods.

"But, as one might counter next, people can always vote independent. And that's true. It's also true that independent candidates rarely get anywhere. You can find a hundred different hot sauces in your grocery store, but you're hard-pressed to find one independent in high office. Why is that?"

The room stirred restlessly, but no one answered. Jack went on. "Would you believe there are laws on the books, designed by our two parties, that all but guarantee that independent candidates don't stand a chance?"

"No way," someone said.

"Yes way," Jack answered. "Just a few examples . . . federal campaign laws allow you to contribute thirty times more to one of the established parties than you can donate directly to a candidate. Try running as an independent with that money disadvantage. Then there's the deadline to even get on the ballot—state courts long ago ruled that early ballot deadlines disadvantage independents, but the two parties are still managing to push ballot deadlines earlier and earlier—so by the time the public is even thinking about the election it's way too late to get anyone new on the ballots. And finally—in some states if you're not a Democrat or Republican you actually need to collect more signatures to get on the ballot.

"Then there's the Hastert Rule, which basically allows the Speaker of the House to prevent a vote on any bill, even if it's a shoo-in for passage. So, you could have a bill with overwhelming public support, perhaps even one supported by independents—but if the ruling party doesn't like it, tough luck; it'll sit there and rot.

"And statistics tell us that the longer major legislation is gridlocked, the more money both parties haul in because their voters are pissed at the other side for holding things up. So, they send more money to 'their' side. Talk about an incentive—donors don't send money when they're happy—they send money when they're pissed off, or afraid. So, really, the more dissatisfied, irate and afraid they can make us, the richer and more powerful the two parties become. There's your incentive."

"So," Keya said, "you're saying a million people marching on Washington probably won't make any difference in the end."

"Unfortunately, in today's system, that's exactly what I'm saying."

"That's messed up," someone else said.

Jack nodded. "Especially because it doesn't have to be this way. Things just kind of devolved into this . . . political death spiral we find ourselves in today, and nobody's got the gumption to pull us out of it."

"It seems like it's impossible to pull out. Isn't it?"

"Not necessarily."

"Okay, professor," said Derek, "what would you do if you were, say—president?"

Jack laughed. "Me . . . in the White House?"

"Why not? Couldn't do any worse, right?"

"All right. Give me a minute . . . "

"Hey," someone called out, "you could take seven months."

Jack smiled and collected his thoughts. "Nothing's as big or powerful as government, right? And we look at that as the problem. Which right now—it is. But what if it's also the solution? Why not *use* the government, to *fight* the government? The tools are already there: the Sherman Anti-Trust Act, the Clayton Act, the Federal Trade Commission Act. Any or all of those could be used to break up the two-party monopoly."

"But weren't those designed to fight *corporate* monopolies?"

"Sure. So what? Just because they've never been used for anything else doesn't mean they can't be. And there's nothing that legally prevents it. They may be political but both parties act more and more like corporations every year. So why not? The president appoints the head of the Justice Department and all ninety-four U.S. attorneys, which basically gives the president control over every federal lawyer in the country. That's ten thousand lawyers and ninety-thousand support staff on an unlimited budget.

And if I were president, I would direct every one of them to focus on breaking that monopoly. Giving people *real* choices at the polls, and creating *real* consequences for elected officials who think they can just carry on with this insanity we see around us. They're not there to get rich off stock trades and fat cat donations, or spend their time auditioning for private-sector jobs when they leave office. They're there for *us,* and it's damn well time someone put a foot up their ass to remind them of that."

A long silence followed.

"Could that actually work?" someone asked. "Like . . . all of

Congress would be totally against it."

"Of course they would be," Jack shrugged. "But fuck 'em," he said, surprising himself.

Someone started clapping, and soon the whole room joined in thunderous applause that continued on. Jack smiled as he looked at them all, realizing he hadn't felt this good in a very long time.

CHAPTER 9

JACK'S CAR GLIDED DOWN HIS TREE-LINED street and pulled into the driveway. He grabbed the bag of Thai food he'd picked up on the way home, and made for the house, hoping things would be okay with Sarah. He hesitated for a moment, then opened the door.

"Is that dinner arriving?" Sarah called out.

"It is," Jack replied, noting the baby clothes were gone from the living room. He joined Sarah in the kitchen. "And me with it." Sarah had already set the table and put out a bottle of their favorite pinot noir.

Sarah turned from the sink and smiled at him. Jack felt a month's worth of tension drain away. Sarah planted a soft kiss on his lips. "Glad you're home. I'm starving." She took the Thai bag and placed the containers on the table. "How was your day?" she asked.

"I said 'fuck' in class."

Sarah grinned. "Off with your head."

"All I need is one to get offended and file a complaint."

"You realize they probably didn't even notice."

"Ummm . . . I think maybe they did." He opened the wine and poured two glasses. "But enough about my blasphemous day. How was yours?"

"I slept for four hours, wrote in my journal for two more, and packed a lot of stuff away." She took a sip of wine. "I want to go back to work next week."

"Okayyy," Jack said, doing his best to read her abrupt turn toward the positive. "If you're sure you're up to it."

"I am," she said, her features turning serious. "And there's something else I've been thinking about . . .:"

The phone inside Jack's pocket dinged loudly with an incoming text. "Don't you dare answer that."

"I wasn't planning to," Jack said.

"I've thought about it all day. I may even have dreamt about it too—"

Jack's phone dinged twice more, then a third time. Sarah ignored it. "I think we should try for another baby."

Jack's phone started dinging again and this time, it didn't stop. "Jesus, sorry," he said, and reached to silence it. Sarah's phone started dinging too. "Oh, for God's sake," she said, and scooped it up.

Sarah looked down at her phone and then back up at Jack, looking utterly confused.

"Are you running for President?"

CHAPTER 10

CLAY OVERTON UPPED HIS JOGGING PACE as he approached the incline at Key Bridge, which stretched across the murky Potomac River. The four-mile loop from his fortified Georgetown home to Arlington National Cemetery and back was the preferred route for his weekly twilight run. This week's jogging partner was Kyle Manning, the junior senator from Kentucky. The man was twenty years younger and could barely keep up.

Four other joggers encircled the pair, all of them Secret Service agents. Opposite the concrete barrier that lined the road, two black SUVs tracked progress dutifully, further congesting the evening traffic.

Overton wore the latest athletic sensor-wear, which would tell him, if he cared, everything he might want to know about his body in motion, right down to analyzing foot pronation, sweat output, and mineral replacement needs after each workout.

Senator Manning, on the other hand, sported common sweats and jogging shoes that looked like they'd been used for mowing the lawn.

"Gotta keep up, Senator," Overton called out, stepping up the pace again. He wanted his running guest good and winded for the next part of their conversation, so he could maximize his advantage. He knew from experience that a breathless adversary was much easier to manipulate, as their brain needed to divert attention from critical thinking to bodily functions.

Senator Manning did his best to conceal his wheezing as he pulled even with Overton. "The campaign . . . is looking . . . . unstoppable," he huffed.

Overton flashed an amused smile as his young colleague tried to sound like he was part of the machinery, or part of anything really. He wasn't. Not yet. But he could be. This was getting too easy. After two years in the Senate, Manning was only modestly beyond figuring out where the bathrooms were. But like most other Congressional newcomers, he'd do whatever it took to gain access to the inner sanctums. That lust for power was easy to exploit, especially among the inexperienced.

"So," Overton said, "you think the race is over, do you?" He gazed straight ahead as he spoke, never looking at his companion.

Well . . . no . . . I mean, it's . . ."

"Do you know what makes a great soldier?" Overton asked. "A truly lethal combat killer?"

Manning remained silent—too out of breath to speak, or perhaps smart enough to know that Overton had served two tours in the Middle East as a Marine and that the question was clearly rhetorical.

Overton continued. "He never doubts his purpose, and so he never wastes time watching a neutralized target go down."

"Sir?"

"Unwavering belief and ruthless efficiency. Before one target hits the ground, the soldier has the next target in his sights. That's the difference between life and death on the battlefield."

"Yeah . . . Totally makes sense," Manning wheezed, starting to resemble a triathlon finisher.

"Totally?" Overton replied.

Manning made a sucking sound as he took a gulping breath. Then his foot caught on a bridge joint and he plowed hard into the concrete. "Ssshit!"

The Secret Service agents stopped only when Overton did.

Senator Manning stared up at Overton. "I'm s-sorry," he bleated, sitting up. Blood and spit dripped from his mouth.

"Son, you need to get outside more."

"Yeah, I know, I didn't . . ."

Overton felt a pang of guilt as he looked down at the junior senator and his embarrassing failure to make the impression he so clearly longed to deliver. But the guilt was fleeting, and it was time to reel in the fish. "You've spilled blood for the cause at least," he said. "Does that mean you're ready for next-level training?"

The young senator's face made it clear he had no idea what Overton was talking about. But at least he was bright enough to say "Yes."

Overton crouched down beside him. "There's a seat coming open next month on EWD, and I want *you* to be in that seat." He hoped there was no need to explain that EWD was the Appropriations Sub-Committee for Energy and Water Development, one of twelve such sub-committees in Congress. A particular member of the current EWD Committee had gotten out of hand, and was about to find herself committee-less.

"Really? Yes, of course! I've actually done some research work on energy and water policy so I can really sink my . . ."

"Wow, you know what, Son?" Overton said, placing a hand on his shoulder.

"What's that, sir?" Manning asked, glimpsing a path back from embarrassment.

"I do not give a rat's dick about your research," Overton said, "because you are being given this opportunity for something much more important."

Manning looked utterly confused.

"At the right time in committee, you are going to share critical evidence that Vice-President Palmer had his own crooked China deal in the works."

"Really? What kind of deal?"

"You'll know when you need to know, Senator, and before the election of course." Overton's sources had established a tenuous connection between Vice-President Palmer's presence at the Southeast Asian Summit, and China's newly aggressive water-damming policies in the region, which were sucking up the region's freshwater reserves.

Normally, Asian water politics would put any US news editor into a coma, but on the heels of one China scandal, any further secret capitulations that involved China would be frothy media chum.

"So . . . you're worried about Palmer in 2048 then?" Manning asked, his face showing his uncertainty. "Cause the Dems ticket is pretty much toast now."

Overton frowned. He hated the ones who thought beyond their station in life. It wasn't an entirely inaccurate calculation by Manning, but this was more about principle. "Son," he said, "when you come back from battle, you don't get rewarded for how much ammunition you saved. Our job, our moral duty, is nothing short of total and utter victory, no matter the cost." He stood, gazing down at his future pawn. "Don't you see? We owe it to the American people to move beyond this terrible shutdown. And that requires total victory—winning every state."

Manning rose, wincing and grasping a knee. "You really think we can sweep the board and win all fifty states?"

Overton ignored the comment and gazed out over the Potomac. "Palmer is a little tethered floatie keeping his boss from sinking to the bottom. Time to set the floatie adrift." He turned back to look at the now upright Manning. "The foundation of greatness is God-given; the rest is sheer will. That's how America was born, and that's how America will prosper." His eyes burned brightly. "Are you with me, Senator?"

The young man nodded.

"Good decision, Senator. Now go clean yourself up. You look pathetic." Overton turned and continued his run. The Secret Service followed.

CHAPTER 11

JACK WAS STUNNED. "Did you just say another baby?"

Sarah looked back down at her phone. "I've got, like, a dozen texts here from people who saw a speech you gave . . . about running for president? What are they talking about?"

"Sarah." Jack stepped forward and put his hands on her shoulders, still thinking about the baby.

"There's some . . . video of you all over the internet. From today."

"What are you talking about?" Jack asked. He could feel his phone buzzing in his pocket like an angry bumblebee.

"Care to tell me a little more about your day at work?" Sarah asked.

Jack leaned in and looked at the images on her phone. "That was today in class. I guess somebody recorded my talk."

"What talk?"

"Someone asked me what I'd do if I were president. It was no big deal. I just answered."

"Look at the views."

He squinted at the phone. "Jesus, does that say four million?"

"That's just on YouTube. This thing, it's all over the place."

"If I'd known that was going to happen, I'd have worn a better shirt."

"The title of the video is *Fight the Government*."

"What?"

Sarah handed him the phone. "Fighting the government . . . Did you say that?"

"I never said fight the government! Well, hold on. Maybe I did . . . sort of." He held up a hand to ward off further questions. "I just said if I were president, I'd use antitrust laws to break the two-party monopoly. Use the government to fix the government . . . something like that."

"The headline doesn't say *fix* Jack, it says *fight*. This was a class lecture?"

"No, it was off the cuff. With the protest turning violent, and one of my students missing . . . When someone asked what I'd do about the shutdown if I were president . . . my mind flashed back to that antitrust article I wrote a few years back and I kind of winged it from there."

"Yeah, it looks like a copy of that article has already resurfaced too."

"Jesus, that's fast."

Sarah looked up at Jack. "Wait, who did you say is missing . . . one of your students?"

"Yeah . . . Max . . . Max Peller."

"Damn . . . So, then . . . you're *not* actually running for president?"

"C'mon, babe. Be serious!"

"Social media thinks you are," Sarah said. "People sure seem to be treating it like some kind of campaign announcement."

"That's beyond ridiculous."

Sarah's phone rang in Jack's hand. "It's Lewis," he said.

Sarah let out a laugh. "No doubt calling to offer his support . . . Here we go." She playfully rolled her eyes.

"Very funny."

Sarah took the phone back and answered the video call with Jack in view. "Hi Lewis, what's up?"

"Jesus Christ, guys," answered Lewis' booming baritone. "First you don't tell me you're running for president, Jack, and then you won't answer my call!"

"Another comedian," Jack replied. He and Lewis had been thrust together as they navigated the trials of first year law at City University of New York, and had remained friends ever since, despite the separate paths their lives had taken. While Jack had pursued the DA's office, Lewis went into private practice and was now lead partner for a highly respected civil law practice in Richmond, Virginia.

The firm made its bones taking down polluters and data privacy violators in civil cases, and the name Lewis Hayes now inspired admiration—or fear—throughout the eastern seaboard. Over six feet, ramrod straight with dark skin and a squared jaw, Lewis cut a figure that would be right at home on the bridge of an aircraft carrier. His eyes held a quiet intensity of someone always studying his surroundings with suspicion. Whenever something new was brewing in Washington, Lewis saw it coming a mile away.

"So, this is not a thing?" Lewis said, sounding disappointed. "Sarah, tell me, is he bullshitting me right now?"

"Our phones started blowing up five minutes ago," Sarah told him. "So, I think it's news to all three of us."

"You know, it's not the worst idea," Lewis noted. "People are sick to death of career politicians . . . " When this drew no response, he said, "So what are you going to do, Jack?"

"I was going to have dinner," Jack said, gazing ruefully at the unopened Thai food on the kitchen table.

"I don't know how to tell you this," Lewis said, "because I know you don't like the spotlight anymore and all that . . . But you really hit a nerve here with this antitrust angle, and as a legal concept I think it could have legs."

"Six million views now," Sarah said, multitasking with her phone.

"And I'm not sure if you've read many of the comments," Lewis said, "but there's already talk about petition drives to get your name on the ballot for November."

"That is absolutely insane," Jack told him.

"More insane than the status quo, Jack? The whole damned country's insane right now, and pissed off beyond belief. So, enjoy your dinner buddy, but this isn't going away anytime soon. Think about it. Politics could use a serious fucking enema right now. Maybe you can be the hose."

"How can I resist when you put it so beautifully?"

"Not kidding," Lewis said. "You want to make this a thing, call me. Immediately."

"Yeah . . . Okay."

"And Sarah," Lewis added, "don't let him do the lone-wolf thing he does and not call until the last minute. I hate that."

"Okay, Lewis," Sarah told him. "But don't hold your breath." The moment she ended the call, Jack redirected their conversation. "Did I hear you say that you want to try for another baby?"

A cautious smile crossed Sarah's face. "I don't want to look back and think "What if." Do you?"

"No, I don't—but the doctor said there could be risks."

"And I could get hit by a bus tomorrow. Life is risk. I'm not saying right now, but I don't want to let fear stop us from being parents."

Sarah's reaction wasn't surprising. Losing her mother at twelve made her realize anyone could be gone tomorrow—so they had to live now. It was part of what he loved about her. Jack grabbed for his own buzzing phone to shut it the hell up, and couldn't help but read the latest text on the screen. *"Oh no . . . Shit."*

"What is it?"

"They found Max."

"Okay . . . Where is he?"

"A DC hospital. In a coma."

CHAPTER 12

JADE RARELY WORE MAKEUP, so it was a struggle to tolerate the layers of powder applied to her face on the set of the AGN 360 morning show. The night before had been a busy one, even after filing her story about President Perez trading military secrets to the Chinese. As expected, her story went up the AGN food chain quickly; first to San Francisco and then overnight to Shanghai. At four a.m. Eastern, AGN shelved the story over confidentiality concerns from China's Politburo Standing Committee about the China/US TAP deal disclosures. By five a.m. the Committee had an apparent change of heart. At six, Jade was told to be in the studio two hours later, where the bombshell story would drop on the web and TV platforms simultaneously. The venue for the reveal was AGN 360, hosted by one of the network's most bankable draws, Chaaya Bandari.

Jade had found her navy-blue pantsuit in the back of her closet that morning, remarkably unsoiled, and had made her way to the twentieth floor of the AGN building just after seven. It was now 7:45—fifteen minutes to airtime. Jade saw no signs of Chaaya Bandari. No one seemed concerned, so she assumed this was normal. Jade felt her phone buzz and checked the number: private. To any DC reporter, that meant answer right away. She answered as the makeup girl finished up. "Jade Xu speaking."

"Jade, this is Angela Dembe." The Chief of Staff's voice was strong, commanding, anything but friendly.

"Yes, Angela," Jade said, trying to sound as if she received this type of call daily, or ever. "What can I do for you?"

"It may be the other way around, actually." Angela's voice softened, catching Jade off guard.

"How do you mean?"

"*Ten minutes to air!*" called a voice in the studio. Still no sign of Chaaya. Jade's heart rate stepped up.

"What I mean is, I know you're about to air a story that will be damaging to the President."

"That may be true."

"It's a little late for cute, isn't it?"

"I guess so."

"I know the story is about the TAP, which has done a lot of good for America . . . but you didn't give us an opportunity to comment." Angela's tone grew darker. "Why?"

"Would you care to comment now?" Jade's heart was hammering, but she kept her voice steady. She hadn't sought comment because the facts seemed clear, and she didn't want to give the White House a chance to kill or pre-empt the story.

"You're running half a story, Jade. Something tells me you know that."

"Why don't you tell me the other half?" Jade suggested.

There was a brief silence. "Running a country is complicated, Jade."

"I think Nixon said that too."

"Goddammit, Jade! Do you really think the President would give the Chinese something that valuable? Think about it."

"So, you're saying the radar technology he gave them is going to be obsolete or something? Is that it?"

A long silence. "Jade, look, this is all off the record. It's complicated, and you know it, but it was the right move then and still is now."

"If this is all off the record, then why don't you just tell me?" Jade said.

"Come meet with the President. Let *him* tell you."

"Is that a firm offer?" Jade's day was getting more interesting by the minute.

"Of course," Angela replied smoothly. "He'll tell you all he can."

All he can . . . There's a dodge-phrase if there ever was one. "I can be there this afternoon."

"Doesn't work," Angela replied abruptly. "It has to be right now."

"You know I'm about to go on-air," Jade replied.

"That's the trade-off, Jade. Now or never."

"Five minutes to air!" They both heard the voice. A door opened across the studio, admitting Chaaya and a gaggle of caffeine-buzzed assistants.

Angela broke the silence. "What's it going to be, Jade?"

Jade's mind spun through the possibilities. A sit-down with a President would be a first for her, if it were to actually happen and this was not just a ploy to buy time while the White House pre-empted the story. Jade knew that Angela Dembe was not one to negotiate, especially with a reporter. Backed into a corner, she did what came most naturally to her. *Throw the punch.* "I'm afraid I've got a story to do," she said.

The line went dead immediately. Jade looked down at her phone, hoping she'd made the right decision.

An AGN studio-tech appeared and pinned a cordless microphone to Jade's lapel. "You're all set, Ms. Xu." She guided Jade to her perch in front of the lights and cameras. Jade's heartbeat found an even higher gear as she settled into the chair.

Chaaya approached in too-high heels and too-strong perfume. "Well, here is our intrepid Jade Xu at last," she beamed. Jade had seen her a thousand times on the screen—her show was AGN's highest-rated news hour—but never in person. She found the intensity of Chaaya's gaze unsettling.

"Hello," Jade said, forcing a smile.

"Please, just call me Chaaya."

Jade nodded, though she'd never intended to call her anything but. Chaaya settled in at her anchor desk, and assistants made final touch-ups to her appearance before being waved away. "Been on TV before, Jade?" Chaaya asked.

Jade shook her head. "Not yet." She'd done some high-profile stories over the years, but nothing on camera. She preferred it that way.

"Well, good way to start with a bang then." Chaaya smiled. "You're in my hands now." She checked the tablet in front of her.

It was an odd comment, Jade thought, her mind conjuring up images of strings attached to her own limbs as Chaaya moved her long manicured fingers overhead.

"One minute to air!"

"Pretty impressive digging," Chaaya said, still looking at her tablet. "You must have some very well-placed sources."

Somehow Chaaya's words didn't seem like a compliment. She felt her cheeks flush slightly under the layers of makeup. "Pretty well-placed, yes," she finally replied. She'd refused to divulge her source to anyone at AGN. Her stubbornness had won out on the matter, despite plenty of screaming over the phone from her potbellied editor, Hal. In the end, AGN had agreed to run the story without exact source confirmation, relying instead on the authenticity of the recording itself after the forensics team had pulled it apart in every possible way, and a source inside the State Department had added their confirmation to the transcript.

"In three . . . two . . . " The producer pointed a long finger at Chaaya and backed away as the studio's background buzz turned to silence.

Chaaya lit up and addressed the camera. "Good morning and welcome to AGN 360 . . . I am your host, Chaaya Bandari, and today we have an AGN exclusive for you that will no doubt shock Washington and become a central issue in the coming presidential election. With me in the studio today is our very own investigative journalist who broke the deeply troubling story that you, our AGN viewers, are about to hear first." Chaaya extended a sweeping arm as the camera expanded its view to include Jade, who for the moment remained an unnamed piece of reporting apparatus on Chaaya's stage. Absent a named introduction, Jade wasn't sure if she should wave at the cameras.

Chaaya continued. "We'll be dedicating most of the hour to this exclusive investigation, so stay right there, and we will be back right after this short message."

"And we're out for thirty seconds!"

Jade blinked in her seat. She knew advertising had worked its way back into news programming because of the audience size, but she'd failed to notice how blunt the reinsertion had been. *Watch this pharmaceutical ad and then we'll tell you about the latest crisis.* Jade found herself half-wondering how long it would be until viewers had to purchase the product in the commercial to get the full story.

Chaaya's voice was instantly in Jade's ear. "Was it Holmes?" she whispered, leaning close.

"What?"

"SecDef, he's your source, right?" Chaaya leaned in closer, the heavy scent of her perfume making Jade recoil slightly.

"Uh . . . no . . . He's not," Jade replied. He was probably Overton's source, but he wasn't Jade's.

"Hmmph." Chaaya leaned away. "That's interesting."

"And we're back in five, four, three, two . . ."

"Welcome back, everyone," Chaaya began, her tone and chin both a fraction lower to better suit the serious moment. "Our top story this morning is an AGN investigative exclusive." She paused for what Jade thought was far too long, her eyes locked on the camera. "We have confirmed," Chaaya resumed, her pace a fraction slower to savor the reveal, "that President Perez, during the US/China summit in 2041, agreed to share top-secret US military radar technology with the Chinese." Chaaya paused for another moment to look at the camera, and Jade half-wondered if dramatic organ music would be piped in to accentuate the reveal.

Chaaya went on for several animated minutes, playing the audio clip from President Perez at the Summit, where he made clear reference to *SCANSAT,* a US military radar system. Just as Jade was beginning to feel like a set prop, Chaaya broke eye contact with the camera and looked her way.

"And we have here in our studio this morning the investigative reporter who cracked this shocking story, AGN's own *Jaaade Schooo*."

Jade did her best to keep from showing the horror she felt at hearing her name presented like she was some kind of fighter being summoned into the ring. "Good morning, Chaaya," she managed, clearing her throat.

"Jade, tell us about the moment you knew the president had stepped over that line by offering classified military technology to China." Chaaya leaned forward with a look of genuine concern, like they were two friends confiding in each other over coffee.

"Good question, Chaaya," Jade said, unsure exactly how to answer. She certainly wasn't going to share that the most critical information was given to her by the Speaker of the House, in a van in a parking lot sometimes used by prostitutes. "The audio file that you played was probably the pivotal moment for me in that—"

Chaaya nodded gravely. "Of course it was. Go on."

"Er . . . well . . . Even though the written transcript had been verified as authentic by a source at the State Department, hearing the actual voice of the president offering to make that deal . . . that was the critical moment for me."

"It certainly is, yes," Chaaya assured her. She then leaned even farther toward Jade, propping her chin on her hand with a look of sympathetic concern, like someone worried about a friend. "Jade, how does it feel . . . as one young reporter . . . and a woman . . . being able to hold an entire administration to account . . . in the way that your work has done here today?"

Christ, don't make me the fucking story Chaaya. Jade knew the angle probably played well for audiences. Petite, attractive female exposes highest office in the land; David and Goliath with heels. But being the story herself, or even part of it, filled Jade with anxiety because making her the story meant sharing feelings—*her feelings.* And Jade would rather puke down her blouse in front of a national audience than do feelings. Sharing feelings would only remind her that each time her investigative reporting disrobed another authority figure, it helped her bury the memory of an abusive stepfather.

"It's just part of the job, Chaaya," Jade replied, "My role as a reporter is to find the truth and bring it to light." She thought about adding, *Just like you, Chaaya*, but she was worried she couldn't say it without sounding sarcastic.

"And you do it so well." Chaaya beamed at her with a thin smile, like an older sister barely hiding her jealousy in front of the parents.

"Thank you." Jade nodded awkwardly, then decided to use the moment to insert some balance into what she felt had been an overly one-sided characterization of the story. "I do think that as this story develops, it will be important to explore *why* the president would offer this technology to China."

Chaaya's smile vanished in a heartbeat, probably at the thought of someone other than herself directing the conversation.

Jade continued. "There's an obvious potential connection to the President's TAP Agreement that came shortly after the summit, but I think the next line of inquiry is why SCANSAT was part of a deal at all. It seems too big a risk for a president to take without reason."

Chaaya lowered her chin further and furrowed her Botoxed brow. "Perhaps so, Jade, but I think what's more important would be to understand what *other* military technologies were also on the table after the summit discussions with China."

Jade stiffened. She had no evidence of any discussions after the summit. Other technologies? How would Chaaya even know that?

Chaaya turned to the camera, a smile edging her lips. "Additional AGN sources have also confirmed that SCANSAT was only *one* of the technologies on the table with China, and that at least one of the additional technologies discussed was related to missile guidance systems."

How the hell could she know that? Jade felt her blood start to simmer. Was someone at AGN running their own side investigation on her story? Was it Chaaya? Could it even happen that quickly—or did Overton share different info with another source? Jade spoke up. "I don't know of any negotiations after the actual summit, so—"

"Of course not." Chaaya's blue eyes seemed to bore into Jade, the implied message clear: *This is my house, not yours. You may know something, little girl, but I will always know a lot more, got it?* She addressed the camera again. "We will have all these details and more on this AGN exclusive throughout the morning. Next up, we'll have our bi-partisan panel of experts break down the potential fallout for President Perez in an election where he is already slipping badly behind in the polls . . . ."

And that signaled the end of Jade's TV debut. She sat like a statue, looking straight ahead as Chaaya wooed the camera. Jade's first real moment of fame felt like something akin to shucking a thousand oysters and then finding out they were all bad. She found herself longing for another commercial break so she could flee the scene.

She may not have been on TV before, but she knew how it worked; the show's producers had apparently concluded, based on less than forty-five seconds of viewer data analysis, that Jade was not the engaging interviewee-type they'd hoped. As a result, Chaaya's earpiece had tipped her to pivot away and stem any viewer drop-off. *Eyeballs.* No doubt Chaaya would remind her producers later that eyeball drops were what happened when she was forced to share the stage with simple mortals.

The cameras were all on Chaaya, but Jade's face grew hot as she looked around the studio. So much for her big moment. She wondered if Woodward and Bernstein's big reveal had felt as shitty as this. *Probably not.*

She caught another unwelcome whiff of Chaaya's perfume. One of the notes sparked a memory that made her flinch slightly; her stepfather's tequila-scented breath as he fondled her at a dark truck stop so many years ago. Even the greatest story of her career couldn't bury the man's pungent memory.

"I'm done," Jade muttered, and stepped from her chair. She unclipped her mic and dropped it in the hand of the nearest set worker as she left. If Chaaya took any notice of Jade's sudden departure, it didn't show.

CHAPTER 13

JADE RODE THE ELEVATOR DOWN from the twentieth-floor studio. She'd automatically pressed the button for the sixteenth-floor newsroom. She watched the doors open and close as she clenched her fists, feeling the impulse to head to the basement fitness center and attack the heavy bag for the hundredth time. Lacking any gym clothes, she pushed the lobby button instead.

Moments later she left the building, interrupted by several cheery congratulations from AGN people she didn't know. Jade let the cool autumn breeze wash over her for several moments. With no idea what to do next, she turned right and started walking. Away from AGN. She even thought about walking away from DC, period. The medium-sized heels she had chosen for her big TV debut clacked on the sidewalk, the sound annoying her greatly. Jade felt like pulling her shoes off and hurling them somewhere, but she wasn't about to walk the dirty streets of DC barefoot.

She paid little heed to where she was going, guided only by a sense of wanting to get as lost as she currently felt. She absently turned off 16th onto Massachusetts Avenue, moving toward DuPont Circle. When she got there, she walked around the circle twice, then set off down a random street.

Through most of the first hour, Jade beat herself up for not getting each side of the TAP deal before breaking the story. Which was probably the way Overton had hoped things would go. Ambition trumps reason.

But how could she break the biggest story of her life and still feel like someone else's pawn?

By the second hour, entering the gates of Rock Creek Park, she acknowledged the obvious answer: One-sided or not, the story had been handed to her—all wrapped up and tied with a pretty bow, and she just did the easiest thing: she delivered it, without ever looking inside. She vowed to be smarter in the future. To not be manipulated.

Somewhere in the third hour, it occurred to Jade that perhaps all that anger therapy in her teens had done some good after all, because she uncovered a more important thought that had been circling in her subconscious:

It just doesn't matter.

She had nailed the biggest story of her career, of pretty much any reporter's career but in the end, it was likely that nothing would change. The investigative reporter in her tried to flick that notion away, several times. But each time, the thought returned like a boomerang with her name on it.

As she walked on, Jade mentally poured over every investigative piece she had written in her entire career, and the events that had followed. Almost without exception, the authority figures she exposed had either remained in place or been replaced by someone similar or worse.

Eventually, Jade was surprised to find herself back at the doors of AGN. She decided to make a phone call. With a measure of atonement that she was unwilling to admit, she dialed the White House line for Angela Dembe's office. Jade had gone against the Chief of Staff's wishes by running the story but had tried to insert some balance into Chaaya's report. Surely Angela would recognize that . . .

Upon hearing Jade's name, the west wing assistant on the other end of the line responded icily. "Ms. Dembe is not available to you." The line went dead before Jade could respond.

She needed sleep after yesterday's all-nighter but didn't want to go home to her dingy little apartment. Jade scanned her work email from her phone and saw two pay stubs instead of the usual one. She opened the second and found an unexpected bonus check. The dopamine-hit was short-lived, however, as Jade's eyes locked onto the modest final sum. She wondered if Woodward & Bernstein got a bonus for Watergate. Probably not, she concluded. They wrote books instead.

After deciding that book writing wasn't in her future, Jade went back inside the AGN building and made her way upstairs. A scatter of applause buoyed her spirits slightly as she entered the newsroom. When she arrived at her workstation, she found that her desk had been replaced with a newer, larger one. She didn't care much for the trappings of office hierarchy, but the gesture gave her mood another upward nudge.

Ten minutes later, when the buzz had settled, she addressed the next inevitable question: *Now what?* She scanned the newsroom, contemplating her next move. It was an unusual feeling, for her at least. She imagined that many of her AGN colleagues spent a good part of their day in this state, like cows staring out at the pasture, without much in the way of expectation. And here she was, doing the same thing. If she was chewing a wad of gum, it would have completed the image nicely, she thought. Reaching into her file cabinet drawer, she popped a piece in her mouth.

Might as well look the part.

She turned to her computer and bit down hard on the gum as she double-clicked the "leads" file, flipping through her notes to see what threads might be worth picking at. She opened the folder on Ethan Bessette, CEO of OmniScientific, one of the world's largest tech companies. He'd given an unorthodox speech several months before at a college commencement, advocating a ban on corporate lobbying so the government could "focus on the serious issue of actually governing." The business press had soundly pilloried his speech as the naïve musings of a trillionaire that could afford such piety, but Jade wondered if there might be a different angle to explore. She opened one of the video files and began to watch.

Before the long-haired CEO could get past his introductions, Jade heard rapid footsteps approaching from behind. She swiveled her chair and was relieved to see junior editor Lenny approaching with a smile.

"Hey . . . *Big Desk Jade*, you got a minute?"

Lenny had been a junior editor at AGN for as long as Jade could remember, but he was the only editor that didn't treat her like she was a caged hen laying eggs. She returned his smile, wondering if a better bonus might have been the firing of their boss Hal who, for the moment, was nowhere to be seen. "Of course, sit down."

Lenny's face brightened at her invitation, and he slid into the new visitor's chair beside the new desk. "The desk in Shanghai has something they want you to take a look at."

Jade rolled her eyes, knowing story 'suggestions' from Shanghai were usually dead-ends, and dead-boring to boot.

"Yeah—I know, I know," Lenny said. "Probably interrupting your victory lap and all that, but they say the diagnostics are hot, it's starting to fly online. So, they really think you'd be . . . well . . . they want to—"

"Lenny, don't pull a friggin' muscle," Jade replied, "just show me." *Besides, it would be good just to do something right now, anything.*

Lenny handed her his tablet. Jade watched a video of someone in the middle of what appeared to be a theatre-style classroom. "Wait, this guy looks familiar . . ."

Lenny nodded. "He's that famous prosecutor guy from New York who took down a bunch of bigshot assholes like five, six years ago. Remember? He was on LiveCourtTV for months."

"Right . . . He was some kind of courtroom messiah, but then he had a full-blown panic attack, with millions watching. Was that him?"

"That's him," Lenny said. "It was during that big trial with the senator. Anyway, he's apparently been teaching constitutional law in North Carolina ever since."

"A little further from the spotlight . . . So what's the angle?" Jade asked. "Why does the Shanghai Desk give a crap about some burned-out prosecutor turned college professor?"

Lenny gestured toward the tablet. "Look at the diagnostics. What he's saying is lighting people up big time. That's about as viral as it gets. They just want you to keep an eye on it, but you might want to run an analysis on the comments feed . . . There's a lot of stuff in there about his idea to use antitrust law against both parties. Also, lots of talk about getting his name on the ballot for November."

"Ballot for what?"

Lenny grinned. "President."

Jade's eyebrows pricked up; that was a wildcard. "Are people that pissed off, that a speech from one sort-of-famous guy with a radical idea gets them started?"

"It looks that way to me," Lenny said. "This thing has almost fifty million views and it's only been up a few days, but, hey, I guess whether it's much of a story is up to the famed Jade Xu to decide."

"Is Shanghai being more empowering than usual, or am I dreaming?"

"Not my department," Lenny replied, looking at the ceiling.

"What's the guy's name again?"

"Jack Sanborn."

She squinted at the screen. "That's right. Pretty boy, isn't he?"

"Also, not my department."

Jade laughed. "Isn't it a little late for people to talk about getting someone on the ballot?"

Lenny puffed up slightly. "I checked that. If people got serious and fast, they could get him on the ballot in forty-nine states. It's about a million signatures, but that's actually not as hard as it used to be if the people behind the ballot drives know what they're doing and don't hit any snags getting the petitions certified and all that."

"What's the fiftieth state?"

"It's Hawaii, but if you mean the state where the ballot deadline is already passed . . . um . . . I actually don't know."

Jade flashed a smile at Lenny. It was nice to talk to an editor who wasn't a pompous prick. "I'll track that down. Be good to know if it's Rhode Island or California." She threw in a wink before thinking about it.

"Hey," Lenny said, crossing his arms for protection. "Speaking of tracking things down, would you like to track down a drink with me sometime?"

Jade fixed Lenny with an amused gaze. "That is the *worst* segue I've ever heard."

He shrugged and tried to hide the blush blooming on his cheeks. "Segues are not really my thing I guess." He pushed himself up from the chair.

"Yeah, I guess they're not," Jade replied as she took in Lenny's mane of frizzy hair. It looked like someone had dropped a toaster in his bathtub, but there was something appealing about it. "But you know what? Yes. To one drink."

"Great. Tonight?"

"Definitely not tonight. I've been up for two days."

CHAPTER 14

DEMARCO CONTI SAT AT HIS USUAL BAR in Queens, thumbing the torn label on his third beer. He squinted at the cracked face of his Casio watch. Almost noon.

"Here we go again," muttered the room's other denizen, the bartender. DeMarco gazed up at the ancient wall-mounted TV. The picture was jumpy, the screen covered with a few decades of grime, and the sound was elusive.

A banner appeared below an image of the White House: *AGN Exclusive: Perez Deals Military Secrets to China*. There were protestors outside the White House, demanding answers that would never come. DeMarco looked away from the screen and back towards more pressing matters. He took a long swig of his Pabst and leaned his fading but still-muscular body against the bar, which had been slowly sinking into the floorboards for several years now.

The front door swung open and thudded into the wall. A large, well-dressed man paused in the doorway, like an old-time cowboy about to enter a rough saloon, except for the cell phone he was staring at. The longer he stood there, the more the sunlight that came with him annoyed DeMarco, who preferred the usual ambiance of dim light, stale beer, and long-surrendered aspirations. He wondered what kind of jackass would make an entrance like that, in a place like this. "Fucking guy," he muttered.

The open door brought fresh air, to which DeMarco's lungs were unaccustomed after years of vaping and steady decline. He didn't know who the new arrival was, but he didn't like him already. DeMarco exploded into a cascade of coughs and hacks that overtook him like repeated jolts from a taser. He raised his hands to his face as if to ward off the attack, and nearly came off his usual perch. *Fucking vapes.*

The visitor stepped inside and chuckled. "Hey, I think you left some of your lung on the bar there." He sauntered past, door closing behind him, and took a seat three stools down.

DeMarco finished his coughing fit. They came often these days, especially at night, which made sleeping more difficult than ever. Not that it really mattered to DeMarco. Despite his less-than-honorable discharge from New York's finest some eighteen months before, he'd managed to hang on to part of his pension. Which afforded a newly divorced "*vilomah*" like him enough money to slowly drink himself to death. Better than waiting on the lungs to do it.

Vilomah was a fancy term for a parent who had to bury their child; the actual meaning having something to do with being against the natural order of things. At least, that's what he remembered hearing, at some point in the jagged haze of the past five years. *Vilomah* meant you were widowed, except your kid was dead and not your wife. Your fifteen-year-old daughter, in his case.

There was no name for the next part, where you lose your wife of eighteen years because she can't stand the sight of you reminding her of what she'd lost. Nor was there a name for the part where you lose your job because a man can't keep ten pounds of being shit-kicked by life in a one-pound tin. Maybe *vilomah* was just God's way of saying you deserved to eat a really big shit sandwich.

Regardless, it didn't much matter anymore. DeMarco was all about the simple life now. He had two main interests: drinking without limits and planning his payback. The latter would come soon enough. He'd been waiting five years. Waiting and planning. Just a few more days to go. What mattered now was the plan, the tools and the location. All was in readiness. And so, he focused his energies on interest number one: drinking.

"The visitor finished looking at his phone and glanced at the bartender. "You have any good Scotch in this dump?" He didn't look like the kind of guy who might become a regular. Not that anyone ever really made that decision consciously.

"Got some Johnnie Walker," said the bartender.

"Black?"

"Just the Red."

"Ah, the red is for shit. You got any Glenlivet?"

The bartender gave the man a look like he had just spoken in Latin.

The visitor sighed. "How the fuck do I celebrate with nothing more than Johnnie friggin' red?"

DeMarco took in the visitor, whose continued presence now rose beyond mere annoyance.

"Up to you," said the barman, wiping down the bar top in a reflex that had nothing to do with cleaning.

The visitor shook his head, "Okay, I guess that'll have to do." He slapped a crisp fifty on the bar and sat down.

"Sorry no cash anymore. Card or tokens only."

"Smallest fucking bill there is and even this shit-dive bar don't take it? What the fuck, man?"

"Owner stopped taking cash last year," the barkeep told him. "Too big a pain nowadays havin' to go across town to make the deposit. Lotta places don't do cash anymore so that makes you old school, pal."

"You got a problem with old school, OLD man?" The visitor's chin jutted forward, and he glowered at the barman like a schoolyard bully.

DeMarco considered getting off his stool then, but his beer was still nice and cold. He didn't want it getting warm. His priorities were not complex these days.

"Look," the bartender said. "I'm just sayin' we don't get cash here, y'know? Technology and all that . . . I don't make the rules." He shrugged and stepped back out of reach, just in case. He tried changing the subject. "So, what's worth celebrating, anyway?"

"My brother just got acquitted."

DeMarco quietly signaled for beer number four, which would clearly be required if this asshole planned to do anything other than just sit there. The barman was grateful for the distraction and headed over. This had the unfortunate side effect of shifting the visitor's attention to DeMarco. He could feel the smug visitor's eyes on him, but he stared straight ahead.

When he concluded that the visitor's eyes had lingered too long, DeMarco took the deepest inhale his ravaged lungs could bear, and started an exchange he knew was unlikely to end well. "What was the charge?" he asked, still staring straight ahead.

"What's that?"

"I said, *What was the charge?*"

The visitor hesitated, appearing to size up DeMarco. "Sexual assault," he announced.

"How about that," said DeMarco, his blood beginning to rise, rousing him from his three-beer Tuesday buzz. He took a swig of beer number four, but this one tasted sour in his mouth. He forced the amber liquid down with a grimace.

"Total bullshit case of course, but my lawyers totally ran circles around the other guy. The chick totally unraveled on the stand. Pathetic."

"Did he do it?" DeMarco asked, finally turning to face the visitor.

"Do what?"

"Rape her."

"Fuck you care. Jury didn't convict."

"That's not what I asked."

"What the fuck are you saying?"

"I'm saying, as his brother I'll bet you know the real deal, don't you. Keep those dirty little secrets in the family. Throw money at 'em if you need to and move on."

"You want to have a problem, friend?" The visitor stood tall, puffing out his chest.

"Depends."

"On what?"

"On whether you're a rapist too, like your scumbag brother."

The visitor was young, lean, quick and sober. He crossed the distance in a step and a half, swinging a haymaker that would shatter DeMarco's jaw if it landed. But DeMarco lunged forward, inside the arc of the punch, driving a lunch pail-sized fist into the visitor's solar plexus with every ounce of energy his two-hundred-fifty-pound bulk could manage.

There was a satisfying hiss as the man's breath whooshed out of him, like a punctured truck tire. He crumpled forward, grabbing his gut, leaving his head exposed. DeMarco grabbed the man's head and bounced it off the edge of the bar, each time harder than the last.

"Jesus, D!" said the barman when he heard something crack. Head or bar, he wasn't sure. "Enough!"

DeMarco froze for an instant, then let go. The visitor slumped to the floor like a sack of potatoes, a tortured howl escaping his mouth as shaky hands grasped what appeared to be his nose—now purple and pointing in multiple directions. DeMarco looked down and saw what he thought were teeth scattered on the floor. Distraction gone, the caustic kaleidoscope of painful memories started up in his head again. The same ones that came each day, until DeMarco drank enough to send them away.

The visitor groaned.

"You better get the hell out of here, D," said the barman.

"Yeah." DeMarco headed for the door.

"And if I was you, I'd stay away a few days."

"Probably right," DeMarco agreed. Just a few more days now anyway. He could head upstate early. Make sure the house was ready for the special guest he had been waiting five years for. DeMarco had taken great care over the past few months, finding a cheap rental house for cash, with the right kind of basement, selected for its hidden access via a connected back-alley garage. And for its excellent soundproofing, no matter how loud the screams. "I'll be out of town for a while anyway," he added. "I'm helping an old friend get settled in a new place."

CHAPTER 15

JACK STOOD AT THE CENTER of his Criminal Litigation 344 classroom, hands in pockets. The afternoon period had officially ended fifteen minutes ago, but as it was the last session of the day and few had moved from their seats, he allowed the discussion to continue.

None of the questions were about the finer points of criminal litigation, but this came as no surprise to Jack. He stopped checking YouTube and TikTok when his 'lecture' views passed fifty million in three days. Because his last moment in the spotlight hadn't ended particularly well, he wasn't eager for a second fifteen minutes of fame. Nor was Sarah, whose mind was on getting back to work and trying for another baby.

When Jack first arrived on the UNC campus four years before, fresh from his LiveCourtTV unraveling, the greetings leaned toward sympathetic. Over the past three days, though, they were enthusiastic, some almost to an extreme. One burly student pointed a finger at him in the hall and bellowed, "Hell yeah, dammit! Sanborn for President!!"

Jack noticed quite a few unfamiliar faces in the classroom this afternoon. A student or two auditing his class wasn't unusual, but close to a dozen certainly was. Every seat was full, including Max's. Jack did his best to compartmentalize the fact that Max remained unconscious in a DC critical care unit.

"But professor," an earnest, red-haired student in the front row said, pulling Jack back from his thoughts. "Doesn't FECA protect the parties from antitrust laws being applied to them?"

Jack shot her an impressed look. "Great question. For those of you that aren't familiar with the Federal Election Campaign Act of—"

He held his hand out, inviting the student to finish his sentence.

"1971," she proclaimed.

"Correct, thank you." He nodded. "FECA is certainly relevant here but has generally been interpreted narrowly against *spending* practices in elections. On the topic of *other* practices restricting competition and causing consumer harm, FECA is very much in the grey zone."

The questions continued for another twenty minutes, until Jack finally signaled an end to the afternoon's proceedings. The room burst to life as backpacks were zipped and slung and students flowed toward the exits. Through the collection of moving bodies, Jack noticed a small, dark-haired woman in a far row, remaining still. She appeared a touch older than the rest of the group and wore stylish clothes that screamed anything but student.

Once the room had nearly cleared, she made her way down to Jack. Her face looked familiar, but for once Jack couldn't place it.

She smiled. "Hi, professor. I'm Jade Xu from AGN." She extended her hand, her eyes warm but already taking stock of Jack. She was almost a foot shorter than Jack, but something about her gaze made her seem taller.

"I thought you looked familiar," he said, and shook hands. "Shouldn't you be out doing talk shows or something? That was quite a story you broke this week."

Jade gave a quick shrug and tugged at the sleeve of her blazer. "Work always suits me better."

Jack unconsciously absorbed several body signals, concluding instantly that there was a great deal more to her clipped reply than met the ear.

As if sensing Jack's assessment, Jade pivoted the conversation. "I tried to reach you yesterday, but you're a hard man to catch."

Jack's phone had been buzzing with unknown numbers over the last seventy-two hours, and he hadn't felt inclined to answer. "Sorry, I'm not avoiding you, just not much for the press."

"Not anymore at least."

Let the sparring begin. "Fair enough," Jack replied, meeting her eyes and avoiding further comment on his LiveCourtTV days. "What can I do for you, Ms. Xu?"

"It's Jade, please. Could we sit for a minute?"

"For a minute, yes." Jack and Jade moved to a couple of chairs in the semi-circular front row. "Is this an attempt at an interview?"

"Well, it's whatever you want it to be, Professor."

Jack replied with an expression that failed to mask his annoyance at the coy remark.

"Look, Professor," Jade continued. "I'm a reporter so I always want an interview, but off the record is fine for now. I'm sorry if it feels like I'm ambushing you here."

Jack eased back in his chair a bit. *No harm in an off-the-record conversation.* "Okay. How can I help you, Jade?"

"Forgive me for being blunt, but are you for real?"

"You don't beat around the bush, do you?"

"I'm sorry, I failed charm school and I know you're busy, so I thought I'd just get to the point."

"I see. And the supposed point is I'm some burned out former prosecutor that's looking to milk his second fifteen minutes of fame? Is that it?"

Jade cocked her head as she considered the question. "Maybe . . . but if that were true, you'd at least have answered your phone . . . And I wouldn't have to pose as a student to be able to reach you."

"So, you came here to check that I'm not?"

"Not what," she replied. "Burned out?"

"No; looking for another fifteen minutes."

"To be honest, I'm not sure why I came. I mean, I was assigned the story and all that. You're well past seventy million views across social media and still climbing, so that's why AGN sent me your way, but . . ." Jade hesitated.

"But what?"

"Well . . . I didn't have to come here and camp out in your classroom to do that kind of story. The second fifteen minutes of fame version is pretty brain-dead reporting, no offense."

Jack thought, *And it's another excuse for the media to recycle that old clip of me having a panic attack on live TV.* "So why are you here?" he asked.

Jade paused. Her gaze was focused on Jack, but she seemed suddenly far away. He saw something flash across her eyes quickly, but like the shadow from a bird overhead it was gone just as fast. "I guess . . . Someone other than the reporter in me wants to know what this moment is really about."

"This, meaning a college lecture that went viral?"

"Is that all this is to you?"

"Well, it's not part of some grand political plan, if that's what you mean."

"Maybe so, but I'm not sure what a speech about using antitrust laws against the political establishment has to do with the second-year Constitutional Law class you were teaching that day."

I see you've done your homework. "So, you think it was planned?"

Jade sat forward in her chair. "Well, the ballot petitions did kick in almost immediately."

"And you think I had something to do with that?"

"The rumors back in New York were that you had political ambitions four years ago. Perhaps they're still lingering."

"Look, Jade," Jack replied, reminding himself that she was a reporter, and even off-the-record he needed to be a bit careful. "We were all a bit upset. A student from my class was critically injured at the SoMAD protest in DC. He's now in a coma."

"I know Professor . . . I'm sorry." Jade's cheeks blushed slightly but she gathered herself quickly. "So, you're saying that, and I get it, you gave an off-the-cuff talk about using the Department of Justice to break up the . . . " Jade looked upwards, obviously trying to recall the exact words Jack had used.

"Two-party monopoly," Jack added, filling in the blank.

"That was it," Jade nodded. She cocked her head. "But a two-party monopoly is really just a duopoly, isn't it?"

"Like I said, not a prepared speech."

"It's a good turn of phrase, though . . . And the reaction since then, the move to get your name on state ballots for November . . . You're saying you had no hand in that at all?"

"None whatsoever. I don't even know how many signatures are needed for ballots. And as you can see, I'm not running around campus with a clipboard."

"It's 953,801."

"What's that?"

"That's how many signatures you need to get on the ballot in fifty states," Jade replied confidently.

"Jeez that's a lot of signatures."

"Actually, it isn't," Jade answered. "Not with online ballots, which all but three states allow."

"You're seriously tracking this?"

"Sure." Jade shrugged. "It's part of the story. It's only been a few days, but the petitions are pretty organized. Looks like they're already getting the required electors lined up too. It's kind of impressive if you ask me."

"You can track how many signatures as well?"

"My job," Jade replied evenly. "Your bigger problem, though, is timing."

"I'm not sure I have a problem, Jade." His voice was laced with sarcasm, but he found himself starting to enjoy the conversation.

"Right. So, you said. This is all just happening. I get that." After a pause she added, "Are you aware that Texas is the one state that has already passed its deadline for third-party candidates to be on the ballot?"

Jack let out a laugh. "That little state huh? No, I wasn't, but again, if this was something organized, waiting until after the Texas deadline would be a pretty poor election strategy, wouldn't it?"

"So, I guess that means you're unaware of the pending lawsuit to challenge that closing date as unconstitutional?"

Jesus Christ. Who are these people doing this? "No, Jade, I wasn't aware of that either." Jack's mind flashed back to political news from the past. Early ballot access deadlines had indeed been successfully challenged in some states as unfairly impeding voter choice, so the Texas lawsuit might succeed.

"This may make for a more interesting story than I thought," Jade announced.

"How so?"

"Well, for starters, *I believe you.* Which is unusual for me. But I do believe that this is all just happening around you."

"So here we are then," Jack patted his thighs, ready to end the conversation. "On the same page at last."

"Come for an in-studio interview." Jade almost blurted it out, like Jack was about to bolt and she needed to get a commitment before he did.

Jack chuckled. "Why would I do that? I have no political ambitions, Jade. I have a full life right here."

"That's kinda the point."

"Meaning?"

"Meaning," Jade got up from her chair and stood in front of Jack, "I think you've said some important things that could put real pressure on the system to end this shutdown."

"I'm not sure a college professor giving an interview is going to end a government shutdown."

"Maybe not. But you're also someone with a pretty badass idea to dismantle the two-party monopoly in politics. People are responding to that in a way I've never seen before."

Jack stood up. *This was a nice fantasy. Time to resume normal life.* "Thanks for the chat."

"I know you don't want the spotlight, Professor. But don't you think Max Peller would want you to use this moment to at least have a conversation?"

Jade's mention of Max's name landed like a slap. His face grew hot at the obvious manipulation tactic. Now he was angry. "Jade–"

"I'm sorry, Professor," she interrupted. "I shouldn't have brought up Max like that, I'm sorry."

Jack could see Jade's face flush as she looked to the floor. "I'm sorry," she repeated, flustered. "Thank you for talking with me today. It's all off the record, completely."

Jack watched her abruptly turn and walk away, half expecting her to look back or offer her number so he could '*just think about it and call anytime day or night*'. Instead, she simply walked out the door.

Jack's face was still warm at the Max comment. *Such a cheap reporter move.* Even if she apparently regretted it. And even if that was exactly what Max would want him to do.

CHAPTER 16

WHEN JACK'S HEAD HIT THE PILLOW that night, he expected to toss and turn for a while. He'd given Sarah a full download on the surreal conversation with Jade Xu, but once they turned out the lights he was asleep in minutes, dissolving promptly into the familiar dream.

The gothic doors loomed before him as he stood facing the back of the courtroom. Waiting. He made eye contact with the bailiff, who looked bored as a stone. Jack tried to scream a warning, but his voice was nothing more than an airy hiss in his own ears. He waved his arms at the bailiff, but the man just looked past him, unseeing. The faintest sound finally escaped Jack's mouth: *Stop her* . . . But it's a sound only he can hear. Jack turned to his counsel's table. Someone has to listen. Someone has to help before it's too late. The person seated at the table is not his co-counsel, but they are familiar. And terrifying. A bloodied Max with hair matted to his temple, looking up at Jack. His eyes are sunken and lifeless but staring straight at him. Jack finally let out a scream.

Sarah's voice finally penetrated Jack's mind. "Jack! Babe, I'm right here! It's another dream . . . Jack!" He sat up in bed, rubbing his face as if that would erase the image of Max, black eyed, calling out to him.

"I'm okay," he finally mumbled into the darkness, feeling Sarah's cold hands on his chest. He let her cooling hands bring him back to the darkness of their bedroom, the fog of the dream still buzzing as it faded.

"Was it the same dream?" Sarah asked.

"Sort of," Jack rasped into the dark, his voice scratched and dry. "Max was there this time."

"Oh," Sarah replied knowingly. "Instead of Gracie?"

"Maybe . . . I think so." Jack wiped the sweat from his lip and swung his legs over the edge of the bed.

"Do you need anything?" Sarah asked, leaning into him.

Jack shook his head. "I just need these dreams to stop."

"I know," Sarah replied. "They will."

"I think I need to go there," Jack said.

"Go where, Babe?"

"For the interview," he mumbled. "To AGN."

"You mean with the reporter you met today?"

"Yeah."

After a pause, Sarah replied. "Can you trust her?"

"I don't know. She's a reporter." Jack was almost fully awake, rubbing his eyes in the dark. "She said it would be a conversation."

"You believe that?"

"No," he replied. "But I think I need to go anyway, at least to stop this circus of speculation." He looked at Sarah through the darkness, feeling the silence of her resistance.

"I think you need to sleep some more," she finally said. "It's not even four."

"I'm awake," Jack replied. "I'm gonna get some water . . . You sleep." He slipped out of bed, grabbed his phone and made his way downstairs to the kitchen. There were still dozens of text messages he hadn't responded to: old friends, new friends, colleagues. There were too many. He saw one from Lewis about his YouTube views passing a hundred million.

This is nuts . . .

He was about to put down the phone, but the sight of Max's name in the body of one of the very last messages to come in stopped him cold. The text came from a number not listed in his contacts, but it hit him like a punch in the stomach.

Professor—Max died at 2 a.m.

Jack felt a numbness as he sat down heavily at the kitchen table and put down his phone. He remained there in the dark for a long time. Listening to faint, normal sounds from inside and outside, in a world that to him seemed anything but normal, at least not anymore. After a while, he picked up the phone again. It took him a minute to find Jade's work email on the AGN website. It took him much less time to tap out his message to her.

Okay. One conversation. When and where?

CHAPTER 17

Late the next afternoon, Jack sat in a chair on the set of AGN News, doing his best to relax. The chair creaked under his frame as he leaned back and submitted to pre-broadcast makeup, feeling the heat of the camera lights as set technicians hurried about. Being interviewed live in-studio directly following the AGN evening news was not exactly what Jack had in mind after agreeing to 'a conversation.' But the thought of Max urging him to use the moment compelled him to continue.

While riding the bullet train from Raleigh to the DC studio, Jack reflected on his last TV appearance. That moment was in court, and lives were at stake. *This is just the news*, he reminded himself now. But he still felt a crackle of nerves, reminiscent of the moment before opening statements in a jury trial. *Channel the energy, Jack. Don't fear it.*

"Professor Sanborn, I'm just going to pin this on you, okay?" A spearmint-smelling production assistant leaned in and clipped a cordless mic on the blazer Jack had chosen for the occasion. No tie. *You're not a politician Jack, don't look like one*, Sarah had reminded him. *And don't sound like one either, Honey*, she added as he dashed out the door to catch the train.

"Say something for sound check Professor, okay?"

"I've changed my mind," Jack deadpanned.

"Funny guy," the assistant replied blandly, as if she'd heard the same reply a thousand times before.

Jack heard the rapid approach of heels. "Well, you may *want* to change your mind," Jade said, as she slid into the studio seat beside him. Her cheeks were flushed. "It won't just be me doing the interview."

"Oh, why's that?"

"Politics about politics," Jade replied, shaking her head and looking down. "And probably the fact that I wasn't that good on TV last time."

That makes two of us. Jack blinked to block out the LiveCourtTV memory.

"So as a result, Chaaya Bandari is joining us in the segment," Jade said. "It wasn't my call, and if you want to pull out, I understand. I don't ambush people; I really hate that approach."

Jack could see the anger and embarrassment in her eyes and concluded that he wasn't about to be played. At least not by her. "We'll be fine," he said, prompting a small smile from Jade.

"Okay," she nodded. "Chaaya agreed to let me open the conversation and I'll do my best to lead it, but . . . "

"I know. I saw your segment with her. So, consider my expectations managed." Jack had also seen enough of Chaaya on TV to know she pulled no punches.

A clackier, faster set of heels approached. Jade mouthed a *thank-you* to Jack and turned to face the approaching Chaaya. She looked arresting in a deep red pantsuit that screamed *center-of-attention*.

"Chaaya," Jade pivoted and extended a palm toward Jack, "meet Professor Jack Sanborn."

"Professor!" Chaaya exclaimed, like someone opening a surprise gift. "Welcome back from the wilderness. So nice of you to join us for a little chat." She settled into her usual chair, Jade in between them. "It's been quite a while out of the spotlight since, well, you know." She wrinkled her nose, as if the memory of Jack's TV flameout five years ago came with a bad odor.

And we're off. "Good to meet you, Chaaya," Jack replied.

"It must feel great to be back in the spotlight after so long."

Jack did his best to smile. "That's not why I'm here, but I'm glad for the chance to have an important conversation with you both."

"Yessss," Chaaya replied, her eyes flashing a look that made Jack think about a tiger ready to eat wounded prey. "A conversation . . . Absolutely."

"Twenty seconds, people!" came the call from one of the producers. An assistant poked at Chaaya's large black hair with a comb until she was waved away like a fly.

"Okay we're live in five . . . four . . ."

Chaaya waited for the final cue and then burst into life. "Hello and welcome to AGN Tonight. As promised, we are leading off with two very special guests here in the studio with me." Chaaya beamed her best smile in the direction of her guests, but Jack was pretty sure she was looking between them. "We have AGN's own investigative wonder, Jade Xu, with us again." Chaaya paused and looked at Jade as if waiting to be thanked.

"Hello," Jade replied, her smile looking rigid.

"And with her tonight," Chaaya continued, "is a very special guest. He's the former New York prosecutor many of you LiveCourtTV fans will no doubt remember . . ." Jack took note of Chaaya's sly 'wasn't-that-a-doozy' eyebrow raise as she jogged everyone's memory of Jack's final moments of TV infamy. "But even more of you may know him from a controversial political lecture of his that went viral last week. Jack Sanborn, welcome to the show."

"Thank you, Chaaya," Jack replied. "And thank you, Jade, for the invitation to be here." He could see Chaaya bristle as someone other than her received thanks on her show.

Jade began the conversation as agreed. "Professor, in a moment we're going to show a clip from your lecture that has been watched over a hundred and thirty million times, but before we show it—can you comment on the groundswell of enthusiasm generated by your idea to use the Department of Justice against the government itself?"

"One hundred and *fifty* million views, actually," Chaaya interrupted, prompting a split-second glower from Jade.

Jack flashed a smile. "Jade, I hate to start with a clarification, but I'm a professor so I'm afraid I have to." Jade nodded her assent. "The idea is to use the Department of Justice against the political *parties* themselves, not the government. The government employs over two million people directly and eighteen million indirectly, most of whom right now remain out of work while the Democrats and Republicans bicker and blame." Jack leaned in closer, feeling like a thoroughbred fast out of the gate. "My premise is that if we break up the two-party monopoly and inject a third option into the mix, politicians will have to go back what they used to do before most of us were born—compromise to get things done, for the benefit of those that elected them."

"As someone who has no involvement in professional politics, Professor," Chaaya interrupted, "I have to ask: what informs your expert assessment on such a complex political matter?"

And the gloves are off, I see. "It's simple game theory, Chaaya." Jack answered evenly. "Even our forefathers understood it. That's why John Adams said what he feared most was two great parties putting all their energy into opposing each other. Whereas with a third party solidly in the mix, once the first impasse gets broken by one of the big parties cutting a deal with enough independents to pass something into law, the dealmaking floodgates open. Otherwise, one party just sits there and watches while their enemy moves some version of their agenda forward."

"I think your key word there was *theory,* Professor," Chaaya replied. "But it could also come across as the naïve musings of someone quite far from real-world politics."

"It's not just theory," Jack countered, ignoring her patronizing tone. "Spend five minutes looking at legislation in most developed nations. Progress is being made on topics that matter as the world evolves." Jack could feel his pulse rising. "This is why, as much as politicians won't admit it, the US has fallen to 49th in the world on the Quality-of-Life Index."

"Forty-ninth?" Jade repeated, obviously surprised at the number.

Jack nodded grimly. "We've been falling about one spot a year for decades now. Our only number one ranking? Space exploration."

"Well, before we venture back into space," Jade inserted with a slight smile as she looked at the camera, "let's show the clip we promised from Professor Sanborn's lecture, which has fired up voters across the political spectrum."

Jack looked down at the floor monitors, grateful for a break after the early barrage from Chaaya. He watched footage of himself explaining why the continued development of politics as an industry had hit certain legal tripwires, rendering it susceptible to antitrust action. If someone in power would be *daring* enough to do it. *Crazy enough might have been the more accurate description to use,* Jack thought.

The footage drew to a close and the floor producer signaled back to Jade, who looked at Jack. "In the past two weeks you've been called, among other things, a visionary, a fascist, a radical and a starved celebrity looking for a return to the spotlight. That's quite a range of public reactions. What would *you* call yourself, Professor?"

"I've been called many things before. But I'd say I'm nothing more than a realist, someone who believes that through legal means we can fix a very big problem that's turning the country against itself."

Chaaya cleared her throat. "One of our live viewer polls goes a bit further, Professor." She held up a tablet for proof, but Jack could see from his angle that the screen was blank. "Thirty percent see you as an anarchist, and twenty-four percent see you as anti-American." Chaaya let the words land as Jack felt the heat rising from his neck to his cheeks. *Did she just make that up?* "Does that bother you, Professor, to be called anti-American?"

"Chaaya," Jack replied evenly, "I came on this program to talk about a serious idea that could address the endless stalemates in Washington that leave people to suffer. People like Max Pellar, one of my students." He felt a slight quiver in his voice as he blurted out the name but pressed on. "He was killed this week at one of the SoMAD protests, just for being there and for speaking out, and do you know why he took that risk?" Jack could see Chaaya about to rebut, but he decided not to give her the chance. "He did that because he knew that every one percent higher unemployment means thirty-seven thousand more deaths in a year, twenty-two-thousand more heart attacks, nine-hundred seventy more suicides, six hundred eighty-eight more homicides, and four-thousand and eleven more mental hospital admissions." Jack could feel his patience fading as he pulled the statistics from memory, but he was careful to keep his tone steady and measured. "Why aren't we talking about that, Chaaya?"

"We will, Professor," Chaaya replied stiffly, "but first I'd like to hear your answer to those who feel that you are down on America?" She wasn't about to back down, especially on her own show. Jack glanced over and noted the look of strained shock on Jade's face, like a bystander watching two shoppers in the grocery aisle pummel each other. "Are you anti-America, Professor?"

Her words hung in the air like an acrid fog. *Okay, the gloves are really off now.*

"Chaaya, do you like Jif Peanut Butter?"

The entire set fell utterly still for a long beat. "I'm sorry, Professor. Did you say *peanut butter?*"

Jack nodded. "I actually said *Jif* Peanut Butter. It's a particular brand. Do you like it?"

Chaaya's eyes flashed a look of alarm, while Jack could see Jade's look of puzzlement in his periphery. "Sure," came Chaaya's uncertain reply.

"Jif has had a great slogan for decades: *Choosy Moms Choose Jif.* It makes you feel smart when you buy it. You've heard that slogan, right?" Jack's eyes bored into Chaaya.

"Um, yes but . . . "

"I read a story recently about that famous slogan that explained the math behind their claim."

Chaaya and Jade seemed unable to respond. "Basically, they give a bunch of moms Jif and some other peanut butters to try, and then they ask them if they prefer one over the other."

"I see," Chaaya replied slowly, still stunned to near silence.

"It turns out that ninety percent of the moms don't care either way; it's just peanut butter! It's peanuts, oil, salt, sugar; that's it. They're pretty much all the same. But of the ten percent who *do* taste a difference, six percent—the so called 'Choosy Moms'—like Jif. So, they try to imply that it's the best, but it's really only six out of a hundred Moms who actually give a damn either way."

"This isn't the Food Network, Professor," Chaaya said, trying her best to look dismissive but still looking a bit panicked.

"No, it isn't, so let me make the connection clear. I've watched your show, Chaaya. The numbers you quote are just slogans. They're not the real math we should be talking about. Here's the real math: 72% of voters didn't vote in the last election, and 90% don't trust the media."

Chaaya's face looked like she'd split a tooth. "So, voters don't care what kind of peanut butter or politician is on offer, because it makes no difference; they're all pretty much the same. Yet here you are Chaaya, reporting what lights up your Twitter-X feed like it's a national referendum."

"We report the facts, Professor, not slogans," Chaaya replied acidly, her black mane quivering as she touched a long finger to her desk.

Jack leaned in closer, catching the smallest glimpse of a smile on Jade's face. "If it's just about the facts, Chaaya, then why would AGN need eight different channels to cover the same news, all at the same time?"

"Well, there's a lot of news to cover, and AGN prides itself on a balanced viewpoint."

"Yes, Chaaya, but that's only balance if your viewers watch all eight shows at the same time. Do they do that?"

"What are you referring to?" Chaaya's face had lost any pretense of a smile.

"I'm referring to this week's coverage of another shutdown riot on the steps of yet another State House. Just as an example." Jack extended his fingers to start counting. "On AGN One and Two the rioters were thugs, and the imagery was largely black rioters. On AGN Three the rioters were white. Here on AGN Four, they weren't rioters at all; they were desperate families. AGN Five, it was a mob provoked by police aggression. AGN Six, Robin Hood-like heroes fighting for their country. And lastly AGN Seven and Eight, which apparently target viewers who don't want the news at all, covered stories about the new Panda at the zoo apparently being gay and a cross-species swinger!"

"Let's come back to your lecture, Professor," Chaaya replied with a pointed finger, looking desperate to get the segment back in her own hands.

"Great idea," Jack replied, "but I want to thank you first, because this discussion was an important reminder."

"A reminder of what?" Jade inserted, obviously eager for the exchange to continue.

"Of something almost as important as using the antitrust laws to break up the two big parties." Jack replied. "The Fairness Doctrine." He could see from Jade's face that the concept was unfamiliar, but the heat in Chaaya's eyes was clear.

"Please explain, Professor," Jade replied to pre-empt Chaaya. It looked to Jack like Chaaya wasn't sure which one of them she'd rather kill first. He continued. "The Fairness Doctrine was in place for decades to ensure the news, in one program, presented a balanced view." Jack held up both palms like a scale. "And when it was in place, trust in the media was very high. Would you believe almost eighty percent."

"And the Fairness Doctrine," Jade said. "I'm guessing it's not in place now."

"Correct. It was repealed in the eighties to make way for twenty-four-hour news."

"You're sounding remarkably anti-free speech right now Professor," Chaaya proclaimed. "And again, quite anti-American."

"Well," Jack replied, "first of all, the Fairness Doctrine was an

American law, so nothing anti-American about it. But without that, here's what happened. News became programming, not news, which was great for a while. But the only way to keep people watching is to make sure it's not boring. Compromising politicians in the middle are boring! But inflammatory politicians at the extremes, preaching ideology over progress? That's just great television, good versus evil."

"That's a very colorful view, Professor," Chaaya replied, shaking her head.

"Are you saying I'm wrong?"

Jade spoke up. "So, Professor, what are you suggesting be done at this point?"

"I suggest that citizens demand reinstatement of the Fairness Doctrine, for their own well-being and the well-being of the country."

"You can't be serious," Chaaya replied. "That's a blatant violation of the First Amendment. That's why it was struck down."

"I am dead serious," Jack replied. "And the Fairness Doctrine has nothing to do with the First Amendment, Chaaya. Having it in place didn't prevent anyone from sharing any view, it only demanded balance so the viewers could decide for themselves how they felt, instead of being told what to feel."

Jack didn't wait for a reply, instead pivoting in his chair to face the camera and looking solemnly into the lens. "Ask yourselves at home, do you feel better off after you watch the news? Any news, not just this station. Or do you mainly feel angry and scared? If you take a break from the news for two weeks, how do you feel then?"

"It sounds like you favor government-controlled media, which is one of the hallmarks of Communism," Chaaya hurled back, desperately wanting to get Jack on the defensive.

"What I am for," Jack replied with his voice rising as he turned back to Chaaya, "is a return to media that is respected and trusted to deliver truth, and I think along with applying antitrust laws to end two-party dominance, a return to the Fairness Doctrine needs some very serious discussion . . . for all our sakes."

Chaaya twitched but was uncharacteristically lost for words. She seemed about to physically explode.

Jack turned and looked out into the studio. "And I'll bet that a lot of you who work hard on delivering the news got into it for the right reasons, and would love to find a way to bring respect back to the news. I hope we can do that, because we sure need it." He shifted his gaze to the camera. "I'm not anti-American. I'm anti-incompetence, and incompetence is pretty much all I see in politics anymore."

When he looked back to Chaaya and Jade, one of them looked like she'd swallowed battery acid, the other like she might burst into applause.

CHAPTER 18

FOR MOST OF THE UBER JOURNEY BACK to DC's Union Station, Jack alternated between elation at how the AGN 'conversation' had gone, and remorse for being on the edge of losing his cool for much of the exchange, which had clearly veered into unplanned territory with the Fairness Doctrine discussion. *And the Jif peanut butter example . . . Seriously?* He could hear Sarah's words now: *Jack, the thoughts that come out of that head of yours sometimes . . .* More than anything, though, he felt he'd done right by Max. And to him, that was as important as anything else.

By the time his Uber dropped him at the west entrance of the station, his phone was buzzing with texts.

Sarah's was first. *You did great. Wake me when you get home. Love you.*

Lewis was second. *Remind me not to piss you off on camera. Awesome job. Count me in if you want to do this for real. PS. Peanut butter . . . ?*

Jack smiled and tucked the phone in his blazer as he walked to the train platform. *Might just be able to catch the 10:05.* After seeing the train on his platform, Jack was about to break into a jog when he saw it lurch and begin its slow exit from the station. He stopped and looked up at the large master schedule panel overhead. He'd missed the bullet train to Raleigh that would have made the trip in an hour, but there was a 10:15. It wasn't an express, but it would get him home sometime after one AM.

"Great interview!" Startled by the sudden voice, Jack looked up to see two commuters in business suits walking past, the second one flashing him a hearty thumbs-up.

"Thanks," Jack smiled back. *Fifteen minutes of fame not quite over yet.*

Jack made his way to platform twelve, which was largely empty but for a few straggling commuters. He saw a metal bench illuminated by thin blue light-strips along its edges. The disinfecting lights had become ubiquitous on and around public transportation, but struck Jack as eerie.

He parked himself on the bench, resisting the temptation to pull out his phone and check for online reactions to his interview. Instead, he let his mind play back the interaction in detail, his adrenaline finally back down to normal after the charged experience. He was surprised to find himself wondering if Jade would be okay after the way the interview had gone. He felt sure Chaaya would have some say in that, and not in a good way.

Jack noticed two serious-looking men in dark, casual suits approaching. They were methodically scanning the platform, but he noticed their eyes returning to him with each pass. Twenty feet out, one of the men stopped walking and took a position against a post, eyes still scanning the platform. The second man walked past Jack and took up a similar position a short distance off.

Before Jack's mind could formulate theories about what was happening, he saw two more figures coming his way. One looked and dressed exactly like the first two, scanning as he walked. But the fourth man was nothing like the other three. He had a slighter build and a more relaxed gait. Unlike his apparent companions, he was focused solely on Jack.

With each step the man took, his face grew more familiar. He seemed intensely serious, but not threatening. The mid-length brown hair that fell loosely around his stubbled face would have looked at home on a surfer, but his entourage and his casual-but-costly clothes made it clear he had not recently departed the beach.

"Mind if I join you, Professor?" the man asked. His voice was pleasant, with the hint of an accent Jack couldn't quite place. "I'm Ethan Bessette," he added after Jack's momentary hesitation.

"Ah, I thought you looked familiar," Jack replied, silently admonishing himself for not recognizing the richest man on the planet, reclusive or not. "Somehow seeing you in a train station threw me off."

"That happens to me more than you'd think," Ethan told him. "I actually prefer it." He extended a hand that Jack accepted. "May I sit?"

"Sure thing." Jack noted that the security detail had tightened their perimeter a bit. *No doubt par for the course when you're a trillionaire.* As CEO of OmniScientific, the largest and an often controversial leader in global big-data analytics, Ethan had a penchant for security of all types, from cyber to physical.

"Don't mind my security detail," Ethan added. "A necessary accompaniment in my line of work." That line included predicting everything from major societal shifts and how nations and industries would be impacted, to what flavor of ice cream someone in Peoria would buy on a Tuesday in March. In the information economy, Ethan Bessette had become the Midas of the past two decades, with every new algorithm churned out by Ethan's company instantly turning to gold. OmniScientific would be the highest-valued company in the world overnight if it went public. But that speculation had ended when, in a rare public statement, Ethan declared that *Omni will never, ever, go public as long as I am alive.*

"You ride the train?" Jack asked. He assumed the richest man in the world moved around by personal air vehicles, and perhaps took the occasional rocket journey.

Ethan looked around. "Hardly; that would be a circus. I actually came here to see you."

"You're kidding."

Ethan cocked his head slightly. "There is a one-hundred percent chance I am not." He glanced around. "I thought it was time to discuss certain . . . probabilities."

Jack was confused. "Wait . . . How did you even know I was here in the station?"

In response, Ethan blinked and gave a slight shrug that let Jack know how rhetorical that question was for a man who likely had access to more up-to-the-minute data than anyone else in the world.

"Jesus, really?" Jack asked.

"Only when necessary," Ethan replied in an offhand manner.

Clearly not the first time. "Well, now that you've located me, Mr. Bessette, what can I do for you?"

"Please, call me Ethan, and I should probably start with what we have in common."

I can't imagine. "Okay, Ethan," Jack replied. "What would that be?"

"My son Max," Ethan replied. His eyes flashed a shadow as he mentioned his name.

Jack stiffened. "Max . . . " He stumbled for words. "You mean Max Peller?"

"I know, different last name," Ethan offered. "As much my idea for security reasons as it was Max's for reasons of personal independence."

"I'm . . . I'm so sorry, Ethan." Through all their interactions, Max had given Jack no hint of his real identity. *I guess he valued privacy as much as his father does.*

Ethan nodded at the condolence. "Thank you. A very unfortunate side effect of the conditions at present."

While Ethan's words sounded like someone describing a rash of inclement weather, Jack could see the hollow pain in the man's eyes. "Your son is actually the reason I'm in DC right now."

"That doesn't surprise me," Ethan replied. "He has that effect on people."

"It sounds like you saw the interview tonight."

"I did. I had already planned to meet you before then, but the early response to tonight's interview makes this discussion even more relevant."

"What discussion is that exactly?" Jack replied.

"The probability of you winning the White House." Ethan said the words as blandly as someone ordering coffee with two creams and one sugar, but they landed on Jack like a ton of bricks.

Jack shook his head in disbelief. "Well, the probability is zero, so this should be a short discussion."

Ethan rubbed his chin. "I don't believe that number."

"You think this is some cooked-up plan I have to run for office?" Jack asked.

"Not at all," Ethan replied. "I deal in mathematics and probabilities, and I believe you care too much to not consider running."

"So, you're a psychologist as well, then?"

Ethan wrinkled his nose. "Heavens no, psychology is such a crude science. I don't study what people say. I study what they do or perhaps want to do."

"Ethan, the mere idea of me running for President sounds . . . absurd."

"Jack," Ethan began, looking him straight in the eye. "From a statistical point of view, absurdity ceased to be a factor four days after your lecture."

"What happened four days after my lecture?"

"Your message had achieved sufficient critical mass in the current environment, that the idea of you as a candidate could override Duverger's Law."

Jack stared blankly at his visitor. "And that means what exactly?"

Ethan flashed an apologetic smile. "Duverger's Law applies in one-winner election systems like ours; it means even voters craving change hesitate to vote for a third candidate in case it helps the other main party win."

Jack nodded. "Which is why third parties never get more than a tiny share of the vote. That makes sense."

Ethan shook his head. "That's only one of a multitude of reasons third parties don't get many votes. But my point is, Jack, that you are now beyond the point where Duverger's Law might otherwise apply, because you would quickly poll high enough to be a credible alternative instead of a long-odds potential spoiler." Ethan showed no hint of doubt in his proclamation. "Of course, the math assumes you run an effective campaign."

Jack's eyes widened. "Look, for starters, there is no campaign. I came here to try to shift the conversation away from what's wrong with Democrats or Republicans to what's wrong with the two-party system they've built into a fortress." Jack's voice was emphatic. "And I also felt your son, who I was fond of, would have wanted me to."

Ethan smiled back. "Max definitely would have enjoyed your lecture, and the interview. But I think he would be especially excited about what's next."

Jack sighed. "What's next is I catch a train home, Ethan. I've got three classes to teach tomorrow."

"Okay." Ethan nodded and pushed up his spectacles. "Thirty-one percent though."

Jack shot him a look. "What does that mean?"

"Thirty-one percent of voters at this point would support you for President over the other two candidates. Does that surprise you?"

Jack laughed. "Can we not indulge in fantasy, please?"

"I am where I am because I deal in probabilities," Ethan replied. "And I assure you none of this is fantasy."

"Okay fine, but the road for political independents is littered with failures, including people with gobs of money."

"You're referring to Ross Perot, back in the 1980s?"

Jack remembered the Perot campaign from his political history studies; his independent candidacy had given the big parties a good scare, polling over twenty-five percent, but he fizzled down the stretch. "Yeah, his campaign issue was the deficit. And the moment that got traction, Clinton and Bush made the issue their own and popped the Perot balloon. Party over, in both senses."

"Yes, but you have to see that the same weakness does not apply here."

Jack paused for a moment to contemplate, and slowly nodded his understanding. "The big parties can't just turn around and say they'll break themselves up."

"Precisely. Given how angry everyone is at the shutdown, your idea has—or could have—the political establishment in check. There is no countermove by these parties that does not achieve the objective you seek."

"Still feels pretty thin though, Ethan," Jack replied. "The two-party system has more walls and moats around it than every castle in the history of the world combined." *And I can't believe we are actually talking about this.*

"Yes, but your idea of using the Justice Department against the two-party system is unique. To use your own analogy: they are already inside the castle walls, are they not? And the higher they build those walls and the deeper they dig those moats, the more they alienate people who will then vote for you."

Before Jack could respond, Ethan continued. "But let me give you another example to think about: Lincoln."

"Really?" Jack felt they were back to absurd, if Ethan was comparing him to Lincoln.

"I'm not saying you're Lincoln," Ethan inserted, as if sensing Jack's reaction. "But people always forget the math. Back then, the Republicans *were* the third party. Lincoln won with only forty percent of the vote. That victory legitimized the Republican Party."

"Forty percent," Jack mused. "That's only nine points more than your models are saying would vote for a college professor from North Carolina."

Ethan nodded. "Perhaps the only fortunate side-effect of the conditions at present. After seven months of shutdown, I see over forty percent of traditional red and blue voters ready to fully support an alternative. So long as that alternative appears viable."

Jack let out a short laugh. "Viable despite having no political experience whatsoever?"

"But that's the point, Jack. After seven months of shutdown, most people have come to the conclusion that political experience is actually a bad thing because, where has that gotten us?"

Jack eyed Ethan warily, mind racing. "Isn't Overton polling fifteen points ahead right now? He looks unbeatable."

"Careful, Professor," Ethan chided gently. "He's leading with current voters, against currently anticipated rivals. But with you in the mix, everything changes. My math says the total number of votes cast in the election would be fifty-two percent higher. Those are people who currently have no intention of voting for either major party. You have the potential to pull people off the sidelines. That renders the current polling data—for Overton versus Perez—almost irrelevant. I'm not saying you'd win; that's impossible to predict at this point. I am saying you'd have a decent chance."

Jack nodded slowly. *How do I argue with the guy who has more data than anyone else in the world?* "You clearly have an agenda here, Ethan," Jack pivoted, deciding it was time to turn the spotlight around. "What's in it for you? Or for Omni? What's your agenda?"

"Well, this is where one could argue I become the naïve one, Jack."

"Meaning?"

"Meaning, that as I've said publicly many times, OmniScientific doesn't deal in government influence or lobbying because that doesn't serve our purpose or create real value."

"I remember that speech. So, you're going to tell me all this is altruism on your part?"

Ethan kicked his white sneaker-toe at the concrete platform and appeared to study it for a moment before looking up to Jack. "There's certainly a part of me that wants to help change the course we are on, for future generations. I also think about what Max would want."

"What about the other part of you? The non-altruistic side? You don't get to where you are without having one."

Ethan's eyes returned to his study of the stained concrete floor, and his expression grew darker. "You have to understand, Professor, my whole company is built around the ability to see around corners. To predict human behavior. Individuals were the focus at first, and then homogeneous groups. But for the better part of ten years we've been working on larger macros that can model the largest societal shifts you can imagine."

"With what intent?" Jack replied, again feeling suspicious about the implications of what was being described to him.

"To predict all types of behavior better than any other company can, so industries and governments can make wiser decisions for the betterment of all."

"You're putting a beautiful spin on something very dangerous," Jack said.

"We only use information that is readily available, with appropriate safeguards."

"Some would argue that level of information shouldn't be available in the first place."

"We deal with the realities of the day, and as I said, we do not attempt to influence policy. We anticipate, adapt, and implement quickly. It's—"

"You still haven't answered my question," Jack interrupted. "What's in it for Omni, and why are you really here?"

Ethan studied him carefully. "As I said when I sat down, this is a conversation about certain probabilities I would like to avoid."

"I wish you'd stop speaking in code, Ethan. What probabilities?"

Ethan sighed. "On our current trajectory, there is a roughly seventy-one percent probability of an economic collapse that will make the Great Depression seem like the good old days."

"*Roughly* seventy-one?"

"Actually, seventy-one point-four the last time we ran the simulation fully, plus a forty-eight percent chance that full recovery takes twenty years, and a twenty-three percent chance there is no full recovery. At all."

"You don't get invited to a lot of parties, do you?" Jack slipped in, immediately regretting his sarcasm.

Ethan ignored the remark. "There is one other element though, if I'm honest, that also factors into my thinking."

"What's that?" Jack asked, surprised to see Ethan's expression soften.

"I'm not prone to emotional decisions, but if the political system had not degenerated to its current state of depravity, my son would still be alive." Ethan looked down at the platform for a moment. When his eyes returned, Jack saw a flash of anger in them. "I very much want to kill what killed him. And you're my best chance of doing that."

Jack nodded.

"And I'm prepared to give you just over two billion dollars for your campaign."

Jack let out a cough. "You want to spend over two billion dollars to try to put a law professor in the White House?"

"Two-point-one to be precise, if you start tomorrow. Jack, I either believe the models or I don't. I deal in datasets and probability, and I've got the best predictive analytics adaptive coding in the world." He brushed a few locks of hair aside. "People know you from your time on TV as a prosecutor. Regardless of what you may think, despite that final . . . episode . . . you are respected."

An episode. It certainly was that.

"And as of this moment," Ethan continued, "you're at thirty-one percent. Which will jump again after the impact of tonight's interview kicks in."

"Yeah, but Ethan, you don't know me!" Jack exclaimed, feeling for the first time that his off-the-cuff classroom speech might have the potential to do more than just shape the national conversation.

Ethan shot Jack a knowing look over his spectacles.

"Oh, right," Jack answered his own question. "Of course, the power of OmniScientific has checked me up and down, I should have figured. Are you reading my thoughts now too?"

"No," Ethan replied. "At least not in the way that you mean."

Jack didn't even want to contemplate the truth behind that statement. "Look, Ethan, even if I was running, which I am *not*—taking two billion dollars from the richest man on earth to run a campaign isn't exactly the high road. What about your heart-stirring sanctimony of 'We don't meddle in government we simply anticipate, adapt and implement?'" Jack's hands made air quotes as he spoke. "Was that a bunch of bullshit?"

"I am prepared to simply give the funds to you personally, not to the campaign. Run, don't run, win, don't win, it's yours to keep and if you prefer, I will sign the equivalent of a restraining order and stay far removed from the campaign."

Jack turned to face Ethan straight on. "So, your plan is to give me two billion dollars and walk away?"

"Yes."

"That's absolutely crazy."

"I'd rather you call me a patriot," Ethan shot back.

"How do you figure?"

"A two billion bet with zero strings attached on a shot to avert a slow crash-and-burn for America? It's not Medal of Honor stuff, but it's up there somewhere I'd say. Some in my position have spent more than that trying to get a rocket to Mars. If things keep going the way they are now, no one will be able to afford a car across town."

Jack saw the headlamp as his train pulled into the station, right on time. He rose slowly, finding himself a bit unsteady given the exchange. He gazed up at the hexagonal pattern that lined the roof of Union Station, and then down the long platform. Jack was glad platform twelve had remained sparsely populated. He didn't need the media reporting that he'd been offered two billion dollars to run for president.

Jack and Ethan stood as the sleek white magnetic-propulsion train glided to stop in front of them. The doors chimed and slid open, disgorging a collection of commuters and tourists, none of whom took notice that the most-viewed man in America and the wealthiest man on the planet were both standing in front of them.

The train gave its three descending melodic pings, which signaled boarding. Jack stepped forward through the open doors and turned around, steadying himself inside the empty passenger car as he gazed back at Ethan.

"Seeing as you have all the answers," Jack called out, "what do you think I'm going to do?"

"Well," Ethan replied, "my math after your interview tells me there's a sixty percent chance you will run for president."

"Is that so?"

Ethan nodded. "It's probably closer to seventy percent now though. I'll run the model again tonight."

"What makes you think it's gone higher?"

"You've spent time listening to me," Ethan said with no air of arrogance. "And the power of suggestion on the human mind is not something to be dismissed."

Jack let out a chuckle as the doors gave a final warning chime. "Thank you, Ethan, for the offer, but my answer is no."

The doors slid shut, separating the two men as the train lurched and began its silent journey through the dark heart of Washington.

CHAPTER 19

IT WAS 1:30 AM BY THE TIME Jack slipped into bed beside Sarah. She pulled him close and planted a soft kiss on his lips, pressing against him instead of going back to sleep. They made love tenderly in the darkness, for the moment not thinking about babies, hospitals, interviews or anything the internet was doing.

"Hey," she whispered, as they settled down against their pillows, facing each other in the grainy darkness. "You did good."

"Thanks . . . What did you think of the interview, though?" He flashed a smile that he could see Sarah return in the darkness.

"Who's the comedian now," she murmured, and planted another kiss on his lips.

"You should sleep," he replied, rubbing her bare shoulder.

"Soon," she nodded. "What was it like?"

There were a thousand ways Jack could answer. "It was pretty great, actually."

"I'm not sure AGN will invite you back any time soon," Sarah said. "But I'm glad you got it done."

"Yeah. I think it might do some good."

"What was the conversation afterward?"

"At the train station?"

"No," Sarah replied, a bit confused, "at the studio. After how you two went after each other, I don't imagine it was friendly."

"Oh," Jack replied. "Chaaya just left the second it was over, without saying a word."

"No surprise there, I guess. She didn't look too happy." Sarah stifled a yawn. "Why did you say the train station, did something happen there?" Jack could see her eyes opening a bit wider.

No point saving this for the morning. "You might say that," Jack said.

Sarah sat up in bed and turned on the bedside lamp. Jack spent several minutes replaying his surreal conversation with Ethan Bessette. By the end of the recap, Sarah was as awake as anyone could possibly be.

"Two billion dollars!?" she exclaimed. "Are you serious?"

"*He* certainly was. I guess for a trillionaire that's a reasonable investment. A billion here, a billion there. There's a thousand billion in a trillion."

"Maybe," Sarah breathed. "But that's still a lot of money."

They sat in silence for a moment, digesting thoughts that would have been delusional mere days before.

"So, what did you tell him?" Sarah finally asked, breaking the silence.

"I said no thank you."

Sarah gasped. "You said no to two billion dollars with no strings attached."

"There's no such thing as no strings attached," Jack replied. "No matter what anyone promises."

"Fair enough, but still. Saying no to two billion—I mean, Jesus." Sarah shook her head slowly as she processed.

"You think I should have said yes?" Jack asked, searching her face for clues.

"No, of course not. I'm so proud of you. It's just hard to imagine anyone turning down two billion dollars."

Jack turned his head and stared at nothing. After several moments, Sarah put a hand on his arm. "What are you thinking, Babe?"

"These petitions are really taking off apparently," Jack replied. "Some of Lewis' staff are tracking them and he texted me some details on the way home."

Sarah furrowed her brow. "Do they think there will be enough signatures in time? The election is only three months away."

Jack nodded. "Lewis says they're moving fast enough they could get there. The early Texas deadline is the main issue, but apparently there's a lawsuit challenging that date for third-party ballot access as unconstitutional. It will file tomorrow."

"That sounds like a Hail Mary pass," Sarah remarked.

"Apparently not," Jack said. "Cases like this have been tried successfully before, so there is some precedent." *I can't believe I'm actually saying this . . . Precedent to get me on the ballot in all fifty states!*

"Jack," Sarah replied as she grabbed his hand, "this all feels a little out of control, doesn't it? I mean, it feels like you're being recruited or something. By millions of people. It's kinda spooky."

"Yeah." Jack stared straight ahead. "*We The People* have chosen . . . And apparently it's me."

"So, what now?" Sarah breathed, looking at her watch.

Jack shrugged. "Work tomorrow. I have two afternoon classes to teach."

"That's good. I doubt those pay a billion each, though." Sarah winked. "Just sayin'."

"Very funny."

"I start back at work this Monday too, don't forget, so we should get some sleep." She yawned and clicked off the light, and they slid under the covers. "Let's see if anyone else offers you a billion dollars tomorrow." She pulled him in close again.

They lay quietly in the darkness for what felt to Jack like a very long time. After a while, he could feel Sarah's breathing settle into the slow rhythms of sleep. He continued staring into the grainy shadows across the ceiling as his mind played back parts of the conversation with Ethan. Despite Sarah's attempt to make light, he knew she'd prefer not to catapult their lives into the chaos of a campaign. Especially one as improbable as this.

The last thought on his mind as he reached for the coolness on the underside of the pillow was: *If Ethan says thirty-one percent would vote for me as President now . . . What would happen if I actually decided to run?*

⌒

The usual dream came without ceremony this time. A thunder of hands banged on the heavy courtroom doors from the outside, the sound almost deafening. Jack stood at the counsel table, the courtroom empty this time. He looked over his shoulder, willing the doors not to open and reveal what lay behind them. But he could feel the inevitable.

The softness of her voice penetrated through the noise. *You said you'd protect me . . .*

The pounding suddenly stopped. There was a click as the door handle turned. The doors opened slowly. Jack wanted to look away but couldn't; he'd been sentenced to watch.

When the doors finally swung open, he saw her there, dangling and twitching.

⌒

Jack's body jerked him awake before he could scream. His heart pounded inside his chest like a hammer. As the gnarled images slipped away like smoke through a vent, Jack felt his breathing start to slow, and his muscles gradually release.

He looked through the darkness and saw Sarah's shape beside him, breathing slowly, somehow still asleep. Jack slipped out from under the covers and went downstairs to the kitchen. He poured a glass of water and sat down at the table, beneath the single pendant lamp above.

He rubbed his forehead, still clammy from the dream. His thoughts shifted back to Gracie, and then to Max. *They can't be the reason I do this.*

"How long have you been up?" Sarah's voice finally echoed behind him, interrupting his thoughts.

"Just a while," he replied, having no real idea how long he'd been sitting there.

She rounded the table and sat beside him. "Did you have the dream again?"

"Worse than usual," he mumbled.

"I'm sorry, Babe," she replied.

"Sarah," he began, "Do you think we choose the moment, or the moment chooses us?"

Sarah slid her hand across the table to meet Jack's. "I'd say it's always some of both. Why, what are you thinking right now?"

Jack met her eyes. "I think if I don't try to do this, I'll always regret not answering when my name was called."

"Could you see yourself being President?" Sarah asked. "I mean, if Ethan's models are actually right?"

"I don't know how to answer that yet. I just know that doing nothing feels wrong."

"Being with your family isn't nothing," Sarah replied.

"You know that's not how I meant it."

"I also know," Sarah replied, "that neither of us have the slightest idea what running a campaign like this would do to our lives."

"I get a sabbatical leave every five years," Jack answered, "and I know you want to go back Monday, but technically you're still on maternity leave and could take another three weeks before going back." Jack saw her wince slightly and immediately regretted his clumsy reminder; she was supposed to be home with a newborn right now. "You said you don't want to live with regret, Sarah. Well, neither do I."

"What about starting a family, Jack? That's not happening in the back of a campaign bus."

Jack smiled, though Sarah had not meant it as a joke. "That comes first, Sarah. I promise you. I want kids as much as you do."

She exhaled heavily and looked into Jack's eyes for a long moment. "All right then, my love," she announced in a matter-of-fact tone, "let's give it a try. But you'd better call Lewis first thing tomorrow. You're going to need someone fierce to watch your back."

CHAPTER 20

The next morning, Jack stepped from the elevator on the seventeenth-floor lobby of Hayes, Chalupka, Shearon and Barbeau in Richmond, Virginia. Despite a scarcity of sleep the night before, Jack hit the I-85 early and headed north. He'd contemplated catching a few winks in his self-driving Ford, now that the technology and laws allowed it, but adrenaline mixed with discomfort at the idea of nodding off at seventy miles an hour kept Jack superfluously focused on the largely empty interstate between Durham and Richmond.

He'd contemplated giving Lewis a heads-up that he was coming, but settled for confirmation from Lewis' long-time assistant Jeannie that Lewis would indeed be in the office this morning. *Some messages are better delivered in person.* Besides, Jack reasoned, the gauntlet he was about to run wouldn't fit many people's definition of fun, so he might as well enjoy the step of enlisting an old friend.

"Good morning," a tall, red-haired receptionist said as Jack departed the elevator. The chic lobby, and the modern office layout visible through multiple glass walls, all screamed *Don't Mess with Hayes, Chalupka, Shearon and Barbeau.* And rightly so, given the firm's track record over the past decade in some of the largest civil, environmental and antitrust suits in the country. "I expect you're Professor Sanborn." She smiled sweetly, her Virginia accent on full display.

"Call me Jack."

"If you call me Tia." She leaned forward, as if about to tell Jack a secret. "I was told we might be seeing you today, but that your visit was on the Q-T."

"Sort of," he replied, "but I'm glad Jeannie told you I was coming."

"I hear you two are old friends. *Thick as thieves,* Jeannie said," a diabolical twinkle in her eyes. "Do you want me to let him know you're here?" she asked. "He's right back there."

Jack peered through layers of glass walls into a large conference room. At least twenty staff were seated around the table. Lewis, unsurprisingly, stood before them, speaking animatedly. The sound-proof glass covered all traces of noise, but Jack could tell from Lewis' arm movements that his volume was at the high end of his range. "If it's okay, Tia, why don't I just walk back there and give him the high sign?"

The receptionist leaned forward again, like secret number two was on the way. "You sure can."

Jack walked slowly toward the glass-walled conference room, doing his best to blend in with the hallway traffic as he enjoyed the moment, wondering how his old friend would react after being called into battle.

He slowed his steps twenty feet from the conference room wall and came to a stop. Standing motionless amid the busy hallway traffic seemed to catch Lewis' eye and he glanced over. A look of recognition quickly followed. Jack held up his wrist and tapped his watch. Lewis stopped speaking and smiled, prompting twenty heads inside the glass conference room to swivel toward Jack.

Lewis was out the door almost instantly. "You sonofabitch," he exclaimed. "You're going to do this, aren't you?"

"Not without you, I'm not," Jack replied.

"I'm in." Lewis grasped Jack's hand and pumped it excitedly. His face turned grave. "What you're doing threatens the whole system. Are you ready to go all-in on that?"

"I'm here, aren't I?"

Lewis gave a satisfied grin. "We'd better get a move on then." He clapped Jack's back as the two men walked to the elevators. "Tia,"

Lewis called out as they passed the reception desk, "mark me down as out of office!"

"Gotcha," she replied. "For how long?"

"Until November 6th!" Lewis called back.

"Uh . . . three months from now?"

"At least," Lewis called back. "Maybe another four to eight years on top of that, but we'll see how it goes!"

The two lifetime friends suppressed the urge to laugh as Tia's jaw dropped. And then the elevator doors closed.

CHAPTER 21

TWO DAYS LATER JACK, LEWIS AND SARAH scanned the growing mass of pedestrians through the windows of Jack's car as the automated drive-assist brought them to a stop in traffic. The light was green, but it didn't seem to matter. They'd traveled from Jack and Sarah's bungalow on their way to the historic Bell Tower, located on the edge of UNC's storied campus.

Normally the journey along Franklin Street would have been routine, especially during summer semester, with less than a third of peak-load students on campus. The Bell Tower would typically have a smattering of tourists hoping to climb its one-hundred-twenty-eight steps to take in a panorama of the Chapel Hill area. But not today.

This was announcement day, planned to take place in front of the UNC Bell Tower with a full media presence. Lewis had made the necessary calls. Given that the view count on Jack's lecture had exceeded two hundred million, spiking yet again after his combative AGN interview that matched the mood of the nation, the media were expected to be out in full force.

"It's probably worth pointing out," Jack had said the day before as the three of them gathered around the small kitchen table, "that we're about to announce a campaign, and other than the three of us, we have no staff."

"Handling it," Lewis replied, his eyes glued to his phone as he messaged his extensive list of media contacts.

"Are we paying these people with legal advice and promises?" Jack had yet to mention to Lewis that he'd turned down two billion dollars from history's wealthiest human. *Maybe a detail for later.*

"Handling that too," Lewis replied just as quickly. "Campaign donation sites are up and running since last night."

"Really," Sarah replied. "Are we taking in much?"

"You'd be surprised," Lewis said.

Jack cracked a smile. He knew that was their private code for "I have no idea yet," but whatever the truth was it would not contradict the answer.

"What content is on the sites?" Jack asked.

"So far, just the two videos," Lewis answered, "from your lecture and the AGN interview. And there's a donation link. We'll get more on there when we have someone on the team to actually think about that."

Jack looked around at the growing crowd. No doubt the number of people gathered at the UNC gates would slow things to a near-halt. They sat for a moment, bumper-to-bumper as the pedestrian traffic seemed to flow from all directions, growing denser by the minute. *One-point-two miles to destination*, Jack's car announced. *Estimated arrival time: unknown.*

"Well," Lewis announced, 'it looks like we have our first campaign snag."

"Ready for a walk?" Jack asked.

"Beautiful day," Sarah said. Jack was glad to see Sarah enjoying the moment. Three nights ago he could feel her reluctance, but there was little trace of that today.

Lewis craned his neck. "We're due there in five minutes, so we do need a Plan B."

Jack jerked the wheel and pulled the car slightly up on the curb. "We'll do better on foot. Let's leave the car here."

The three of them exited the car and made their way along the crowded sidewalk. As they neared the edge of campus, the sidewalk crowd spilled over into the streets. By the time they hit the intersection of Franklin and Columbia, the road was a sea of bodies. Everyone headed in the same direction, no one really getting anywhere.

"How many people did you tell?" Sarah asked.

"A few,' Lewis admitted. "And the media did the rest."

"Professor!" someone shouted. Jack recognized one of his students and waved, as there was no possibility of getting closer.

"Jack," Sarah said, "I'm not sure we're going to make it to the tower before sunset."

"We're with you, Professor!" came a voice that prompted a cascade of cheers when the crowd realized the person they were coming to see was already among them. "All the way to Washington!" another voice shouted.

"Let him through!" a man called out, but the mass of pedestrians might as well have been crammed into a subway.

Jack was tall enough on tiptoe to see up Columbia Street and verify that their odds of getting to the Bell Tower were less than slim. *Where the hell are all these people coming from?*

The crowd began to press in, unable to move and unsure of what to do about that. The large intersection had to have close to a thousand bodies packed in, pushing in from three directions. "Jack, Jack, Jack," the crowd chanted as word spread that he too was stuck in the jam.

"Looks like we need a Plan C," Jack announced.

"Any ideas?" Lewis replied.

Jack saw a nearby student with a megaphone clutched to her chest. "Just one," he replied. He slid past several supporters who patted him on the back. "Can I borrow that?" he asked the student with the megaphone. She gave him a bewildered nod and handed it over.

Jack made his way to a parked car and muttered under his breath, "Sorry for whoever's car this is." He stepped on to the hood, and then the roof. Fortunately, it didn't buckle under his weight.

It was Jack's first clear view of the crowd. There were more people than he'd thought. Several thousand at least. *We're gonna need a bigger boat.*

A sustained cheer rose from the crowd like a rushing wave, the moment they saw Jack on the rooftop. He gazed down at Sarah and Lewis, now beside the car.

"What's the plan?" Sarah called up to him.

"This *is* the plan!" Jack shouted back and smiled. He thumbed the power switch and blew into the microphone, sending out a loud *pop*. He could see several phones held up to record him. Even better, he spotted what looked like a reporter with a proper video camera trained on his position.

"Hello, Chapel Hill!" Jack shouted into the megaphone. "Can you hear me?" A thunderous cheer burst forth from the crowd in multiple directions. *Here we go.*

"So, I've been reading a lot lately about a lot of petition signatures to get someone new on the ballot for November." More cheers as Jack swung the megaphone around to make sure his words hit all corners of the packed intersection. "And I think it's pretty clear that many of you have decided that I need to run for President of the United States!" The crowd gave its loudest cheer yet. More phones and cameras appeared. "And while my plan was to get to the Bell Tower today, it looks like many of you have decided that I should announce right here, right now on top of this parked car. Is that right?"

The crowd exploded with enthusiastic cries that went on for almost a minute.

"That feels just about perfect to me," Jack shouted into the loudspeaker. "Because this is not a campaign. It really isn't. This is a rescue mission!" Whoops from the crowd filled Jack's ears. "It's a rescue mission for all of us. Democrats, Republicans, Independents, Libertarians, Conservatives, Liberals. This rescue mission is for anyone who has come to the same conclusion that I have!"

"What's that, Jack?" came several replies from the crowd.

"I've come to the conclusion that the two-party system that our forefathers feared, is now business-first, public-last. And that must change! NOW!"

The crowd thundered its approval like cannons letting loose.

"A seven-month shutdown with no end in sight. This must be our tipping point. It must be your tipping point. And my pledge to every American right now is that I intend to unleash the full power of the Department of Justice to use our American antitrust laws to bring the establishment to heel! They've wasted their moment—and now it's ours!

"We believe, Jack!!" cried a large woman holding a SoMAD banner with Sanborn scrawled across it.

Jack's heart hammered as he fed off the crowd. Compared to this, closing arguments in front of a jury seemed about as exciting as a phone call. "So, the answer to your question is YES. Absolutely YES, I am running for President of the United States of America! And I ask everyone, no matter who you are, to join me in this mission to rescue America!"

The voices of the crowd made the air feel like it was crackling with electricity. Jack held both hands in the air and turned to each side of the intersection to acknowledge the overwhelming support.

As he turned to climb down, a nearby reporter shouted over the crowd. "Professor! Are you still going to make your official announcement today!?"

"A rescue mission doesn't have time for formalities! That was it!" Jack hopped down by Sarah and Lewis, and they began the very slow process of making their way back home.

President Perez sat in the dimming afternoon light of the Treaty Room, alone. The large square room on the second floor of the White House residence had served different purposes through various administrations: cabinet room, private office, studio for TV addresses, a simple waiting room for those visiting the President of the United States.

Today it was certainly a waiting room, but it was the President doing the waiting. Not for a person, but for some break in the race that might illuminate an improbable path to a second term.

The television was on. A panel of talking heads was opining on the new horse in the race as images of Jack Sanborn standing on a parked car played on repeat. The scrolling headline along the bottom of the screen read *Three Horse Race: Yes or No?*

The President stifled the impulse to spit as he watched the panel conclude unanimously that it was a three-horse race, and that Perez himself was clearly the trailing horse. He muted the sound in disgust after one commentator said the third horse had pulled up lame and needed to be put out of its misery.

Michael Perez was not surprised that the press was eating up the excitement of a legitimate third-party contender. Jack Sanborn may have excoriated the media during his recent AGN interview, but the business of news was clearly looking past that for the moment. *They always turn on you eventually*, he thought bitterly.

A knock sounded at the door. "Mr. President," a grey-blonde secretary said in a hushed tone, stepping inside the room. "You have the phone call with the Prime Minister in three minutes."

"Which one?"

"Great Britain sir," she replied. "But you also have an incoming call from Ethan Bessette. He says it's urgent."

Perez's gaze shifted from the TV to his secretary. "Delay the Prime Minister by fifteen minutes."

'Yes sir. I'll have Mr. Bessette's call transferred to your line now." She handed the President a small note card and left.

"Thank you." Michael folded his hands under his chin as he contemplated what the world's richest man would want with him. *Probably not calling to make a donation.*

The black phone on his desk chirped softly, and he raised the receiver to his ear. "Yes?"

"Good afternoon, Mr. President," Ethan began. "Thank you for taking my call."

"Of course, Mr. Bessette."

"Please, call me Ethan."

"Fine," the President replied, not feeling inclined to reciprocate. "Can I start by expressing my deepest sympathies for the loss of your son Max." The notecard from his secretary had told him all he needed to know; he was still a politician, after all.

"Thank you for that. You're very kind."

"I'm a bit surprised to receive your call, Ethan," the President pivoted. "You've been a vocal proponent of keeping big business far away from politics."

"Indeed, Mr. President," Ethan replied. "A vocal but lonely proponent of that separation, yes."

"And I'm sure you're not calling to share that you've changed your mind," the President added. Hearing the chuckle on the other end of the line, he continued. "How can I help you?"

"Mr. President," Ethan began, his voice grave, "I believe you came to your office with the greatest of intent to reverse the pattern of political gridlock in this country."

The President nodded. "Yes."

"But I don't believe any human being can achieve that from within the confines of a two-party system designed to protect itself at all costs. No matter how strong the man."

"If you're calling to hear me complain about Congress or the opposition within my own party, Ethan, I'm afraid I'll let you down."

"Mr. President, I would not waste your time with such obvious matters."

"Then what exactly is on your mind?" Perez wasn't up for a long game of cat-and-mouse, especially when it wasn't yet clear which was which.

"I called you, Mr. President, because I am ninety-seven percent certain that this race is over for you."

There was a long pause. "Ninety-seven?" Perez replied, a weariness lacing his voice as the political commentator's *lame horse* analogy reinserted itself into his thoughts.

"Ninety-seven-point-six, actually," Ethan replied, "but I don't round up. The entrance of Jack Sanborn shifted your probability of losing from eighty-eight percent to nine points higher."

"Is that so?" Despite his questioning tone, the President knew, as others did, that Ethan and OmniScientific's data were known for extreme accuracy.

"Yes, Mr. President. Every possible scenario I can produce shows it would take eleven months at minimum to recover from the China scandal. And you have less than eleven weeks. The timing, for you, could not have been worse."

"I think I can get that gist myself from watching the news," Perez replied, the weariness in his voice growing heavier. "Is that what you wanted to tell me?"

"No," Ethan replied. "I called to ask you one of the more important questions in recent history."

"And that question is?"

"With this race over for you, Mr. President—what do you want to do with this moment?"

Michael kept the receiver to his ear, but remained quiet as the question sunk in.

⌒

Three-hundred-eighty miles to the north, on the outskirts of Buffalo, a wheeled gurney was pushed down one of the many dank grey corridors of Wende Maximum Security Prison. A sheet that had once been white was draped over the gurney. As usual, the guard pushing it was in no particular hurry. He ignored the questions shouted from the cells he passed, the hint of a smile tugging at his mottled cheeks. *Looks like justice has a sense of humor after all.*

One of New York State's most infamous inmates was about to exit the penal system exactly one day before his scheduled parole. But not in the way he'd hoped.

CHAPTER 22

THIRTY HOURS LATER IN MIAMI, Jack huddled in the large basement dressing room of the BankOne Arena. Sarah and Lewis were with him, along with a half-dozen campaign staff Lewis had lured into action with a few quick phone calls. The brightly lit room was quiet for the moment, the rumble of the expectant crowd audible from somewhere above them. Jack and Sarah swapped glances as the noise seemed to rise and fall. *Perhaps they're doing the wave.*

The first major event of the Sanborn campaign had undergone three venue changes in less than a day, as registration had twice exceeded available capacity. Lewis had fed this news to the press, which only served to enlarge the Miami-based audience. Florida was chosen because its signature requirements for the online ballot petition were one of the most stringent in the country.

"How did we get this big of a venue on such short notice?" one of the staffers asked.

"A friend of Ethan's," Jack replied with a smile. "We were going to start small, but Ethan saw the number of people coming in and booked us in advance."

"I hope they all show up," Lewis said, massaging his brow. "If we don't get the crowd we expected, we'll look delusional."

"I've got the door count here," one of the staffers beamed, holding up a tablet. Attendance is 10,234 so far." Someone let out a low whistle.

"All right then," Lewis said, and looked to Jack and Sarah. "You guys nervous?"

Jack wore a casual blue suit with no tie; Sarah a smart-looking pantsuit. Her blonde hair was pulled back into a loose ponytail. The group agreed Sarah would be the ideal person to introduce Jack, especially since the public needed to get comfortable with her as well. She'd spent much of the past twenty-four hours honing her 'Jack introduction' and practicing with a speech coach Lewis had hired.

Jack shrugged. "This is all somehow still a bit surreal. So, I guess I am nervous, but probably not as much as I should be."

"Now I know why people fear public speaking more than death," Sarah announced. "but I'll be fine. At least I know the subject matter pretty well, so I can ad-lib if I mess up." She flashed a nervous smile at Jack.

"Well," Lewis said, "you'll be doing this a couple times a day for a while, either in person or virtually, so it'll be second nature in no time."

"Nine cities in five days," Sarah replied. "I hope you're right."

A knock sounded and the dressing room door opened, admitting two intense-looking men in dark suits and ties. The two men approached. Jack had the strange feeling he was about to be handcuffed.

"Sir," said the first man, "I'm Special Agent Jonah Mullen and this is Special Agent Terrence Franklin." The second man nodded and folded his hands in front of him, as if presenting himself for inspection.

"Is there a problem?" Jack asked.

Special agent Mullen cracked the faintest of smiles. "No, sir. We're Secret Service. We're part of your assigned protection detail."

"Secret Service?" Lewis asked.

"Correct." As if by reflex, both men held out their identification for inspection.

Lewis stepped forward and examined them both. "I assume you don't mind if I verify these."

"Absolutely fine," agent Mullen replied. Lewis dialed the number of an old contact in the Secret Service and stepped away from the group with the IDs in hand.

"Do we need protection?" Sarah asked, a look of concern blanketing her face.

"Standard procedure, ma'am," Agent Mullen replied.

Jack's instincts at reading witnesses and jurors caught the second agent glancing downward at his partner's reference to standard procedure. *There's more to this story,* he thought.

"Are you sure standard procedure is all this is, Special Agent?" Jack asked.

Agent Mullen pressed his lips together and hesitated, making it obvious he was deciding how much to share. "Sir, the regs are that once a third-party candidate is polling above twenty percent nationally, protection is assigned."

"He's over thirty-three and climbing," one of the staffers interjected. "That's pretty clear, no?"

They both nodded. "Is there something else, though?" Jack asked, his radar still up.

"The regs also say polling over twenty percent for thirty straight days," Agent Franklin added. "So, this is in the grey zone."

"I'm glad you're both here," Jack said, nodding. "But a bit surprised to see the Secret Service deviate from procedure. I don't imagine that happens a whole lot."

Agent Mullen nodded. "It was the Director's call, sir." The look on his face told Jack there would be no further details on the matter. *They're here,* he thought. *That's all that really matters.*

"After the event today," Mullen continued, "we can go over some protocols and explain how your detail team will work and what that means for you and Mrs. Sanborn day to day."

"Are you moving in with us?" Sarah said with wide eyes. "We're a bit tight on space."

"We're aware," said Agent Mullen. "We'll have to talk about that, Mrs. Sanborn."

Jack could already picture the locked-down street access annoying their neighbors. "Okay," he said. "Let's talk about all of this afterward."

"These guys check out," Lewis announced, handing back the IDs. "Jack," he added, leaning in close, "we need to talk the VP candidate list on the way to Atlanta tonight. I've got some potentials."

Before Jack could reply, one of the staffers stepped in from outside, "Excuse me, Professor? There's a Jade Xu outside, asking to see you."

Jack saw a look of discomfort cross the agents' faces. They'd been dropped into the middle of an event they hadn't planned for, and already there were unexpected visitors. "It's okay, I know her," Jack replied.

Agent Mullen nodded, still looking a bit uncomfortable. "The team will be fully in place by tomorrow, sir, all twelve."

Jesus . . . twelve agents? This is moving so fast. Jack nodded at the staffer to let Jade in.

Stepping into a room with a dozen unfamiliar people would imbalance most anyone, but Jade showed no sign of surprise at Jack's new entourage. "You draw quite a crowd, Professor," she said with a crooked smile.

"So I've discovered," Jack replied, shaking hands. "Let me introduce my wife Sarah, and Lewis Hayes, the head of my campaign."

Jade shook hands with both of them, then turned back to Jack. "Thanks for seeing me, Professor."

"Why wouldn't I see you?"

"You were ambushed back at AGN," Jade replied, "so I probably wouldn't see me if I were you."

"Forget about it," Jack replied. "The ambush wasn't from you, and I thought things worked out fine in the end."

"I guess that's true," Jade noted. "Your poll numbers jumped several points after footage of you tearing a strip off Chaaya made its way around the internet."

"Are you here for a thank you?" Lewis interrupted, his own protective instincts kicking into gear.

"It's all right, guys," Jack said. "I don't think that was any of Jade's doing. What I saw off-camera made that pretty clear."

"Look, Jack," Jade said. "I came here to apologize for what happened in the studio." She wrung her hands, suddenly appearing nervous as she looked at all three of them. "I had no idea Chaaya was going to go after you like that. That wasn't . . . It wasn't how news should operate as far as I'm concerned."

Jack nodded. "We can make sure it's real news when you do your next story," he said, ready and willing for a fresh start. "I assume that's why you're here?"

Jade's mouth wrinkled at the question. "There actually won't be a next story, not for me anyway."

"How's that?" Jack replied, fearing she'd been fired after their on-air performance with Chaaya.

"I quit AGN last night," Jade announced with a look of finality.

"Why would you do that?" Lewis asked. "You broke one of the biggest stories in a decade less than two weeks ago. You should be riding high right now."

"I hope it had nothing to do with my interview," Jack added.

"Far from it," Jade said. "Your interview was one of the highlights of my year."

Jack nodded as his mind flashed back to their first conversation, when Jade had sought him out at UNC. He sensed what was coming next before she said the words.

"I'd like to try building something meaningful," she said earnestly. "Instead of tearing things down."

"Meaning what exactly?" Lewis asked.

"Meaning," Jade said, her eyes focused on Jack, "I'd like to work on your campaign."

"Do you mean covering the campaign, as a freelancer?" Jack asked.

"No," Jade replied. "I mean working *for* you, as part of the campaign team. Doing communications, or whatever you need."

Jack studied her face, reading her like a witness on the stand. "So, you'd leave your career at its peak, to work on a campaign that might be over in a few weeks?"

"Jack," she began, "most of the media are loving you right now, because you just gave the election a whole new trajectory. So right now, you mean ratings, but you also declared war on the news by suggesting the Fairness Doctrine come back." Her eyes almost glowed with intensity. "After a few weeks of ratings, if you're still in this, it won't just be the two main parties wanting to take you down. You're a threat to the whole system now."

"So, you came here to warn us?" Sarah asked, her tone skeptical.

Jade shook her head, unfazed by the questioning. "I just don't want to be part of that anymore. I've had enough of tearing down people, whether their intentions are good or not."

"Very noble," Lewis replied. "But how do we know you're not just a mole for AGN or another campaign?"

Jack could see Jade's eyes spark for a moment. "I know I can't prove it to you," she said, "but I can promise you the reasons I want to do this are personal, not professional. And that those reasons are mine and mine alone."

The conversation fell silent. Jack studied her a moment longer. The only sound between them was the steady rumble of the crowd above them, like the noise of a distant subway that rose and fell.

A staffer leaned in the door. "They're ready for you upstairs, Professor," she said.

"I'm glad it's personal," Jack finally said to Jade. "Because that's exactly what it is for me."

Jade's expression turned hopeful. "So . . . That's a yes then?"

Jack nodded, and watched a broad smile transform Jade's normally intense disposition. He turned to head upstairs, where over ten thousand frustrated Americans were hoping for a new way forward.

"When do I start?" Jade called after him.

"You just did," Jack told her.

CHAPTER 23

DEMARCO CONTI STOOD at his kitchen counter, still wearing last night's clothes. He let out a sour belch. He'd been staring into the dank kitchen cupboard for what seemed like a very long time. He went there out of habit, though his numbed memory warned him there was no breakfast to be found there. He gazed at a lonely jar of artichoke hearts and wondered why he'd bought such a useless item.

"I like it when you at least *try* to cook, Dad."

The grainy memory seeped through the outer edges of the roiling alcohol-laced fog inside his brain. *They were for her.* He'd bought them for Gracie to try on the weekend nights when they cooked together. It wasn't something DeMarco did remotely well, but he tried to make an event out of it to keep his teenage daughter interested. It even worked occasionally, especially if he let her invite a friend or two.

It also kept DeMarco out of the bars on Fridays and Saturdays, which were by far the hardest nights for him.

Like many things along his life's path, Gracie had not been planned. But there was little doubt that in many ways, she'd become his salvation. DeMarco's history boasted a notable litany of screwups over the course of what might generously be called a career. Somehow, through all his shortcomings as a police detective, he'd managed to rise to the occasion of father surprisingly well. Not that Gracie was an easy kid, having her fair share of dustups and transgressions, but DeMarco saw her through every scrape. He was there to pick up the pieces when they needed reassembling. He was there with a firm word when that was needed too. And while there were times when lines were crossed and he could think of nothing more deserving than a backhand across her face . . . He never, ever laid a hand on her. Each milestone they passed through together had helped DeMarco get that much stronger, and through it all he never doubted she was going to come through her youth okay. Until one day, all that changed.

"Fuuuuck . . ." he said with a long sigh. His stomach let out a tormented growl, still protesting last night's abuse at the hands of another bottle of . . . something. It didn't much matter anymore. He'd managed to hang on to a partial NYPD pension despite the dishonorable discharge, but partial didn't get him very far so whatever he bought came cheap, and food was never at the top of his list. He needed some today, though. For the trip.

He looked around the apartment, but there were no take-out containers with remnants to quell his stomach rot. So he checked his watch and began the search for his shoes and coat. He concluded he had time to head down the block for a greasy plate of something before heading upstate in the old windowless panel van he bought for cash a few weeks back.

In times past, shoes would be on the doormat by the door, coats on one of the hooks in the hall. Things tended to be in place then, but nothing about his current world was where it should be, save for the Sig Sauer P320 tucked into its holster. Still part of his daily wardrobe. They'd taken his badge but, in the chaotic mess of his dismissal, had somehow managed to leave him with his retired cop carry permit. A mistake that would one day come to light, but not today.

Gracie's assorted shoe collection had typically resided in a jumbled pyramid on that doormat, often burying DeMarco's dingy footwear. The hooks had always carried a colorful array of coats for every season. Those belonged to Gracie, and to Janise, his wife of seventeen years.

The coats and the shoes were long gone. Gracie's went first, of course. Janise's departed ten months later when she realized that DeMarco the co-widower was not the man she could spend her future years with. New York's finest reached the same conclusion shortly afterwards, and the downward spiral had proceeded from there. He'd taken a couple runs at private investigation work, but had burned too many bridges in every precinct that mattered to make him effective.

He pulled on the battered, unlaced Reeboks that now sufficed as his year-round footwear, but his coat was nowhere to be seen. He looked at the hooks and laid a hand on the only item that still remained. Gracie's frayed jean jacket. The last time he saw her, she was wearing it. He never saw her again, not alive anyway. Not long afterward, the jacket was handed to him in a plastic bag along with the rest of what she had been wearing.

At his feet, where Gracie's assortment of shoes used to be, was a heavy-grade duffel bag. DeMarco looked down at it for a moment. He had no need to look inside, the contents having been carefully assembled and packed for some time now. Duct tape, several lengths of chain, bolt cutters, carving knives, steel clamps, a car battery, enough chloroform to sedate a linebacker, and a bone saw he found at an old medical supply store. There had been ample time to plan. That was where his mind went nightly, at least when he wasn't simply blacking out. But now, after almost four years, the waiting was finally over. It was time to execute.

DeMarco heard the sudden wrench of a twisting guitar riff break the silence, which was unmistakably his phone. "Shit," he muttered as he patted his pockets, his throbbing head unable to determine the location of the familiar ringtone. He scrambled through his living room in search of the device, finally finding it in the pocket of his waylaid coat, tucked between the wall and the tattered sofa late last night after being tossed aside.

He slid the small vibrating panel and tapped the screen. "Yeah?"

"Uh, hello, is this DeMarco Conti?"

"Yes."

"Great. Um . . . okay. Before we proceed, can you verify your social–"

"Proceed with what?"

"Sir, I just need to—"

"Look fuck-stick, you called *me* so don't give me any shit about verification. Just talk."

"Um, well I'm not sure then—"

"Who is this?"

"Sir, this is Elijah Simmons from the DA's office."

"Oh, okay," DeMarco replied, softening his tone. "What's happening, is he out early or something?" He could feel the adrenaline start to course in his veins, lifting him from the sweaty grey fog that enveloped his every morning. He looked down at the duffel bag again.

"I assume you mean Dean Elenestro, and he is certainly *out* Mr. Conti, at least in some sense of the word." The caller chuckled. "I had a note in the file to call you before we closed it today."

DeMarco stiffened. "Closed it? Why would they close Elenestro's file? He'll still be a convicted felon."

"Well, it's uh, standard procedure once the suspect, I should say felon, is deceased."

"Deceased?"

'Yeah, apparently a heart attack. One frickin' day before parole. How 'bout them apples, huh?" The caller's voice sounded almost giddy. "Got what's comin' to him, hey?"

DeMarco stood motionless, halfway down the hallway, not fully aware he'd slipped the Sig Sauer P320 from its holster the moment he heard Elenestro's name.

Not even close to getting what he deserves . . . And now he never will . . . Fuck.

The caller bid a cheery farewell and ended the call. DeMarco numbly dropped the phone into his pocket and turned to face the coat hooks on the wall. As he reached out and touched the sleeve of the jacket, he simultaneously put the Sig's muzzle squarely under his chin, taking care to get the angle just right.

He'd come close to this moment many times since Gracie was taken from him. Each time, the thought of a just revenge had kept his finger from pulling the trigger. Today, there was no hesitation.

Click.

DeMarco flinched at the misfire and pulled the trigger again.

Another click.

"MOTHERFUCKER!" His face twisted with rage as he reared himself back and hurled the gun at his apartment door with every ounce of strength he could muster.

The sound and flash as the Sig hit the wall and fired registered at the precise instant DeMarco felt a searing pain crash into the side of his head like lightning. His body careened into the wall and he tumbled onto his hands and knees. The acrid smell of gunshot invaded his nostrils next, reminding him he wasn't dead. Yet.

His trembling fingers moved to the side of his head and touched what felt like a deep burn, like a hot poker had been pressed against his flesh. *It fucking grazed me.* One more disappointment in his already dismal day. DeMarco stood unsteadily and turned to look at the bullet hole in the wall.

With no idea what to do next, DeMarco stepped over the duffel bag and the warm Sig pistol and made his way downstairs. His head was still spinning from adrenaline and shock as he squinted and made his way up the block.

"You okay, D?" the bartender called once DeMarco finally found himself inside the familiar Thirsty's Bar, the only place his mind could think to bring the rest of him.

"Bourbon . . . any," he replied as he dropped himself onto the nearest barstool.

"What happened to you?" the bartender asked, "you got a bit of blood there on the side of your head."

"I got jumped outside my apartment."

"You want me to call someone, D?"

DeMarco shook his head. "Definitely not." He took the shot of bourbon down. "Another."

"Hey, weren't you supposed to be upstate or something?"

DeMarco ran a rough hand across his mouth and shrugged. "Guess it wasn't meant to be." He closed his eyes and left them closed long after downing the second shot of bourbon. The bartender seemed to take that as a cue to back off, despite DeMarco being his only customer this midday.

As the bourbon made its way through his bloodstream, DeMarco's brain finally slowed enough for his synapses to place a familiar voice. He opened his eyes, turned and looked at the worn TV screen that hung opposite the bar. He blinked and tried to focus. The voice looked like it was coming from a politician on screen, but something about the figure wasn't right. That was a face he'd seen in person, up close.

You gotta be shitting me.

DeMarco squinted toward the TV image of Jack Sanborn, at what looked like a large campaign rally.

It's him. Today of all days. Right now.

"You want another shot, D?"

DeMarco shook his head, feeling instantly sober as he watched Jack on stage, smiling. "I thought that fucker crawled down a hole somewhere and killed himself," DeMarco muttered aloud, oblivious to the hypocrisy in his critique.

"You know him?" the bartender asked. DeMarco ignored the question.

How did I not think of you before? His mind started turning quickly. *Elenestro may be gone, and I was almost right there with him. But I'm not. I'm still here, and you show up. Like the universe is trying to tell me something.*

DeMarco wasn't religious, and he certainly didn't care much for fate, but this moment was the furthest thing from random coincidence his brain could imagine. He reached into his pocket and withdrew his phone. After scrolling his contacts for several seconds, he thumbed the number and put the phone to his ear.

"Jimmy . . . ? Yeah, it's DeMarco . . . Yeah, I know . . . Listen, you still got some good contacts in DC that do opposition research on politicians . . .? Yeah, finding dirt, exactly. Send me his number, would ya . . . ? Yeah, look just do it would ya, and tell him to take my call. I can promise he'll be glad he did."

CHAPTER 24

"WE'RE ALMOST AN HOUR LATE," Jack said. The large SUV with Jack, Sarah, Lewis and two staffers snaked its way through the streets of downtown Sacramento, the next urgent Sanborn campaign stop. "Are we close?"

"Less than five minutes to G1," the agent at the wheel replied, referring to the Golden 1 Arena, where over twelve thousand noisy SoMAD supporters awaited. Ethan had offered the use of one of his personal air vehicles to bypass traffic from the Sacramento airport, but Jack had wholeheartedly agreed with his Secret Service detail that such a mode of transport would be a bad idea. Money may have been flowing in quickly from GoFundMe donation sites, and now directly to the hastily assembled campaign website, but Jack knew to treat every penny like his own.

"Jade will be at the back door to escort you both to the stage, so we're not far off schedule," Lewis said.

"I hope the warm-up band doesn't run out of songs," said the burly, dark-haired staffer Jack barely knew. He'd managed to cram his large frame into the back row of the SUV, and had a phone pressed to his ear.

The past two days had been a blizzard of activity as Jack's campaign targeted the states with the biggest petition requirements, doing in-person rallies and interviews, and packing virtual town halls. The idea being to make it seem like Jack was everywhere, all at once. He had yet to shake the surreal feeling of thousands of voices chanting his name at each stop, but even Jack himself was surprised at how calm he felt when he worked the crowds. He did his best to sound Presidential, in his own way.

"Any word out of Texas?" Jack asked, "If they rule against us there, the media will be quick to write us off as a spoiler, but if we get on the ballot a lot of fence-sitters are going to jump-in."

Opening arguments in Austin had begun two days prior, with forty electoral votes in the balance as the Texas Supreme Court weighed the unconstitutionality of the very early third-party ballot deadlines. Being on so many ballots made Jack the biggest threat the American two-party model had ever faced. At least since the Whigs and Democrats were confronted by the newly formed Republican party under Lincoln.

Lewis cleared his throat. "Arguments will take a while, especially as the establishment tries to drag it out. But my guys still like our chances there."

"We set for Houston for tomorrow?" Jack asked.

"Yep, maybe Dallas in the evening as well . . . Still firming that up."

"I'm starting to forget what day it is already," Sarah remarked.

"Jack," Lewis said. "How about your thoughts on the VP list you've had since yesterday."

Jack exhaled and looked at his friend and campaign general. Lewis was someone he'd trust with his life. "I did review them."

"Any preferences?"

Jack paused for several moments, eyeing the downtown Sacramento traffic and wondering where this many people were going in the middle of the day. "None of them."

Lewis' face dropped. "I gave you a list of ten names. Are you saying no to all ten?"

Jack nodded calmly. "And the back-up ten you probably have ready just in case."

Lewis seemed stunned. "Why?"

"Because I see way more risk than upside."

"Jack," Lewis replied, "Americans have been voting for the top and bottom of Presidential tickets for almost two hundred years. That's a huge gamble."

"This whole campaign is a gamble, Lewis," Jack said.

"Not to mention the fact that it adds to the legal headaches of getting on the ballot in about half of the states. The clock is not our friend."

"Hire more lawyers if we need to, Lewis. I don't want to make a rush choice that could bite us. Vetting and defending a hasty VP pick pulls our focus from getting on the ballot at all."

"You've got a point there," Lewis ceded. "But I assume you haven't forgotten, Professor, that the twenty-fifth amendment requires a sitting president to have a backup?"

"Seriously?" Jack replied with a look of mock surprise.

"Or that congress would make your life a living hell during any confirmation process . . . Assuming who you eventually pick even gets through."

"We've got an idea on how to handle that," Jack answered, winking at Sarah who fought to conceal a smirk.

"Okay," Lewis replied. "So, we sleep in separate bedrooms, but you two might want to fill me in on any late-night brainstorms."

Jack leaned forward. "This whole campaign, this rescue mission, is about giving people more to choose from than just the usual two suspects, right?"

"Sure," Lewis replied warily.

"Well then," Jack replied, "let's give them a choice. We announce that if I'm elected, we'll publish a ballot of, say, three VP candidates. And before inauguration, voters can choose the VP who'll serve with me. It's like *they* designed the ticket. So, Congress can vet all they want, but the people have already chosen."

"Risky . . . but that's actually not a terrible idea," Lewis replied, rubbing his chin as he digested the unusual concept. "It could work. And it definitely fits our narrative and keeps us on the front foot, if you're not going to actually name someone."

"Exactly," Jack responded.

"You sure you weren't planning this whole thing before you gave that lecture?" Lewis inquired with an arched brow.

"That's what I'm talkin' about, yeah!!" cried the burly staffer sitting behind Jack and Sarah, his booming voice making them jump in their seats and stare back at him in surprise. "Sorry!" he exclaimed with a clenched fist held in the air, "but we just passed the signature requirement for California!!"

A cheer rattled the SUV windows from the inside as they pulled up to the back entrance of the arena. The passenger door was pulled open, and an impatient looking Jade peered inside. "Finally! I think the band was down to their last song." She waved her hands, beckoning them from the SUV. "And what's all the yelling about?"

"All good," Jack replied as he and Sarah climbed out of the back seat. "We have some news to share that the folks inside will be glad to hear!"

CHAPTER 25

CLAY OVERTON SAT AT HIS congressional office desk, intently study-ing the file of papers splayed before him. He enjoyed many things about his job, but none more than the moment before launching an attack against a known adversary. To him, the feeling was akin to the moment a fine porterhouse steak was laid before him; the anticipation of the first bite was to be savored.

The junior senator Kyle Manning and several other campaign staffers leaned forward in the club chairs surrounding the Speaker's massive desk, like pawns scattered around a king.

"This will suffice," Overton announced. He leaned back and cast an eye upon his charges, all of whom exhaled. "Were there no recordings of the meeting?"

Kyle Manning, the junior senator Overton had installed on the Energy and Water Development SubCom for expressly this reason, grimaced. "No, but the notes are clear that he was in the room when the downstream implications of China's water policy were raised, so he effectively signed off on their plan."

The Speaker nodded his acceptance as he looked back down at the evidence on his desk. A recording would have been ideal. But just being in the room and allowing China to dam the living hell out of every river for their own use while their southern neighbors suffered catastrophic droughts was enough to paint Vice-President Palmer as another China lackey. Just like POTUS. "It's not the mortal wound that rules him out for 2048," Overton said with a furrowed expression. "But like I said, Kyle, you don't get credit for the ammo you bring back from battle." A scorched Democratic ticket had been in Overton's sights for the past four years, and now he could almost taste the smell of burnt hair wafting from the smoking rubble of a campaign that was twenty points down and falling. "Release it all."

Kyle and the staffers rose from their seats and turned to exit.

"You stay," Overton directed.

Kyle turned back expectantly. "You mean me?"

Overton flicked a finger. "You can run along," he said, and pointed at one of the staffers to Kyle's right, momentarily forgetting his name. "You . . . John. Er, Jim. You stay."

"Yes sir," Jim replied, and settled back down in the club chair. "What's next?"

Overton waited until the others had left. "It's time to wipe some dogshit off my shoe," he began, his expression sour. "It's only a smear, but the smell won't seem to go away."

"I assume you mean Jack Sanborn," Jim replied.

Overton stared blankly back and said nothing. *We already talked about this. Don't make me repeat myself.*

Tentatively, Jim continued. "If that is who you mean, we've worked up some ads that show him melting down on TV during that Elenestro case a few years back. He looked pretty pathetic if you ask me."

"Christ's sake!" Overton exploded, his palm smacking down on the desk with a sonic clap that made the air in the room shift. "Everybody's seen that online already! I need something original to take his fucking legs out! This imbecile might be the only thing standing in the way of a landslide ten years in the making!!"

"Will he make it on enough ballots to be a real problem?"

Overton seemed poised to spit. "Not sure. But his even more imbecilic SoMAD followers may get him close."

"And Texas?"

Overton sighed. "We've got an army of lawyers in Austin, but no guarantees. Reagan nearly got tripped up by Anderson winning a court case to get on the Ohio ballot back in the eighties. Had he not been running against Carter that might have screwed him." Overton flinched suddenly. "But why the fuck am I explaining this to you? The point is, this clown is threatening to turn the government on itself. I want him buried so deep I can smell worm shit on his breath!"

"Well," Jim began, his cheeks flushing. "There is one lead that came in today, but I haven't had a chance to vet it yet." He pulled out a folder and opened it on his lap. "I know you don't appreciate speculation."

"Let's go there, just this once," Overton replied dryly.

"I've not seen the evidence yet, so I can't speak for the—"

"Out with it already, for God's sake." Overton interrupted.

"There's a detective out of New York. Came through a good contact of mine. Says he's got something that can take Sanborn down."

He studied the man for a moment. "How far down exactly?"

Jim looked at his file and then back at the Speaker. "Down as in prison-level down. If it checks out."

"Get it for me," Overton commanded. "Every bit, immediately."

"There's one thing, though, that you may not like. In order to hand over the evidence, the cop said he needs to meet you in person."

"Bring him in tonight."

Jim shifted uncomfortably in his seat. "He's still in New York, Mr. Speaker."

Overton let out a disappointed sigh. "Then what are you still doing here? Go fetch him."

CHAPTER 26

JACK, SARAH AND JADE WALKED at a brisk pace behind Agent Jonah Mullen as they followed the arcing tunnel toward UNC's famed Dean Smith arena. It was Jack and Sarah's first hometown rally, aside from Jack standing on a parked car on Franklin Street announcing his candidacy. They were both nervous with excitement. "You sure you know where this tunnel is going, Agent?" Jack quipped, "I heard the UNC coach got lost down here when they first opened it, and nearly missed the tip-off."

"Not much farther now," Agent Mullen replied, his eyes scanning the service tunnel ahead. This would connect to the "Dean-Dome," where a large crowd awaited.

"Was there something wrong with just pulling up to the back door?" Sarah asked.

"Pretty big crowd outside the street-level entrances," Agent Mullen answered, keeping up his pace.

"I could just do the megaphone thing again," Jack said.

"With the level of media coverage you're getting," Jade replied, "I think you could sit on your front porch and just give speeches from there."

"Our neighbors would love that," Sarah said.

They rounded a final archway, and the tunnel expanded into an open area. Security doors led up to the arena. Jack saw Lewis ahead, chatting with a man and a woman, both of them smartly dressed.

"Jack," Lewis called as the two groups came together outside the security doors. "Let me introduce you. This is Lisa Dunmore, our new campaign director, and Patrick Lee, our field manager."

Jack shook hands and introduced Sarah and Jade. "Welcome to our small but scrappy team."

"I'm afraid I don't know what a field manager does," Sarah added as she greeted them.

"Ma'am," Patrick replied. "My only job right now is to harness a huge but unwieldy volunteer network to get us enough signatures filed and certified in fourteen days."

"It's thirteen days until the ballot deadline, actually," Lewis corrected. "Yesterday you had two weeks. Today, you have thirteen days."

"What does it mean to have signatures certified?" Sarah asked.

"It's state bureaucracy," Patrick replied, "but the certifications are coming fast. We have a big advantage that others never had."

"What's that?" Jack replied.

"The state bureaucrats are just as pissed about the shutdown. With the government closed this long, the states don't get their usual flow of fed money, so most are behind on paying non-essential state employees."

"So, it's all politics as usual until you screw with my paycheck," Jack summarized.

"Precisely. They want you on the ballot, sir, to put a large foot up DC's ass—metaphorically speaking, of course."

Jade made a noise and looked up from her phone, smiling. "Can't argue with that."

"Meaning?" Lewis replied.

"Meaning they just certified us in North Carolina. We're on the ballot." Jade's grin widened as she held up her phone as proof. "And the petition only went in two days ago!"

"That's motivation, all right!" Jack exclaimed with a fist pump.

"That makes twelve states," Lewis concluded. "Thirty-eight more in thirteen days."

"I like our chances, sir," Patrick said with confidence. "The petitions are literally flying."

"They're ready for us," Jade announced, checking her phone.

Jack and Sarah followed Agent Mullen through the security doors and made their way up a staircase that opened on a short hallway. The rumble of the crowd rose in their ears like an oncoming wave. They reached the side of a stage framed by massive curtains and two large video screens.

Jade waited for the ready nod from Jack, and proceeded through the curtains and out onto the large stage. The crowd applauded enthusiastically as Jade began her commentary, which would conclude when she introduced the 'next First Lady of the United States,' Sarah Sanborn.

Jack let his fingers entwine with Sarah's for a moment as he listened to Jade's now-polished campaign introduction. "Hey," he nudged, "you've been pretty quiet today. You okay?"

Sarah took a deep breath. "Yeah," she replied with a smile that Jack knew was forced.

He squeezed her hand. "You sure?"

"I'm about to speak to fifteen thousand people," she replied. "I'm probably just tired. So, let's talk later, okay?"

Jack could see the strain on her face. "Sure. At least we'll be at home tonight." Which would be the first time in a week.

"I'm not sure it feels much like home right now, but sure. Fine."

"Babe, you don't need to do the daily campaign slog," Jack whispered. "You really don't." Upon looking at the punishing schedule a week ago, Jack had suggested that Sarah attend only a few events. But with Sarah's midwestern work ethic, she wouldn't hear of it.

The crowd clapped wildly and waved SoMAD banners in the air as Jade transitioned into Sarah's introduction. Sarah looked at Jack for a long moment, and his instincts told him she was holding back an uncomfortable truth. "What is it?" he asked.

"I don't think I've fully wrapped my mind around what life will be like if we win."

"—your next First Lady of the United States . . . Sarah Sanborn!!"

Sarah gave Jack's hand a final squeeze that said *to be continued,* and strode out to center stage. She thanked Jade and turned on a broad smile, waving to the crowd. After the applause died down, she delivered the opening line she'd ad-libbed at her first campaign event.

"Does anyone out there fear public speaking more than jumping out of an airplane . . . without a parachute?" Jack watched the entire crowd laugh and immediately sway her way. "Well, I sure sure do. But I'm getting used to it," she said with a smile.

Jack watched from stage-right with a mixture of affection and concern as Sarah talked about her Minnesota roots, and eventually made her way to talking about him. Her phrasing was a little more clipped than usual and she tripped on a couple phrases, but the local crowd ate up every word.

"And now it is my pleasure to introduce you to the—" Sarah's body flinched slightly as she stopped mid-sentence, her mouth open. For a moment, Jack thought she was drawing out the introduction to work the crowd, but a split-second later, Sarah's body seemed to turn off like a switch had been flipped. She slumped sideways and sank to the floor.

"Sarah!" Jack cried. He ran toward her, only to feel himself tackled to the floor and covered by two large bodies. *Jesus fucking Christ. What just happened?* He tried to break free but couldn't move. "Sarah!!"

He heard panicked cries from the crowd as the chaotic scene played out on the big screens for all to see. Some scrambled for the exits.

The Secret Service swarmed the stage, shouting at each other. "Shooter!? Where's the shooter!?"

Jack saw two agents by Sarah's still body, guns drawn as they tried to examine her. "I can't see any blood!"

Jack heard Agent Mullen shout, "Get them out!" A stretcher appeared by Sarah's side. Agents seemed to be coming from everywhere now.

Jack felt himself hoisted from the floor as if he were weightless. The second his feet touched the ground, he was propelled off stage. "Tunnel!" shouted one of the agents.

"Stop!" Jack shouted, feeling like his body had been commandeered. "Not without Sarah!"

"Sir," one of the agents replied as they continued to force him forward, "we need to get you out of here now!" They were backstage and headed for the nearest exit hall.

It took all of Jack's strength to wrench himself free of the agents' grip. "GET OFF ME!" Jack looked to his left and saw the stretcher with Sarah disappear into a different hallway. He looked back at the agents with a menacing glare. "I'm going with that stretcher. If you don't like it, shoot me." He turned and ran to catch up with Sarah. Agent Mullen and the others had no choice but to follow.

Jack's adrenaline helped him close the distance quickly on the younger agents carrying Sarah's stretcher. "What the hell happened?" he asked.

"We don't know, sir," one agent answered without breaking stride. "No blood that we can see."

"Where are you taking her?"

"Ambulance is standing by. Less than five minutes to UNC Med Center!"

Jack looked down at Sarah's face as he ran beside them. He stumbled, grabbing an agent's shoulder to keep from falling. *Jesus these fucking tunnels never end.* "Is she breathing?"

"I can't tell," replied another agent.

They rounded the corner. Up ahead, several agents held exit doors open. "They're coming out!" The back doors of the waiting ambulance flew open, and Sarah's stretcher was thrust inside at high speed.

Agent Mullen caught Jack by the elbow.

"Don't even think about it, Jonah," Jack replied. "I am getting in that ambulance!" He pushed past and almost flung himself into the back of the ambulance before the doors closed. "Let's go!" Jack cried, but he sensed the pedal hitting the floor before his second syllable.

"Sit back, Mr. Sanborn, right there." the first medic commanded, and Jack complied. He watched as the two medics tended Sarah. "Got a pulse . . . Respiration shallow."

"I can't see any entry or exit wounds."

"She wasn't shot?" Jack asked, his face wet with perspiration.

"Not with anything I can see at this point."

"Pupils not responding," the second medic added. Jack looked up through the small access window to the front seat, just in time to see them follow their escort vehicle through a red light.

"Go faster," the first medic called out to the Secret Service agent at the wheel. "We still don't know what we're dealing with here."

"Flooring it," replied the agent tersely. He spoke into a radio. "We're only a minute out."

"Mr. Sanborn," the first medic said. "Is your wife on any new medications? Anything not in her file?"

"No," Jack replied hoarsely. "But you saw in there she had bleeding problems during childbirth?" *Stillbirth*, the echo in Jack's mind reminded him, as always. He saw the medics look at each other momentarily.

"How long ago was that?"

"Eight weeks," Jack said.

"We'll need that blood panel," one medic said to the other, "and anything they administered then."

"What do you think is wrong with her?" Jack asked.

Before either medic could answer the ambulance screeched to a halt. The doors were flung open, and Sarah's stretcher was whisked away by two more agents. Jack leapt out and was right behind them. He was joined by Agent Mullen before he had cleared the second set of sliding doors. The lead medic shouted as they ran. "Clear a path!"

"Sir," Agent Mullen's familiar voice beckoned from behind Jack's ear as they ran. "We're not secure here."

"Then make us secure," Jack said as they approached the hulking ICU doors.

"Get those doors open!" one of the agents called out. The orange doors buzzed and swung open before them. A half dozen medical team members took over. "We've got it from here."

Jack was about to press on through the doorway himself when two agents and a doctor blocked his path. "Mr. Sanborn," the doctor said. "You need to let us help your wife now."

"Tell me what's going on!"

"You'll know when I do," the doctor replied, "now stay here and let us help her." He shot a concerned glance at the agents, and Jack could sense their hands ready to grab him if he let his instincts take over.

Jack exhaled heavily and ran a palm over his clammy face as Sarah was wheeled away. The heavy trauma unit doors closed between them with a final deep *thunk* as the magnetic locks engaged.

Jack recognized the familiar sound and flinched. It was the same sound he'd heard two months ago when Sarah was rushed from the birthing unit into the O/R after hemorrhaging during their daughter's stillbirth.

"Sir, I think you need to see this."

Clay Overton looked up from the speech notes he was reading. His convoy of black SUV's was rolling through the hills of western Pennsylvania, on its way to an "America Always" campaign event at a large tire factory. "What is it?" he asked, ready to lay into the aide if the interruption proved unimportant.

The aide handed him a tablet displaying a newsfeed. "Something happened to Sarah Sanborn."

Overton studied the scene at the Sanborn event; Sarah collapsing mid-sentence, Sanborn thrown to the floor and a jumble of moving bodies as whoever held the camera was jostled by the crowd. "Look at that chaos!" he said, feeling a confusing mixture of wonder and alarm. "Was she shot?"

"It doesn't say," the aide replied. "And it's hard to tell, the way she stays upright for a second."

"When was this?"

"Just a few minutes ago."

The Speaker watched handheld footage of Sarah's stretcher being wheeled into a hospital. *So many possibilities with this...*"We need to find out her condition. Right now."

"Sir?"

Overton shot a cold look at the aide. "So we can game out the options."

The aide shrank slightly in his seat. "Options depending on?" he responded timidly.

The Speaker glared at the aide. "If she just collapsed, then he either forced her into something she wasn't ready for or, even better, she's got drug problems," Overton started counting on his fingers. "If she has something serious but makes it, he'll be the village asshole if he keeps campaigning. And if she dies, it'll bump him at least five points that'll last way too long this close to the election."

"Well," the aide nodded. "Let's hope she recovers then."

"Hope is not a strategy," Overton announced, and rubbed his chin thoughtfully. "Just find out exactly what happened," he said, jabbing a finger in the air. "And if I have to hear it on the news first, we have a problem."

"Understood," the aide replied, looking pale.

CHAPTER 27

SEVEN HOURS LATER, Jack and Lewis stood inside Sarah's ICU room, trying to absorb what the doctor was telling them. Jack blinked his eyes hard, as if somehow that would help his brain to better process the words. The figure on the bed barely looked like Sarah. Her face and head were obscured by ventilator tubes, electrodes, and bandages that held everything in place. The only recognizable features were an exposed cheek and the slender hand at her side.

"It was a brain stem stroke," the tall, silver-haired doctor announced. He traced his finger along a monitor that displayed a three-dimensional image of Sarah's brain. "They're not common, but they often result in a sudden loss of consciousness, which is why your wife collapsed so quickly."

Jack stepped to the bedside and slipped his fingers around Sarah's. He gave her limp hand a gentle squeeze, hoping she'd squeeze back. *Please no. Not Sarah. Not her too.*

He finally looked back at the doctor. "What's the . . . prognosis?" He struggled getting the last word out, as if it were an open invitation to have what he valued most taken away.

The doctor's face was grim. "It's very difficult to say, Mr. Sanborn. With brain stem strokes being so rare, it is harder to give an accurate assessment of potential damage. The good news is the brain stem is not where most motor, memory and reasoning functions reside in the brain."

"So, what's the bad news?" Jack replied, not sensing any optimism in the doctor's demeanor.

"The brain stem controls the vital functions of the body like breathing, heart rate, digestion. Basically, all the things you and I take for granted, and we don't yet know how those functions may have been impacted."

"So that's why she's on a ventilator then?" added Lewis.

"Yes. At least for now."

"What can be done for her?" Jack asked, an edge of desperation in his voice. "There must be something . . . "

"Well, the blood clot in the brain stem has been removed, which will prevent further damage. And medication will help prevent additional clots. But the normal treatment options for this type of stroke are," he hesitated, shifting his weight uncomfortably. "Slow-going."

"You said *normal* options," Lewis observed. "Does that mean there are *abnormal* options?"

The doctor exhaled and studied the two men for a moment before nodding. "There's an experimental treatment out of UCLA that has been trialed successfully. But I believe the phase three trial is complete now and they are waiting on FDA approval to release."

"Are you saying it helps with recovery from stroke?" Jack asked, finally letting go of Sarah's hand and facing the doctor head-on.

"Apparently the treatment helps restore damaged brain tissue in areas affected by the stroke. And I've read it can work quite quickly."

"We need to get her in that trial," Jack said. "Right now."

The doctor flashed a look that Jack sensed was regret for raising his expectations. "I believe the trial is closed and they're awaiting approval. I'll make some calls right away and find out. But Mr. Sanborn . . . I'm sorry, but I have to say, please don't get your hopes up on the treatment."

Not much chance of that. As the doctor excused himself, Jack struggled to control his thoughts. He felt like he'd endured a lifetime's worth of hospital trauma in just a few months. "Lewis," he said, "what if the stress of this whole thing caused her stroke?"

"I don't think two weeks of stress brings on a stroke, Jack."

"Maybe so, but given what Sarah went through already with the pregnancy . . ." Jack exhaled heavily. "I'm afraid the stress of the campaign may have put her over the edge." *And it was me who pushed her.*

"Stop speculating about things you can't possibly know," Lewis replied firmly, driven as always by hard facts. "Let me see if I can reach a few folks who might be able to get the treatment approved. I don't give a shit about the FDA. That's another outfit we should take a sledgehammer to."

"Thanks, Lewis," Jack replied. "And while you're at it you'd better tell the team to shut down the ballot petitions. This thing is over."

"Don't even waste a minute thinking about that right now, Jack. I'll handle it."

———

Jack woke the next morning and felt an immediate ache in his lower back from sleeping in the hospital-grade recliner beside Sarah's bed. He stretched, rubbed his face and—with more effort than he expected—pulled himself from the chair. "Good morning," he murmured to a motionless Sarah. She didn't appear to have moved so much as a finger since yesterday. *Come on, Sarah. Come back to us.*

A barrel-chested Secret Service agent appeared in the doorway. "Mr. Sanborn. A couple of visitors are here to see you."

Jack looked up as Lewis peered over the agent's shoulder. "Mind if we come in? I brought someone."

"Of course," Jack replied groggily.

The agent stepped aside to allow Lewis in. Ethan Bessette followed. "I'm so sorry about all this, Jack," he began. "I thought you could use some coffee and a change of clothes." He offered takeout coffee and a shopping bag. "You're about my size," he added as Jack accepted them.

"Thank you. Both are welcome."

"He's got something else to share," Lewis added, the hint of a smile in his eyes.

"Oh?"

"It's not final," Ethan said. "But by close of business today, I will have bought the company behind the UCLA medical trial you heard about yesterday."

Jack nearly spit out his first sip of coffee. "Are you serious?"

"Dead serious," Ethan said. "They're obviously on the west coast, so when Lewis told me about it, I had my people make contact last night."

"You can't acquire a company in a day," Jack countered. "Can you?"

"Actually, you can do it quite easily. If it's privately owned and your offer is ridiculous enough. The transaction will be done by tonight."

"And that means they would treat Sarah immediately?" Jack asked, prompting a placid return stare that said *Ethan's companies do precisely what Ethan wants, when he wants it, how he wants it, as many times as he wants it.* "Right. Of course."

"Pretty damn good way to start the day," Lewis concluded.

"Ethan, I don't know what to say other than thank you," Jack added.

Ethan shrugged. "It's a good investment."

"In the company?" Jack found himself saying. "Or in something else?" He immediately regretted the blunt question, which likely appeared ungrateful.

"The company," Ethan replied, seemingly unconcerned. "Though I have to admit that a world without Sarah in it has far fewer . . . exciting probabilities."

The three of them stood silent for a moment, watching Sarah. A rush of footsteps announced the arrival of one of Sarah's doctors, a bit breathless. "Mr. Sanborn!" he announced, "you'll never guess the news."

"Then you'd better tell me," Jack replied, wondering how the morning could get even better.

"The angiogenic treatment protocol was just FDA approved!"

"You mean the stroke recovery treatment, from UCLA?"

"Yes!" he replied excitedly. "And the company is already sending everything via air courier, so we can start your wife's treatment tomorrow."

Jack and Lewis looked at Ethan expectantly. But he held his hands up. "Not me," he murmured. "Remember, I don't interfere with government policy. I'm merely buying the company."

"There's no way that's normal FDA approval timing," Lewis said. "That's months, even a year ahead of when it should be."

"Who cares," Jack said. He looked to the doctor. "Let's do it."

"Ethan," Lewis began. "Do you think your people can find out how that FDA approval happened?"

"Sure," Ethan replied. "Once I own the company."

"You're still planning to buy them?" Jack asked. "I mean, you probably don't need to now, and with that FDA approval the price may have just gone up."

"98 percent likely, yes," Ethan shrugged. "But I'll buy it anyway. Just in case."

CHAPTER 28

CLAY OVERTON TOOK AS LITTLE NOTICE as possible of the two visitors sitting in his office, choosing for the moment to focus his attention on the weighty crystal glass he held in his hand. He squeezed it tightly. It was palladium micro-alloy crystal, one of the hardest substances on earth, so the only surrender in his grip was from the flesh of his fingers squeezing into the crevices of the ornate crystal.

The rare crystal glasses had been a gift from the Kenyan President after Overton's trade mission there several years ago. The trade mission was forgettable, but Clay appreciated the craftsmanship of the glasses, so the set found its way into his congressional office wet bar. Instead of being catalogued and filed like so many other gifts, into the dark recesses of the National Archives and Records warehouse.

Overton looked up from his glass at the nasal-sounding visitor who was still droning on while the second visitor sat in silence. For a moment, he contemplated hurling the glass at the billboard-sized forehead of the motormouth before him. His college fastball had been well above ninety, and he briefly visualized the heavy glass ripping the man's skull open and silencing the interminable noise.

"Mr. Speaker," the forehead said in a louder tone, interrupting his thoughts. "Do you want us to continue to investigate Sarah Sanborn?"

"No," he replied, "I've opted for another path there." A loud knock on the door sounded before the forehead could ask for details. "Come!" Overton called.

The door swung open and a large figure entered, his feet closer to sliding than stepping across the floor. "Good afternoon, sir," the man said in a raspy baritone. "I'm Grady O'Shea."

Overton took stock of this bulky new visitor. He figured him for two-hundred seventy. His wavy red hair made him look like he'd just stepped out of a wind tunnel. "You're Peterson's guy?" he asked the man.

"Yes, sir." Grady seemed to pull his chest back, which only succeeded in making his gut stick farther out.

Sid Peterson had the largest cumulative career margin of victory in US Senate election history, and he did things the way they needed to be done. Ugly and without mercy. He was turning eighty-four and was finally retiring. Over a few glasses of Haydens, he'd agreed to send O'Shea to Overton's camp in return for a little extra DC-style pork for Peterson's home state, whenever the federal budget actually did get approved. Not that O'Shea didn't have a say in his own endeavors, but Sid Peterson's will was hard to buck, and the cash on offer to work for Overton was more than sufficient.

He motioned O'Shea forward. "We were just settling the matter of Mrs. Sanborn."

Grady sniffed indifferently. "She's a sideshow." Overton noticed that the man's dress shirt was fighting to keep several dozen pounds of flesh from spilling out. "We've got bigger problems to deal with."

The room fell silent, awaiting the next words in the conversation.

"I see you come just as advertised: straight to the point," Overton remarked. "Let's hear it."

"For starters, Mr. Speaker, you've overplayed your hand."

"Not possible," he replied tersely, "but permission to entertain me."

O'Shea shook his head and moved directly in front of the Speaker's large desk. "Sir, you need to end the shutdown now, and allow Perez to take the credit."

There was an intake of breath as the staffers reacted to these unexpected words. "This had better be good," Overton said.

"You're well beyond Duverger's Law," O'Shea began. "Your own desire for a landslide has put your campaign in danger."

"Who the hell is Daverger and why should I care?"

"Duverger," O'Shea corrected. "He's a French economist and a master of election theory."

"French economist sounds like an oxymoron, Mr. O'Shea, all they do is go on strike over there. You're not helping yourself."

Grady tugged at the waistline of his pants, which seemed to have trouble staying in place. "Look at it this way. In a close race, no Democrat or Republican risks voting for a third candidate, given that may help the other major candidate win. People still remember Nader accidentally helping Bush beat Gore. But in your case, you've made it so damned obvious the Democratic ticket is toast, you've now removed that risk for any Democrat voter."

"Your point being that a bunch of sore-loser Democrats will flock to some half-nobody just to fuck me over?"

"I think you've summarized it perfectly."

"And so," Overton replied slowly, "your masterful suggestion is for me to cut a deal with the Democrats to end the shutdown, and then actually give Perez the credit, so more voters will go *back* to the Democrats?"

"If you want to make sure you win . . . yes."

"I'm fucking twenty points up!" Overton replied, his cheeks starting to flush.

"On Perez you are. But you're not watching the inside rail. You're only nine up on Sanborn, and he's gaining." O'Shea's upper lip started to glisten with the apparent exertion of standing, moving and speaking at the same time. "By beating the hell out of Perez, you opened the door for a ton of Democratic voters to flow to Sanborn. But guess what? Bad as that sounds, that's not even your biggest problem anymore."

"Is that right?" Overton said dryly. He was not accustomed to being on the receiving end of tough love. "Do tell: what is my biggest problem?"

"For every Perez voter that gives up and goes to Sanborn, there are two more pissed-off non-voters getting off the sideline and deciding it's time to give a shit and find a ballot box. And you're not lookin' so good to them either."

The Speaker waved his hand dismissively. "Polls this far out are about as useful as toilet paper."

"Believe me, Mr. Speaker," Grady replied, "this election will shatter turnout records. You're the big fish in this pool. But the pool's about to get a whole lot bigger. And your best play in my opinion, is to end the shutdown right now. Today."

"That's impossible."

"Not for you. Do it, and I guarantee it takes the wind out of Sanborn's sails. Without the shutdown, Jack Sanborn doesn't even exist."

Overton sat for a long moment, doing the mental calculus on all the possible compromises required to cut a deal with the Democrats and end the shutdown. The taste of bile threatened to climb into his throat while he chewed on the advice he'd already paid a tidy sum for.

"There was a time during the Revolutionary War," he said, "after so much bloodshed, that many Americans favored a compromise with the British." He stood up from his desk to look his new adviser in the eye. "Had the forefathers allowed that putrid sentiment to fester, we would not be the America we are today." The Speaker stabbed his desk with a thick index finger. "The mere thought of that type of weakness and what it could have done to this country sickens me."

"I'm not quite sure who represents the British today in your analogy, Mr. Speaker. But either way, you paid me a lot of money to ignore my advice."

"Wrong." Overton smiled at his newest advisor, appreciating that he apparently had the balls to match his body size. "I paid a lot of money for you to come up with advice I can actually use. So, sit down and let's get to work."

CHAPTER 29

LATE THE NEXT MORNING, Jack stood at Sarah's bedside. A doctor stood behind him facing a panel of monitors. He was one of several that had flown in overnight from UCLA and had wasted no time injecting the angiogenic material into her brain stem just before sunrise.

Now, all that was left was the waiting.

The doctors had taken Sarah off the ventilator late last night. Jack was grateful to be able to see Sarah's face again. The residue lines from the tape were still visible, but he could almost imagine her just being peacefully asleep—minus the dozens of wires still snaking through her hair, each one connected to a tiny electrode that measured her brain's response to the angiogenic material.

Jack turned around to the doctor studying the set of six monitors. Five of them displayed charts with undulating lines and various numeric data, while the sixth showed a three-dimensional image of Sarah's brain, with colors that slightly pulsed and shifted.

"What are you looking for exactly?" Jack asked.

"A lot of things. Blood flow, synaptic activity, chemical markers that indicate cell regeneration."

"Can the treatment work that fast?" Jack asked, "it's only been six hours."

"It can vary quite a lot," the doctor replied. "The phase-three trial had close to a thousand patients, and initial response times to the axonal accelerant medication ranged from hours to weeks. We're not sure why the wide range yet, but the accelerant definitely works."

"That's great. Congrats on the FDA approval, by the way," Jack added.

The doctor smiled. "Thanks. That was quite a surprise to us."

"That it was approved?"

"No. That it was approved so quickly."

Just in time for Sarah. "Any early signs?" Jack asked, scanning the doctor's face instead of the screens. He knew the answer lay there and not in multiple displays that made no sense to him.

"There's clearly some progress, but it's still early, Mr. Sanborn. Be patient."

"Hey there," Lewis said from the doorway. He came in and handed Jack a cup of coffee.

"Thanks, Lewis, much needed."

Lewis nodded in Sarah's direction. "So far so good here?"

"Apparently. Still early." Jack said.

"So, there's going to be an interesting bit of political news hitting in the next hour," Lewis said, his voice uncharacteristically tentative. "I know it's not relevant at this moment, but I thought you should know."

"Okay . . . " Jack shifted to the corner of Sarah's room and Lewis followed, while the doctor continued to focus on the monitors.

"Justice Faber apparently commented on your theory about applying antitrust laws to the two-party system."

"Publicly?" Jack replied. It was unusual for Supreme Court justices to comment officially on anything; they generally let the court's rulings and dissents do the talking. Faber in particular was known for his low public profile.

"Not exactly," Lewis replied. "He was in a Q&A session at Harvard, and someone asked him if your idea had any merit. And it turns out he was being recorded."

"A familiar theme," Jack commented. "What did he say?"

"That your argument is a critical one for the situation we find ourselves in."

Jack's eyebrows pricked up. "That's quite a statement from him, or anyone on the Supreme court."

"It is. And it means your idea can get momentum . . . " Lewis trailed off, apparently unsure how to finish the sentence.

"Where are we on getting the petitions shelved?" Mention of the outside world reminded Jack he had a runaway train he needed to stop.

"It's not like flipping a light switch," Lewis said, looking away. "But it's in the works."

Something about Lewis' expression told Jack that there was more to the story. "How many state ballots were we up to before hitting the brakes?"

Before Lewis could answer, they were startled by a sudden gasp behind them, followed by the sound of machine alarms. Jack spun around to look at Sarah.

Her eyes were open for the first time since the stroke, but they were rolled back in her head. Her body pitched and twisted wildly, like a woman possessed. With all the wires, she looked like a woman being electrocuted. She let out a guttural cry that filled the room.

"What the hell is happening?" Jack cried.

A nurse and two more doctors rushed in. "Give five milligrams of lorazepam now!" the first doctor commanded. The nurse rushed out while two of the doctors held Sarah's arms and legs.

"Let go of her!!" Jack bellowed. He grabbed one of the doctors by the shoulder.

"Mr. Sanborn, please!" Jack felt strong arms encircle him and haul him backward. "Let them handle it. They know what to do."

"Make it stop! For God's sake, she's—"

"She's having a seizure, Mr. Sanborn," the doctor now facing him replied, "It can happen when synaptic regeneration happens rapidly."

The nurse returned, syringe in hand. "Five milligrams lorazepam going in now." She emptied the syringe into Sarah's IV port.

"The seizure itself is not dangerous," said the doctor that was still facing Jack, blocking his path. "We just need to keep her from going into status epilepticus."

"What does that mean?" Jack said. Sarah was still thrashing on the bed.

"It's a type of seizure that is very hard to stop."

Jack steadied himself against the panel of screens that had been pushed aside, cursing himself. *What have I done to her?*

CHAPTER 30

CARMEN MARINAS COVERED HER MOUTH as she yawned in the back of the crowded bus. It had been another long day of clerical servitude at the New York County criminal courthouse. Now it was being made longer by everything New York's Metro-Transit-Authority guidance system did to re-route the transports around the SoMAD protest areas that sprang up on an almost daily basis. Despite the satellite guidance, Carmen's thirty-minute commute back to Queens was now closing in on an hour. She shook her head with irritation, ready to be back in her apartment.

She slipped the MS Slimfold phone from her purse, and the screen sprang to life as she opened it. With a couple taps, she arrived at a series of beach-view terrace photos. Carmen drew them in like a slow breath, her lips curling until she forced herself to stop and look around. Only five more weeks until she and her new boyfriend would be on the beach in Ixtapa sipping the local tequila. She was eager for a break from the shouting in New York, and with the long-running border dispute finally settled, she could get back to her favorite little piece of paradise. Carmen's sister had agreed to take her son Paco for a few days; she had three kids of her own, which meant Carmen would soon repay her sister's favor in triplicate, but that was okay. She was desperate for a break.

The bus finally chimed, announcing Carmen's stop. She tucked the phone away and slipped out the door as the virtual assistant thanked her for riding. At least she didn't have a long walk at the end of the long ride; the stop was only a few doors from her apartment.

She climbed the steps up to her building's front door and was about to press her thumb to the scanner when a voice spoke behind her.

"Are you Carmen Marinas?"

She jerked at the sound and whirled around.

"Quién-w-who are you?" she stammered, clutching her purse. The man moved up the steps behind her. She had no idea where he had come from. She scanned the street and saw no one else. Not good.

"I'm not going to hurt you," DeMarco told her. He held up his phone, displaying Paco's photo. "Is this your son?"

"I don't understand . . . Is he . . ."

"Your son is fine, Carmen, for now." With that he returned the phone to his pocket.

Carmen's heart pounded in her chest.

"You work at the New York County Criminal Courthouse. A clerk in the records department." It wasn't a question. DeMarco still had plenty of contacts able to tell him who to lean on for a given piece of information. And he still had sources skilled in digital dumpster diving. Together, they'd given him all he needed to know about Carmen Marinas, well before he planted himself by her front door to await her arrival.

"Yes," she replied, her voice trembling.

DeMarco reached into a pocket and pulled out a fingernail-sized USB-Tetra drive. He held it out. "Take this."

"What is it?" Carmen asked. DeMarco thought she looked like she was staring at a bloody knife.

"By tomorrow night, you will bring me the full evidence files from the Elenestro case. The case number is on the drive."

The woman was desperately processing, her breath shallow and growing rapid. "You w-want case files? I . . . I don't know any Elenestro case. I've only worked there—"

"Two years." DeMarco had done his research. He needed someone on the inside, but someone he knew he could manipulate. "I know. The case is from 2039, before you were there, but you'll find it easily enough."

"What do you want with them? What are you—"

"Let's just say you'll be helping to right a wrong." DeMarco replied, still holding out the drive. "You believe in justice, don't you, Carmen?"

She extended a trembling hand, and DeMarco dropped the drive in her palm. "Now Carmen," he added, "I want you to consider two things before you go inside. If you flush that drive down the toilet in hopes this was just a bad dream, and then go down the hall to hug your son Paco—"

"Mm-how do you know his name!?" she recoiled as if slapped hard.

"—and then decide to call the cops," DeMarco continued, stepping close enough to smell the coffee on her breath, "keep in mind that I know all the cops, and you can be sure one of them will tip me off."

He held up his phone again, with a second photo of her son, this one taken as he was walking out of school, all smiles. "Paco is a good-looking boy. He's got very nice skin. Handsome."

Carmen's eyes grew wide at the idea of this man following her son. Her throat felt like it was in a vice. "P . . . please, why are you—"

"It's okay, Carmen, he's fine upstairs." DeMarco swiped to another photo. "But you should know that this is what a face looks like after an acid attack."

Carmen recoiled in horror at the grisly image.

"It only takes one second, passing by anywhere, and Paco's handsome little face gets erased forever." DeMarco didn't love the idea of threatening a child, but he also knew it was the only sure way to get what he wanted.

"Y . . . you can't—"

"By tomorrow night I want the evidence files," DeMarco told her. "I will send you a message where to meet."

"Mister—I can't remove—"

"Do this one thing, Carmen, and you can enjoy Ixtapa with your new boyfriend in peace. And you have my word you'll never see me again and your son will never, ever have to meet me."

Carmen inhaled sharply at the mention of her vacation plans.

Getting a tap on Carmen's phone had been an easy favor to call in with one of the digital pirates he'd known when he was still a cop. "*Don't* bring me the files tomorrow night, and any day now you'll be begging for money to fund skin grafts for little Paco. You have my word on that too."

CHAPTER 31

Jack dwelled on the narrow edge of evening sleep, the dull aches from hours in the reclining chair at Sarah's bedside making it difficult to nod off. The steady flow of staff in and out made it all but certain that anything more than a thin veil of sleep was impossible. Which suited Jack just fine. After Sarah's seizure, which the medication quickly interrupted, he wasn't about to step away from her bedside unless he was cuffed and dragged away.

He was hesitant to believe the neurologist's assessment that the seizure was actually a good sign, that it was a side effect of her brain responding faster than expected and rebuilding neural tissue at a rapid rate. One of the UCLA doctors had also shared with Jack that certain patients in the trial phase emerged from the treatment with *higher* brain function than before the stroke, and Sarah's early indicators thus far were positive—something about developing stronger neural network density. He found it all a bit hard to believe. *But sometimes believing is the only option.*

By Jack's count there were three doctors and four nurses rotating in and out of the room, monitoring Sarah's progress around the clock. Even with ear plugs in and teetering on the edge of sleep, Jack could distinguish each of their voices as they spoke in hushed tones. It was comforting to know Sarah was being looked after.

He could feel himself settling deeper as the two most familiar voices continued their steady rhythm. After a time, his brain became aware that the voices had stopped. And that a third sound, low and intermittent, had taken their place. *That sound is different.* The moment the thought formed in Jack's brain his system shifted to full alertness. He sat up and pulled out his earplugs.

"What's happening?" he said to the two doctors; one was tall, reedy and serious looking, the other with a frizz of red hair that gave the impression of someone fresh out of medical school. Sarah still lay peacefully in her bed, which eased Jack's panic before it could gather any steam.

The reedy one gave Jack a smile and spoke low. "She's talking in her sleep."

"Is that good?"

"Well, talking at this stage of the treatment is definitely a good sign," he replied. "We've seen it before. Her brain is reprocessing and storing things as the neural networks repair themselves. From the outside, it looks like she's dreaming." He gestured to the bank of flat screen monitors by the bedside. "But from the wave patterns, we can see that she's not in a dream state, which would be theta-type waves. She's in a delta wave state, which the medication is keeping her in because that's where the most regeneration happens."

Sarah interrupted them with soft mumbling. Jack leaned close, trying to make out the words. For a moment it sounded like nothing more than muffled gibberish, but after a time he recognized something else entirely.

"That doesn't sound like English," he said, utterly confused.

The red-haired doctor nodded his agreement. "Did your wife study languages?"

"She studied some Spanish and a bit of Mandarin in high school and college."

"That could be it. Her brain is reprocessing, trying to reorganize a lot of information right now, including things she probably doesn't even know she remembers."

"So, she's progressing, then?" Jack said excitedly.

"It's hard to say the level of progress, but the mumbling while in a delta wave state is a good sign that we're seeing axonal sprouting at the right levels."

"What is that again?"

"It means," the reedy one replied, "that her brain is generating new connections and restoring damaged ones at an accelerated rate. It's a sign that your wife's brain is responding very well to the treatment."

Jack heard a soft knock at the door. He turned to see a fresh-looking Jade in jeans and a black blazer. Her hair was down around her shoulders, which made her look much softer than her usual pulled-back style. She smiled. "Hey, I hope you don't mind me coming by."

"How long were you there?"

"Couple minutes. Secret Service let me in." Her eyes shifted to Sarah. "I heard what the doctor was saying. Sounds promising."

"It does," he replied, as the doctor went back to watching the monitors.

"It looks like retirement from AGN agrees with you," Jack said.

"Thanks. I think so too."

"So, what's next for you, Jade? Any plans?"

"I'm going to freelance for a while, do the stories I want to do. See where that takes me."

"Good decision." He was happy to see Jade looking content, something that didn't strike Jack as her typical state of being. "So, where's your first story going to take you then . . . Any idea yet?"

"I do, actually. The story's right outside."

Jack fixed her with a quizzical look.

"I guess you haven't looked out the window lately?"

Jack hadn't even realized there was a window in the room; it had been opaqued the whole time he'd been there. It looked like a wall. "You switching to the weather business now?" he asked. He found the button to clear the smart-glass window and looked outside.

For a long moment he squinted into the evening light, craning to see through the rectangular window that framed the scene below. For a moment the scene looked like a blanket of fireflies, but Jack quickly realized it was a sea of candles, flickering. "What's going on?"

"They're holding vigil for Sarah."

Jack inhaled deeply to steady himself. He took in the array of lights and the faces above them, beginning in the parking lot three stories down and spreading like a twinkling river across the hospital grounds, extending over the main road for as far as he could see.

That night, Jack slept more than he had in days, the news of Sarah's progress easing his troubled mind. He stretched and pulled himself up from the recliner chair. His body seemed to be getting used to it.

Sarah looked peacefully asleep. The same reedy doctor stood by the monitors, making Jack wonder if he'd been standing there all night.

"Good morning," Jack said.

"Hello, Mr. Sanborn. You slept."

Jack heard a noise from outside and moved to the window, which was still transparent. A chill washed over him. *Jesus . . . They're all still there.* In the light of day he could see the chairs, sleeping bags and coolers scattered among the crowd of supporters.

When he first watched the scene the night before, it was with a sense of awe and reverence for the outpouring of support for Sarah's recovery. This morning, though, he sensed something entirely different. Expectation.

His heart seemed to flutter in his chest. *They're hoping I keep running.* The obvious thought that hadn't dawned on him the night before suddenly hit him like a ton of bricks. *They want her to get better because they want me to stay in the race.* He swallowed hard at the thought. *But I can't run! This whole thing nearly killed Sarah. It's over!*

Jack slipped the phone from his pocket to text Lewis about officially terminating the campaign. No more waiting. "Shit," he muttered as he remembered the lousy phone reception in this part of the hospital.

"Mr. Sanborn?" the doctor spoke, interrupting Jack's pinwheeling thoughts. "Can we talk for a moment?"

Jack sensed his tone and stepped forward. "What happened?"

"Nothing has happened, Mr. Sanborn. We're still seeing strong regeneration patterns."

Jack waited. Reading faces like a book meant sometimes he didn't need to ask. He just knew it was coming.

"The concern I have is what I am seeing here." The doctor pointed to the whole-brain image in multiple colors. "The left mid-brain section of the brain stem."

"What's the problem?" Jack asked, his anxiety rising. "I thought the regeneration was going better than most patients you've seen in trials."

The doctor sighed. "It is going well, that's absolutely correct."

"So how can there be a problem?"

"This part of the mid-brain controls the reticular activating system." The doctor indicated another area of the brain. "Which controls whether we're awake or asleep."

"Okay."

"The chemical markers and synaptic activity I see right here indicate the healing in that part of the brain has plateaued."

"But, if she's recovering well, is that bad?"

"No, not necessarily . . ." He paused, looking unsure of what to say.

"Doctor . . ."

"It's just that . . . I had hoped with the chemical markers I'm seeing that she'd show signs of waking up by now. I actually thought she was going to wake up last night. That's why I'm still here."

"Are you telling me that even though every other part of her brain is responding well . . ."

The doctor nodded back and finished Jack's sentence. "Yes. There is a chance if that section of the mid-brain doesn't fully heal, Sarah's otherwise fully recovered brain may not actually wake up."

Jack pushed away a torrent of horrifying thoughts: Sarah forever imprisoned in a sleeping body that would slowly waste away as the months and years went on. He shook his head. "No. There must be something you can do."

"We are trying, Mr. Sanborn. Please know that. We'll do everything we can . . . For both of them."

Jack flinched like he had been slapped. "What do you mean, both of them?"

The doctor's thin face went slightly pale. "I'm sorry, Mr. Sanborn . . . I shouldn't have assumed you'd know by now given the hormone signature was pretty faint in the blood panels . . . but your wife is definitely pregnant. No more than two weeks, I would say."

CHAPTER 32

CARMEN MARINAS FUMBLED NERVOUSLY in her purse for her ID badge. She was proud of her job at the New York County Criminal Courthouse—the largest of its kind in any state—having made the move to New York with her now deservedly ex-boyfriend, who'd left her penniless and pregnant in one of the most expensive cities in the world.

She'd worked three terrible jobs for an equal number of years while completing her college diploma in legal studies at Kingsborough Community College in Brooklyn. She'd then parlayed that into a potential career as an administrative support clerk in what was generally considered the second most prestigious courthouse in America. All while raising her son Paco, and with no family within three thousand miles to lean on.

"Where the fuck?" Her fingers finally located the slim badge that normally would have been clipped to her blouse. She took a great deal of care with how she dressed, and each accessory was chosen to match. But she was always pleased to wear the perennially clashing ID badge like a jewelry showpiece. Not only was it an outward declaration that she belonged, but wearing it saved fumbling around in her purse at the screening station, while fellow commuters queued behind. With good reason, today was the first day she had failed to follow her routine.

"Good morning, Carmen." The large security guard nodded from behind his console. His presence was altogether redundant nowadays, as was the actual badge that Carmen wore. Fingerprint technology and wearable device monitoring meant that any employee not trained in spycraft trying to go where they shouldn't, could be stopped automatically.

"Hi, Gopal," she replied with a forced smile, doing her best to make today feel like any other day. She scanned her ID badge over the reader, and it responded with an off-tone bleat followed by a red flash. Carmen produced a sharp exhale that stifled the curse on her lips. *Bleat.* After the second flash of red denial, she could feel the blood rushing to her cheeks.

The guard smiled. "Try it a bit slower, Carmen." He sat up higher in his seat, happy to be useful for something.

She passed the card as slowly as her adrenalized system would allow and was rewarded with an affirming chime followed by a green light. "Sorry. I'm running late, I guess." She reached toward the thumbprint scanner.

"How can you be late, Miss?"

"Sorry?" she replied.

"How can you be late, when you're twenty minutes early?"

Carmen opened her mouth, and then closed it with a soft pop, unsure what to say. *You are blowing it already . . .* she cursed herself silently.

"Unless they're working you too hard, Carmen. You better make sure you get overtime if they make you come in so early."

Carmen laughed more naturally than she expected, relieved her slip-up didn't matter. She'd forgotten how chatty Gopal could be when he had the chance. "You bet I will," she said, and headed for the escalator that would take her down to the second basement. She didn't go there often, but her security clearance should be good enough for what she needed.

Carmen's heels sounded too loud as she stepped off the escalator and strode down the echoey hall toward the evidence locker. It wasn't much of a locker anymore, so she wasn't sure why they still called it that. Gone were the days of padlocked cages with boxes of manila files, murder weapons and fingerprinted glasses that anyone with the right connection or a thick enough cash envelope might peruse. Those items were all stored three floors farther below now, and like almost everyone in the New York County Criminal Courthouse, Carmen lacked the clearance needed to access sub-basement level five. What she did have access to were the bank of restricted terminals that sat in a largely empty, stark grey room that had been part of the old evidence locker system. Those would be good enough for what she was looking for.

Carmen extended her thumb to the authentication pad by the entrance. This time, the steel doors unlatched. She exhaled and pulled the door open. The room was empty. She checked her watch. In fifteen minutes, the building's legal staff would be showing up for work. She'd have to move quickly.

Carmen sat down at the first terminal. After two failed attempts where her nervous fingers betrayed her, she entered her credentials properly. Her finger hovered over the Enter key. She'd leave a digital trail, but there was no way around it. An image of Paco flashed in her mind. "Fuck it. I can get another job."

Not with a criminal record for stealing state's evidence. The voice in her head always sounded like her mother.

She chewed her lip for a moment, then placed the thumb drive into the port on the side of her terminal. The drive light flickered as she typed the name Elenestro. She thought the case name sounded familiar.

Focus, Carmen. Focus on Paco.

She'd convinced a friend in Jersey last night to come get Paco and take him upstate for a few days. She sent him off with his blanket, several toys and more than a few confused tears. Paco went on a "little adventure" she dearly hoped he'd never comprehend.

She hit Enter, but the files she wanted were nowhere to be seen. She did as the man instructed, accessing the thumb drive and running a level-seven file recovery program to search for the Elenestro evidence files.

It took less than a minute. *Thank you.*

Carmen tapped the glass panel and with two fingers slid the first file icon into the transfer bin, which would copy the files to the thumb drive. The terminal bleated loudly, and the folder bounced back to its original location, giving Carmen a jolt. She tried again. Another bleat. This one felt louder, and Carmen jerked in her seat. She felt her pulse speed up. "What the hell?" she breathed, feeling her scalp prickle with sweat. She checked her watch again. *Running out of time.*

She pressed her finger hard on the file icon to bring up the file properties. It was Level 3 access. Such files were usually restricted to cases in progress. But these files were five years old. It made no sense.

There was only one way to access Level 3 files, and it was a really bad idea.

She logged out of the access system and moved to another terminal. She tapped the screen and entered the credentials for Judge Malcolm Creemore.

Carmen was one of the first to know how any new system worked, so when software changes happened everyone leaned on Carmen to be their personal help desk. She was happy to do it; she took pride in being helpful. She hadn't expected Judge Creemore to share his password so she could handle his software updates, but men like that hated menial distractions. She would have forgotten it, but she had to ask him for his current password several times, to update programs and untangle various IT snags that came up. She eventually noticed the pattern he was using. It was his dead son's name backwards, followed by the number of months he would have been alive at the time of the password change. The last time she used it was only two months ago, and she knew the system only reset passwords every six months.

Carmen took the most likely option and typed in the last password she had used and hit Enter. The login window disappeared without fanfare. She waited for a bleat or something else to happen, but nothing did. Only silence. She tried moving the file again, and it worked.

"Thank God!" she proclaimed and then nearly jumped out of her seat when the door opened behind her.

"Well, someone's excited to be at work early today."

Oh God, not that voice. Any voice but that one. Carmen turned in her seat and found herself staring up at Judge Malcolm Creemore.

She did her best to smile. Judge Creemore was at least six foot four and was not slim by anyone's sense of the word. He cast an imposing figure on any occasion and especially now. Carmen fought a primal instinct to flee. This was going worse than any of the scenarios she'd played out in her head the night before. She'd never known Judge Creemore to venture down to the evidence locker.

"We must be working you hard, Carmen," he said warmly. He was always friendly with her, even more so since she'd become his unofficial IT helpline. In addition to fear, Carmen felt a sudden overwhelming surge of guilt for abusing the trust of the judge who'd bestowed her with greater responsibility. The impulse to blurt out her impossible predicament nearly made its way to her lips, but the thought of Paco stopped her.

"Just catching up on some backlog, Judge," she said, trying to sound bored. "You know how it is. I just got here a few minutes ago." She held his eyes and continued to smile. He did the same for an extra beat that seemed to last an eternity. Was he glancing over her shoulder at the terminal? She suddenly couldn't remember what was on the screen, so she hoped for the best. "You've had a busy week too, huh?" she asked, desperate to divert his attention. She shifted slightly in an effort to conceal the terminal behind her.

The judge smiled. "Quite so. Plenty of misdeeds to keep us all quite occupied." There was yet another pause, this one longer than the last. His grey eyes never left hers. After a moment he looked away, and she hoped he'd get on with whatever business had brought him down here. What came next made her heart skip a beat. "I've enjoyed the chance to work together, Carmen."

He fixed her with a strange smile, one she hoped she was

misinterpreting. "Um, me too, Judge," she said. "I really like the work here."

"I can tell you care about that," he said. "That means a lot to me."

"Thank you."

"It means a lot that I can trust you," he added, his weathered face widening into a smile that looked to Carmen more like a gash with teeth growing behind it.

Carmen's heart was hammering like it would burst at any moment. She could feel beads of sweat trickling down her scalp.

"I don't want to make you uncomfortable, Carmen," the judge said, his tone turning serious. "But perhaps we could share a drink some time. I'd like to get to know you better, if that's all right."

Carmen's mind spun like a Tilt-A-Whirl, her instincts fighting her fear. She had no idea what her face might be telegraphing to the judge.

"I'd like that too," she said at last. The fact that he was married, and that she had a boyfriend, made the whole proposition wildly inappropriate.

"That's good." His eyes traveled down to her waist and below, then back to her eyes. Carmen's sense of guilt for using the Judge's password quickly dissipated, and she just desperately wanted to leave.

She did a half turn in her chair, back toward the terminal. "I guess we'd better . . . "

"Yes, of course," he responded and sat his heavy frame at the terminal beside her.

Carmen's mind clicked back to business and she went cold. *Shit! His login can't be used on two terminals at once!* She raced to copy the second Elenestro file as the judge started tapping his own screen. Carmen slid the second file down to the transfer bin and released, only to have it pop back to its original position on her screen. *Goddammit!* Had she not positioned it correctly? She tried again, moving slowly and deliberately though she knew she had only seconds left before the judge's terminal bleat and flashed a message like *'Your password is being used by your desired mistress, five feet to your left.'* She exhaled quietly when the second folder finally started copying to the transfer box and onto the thumb drive. *Come on, COME ON...*

The second the operation completed, she logged out. Thank God she was familiar with the system. She could hear the judge still tapping away slowly. She palmed the thumb drive and rose to leave.

"Done so soon?" Judge Creemore asked, a mock look of pouty disappointment on his face.

He was laying it on a bit thick. Which certainly made it easier to not feel guilty, at least as long as she wasn't caught. "I'll see you soon, judge," she said, mustering a slight smile and buzzing herself out.

Don't run, she told herself as the door closed behind her. She rode the two-story escalator up to the main level, using a tissue to dab the sweat from her forehead.

She approached the security entrance, her eyes on the outer doors and safety. She fumbled again for her ID badge.

"You okay, Carmen?" came a sudden voice. She almost dropped her ID badge. She turned to see Gopal looking concerned. "You look like you've seen a ghost," he said.

"Suddenly not feeling well, Gopal." She shook her head. "Best I don't share that around."

With that the glass panels opened, and she left the New York County Courthouse, hopefully not for the last time.

～

The secure phone on United States Attorney General Susan Pericote's desk chirped intermittently. The AG furrowed her brow at the sound of her secure line; it was seldom used, and never brought good news. "Would you excuse me," she said to the gaggle of visitors that had assembled in her office, deep inside the RFK Department of Justice Building in Washington. "I need to take this call."

When the visitors had been shuffled back to the outer office, she lifted the receiver. "Yes?"

"General," said a man who didn't need to identify himself. "You asked me to keep a log on the Elenestro files . . ."

"Listening."

"Seven minutes ago, a level seven recovery program was run. We believe the complete case and evidence files were copied."

Susan tightened her grip on the receiver. She'd hoped this call would never come. "Copied by whom?"

"A Judge Malcolm Creemore. He's on the New York County—"

"I know who he is," Susan interrupted. *But what in the hell does he want with the Elenestro files?*

"Strange timing given Elenestro just died a few days ago, shortly before his release date."

Susan nodded, deep in thought. She ended the call and tapped her intercom for her assistant.

"Yes, General?"

"I need you to clear tomorrow's schedule and arrange transportation."

"Of course. Is this an official trip?"

"No," Susan answered.

"Got it. Where to?"

"Chapel Hill, North Carolina."

CHAPTER 33

JACK STARED OUT THE WINDOW of Sarah's hospital room and blinked hard at the sight. *Is that crowd bigger than it was yesterday?* The scene looked like the view from an outdoor concert stage. He took note of the food trucks and port-a-johns, which hadn't been there the day before. If the crowd had plans to go anywhere soon, it didn't show.

Where the hell are you, Lewis?

Jack contemplated heading downstairs and simply making the announcement himself: *I'm out of the race.*

He looked over at Sarah, still peaceful in her bed, a lone doctor checking the monitors. Jack wondered if this was what purgatory felt like: everything you want is visible, but just out of reach. It had been eight days since Sarah collapsed at the rally, and Jack had barely left her room.

"Knock, knock," came Lewis' voice, interrupting his thoughts.

"You're here!"

Lewis stepped into the room with Jade close behind. "Both of you—good." Jack waved a hand behind him at the window. "We need to put an end to all this, today. Stopping the petitions doesn't seem to have mattered much. Jade, are there reporters downstairs? We need to do this now."

Jade immediately shot a glance at Lewis that Jack didn't need jury-reading skills to interpret. "The petitions have been stopped . . . haven't they?"

"Look, Jack," Lewis said. "It's a little complicated."

"You said it was being handled. What happened?"

"It's not like blasting out a group email gets everyone to stand down," Lewis said. "Turns out it's a lot harder to stop something you didn't start in the first place. These petitions all have a life of their own."

"Bullshit," Jack replied. "What happened to the firm of Hayes and company being able to handle mountains of red tape bigger than Everest?"

"Jack," Lewis said, stepping closer. "You were in no condition to make that call. You've barely slept in days. From the look and smell of you, you haven't showered in a week. And run or not, you don't have to abandon the cause."

"What are you talking about?"

"I'm saying, with that backhand endorsement from Justice Faber, your antitrust idea has real legs. But if you're not at least on the ballot, the air starts leaking out of the balloon."

"How many?" Jack replied, practically glowering at Lewis.

"How many what?"

"How many state ballots have we qualified for?"

Lewis paused. "Forty-three."

The hair on Jack's neck stood up straight. "Jesus."

"Six more in five days," Jade added, "and they're all within reach."

"And Texas?" Jack asked.

"No decision yet," Lewis replied. "But soon."

"So, you want me to . . ." Jack walked back to the window and waved his arm, his knuckles whacking against the glass, ". . . let these people think they have a candidate to vote for in November, when I know damned well that's not going to happen?"

"Yes," Lewis replied firmly, "I do."

"Easy for you to say."

"Jack," Jade said, "none of this is about faking it. The more weeks of pressure the mere *idea* of you can apply, the more likely change will happen. The shutdown at least. And maybe more."

"The Democrats aren't even on the map right now," Lewis said. "And even without having campaigned in a week, you're breathing down Overton's neck in the polls."

"It's like I'm not even here," Jack said, exasperated. "It's like I'm a brand name or something that doesn't even need the person. We should just put cardboard cutouts of me on every corner, smiling and waving. Maybe you already did!"

"Jack," Lewis said, "you need some real sleep."

He let out a long exhale. "You still should have talked to me. Both of you. Asleep in a chair or not . . . I've been right here."

The three of them stayed silent for a moment, the only sound in the room the faint beeps of Sarah's monitoring equipment.

"I'm sorry, Jack," Lewis said. "I was not trying to completely ignore your wishes."

"Just partly," Jack said, his tone softening.

"So, what do you want to do?" Lewis asked. "All options are still open; it's your call."

Jack looked at Sarah in bed, then back at Lewis and Jade for a long moment. "I want to go downstairs and tell everyone the truth."

Jack's words hung in the air, leaving Jade to break the next silence. "A shower and a shave before you do that might be a good idea." Jack smiled back at both of them.

"Hon . . . " The word was a raspy whisper.

Jack looked toward the door, confused until he realized whose voice it was.

"Sarah?" He hurried to her bedside, leaning close. "Babe?" Sarah's eyes were closed but her nod was unmistakable. Jack teared up, feeling like the greatest weight of his lifetime had just been lifted. "You're back," he whispered. He took her hands in his and kissed them. He could see Sarah's lips moving, but no words came forth. "Babe, I'm right here," he said. "Don't try to talk, okay? I'm right here."

Sarah kept straining, her dormant vocal cords rasping as she tried to push the words out. Jack leaned in closer, until he heard what she was trying to say . . .

"Don't quit . . . Run."

CHAPTER 34

JACK SQUEEZED SARAH'S HAND as he sat at her bedside. Sarah squeezed right back while Lewis and Jade looked on and doctors streamed in and out of her room.

"Babe," Jack said, "How can I run when nothing in my life matters without you? I need to stay with you. For us. For our family. We have a future to think about."

Sarah finally opened her eyes, squinting in the bright light then focusing on Jack. "I know, Jack. We do have a future to think about . . . That's why you have to run."

Jack studied Sarah's face, searching for clues that might help him understand how she could wake up from a stroke, learn she was two weeks pregnant and yet still urge him to keep running for President. "You had a stroke on stage," he said. "A big one. I don't think—"

"I know I did," Sarah interrupted as she cleared her throat, "I could hear the doctors talking, and you as well. I just couldn't wake up . . . until now."

"That's incredible," Lewis said. "This treatment is unbelievable."

"But Sarah," Jack protested, "I can't go running all over the country with you here recovering."

She pushed herself up in the bed as one of the doctors came to her bedside to test her pupil dilation with a pen light.

Sarah smiled as she blinked. "Something tells me I'll have plenty of people around to guide my recovery. I don't want to live with regret, my love. We just got a second chance, at everything. Let's not waste it by being afraid."

Jack smiled back at her. "Okay. No fear it is."

"Mr. Sanborn, can I get in here?" another doctor interrupted. "I need to check some vitals and motor responses."

Jack stepped back.

"Sarah," Lewis said, "we can do more than half the events virtually and be home every other day."

"Well, aren't you the responsible one," Sarah said with a crinkled smile as the doctor had her wiggle each finger one at a time. "That sounds great."

Jack, Lewis and Jade stepped out into the hallway to let the doctor attend to Sarah. "Look, Lewis," Jack said. "What I said in there about you ignoring my wishes. I was a bit harsh."

Lewis beamed. "But you're liking me now, aren't you? Forget it. We have work to do."

"So now what?" Jade asked. "Other than a shower and some decent clothes?"

"Yeah . . ." Jack looked down at himself. "After that, we stick to the plan: go downstairs and talk to the press."

"With a very different message than you were planning," Jade added, with the biggest smile Jack had seen on her.

"You better believe it."

"There's some press down there now," Jade said. "But by the time you get cleaned up, I'll make sure there are plenty more."

"Good."

"One suggestion, though," Jade added. "Don't do it like a normal press conference, inside the hospital. You've got close to a thousand people out there, camped out for Sarah and for you. Talk to them. Tell them about Sarah. Let the press cover that."

Both men nodded. "I love it," Jack replied.

⌒

Jack, Lewis and Jade stepped into the hospital elevator thirty minutes later and descended from the sixth-floor intensive care unit.

It dawned on Jack that he hadn't left the hospital in eight days. His nerves thrummed with anticipation.

"You're going to need to re-assemble the team," Jack said, his eyes forward.

"Consider it done," Lewis announced.

Jack looked over at his old friend. "You never actually disbanded them, did you?"

A grin spread across Lewis' face. "You're *really* liking me now, aren't you?"

"I suppose I'll have to."

The doors opened and they entered a small service hallway where Agent Muller waited with several other agents. "Good to see you, sir."

"You guys must have been getting bored," Jack said as they moved down the hall. He checked his buzzing phone and answered a call from Ethan Bessette. "Thanks for calling me back. Yeah, the treatment worked beautifully . . . I think you've bought yourself quite a technology there . . . She'll be in hospital for a while still, just to make sure that she's a hundred percent . . . We're about to make an announcement right now, so I don't have a lot of time. Let me get right down to it. Remember that two billion dollars you offered at the train station? Well, here's the thing. I still don't need it, but I have another idea."

Jack talked to Ethan for another minute, ending the call as the group stepped into the hospital's main atrium.

Lewis was the first to speak, his eyes saucer wide. "Did I hear you say something about Ethan offering you two billion dollars?"

"It's a long story," Jack said, doing his best to conceal a smirk.

"And one you *will* tell me," Lewis stated.

Once outside, Jack stepped onto a construction lift Jade had arranged as a makeshift speaker's platform. The press fired off a dozen questions. Instead of answering, Jack grabbed the waiting megaphone and hit the UP switch on the lift. The crowd roared when it saw him rise twenty feet in the air. Press photographers pushed back to get clearer shots.

Jack waved, then brought the megaphone up. "Patience and persistence are way too underrated in this world!" he shouted. "But let me tell you . . . today, patience and persistence have been rewarded!" The crowd whooped, despite the fact that he hadn't really said anything yet.

"I'd like to first express my thanks to the wonderful staff at UNC Hospital and the team of doctors who joined us here from UCLA to help Sarah make an incredible recovery."

The crowd exploded like their team had just won the Super Bowl. "That's right! She's upstairs right now, chatting away and asking when she can get out of bed!" The crowd howled with delight. Jack wondered if Sarah was watching from the upstairs window behind him.

"I am so eternally grateful to all of you for your support these past eight days. Your will and your resolve have kept me strong. And I'm here to tell you now that we're not in this race just to compete anymore, or just to shift the conversation! That moment is gone. Now, you and me, we're in this race to WIN!"

The crowd thundered its approval, making the air feel electric. Jack held up a hand for quiet. It took a while before he could continue. "This campaign, this rescue mission, is not about me. It's about having NEW ideas, NEW choices, a NEW approach to solving problems in this country, and not just two parties bickering endlessly!"

More cheers.

"So, I have another idea. As you know, my campaign will not accept large donations, because we'll do just fine with the help we get from each and every one of you. But changing America is not just about changing who's in the White House! We need independents—a lot of them—elected to Congress in the next midterms!" The crowd cheered every time Jack took a breath.

"I received a pledge call this morning from Ethan Bessette, who is just as sick and tired as you are of the lack of progress in Washington. His son Max, who also happened to be one of my best students, was killed at one of the recent SoMAD protests as he tried to help his country. So, Ethan has asked me to share with you today that after you put me in the White House, he will pledge up to two billion dollars to triple every dollar you donate to independent candidates in the next midterms!"

Jack saw the mouths of several reporters fall open. One of them nearly dropped his camera while fumbling with his phone.

"The time is now. After close to two hundred years of the same two parties trading power and corporate donors in the darkened halls of what was once the 'People's House', the lights are about to come back on . . . and there will be nowhere to hide!"

CHAPTER 35

DEMARCO CONTI SPREAD HIS THICK arms wide. "Before you lay a hand on me, you need to know I'm carrying," he told the two suits about to frisk him outside Clay Overton's hotel suite.

"You brought a weapon to a meeting with the next President of the United States?" one of the men said. The other took a half step back and rested his hand on his own concealed weapon.

"Once a cop, always a cop so, yeah, I'm always carrying. I didn't want you and Barney here to be surprised when you found it."

"Where?"

"Back waistband."

"That's no cop carry," the suit noted, taking the gun. "Sig 320. Decent piece. I'll just hang onto it for a while."

Suit number two stepped closer. "Okay, Boy Scout, let's make sure there's not another, shall we?" He twirled his finger for DeMarco to assume the frisk position.

DeMarco shrugged. "That's not necessary, but I can—"

"Mighty gracious of you," he interrupted, his powerful hands helping DeMarco's cheek find the wall.

"Fucking prick," DeMarco muttered, doing his best to stay calm and avoid a coughing fit that might debilitate him in front of these two hired goons. They didn't look like Secret Service types to him.

"Clean. You can go in."

DeMarco scanned the elaborate foyer of the penthouse suite perched atop the Baltimore Four Seasons. There was only one door, and dark suit number one was planted firmly in front of it. DeMarco took three steps and then stopped, virtually toe to toe with the slab-like figure in his path. "You want me to climb over?"

The suit finally turned, knocked, and opened the door. DeMarco brushed past into the sprawling suite and was unsurprised when the two suits joined him inside.

Clay Overton was seated at the head of a glossy twenty-foot conference table with four others. Beyond him through the bank of windows, DeMarco could see the fading light settling across Baltimore's Inner Harbor. "Detective Conti," said Overton, "how nice of you to come."

He invited DeMarco to sit. "You can leave," he told two staffers at the table. "Jim and Grady, you stay."

DeMarco scanned the remaining pair quickly. One looked like a typical DC type, expensive suit trying to distract from the receding hairline and bulging waistline after a decade of power lunches. The second man had unkempt red hair and looked like lunch was all he did, other than avoiding personal grooming of any kind.

DeMarco sat two seats from the Speaker. He could care less about security protocols, but he didn't need any static from the suits, who seemed a bit too eager for battle.

"Jim tells me that you now have some very usable information," Overton said.

"That's right." DeMarco resisted the urge to tap his jacket pocket where the thumb drive was. Carmen Marinas had complied in full in order to protect her son. DeMarco imagined they were already on their way across the country to start a new life somewhere.

"Yet you wanted some assurances, I imagine," Overton said. "And so here we are."

"Hmph," Grady mumbled, looking at his phone.

"Something to contribute, Mr. O'Shea?" Overton asked acidly.

Grady flashed his phone at the Speaker. "Sarah Sanborn is awake. Looks like no widow bump for Sanborn. Caught a break there."

"A break," Overton repeated. "Funny how fortune smiles on some."

"I just need to know, Mr. Speaker," DeMarco interrupted, anxiety getting the better of him, "that the information I have on Jack Sanborn will be used. To the fullest extent."

Overton brushed imaginary lint from his sleeve with a *Tch*. "Know your audience, Detective. In matters of political pursuit, you should know that for me there is *only* the fullest extent."

"This isn't just a political hit job for me, Mr. Overton. What I have can put that bastard in jail for ten to twenty, and that's what I want to see."

"Yes," Overton replied. "I understand you have evidence that dear Professor Sanborn may have tampered with federal evidence in the case against our recently departed Senator Elenestro, the man who attacked your daughter Gracie, God rest her soul. Am I correct so far, Detective?"

"All except the word *may*. There is no *may*. The DNA evidence was faked. It's a duplicate from another case file against Elenestro. I have the proof. And it's a federal crime."

"I see," Overton replied, flashing a look at his two associates. "But Detective Conti, you must fill in some blanks for me." His tone toward DeMarco was soothing, almost coaxing. "Your daughter's attacker was convicted and is now dead. So, skipping over the question of why you would wish to exonerate your daughter's deceased attacker—how can you be certain the evidence was faked?"

DeMarco looked the Speaker in the eye for a long moment, finally deciding that if this was going to work, he'd have to be completely honest. "Because I had the original DNA evidence in her case destroyed before the trial."

Overton's eyes flickered for a moment. The other men's faces did nothing to conceal their shock at DeMarco's revelation. Overton leaned forward in his chair. "Detective, let me clarify. You destroyed evidence that was certain to convict the man who raped—your own daughter?"

"Yes," DeMarco replied, his voice steady. "I couldn't stand the thought of a guy like him doing soft time for what he did." He sniffed loudly, his face curling up in disgust. "A few years in prison for a guy like that, with his money and political connections, would be like a stay at a country club. He deserved much more than that."

Overton almost smiled. "Meaning, something only a father could provide," he said, studying his visitor closely. "I must say, I greatly admire your commitment to principle, no matter how difficult the path. America needs more men like you."

"Thank you."

"And so," Overton said, leaning back again, "as the conviction rested on the very evidence you destroyed, the evidence used to convict could only be falsified."

"Correct."

"By our ambitious Mr. Sanborn, I take it."

"Also correct. It's all in the file."

"And for denying you this opportunity to properly avenge your daughter, you would like to see Mr. Sanborn behind bars for his crime."

"Yeah, but that was not his crime," DeMarco replied. The burning in his eyes grew stronger as he fought to keep his emotions from taking over. "His real crime," he said, his voice wavering slightly, "was bungling case procedure so badly that Gracie had to take the stand a second time." DeMarco bowed his head as a single tear rolled down his cheek. "It was more than my little girl could bear, so she . . . she . . ."

"I know, Detective," the Speaker said soothingly, exuding the grace of a mortician while grasping the final piece of his visitor's motivational puzzle. "I know that your daughter took her own life during the ordeal. Such a terrible, terrible loss to endure but certainly there was no way for you to anticipate Sanborn would turn out to be corrupt as well as incompetent."

DeMarco finally brought a fist to his mouth to choke back a sob.

"The pain you have lived through, I cannot imagine. I am so sorry, Detective."

"One man raped her," DeMarco rasped, "and then another left her unprotected on the witness stand to die. That's how I see it."

"That is exactly how I see it as well, Detective." Overton leaned forward again and slid a hand across the table. "Justice will be served. I can promise you that."

DeMarco reached into his jacket pocket, withdrew the thumb drive, and placed it on the table. "I want fifteen minutes alone with him, before he gets sent away."

"Make it thirty," the Speaker replied, his grey eyes suddenly glassy with emotion.

CHAPTER 36

AFTER THE IMPROMPTU PRESS CONFERENCE outside the hospital, Jack spent two dizzying days doing media interviews and attending a few rally events via hologram. "Technology allows me to be everywhere," he noted to his team as ballot deadlines loomed, "so I *will* be everywhere. *And* I'll be with Sarah by night." Based on the narrowing gap between Jack and Overton in the polls, voters didn't seem to care *where* they saw Jack, so long as he was out there and in the race.

Early the following morning, Jack stood alone in the hospital elevator, feeling a swirl of emotions as it descended. To his great relief, Sarah had passed every neurological test with flying colors, surpassing every expectation of the UCLA medical team. Jack had also been quick to feel comfortable in the skin of a serious presidential contender, something unfathomable just weeks ago.

What was harder to fathom, however, was why the Attorney General of the United States was concerned enough that she insisted on meeting in person this morning.

It had been nearly five years since Jack had been face to face with Susan Pericote, and close to ten since the time when their working relationship in the New York County DA's office became something more than work. Then Sarah came along.

Despite running a campaign that could land him in Washington, Jack hadn't felt the need to reach out to Susan. But when the Attorney General of the United States requests a meeting and was willing to come to him, yes was the only answer.

Jack's memory flashed back to his early days as a prosecutor. After wrestling several high-profile convictions from the clutches of certain defeat, against Leviathan-sized defense teams, Jack's career went through a halcyon-like period where it seemed he just couldn't lose. Jack could read the jury members one by one, knowing just the right words to sway each heart and mind. Man or woman, black, white or brown, angry or disinterested—he found a way to bring them all along. Most important, though, he was just so damned believable. And it didn't hurt that he had the truth on his side.

Jack stepped off the elevator and nodded at the two Secret Service agents that awaited his arrival. The three men made their way through the cafeteria doors. Four obvious FBI agents were positioned throughout the room, making no attempt to blend in and making it plain that Jack's one-time boss Susan Pericote had indeed arrived for their scheduled meeting.

Dressed in a trim navy-blue pantsuit and cream shoes that weren't long off the rack, Susan sat with long legs crossed. She leaned over a tablet, reviewing something intently enough to take no notice of Jack's approach, which gave Jack a chance to observe her briefly. Wisps of dark hair fell gracefully around her face, with the rest pulled back into a tight ponytail, adding a youthful quality to her stately demeanor. He thought she looked a bit tired, but not much older than the woman he remembered. "Hi, Susan," he said warmly, approaching the table.

"Ah . . . Jack." She rose and took his hand without shaking it, and to his surprise pressed a cheek against his and made a soft kissing sound. He returned the gesture clumsily. Susan stepped back and took in his appearance. "You look exactly the same."

"So do you."

"That's a lie," she replied with a slight smile.

They both sat at the small corner table.

"I saw you on TV," Susan said. "The news about Sarah is such a relief . . . I can only imagine."

"Thanks," he replied. "Been seeing you on TV a lot too." Susan had risen quickly in the New York County ranks; Jack's string of victories having assisted her in catapulting from Chief of the Trial Division to Manhattan District Attorney in record time. Jack had watched from North Carolina as Perez tapped her for US Attorney General. Susan's confirmation was an early victory that would end up being one of very few for President Perez in the bitterly divided trenches of Washington. His success there came largely on the back of Susan's independent political leanings and lack of official party membership, both of which—along with her impeccable legal record in New York—carried her through the confirmation process.

"How's life in Washington?" Jack asked.

"A mess."

"I assume you mean professionally."

"I assume you do too," she said, her expression making it clear that personal talk was not on the agenda.

"So, what brings you here?" Jack asked, taking her cue. "Did you have other business in the area?"

"I came here to see you."

"Well, that sounds serious."

Susan paused, her lack of immediate deflection only adding to Jack's concern.

"I don't want to add to your worries right now, Jack, but I'm afraid I have to." She pressed a finger down on the tabletop, as she often did to focus attention. "If the Texas ballot decision goes your way, you have a serious chance of pulling this thing off."

"That's what you came to tell me?"

"No. I came to warn you, so you can be prepared for something."

"Okay . . . " Susan's eyes flickered, making him wonder if she regretted coming.

Susan put her palms flat on the table "Someone accessed the restricted evidence files for the Elenestro case."

"Oh." He felt a twinge from somewhere and looked away. Jack knew full well that the Elenestro case and the LiveCourtTV footage were continued chum for the media but had resolved to ignore both as there was nothing he could do about either. "Wait," he said, thinking more carefully about her words. "Why the evidence files?"

"This isn't about what happened in court that day, or the girl." *Her name was Gracie*, Jack wanted to say but didn't. "There were some . . . irregularities, in the DNA evidence."

"What kind of irregularities? The DNA evidence was pretty cut-and-dried, as I recall."

"It was until it went missing."

"Missing?" Jack's voice rose slightly. "I don't remember this at all. Jesus, was I in that bad a mental state that I can't remember?"

Susan shook her head and looked away for a moment. "You remember it fine, Jack."

He stared back at her, wondering where this was going. "So what evidence was Elenestro convicted with?"

"DNA evidence from another case," Susan replied, almost casually. "Elenestro's other victims, the ones who never made it to trial, made that option available to us."

"Option?" Jack said. "Us?" He thought for a moment. "Or do you mean available to you?" He could feel the heat rising on the back of his neck.

"I wasn't about to let someone we knew was guilty get off on a mistrial."

"He hadn't been convicted in the other cases, Susan . . . You know that doesn't work."

"I'd seen all the evidence, and you know it too. He was a fucking predator, Jack."

"Why do it behind my back then? And don't say you did it to protect me because I'm pretty sure the reason you're here is that the falsified evidence files are still in my name, not yours . . . Aren't they?" He fought to control the edge in his voice. "Is that why you came to warn me?"

"Goddammit Jack. You were imploding during that trial. And yes, I should have pulled you off the case, and yes, I should have told you about the missing evidence but that was the day the girl—"

"Her name was Gracie," Jack interrupted, barely keeping his voice down.

Susan exhaled heavily, and they sat in silence for a long moment. "I'm sorry, Jack. I know you think I did it all for my own ambitions. Yes, it was wrong. But if I submitted evidence under my signature, it would have raised immediate flags and made the whole thing pointless." After another long pause, she added. "Anyway, I couldn't let you go unwarned and unprepared. For what it's worth, I'm sorry."

Jack shook his head. "I'm not sure how we prepare for this. We'll just have to hunker down and ride it out." He could immediately see a look of hesitation on Susan's face. "What else aren't you telling me?" he asked.

"Jack," she said, her voice serious. "That case was less than five years ago, so the statute of limitations hasn't expired."

"Jesus," Jack said softly. "So, whoever accessed the files doesn't just want me to lose. They may want me in prison."

"Quite possibly, yes."

CHAPTER 37

Fifteen Days to Election Day

"It's been a while since I've taken the bus," Ethan remarked, scanning the interior of the hastily arranged campaign vehicle. They traveled along the I-40, on their way to a rally in Charlotte. Jack, Lewis, Jade and a handful of staffers sat around a conference table at the back.

"A while as in your entire lifetime?" Lewis asked.

"No," Ethan replied. "About thirty-one years ago though. Maybe closer to thirty-two."

"No probabilities on those?" Jack asked.

"Fifty-fifty."

Jade grinned. "Not sure I'd call this a bus," she said, looking at the blackout-mode windows. "Feels more like a submarine right now."

"So, what sayeth the oracle?" Lewis asked, looking at Ethan. "Is the gap to Overton down to eight points as CNN is reporting?"

"AGN said seven points," Jade added.

"It'll be back to nine points by the end of the week," Ethan replied. "Sarah's recovery has that effect I'm afraid."

"Voters prefer widowers?" Jack asked, a confused look on his face.

"Not long term," Ethan replied, "but the concept of the sympathy vote is certainly real. The thing that can bring us back will be non-voters getting off the sidelines. That's just over half the country. The network polls don't capture that."

"And yours do?" Jade asked.

Ethan's look was answer enough. "There's something else to share, though," he said. "A bit of news that I didn't see coming."

The entire bus grew silent; few things surprised Ethan and his algorithmic behemoth.

"What is it?" Jack asked.

"I completed the acquisition of the UCLA-based start-up that treated Sarah's stroke damage."

"Did you find out how they jumped the queue and got instant FDA approval?" Lewis asked.

"Yes," Ethan told him. "Through the personal intervention of Clay Overton."

"Seriously?" Jack said, eyes wide. "Hard to see that one coming . . . Maybe there's more to the Speaker than I gave him credit for."

"Yeah, or maybe there's less," Lewis noted.

"How so?"

Lewis wrinkled his nose. "Meaning, this guy will do anything to win."

"So, he had the FDA fast-track a drug approval so I wouldn't get a lasting bump in the polls?"

"Welcome to big campaign politics," Lewis said.

"There's a decent probability he's right," Ethan added. "But the Speaker is a harder one to model at the individual level. He seems to do a lot off the grid, so I can't model him accurately."

Before Jack could fully digest the implications of Overton's act or Ethan's comment, Lewis grabbed him by the elbow. "Can I see you up front for a minute?"

The two men stepped from the table and moved to the front of the vehicle. The windows remained opaque, but Jack felt the bus take an exit ramp. "I was going to tell you about Susan coming to see me," he said.

"I hope so," Lewis answered. "Because it's hard to keep a visit from the Attorney General of the United States a secret."

"It wasn't a secret, Lewis; we met in the middle of the damned cafeteria."

Lewis shook his head. "When you're running on a platform that says the establishment needs to go, it doesn't help to be seen cozying up to one of them."

"She's not *one of them*," Jack replied.

"She's part of a Democrat administration. I'd say that makes her part of the problem."

"You're being paranoid, Lewis."

"Right now, with what we're trying to do, paranoid is just good thinking."

"So, we're endorsing paranoia now?"

"And the fact that you two have a history. The media would love this."

"Forget the history, Lewis. It doesn't matter."

"So, what did she want?"

Jack stepped a bit closer. "She wanted to warn me."

"Yeah, so does everybody. What about?"

"Something from an old case that is going to come out and bite us."

"How hard?" Lewis replied.

Before Jack could answer, the bus came to a stop and a loud cheer from the back jarred them from their conversation.

"What happened?" Jack called out.

"It's Texas!" Jade answered. "The court ruled the early ballot deadline was unconstitutional. You're on the ballot in all fifty states!"

Lewis spoke into Jack's ear as everyone on the bus celebrated around them. "How bad?"

"We'll talk about it after the rally."

Jade checked her buzzing cell phone and saw an encrypted email. She tapped in her code and read the message from one of Overton's pseudonymous emails.

In Charlotte. Meet me tonight. 11:30. Urgent. Will send location.

CHAPTER 38

FIVE HOURS LATER, the elevator of the Charlotte Ritz-Carlton opened up on the fifteenth floor, depositing Jade at the brass-doored entrance of The Punch Room. Two men from Overton's protection detail stood outside, obviously awaiting her arrival.

After being given the rendezvous point, a quick search on the Punch Room revealed why it was not her taste; another concocted old-world speakeasy with few tables but enough money sunk into the décor to build a dozen houses or a decent school or two. Being located on the fifteenth floor—without any signage to alert casual passersby of its existence—kept unwanted observation of The Punch Room's patrons to a minimum. Jade did like the name though; Punch Room conjured images of what she'd like to do to more than one jaw from the past and present.

She stepped towards the doors, choosing to ignore the two suited slabs watching her.

"No hello, Ms. Xu?"

She craned her neck and recognized the face of Anton Reverdy, Overton's closest protector. "If it isn't Lurch, the human totem pole. Somebody leave the cage door open?"

The second man, much shorter than Anton, let out a grunt. He had a round, puffy face that would have looked more at home on an alcoholic accountant than a Secret Service agent. He smiled at Jade, but to her it felt more like a grimace.

"I need to check you for weapons," Anton said.

"Don't you fucking touch me," she hissed. "*He* asked for this meeting, and I'm a reporter, not an operative, so your hands aren't going anywhere. I'm not carrying anything. I can't even *pen* him to death."

"You mean you *were* a reporter," Anton corrected.

Jade was about to fling back a response, but paused when she realized this was a truth she had yet to acknowledge. The thought almost made her flinch. *I hope you know what the hell you're doing, Jade.*

Before the sparkling conversation could continue, the heavy brass door was opened from the other side.

"How lovely to see you, Jade," Overton announced, his fabricated charm seeping from every pore while he sized her up like prey. "Do come in."

Jade stepped inside the small, shadowy bar. It suited him, she thought. The room was empty but for the two of them. *Not even a bartender to keep watch. Bad sign.*

"Please," Overton said, leading her to a leather sofa in one of the room's darker corners. "I hope you don't mind; I relieved the staff so we could talk privately."

Jade winced slightly, his soothing tone reminding her of being trapped with a drunk father at a truck stop parking lot long ago.

"I had them prepare you a Manhattan before they left," Overton added, gesturing to a pair of crimson-filled martini glasses. "You prefer it sweet, isn't that right?"

Jade said nothing and tried to maximize her distance from the Speaker. While her body could have used it, she had no intention of touching the drink, signaling as much as she folded her hands carefully in her lap.

Overton flashed a pout below his reptilian eyes, then raised the glass to his lips and took a long pull. "Waste is such a shameful thing, I find." His eyes bore down on Jade, his expression making her want to leave before the conversation began.

"Why am I here, Mr. Speaker?"

"All business, I see. Does the dear Professor know you are here?"

"No."

"I thought not."

"If you're trying to get information, Mr. Speaker, then you're wasting your time."

"Quite the opposite, my dear Jade," he corrected, moving slightly closer. "I'm here to prevent a friend from wasting her career on a lost cause."

"You're still thinking lost cause after the news out of Texas today?"

Overton waved his hand dismissively. "I have no need of information, Jade. As you well know, in our history of information flow, you have been more the beneficiary and I the benefactor. Can two old friends agree on that at least?"

Jade studied his face. If he was the least bit concerned about Jack making the ballot in all fifty states, her reporter's instincts couldn't pick it up. She half-shrugged, signaling indifference.

"You disappoint me, Jade."

"Gosh, not the disappointment speech, please. You'll devastate me." He continued to inch closer. She readjusted her folded hands, curling the one underneath into a concealed fist, just in case.

"I'm surprised that someone of your convictions would take up with someone who stands for . . . nothing at all, really."

"If you want to call the dismantling of a destructive two-party monopoly nothing."

"And what would that leave in its place, Jade, other than utter chaos?"

"Oh, I don't know. How about a Congress that actually works together to solve America's problems?"

"America didn't rise to lead the world through weakness and compromise," Overton scoffed. "If our forefathers had taken that approach with the British monarchy in the seventeen hundreds, where would we be?"

"In a better version of Canada, with nicer weather?"

He ignored the comment and studied Jade for a long moment, his face frozen in curiosity. "You actually think you have a chance here," he said, his incredulity either genuine or perfectly played. "Look, with little platform to ride upon other than some legal prayer . . . I actually called you here to give you a choice, out of fairness."

"Fairness. Now there's a big word for you, Mr. Speaker," Jade replied. *I may be the mouse, but enough of this cat-and-mouse bullshit.*

Overton shook his head. "You've changed, Jade."

"I don't need your stories anymore, so you get the real me."

"Well, let's talk about that, because the choice I'm offering is all about being the real you."

"I can hardly wait."

"Your choice, Jade, is to come back to the winning team and be my communications director in the White House. Or be on no team at all, after our dear Professor learns that the *real* you has been playing on team Overton for years." Overton paused for a moment, then broke into a smile that looked like two hidden strings had suddenly been activated, pulling the edges of his mouth back to reveal his too-white teeth.

'You're joking."

"I assure you I'm not."

Jade first imagined Jack's face as he fired her for not sharing her ties to Overton. Then she imagined her former tobacco-stained editor leaning over some ass-wipe cub reporter, gleefully dictating a story about Jade's firing from the Sanborn campaign. *Fuck that.* "You're desperate, Mr. Speaker, and you're going to lose."

"Jade." Overton shook his head with a pitying half-smile. "Do you truly believe that I don't have every eventuality, every consideration, every path that could deliver victory covered, no matter the sacrifice required?" His hollow eyes regarded her with a look of placid curiosity that conveyed absolute confidence in the election's outcome.

"No," she finally said. "I don't believe you do. Not at all."

"Well, my dear," Overton inhaled deeply and stood. "Then I suggest you consume that drink in front of you and come up with a plan B of your own."

"I'm not the one who needs a plan B," Jade replied.

"Hold that thought," Overton said, and turned away.

CHAPTER 39

Ten Days Until Election Day

DeMarco woke in his stale DC hotel room with a very unfamiliar sensation. It took him a few moments to discern that the strange energy he felt was an optimism strong enough to block out the constant craving for alcohol that thrummed inside his head after three days of abstinence.

He showered and shaved quickly, wolfed down an extra-large free breakfast and set off early on the two-mile walk to his seven AM meeting at Overton's congressional office. It was going to be a good day, and he didn't have many of those.

This was the beginning of Jack Sanborn's end. The shame of a grand jury being convened would be enough to destroy his campaign, and the strength of the damning evidence would likely send him to prison for federal evidence tampering. *Ten to twenty years. Not bad.* And if a former assistant DA actually survived prison, and DeMarco lived long enough—perhaps he could arrange a proper coming-out party.

After three separate security checkpoints, he finally found himself being ushered through the towering doors of the Speaker's office.

"Ah, Detective Conti," Overton said. "Thank you for joining us again today." He waved DeMarco forward. "Please, sit down." He flicked his fingers at one of a dozen aides, who promptly vacated his chair. "We were just wrapping a few things up here."

DeMarco scanned the room. Other than the large frumpy redhead named O'Shea he thought, the faces were unfamiliar.

"You were saying?" Overton said to Grady O'Shea.

Grady stood, his abdomen threatening to burst through his over-sized dress shirt. "I think even with Sanborn under grand jury investigation, a lot of Democratic voters would still rather vote for Sanborn as a message to you and the Republicans."

"So, they would cast their votes for someone likely headed to prison?"

Grady shrugged. "Nobody assumes dirt sticks to politicians any-more until they hear the sound of the prison bars clang. You know that, Mr. Speaker."

DeMarco watched as Overton contemplated this obvious truth from his advisor. "We're still seven points up," he finally replied. "If you're trying to tell me a grand jury doesn't put us up by at least a dozen points on this fucking schoolteacher, then consider yourself fired."

"Mr. Speaker, I'm not saying the grand jury isn't a masterstroke; it is. I'm just saying that despite that, there's still a chance we end up short of two-seventy on election day, if enough non-voters get off their asses and find a voting booth."

"Even so, in that case the House decides," Overton said. "So, either way, we've got it."

DeMarco finally spoke up as his curiosity got the better of him. "You mean if there's no winner, the House of Representatives decides who wins?"

"It's a beautiful system, isn't it?" Overton said with satisfaction. He then turned his gaze to a trio of suits who had lawyer written all over them. "Enough about predicting the math; we control all the math right here with what the good detective has provided. So, gentlemen—is all in order for this afternoon's bombshell?"

The trio all bobbed their heads in unison before the tallest spoke. "Mr. Speaker, are you sure the New York AG will run with this once we announce the evidence?"

"Of course she will."

"But she's, ummm..."

"A Dem-o-crat. Yes, thank you for that. With what I have on her, she'll pounce on this like a fly on a fresh turd. We just need to start the ball rolling. And don't forget, the Dems want Sanborn gone as much as we do."

DeMarco felt a smile spread across his lips. His mind drifted to images of being alone in a cell with Jack Sanborn, moments before he was locked away for ten to twenty.

CHAPTER 40

JACK STEPPED OUT INTO THE MAIN HALLWAY of UNC's intensive care unit, the bright overhead lights forcing him to squint. The dark recesses of a hospital storeroom had become his temporary sleeping quarters, which suited Jack fine so he could be close to Sarah when in town.

Jack nodded across the hall at Special Agent Mullen, who looked as fresh as ever despite the rigors of the campaign blitz. Meanwhile, Jack was adjusting to five hours of sleep a night. At least this was a virtual campaign morning and would be a bit easier on the system. Like a global CEO, Jack could be everywhere in a day, at least in hologram form.

"Morning, Sir," Agent Mullen said. "Sleep well?"

"You'd better stop asking me that," Jack replied as Agent Mullen handed him the usual cup of steaming black coffee. Jack would have rather fetched his own but as he was learning, these were the precautions of his newly public life. He took a sip and started in the direction of Sarah's room, his thoughts starting to whirl.

The prior night, after Sarah had fallen asleep, Jack huddled with Lewis and Jade outside her room. He gave them the download on Susan Pericote's warning. "It doesn't seem that uncommon for a Presidential candidate to be at risk of prosecution anymore," Jade said. "As you had nothing to do with the falsified evidence, I'm not sure you do anything other than deny it and keep moving."

"The problem is," Jack said, "is that on paper it's all true. It's my name on those documents, even if I'm not the one who signed them." The three of them had agreed to sleep on it and confer in the morning. But after five hours of sleep, Jack wasn't seeing anything better than a cliché denial. *Which no one will believe*, he thought. Jack checked his watch. The virtual campaign events didn't start until mid-morning, so there was still a little time to brainstorm options.

"Hello, Professor," Sarah said from her room, jarring Jack from his thoughts. "Are you pacing out there to guard my door or do you want to come in?"

Jack beamed a smile. "I was leaving you in peace for the moment."

"Or you were so deep in thought you hadn't the faintest idea where you were."

Jack stepped inside. "How are you feeling?"

"Much better than I should," Sarah replied. "Especially for being three weeks pregnant."

"More memory testing today?" he asked. "I gave them a big download the other day, complete with incriminating pictures to test you with."

"I may get time off for good behavior. I scored one hundred percent yesterday. I also made you sound much more impressive than you actually are."

"Thank God for that."

Sarah studied Jack for a moment, and an easy silence settled between them. "Is something bothering you?" she asked.

"You mean other than running for President?"

Sarah seemed to study him. "That certainly qualifies, but I don't think that's it."

"What do you mean?"

"I'm not sure. Just a feeling I'm getting from you. Are the dreams back?"

Jack shook his head. "Not in a while. Maybe the thought of losing you rattled me enough to chase them off."

Sarah shook her head. "I don't think that's it either."

"I did get some news the other day," Jack began.

"About the Elenestro case," Sarah added, seeming surprised by her own words.

Sarah had always been great at reading Jack, but he thought this felt very different. Way too random. "Did you hear us outside your door last night?"

"No. I slept like the dead."

"Pick another phrase, please."

"I didn't hear a thing. That old case just popped into my mind when you said you had news."

Jack's mind flicked through the past couple of days. He came up with no moments around Sarah where he would have mentioned the Elenestro case.

Before Jack could reply, they heard running footsteps in the hall. Lewis appeared in the doorway, his cheeks flushed. "Do you not look at your phone?" he said, looking flustered.

"It didn't buzz. The signal barely works in here." Lewis moved to the wall-mounted TV and switched it on, then stepped back when he saw a newscast. "Is it Overton?" Jack asked.

Lewis shook his head. "The Attorney General called a press conference."

Sarah sat up straighter in bed. "Any idea what about?"

Jack looked at her. "She came to see me a few days ago."

"Sir?" One of the Secret Service agents appeared in the doorway. "I just received a message from the AG's office that she's been trying to reach you."

"Why would the Attorney General come to see you?" Sarah asked. "And why does she need to get a hold of you the morning of a press conference?"

Jack looked up at the TV as Susan descended the steps outside the Robert F. Kennedy Department of Justice Building. "We're about to find out."

Lewis turned up the volume. The talking heads were busy tripping over each other as they speculated furiously about a press announcement from the AG ten days before the election.

. . . we don't know the subject of today's press conference or why it was

urgently scheduled just forty-five minutes ago . . . the Attorney General of course has been the target of harsh criticism from many sides lately for the use of heavy-handed crowd control and digital suppression tactics in silencing SoMAD protestors, and there have been rumors swirling about an investigation into Susan Pericote's potential linkages to the China water rights scandal, but with insufficient proof she appeared poised to survive yet another threat to her position as AG . . . and here she comes now . . . the Attorney General of the United States Susan Pericote. Let's hear what she has to say . . .

Jack could see the strain on her face as she stepped to the podium. "Ladies and gentlemen, thank you for coming on such short notice. I'll get right to it. I am here to announce that I am resigning my office with immediate effect . . . and Americans deserve to know exactly why I have made this decision. I have had the honor to serve each day by seeking to do nothing more than uphold the principles of law that our founders envisioned for this great democracy. Those principles were established for the greater good of our union, and to ensure that all are treated as equals. I'm proud of the work of my tireless colleagues at the Department of Justice, and while I have risen to the privilege of this office under a Democratic administration, in my best days and worst days I have truly only aspired to one ideology, and that is the rule of fair treatment for all under the law."

"Where is she going with this?" Lewis said.

Susan continued. "But it saddens me to admit that I am not without fault. While my pursuit has always been justice for those who suffer at the hands of others, my methods have not always been pure. And while the crimes and the cases where I strayed from the standard I swore to uphold were barbaric in the extreme, and were also some time ago, that does not justify the actions I took to falsify evidence in order to secure the conviction of a guilty predator who shattered many lives, and ended at least one."

"She's talking about Elenestro," Sarah said. "Isn't she?"

"Yes." Jack's gaze remained fixed on the screen. "She came to warn me that someone was digging into the files and had proof that the evidence convicting him was doctored."

"Jesus," Sarah breathed. "Doctored by who?"

"By her," Jack replied.

". . . While I have lived with the knowledge of a rightful conviction wrongly secured, I cannot allow my actions for the greater good to now be turned against what I feel, for our union, is an even greater good for a better future. To this end, I would like to share the following with all of you here today . . . "

"Here it comes," Lewis said.

"While I willingly submit myself to the full force of the law for my misjudgments in prosecuting the Elenestro case with falsified evidence, that same force of law must be applied to those who have illegally accessed New York Justice Department files to try to smear a promising independent candidate, Jack Sanborn. I acted alone and without Jack's knowledge to ensure a predator was convicted by any means. I have to live with that. But I cannot live with Jack Sanborn being wrongly accused by the two-party duopoly that so rightly fears him."

"I can't believe she's saying all this," Lewis remarked.

"As a lawyer and a patriot wanting only prosperity for our country, I would also echo Justice Faber's comments in saying that the application of antitrust laws to our two-party system is something that warrants serious consideration. Not someday . . . Right now. Today."

"Wow," Lewis said. "If she wasn't going to jail, she'd make a great running mate."

"More like Secret Service agent," Sarah said. "Sounds like she just took a bullet that was meant for you, Jack."

Overton spoke slowly, his fingernails tapping the surface of his desk. His grey eyes bored into DeMarco, who was still in the midst of grappling with what had just taken place. "I would like everyone to leave please, except for my Detective friend here."

Less than an hour before, the room had been vibrating with excitement as final preparations were being made to announce the grand jury investigation into Jack Sanborn's falsification of evidence in a capital trial. AG Pericote's bombshell had laid waste to those plans in an instant.

Overton cast a look at Anton, his pale-eyed bodyguard, who obligingly remained and settled noisily into a chair directly behind DeMarco.

Looking down at his still shiny Edmond Allen shoes, DeMarco fought the urge to run. Just days ago, alluring images of an improbable return to something resembling respect or even purpose had him brimming with an energy he'd not felt in a long time. Today was to be the start of something special in his life, something healing. Something that could honor the memory of his Gracie in a way he'd never thought possible.

He'd awakened that morning with the lightness of great anticipation. And now, just hours later, his body felt like a lead weight that might pull him through the floor and straight into hell. His heart pounded inside his chest like a thudding fist. As insane as the thought was, he half-wondered if he was about to be garroted in the office of the Speaker of the House. He resisted the urge to turn around, but his senses were fully fired, ready to detect and react to any sound of movement behind him.

"Not quite the morning of glory we had envisioned for ourselves, isn't that right, Detective Conti?"

DeMarco looked to Overton, trying to interpret his paternal tone. "Far from it," DeMarco replied, his head slightly bowed. "I truly don't know how—"

"Detective Conti," Overton interrupted, leaning forward behind his massive desk, "do I look like the kind of man assuaged by atonements or prone to exonerations?"

"Um, excuse me?"

"Let's spare each other the indignity of such shameful weaknesses." Overton grimaced, as if the words he spoke left grit in his mouth.

"The New York AG clearly leaked our plans and will pay a price for that. And our little lost professor has inexplicably persuaded the AG to lob her beautiful frame onto the grenade meant for him."

DeMarco blinked at the Speaker's calmness.

"Incredibly misguided on her part, but there is great nobility in sacrificing all for a cause one feels is just." He studied DeMarco evenly. "And it's true what they say. When one door closes, another opens." Overton flashed a satisfied glance at his bodyguard, then glanced at the news coverage on the large flatscreen behind DeMarco. The media were still in a frenzy over the press conference.

"I'm not sure I understand."

"PLEASE!" Overton bellowed and slammed his palm down on the desk. "Do not mistake this for conversation, Detective. We are not *unpacking this* here together, you and I. Your purpose at this moment, if you still have one at all before your lungs expire . . . "

Overton paused as DeMarco's eyes widened at the violation of his medical privacy.

"Oh yes, Detective, I am well aware that the hour is near at hand for you."

DeMarco sank deeper into the leather chair, and again looked down at the shiny shoes he'd scrounged up to create the façade that he was something other than what he was: a desperate, slowly dying man who sought revenge at any price. "You used me," he finally said, looking straight ahead.

"You make that sound like a negative thing," Overton replied. "No less than you used me. I gave you an opportunity, didn't I?"

DeMarco sighed heavily and looked at the Speaker. "What now?"

"In a way that's up to you," Overton told him.

"I don't know what that means, Mr. Speaker."

"It means, Detective, that your improbable but noble cause need not end here." Overton nodded at his bodyguard to escort DeMarco out, and then swiveled around in his chair, turning his back. "I'll be in touch."

CHAPTER 41

JACK SAT AT A SMALL TABLE in the far corner of the hospital cafeteria. The space was largely empty. Agent Mullen and a second agent stood nearby. Jack tucked an earbud in and placed the video call he had slipped away to make in relative private. Immediately, Susan Pericote's face filled the screen of his phone.

He skipped the preliminaries. "I really wish you hadn't done that, Susan. There could have been other options."

"I had to, Jack. You didn't deserve to take one in the chest on this. The Elenestro case has caused you enough pain already."

"Have you talked to the New York AG?"

"I can't. Not anymore."

"But I'm assuming she tipped you off that they were about to announce the falsified evidence?"

Susan didn't answer. She merely looked at Jack and blinked.

"Do you think she'll convene a grand jury? I mean, nobody in New York gives a damn about Elenestro case proceedings anymore. Like you said, he was a predator. And he's dead now anyway . . . Or don't you think she has a choice?"

"Overton apparently has her pinned in a corner, I don't know with what. But I think she'll be forced to act, even if it's me now and not you."

"God, he is a Grade A Certified son of a bitch."

"Yeah. And given I just blocked his kill shot on you, he's going to be out for blood."

"Jesus, Susan," he replied, "you could do serious time. I feel terrible about this."

"Jack, don't." Susan replied. "It was my choice to fake the evidence, not yours."

Jack was surprised that she somehow seemed serene about what was to come. Maybe the whole thing had weighed on her for years.

"Besides," Susan said, "what you've started here is worth protecting. I've gone as far as I could here and none of it really seemed to matter anymore, given the state of the government in general."

"I just wish there'd been another way," Jack said.

"There wasn't, and there was no time. I needed to strike first."

Jack understood. Susan's tactical analysis of every situation was what had allowed her to rise to the top law enforcement job in the land.

"I've got my legal team ready for whatever comes," Susan said. "And besides, I know a guy who might become president. Maybe he'll pardon me before I get too used to life behind bars." She cracked the first hint of a smile. It brought back memories of a simpler past.

"I hope you like dark horses," Jack said, "because I'm still eight points back."

"I like them very much." Susan looked at him for a moment. Jack could see her holding back a thought, likely one they both thought was best left unspoken. "Good luck, Jack," she finally said.

"You too."

They ended the call. Jack closed his eyes for a moment, then felt like someone was watching him. He opened his eyes and saw Jade standing a few tables away. "Can we talk?" she asked. Her lowered eyes and posture were a marked contrast to her usual combative demeanor. "What did you do?" he asked, the hint of a smile on his lips.

"Something you should probably fire me for."

"Well, you have my attention. Is this something Lewis knows about?"

"No. And he would definitely fire me if he knew what I'm about to say. Clay Overton has been one of my sources for a while now." She looked away and then back again. "Among other things, he was my source for the Chinese TAP deal leak on the President."

"That explains a lot," Jack replied.

"Like what exactly?"

"Why you came to my class that first time," Jack answered. "You were disillusioned that your big story was going to put somebody worse into office."

"Was I that obvious?"

"Not to someone unaccustomed to reading faces for a living. So why are you telling me now?"

"I'm guessing you already know why."

Jack nodded. "What did he want?"

"He wanted me to be his communications director."

Jack chuckled. "Join or he'd expose you, nine days before the election . . . Great recruiting strategy."

"So," Jade said. "What now? I mean, I don't think I would trust me in your shoes, so I assume I should just resign."

"But you already passed the test."

"What test?" Jade asked.

"We put tracers on all the files shared with you since you joined. So, if they were shared or opened by anyone other than you, we'd be able to trace their location."

"Fuck me. You did that?"

"Ethan helped."

"You didn't trust me, so you violated my privacy."

"Says the Washington investigative reporter. And technically they're my files, so tracing their whereabouts when not in your hands has nothing to do with your privacy. If you'd shared them, you'd be violating my privacy."

Jade thought about it for a moment. "Fuck me."

"You said that already."

"That's pretty dark, Jack. Like mafia dark."

"Let's just call it proper document control. Anything else?"

Jade's black-pearl eyes studied Jack for a long moment, seeming disappointed. "You really did that?"

"Actually, no. I made it up. That was the test just now. To see how you reacted to learning you were being watched."

"Seriously?"

"You spend as many years as I have questioning witnesses and jurors, you learn how to tell who's being straight and who isn't."

"I think I'm supposed to feel better right now but jeez, Jack."

He broke a slight smile. "Well, the good news is I'm satisfied you're not playing both sides. The bad news is I've learned you're a bit gullible."

"If you were anyone else, you know I'd tell you to fuck off."

"I knew you'd say that."

Jade shook her head, exasperated. "Now you can officially fuck off," she said, "because I have work to do." And with that, turned and strode off.

CHAPTER 42

Seven Days Until Election Day

"THE VICE PRESIDENT IS HERE SIR," a nasal voice announced over the president's intercom. Chief of Staff Angela Dembe sat across from him, like an attending physician who was out of options and could only wait for her patient to die.

Perez was in a suitably dark mood, drained by the futility of three in-person rallies, two more via satellite and four media interviews, none of which would do a damned thing to avert the coming disaster. He was sixteen points down and still sinking. He'd seen his own staffers filling open audience seats at recent events, hoping to make the situation appear less dire than it was.

"Send him in," he said, and flicked an imaginary speck of dust from his sleeve.

The door swung open, and Vice President Reid Palmer stepped into the Oval Office, his nostrils already flaring. "Michael, Angela." He nodded as he approached the Resolute Desk. "Why am I here?"

"You mean Mr. President," Perez said dryly.

"Really?" Reid answered. "We're still doing that?"

"Yes, Mr. Vice-President," Perez said. "Some of us still respect the offices and duties to which we were elected."

"Christ, Michael . . . Mr. President, Your Lordship, whatever. It's seven days to political oblivion. Why did you call me here?"

Angela Dembe was also curious about that.

"I wanted to ask you a question, face-to-face."

"Fine then."

"Is it true that you were considering your own challenge to my renomination?"

Palmer exhaled and waved a hand, apparently unconcerned with pretenses. "Yes. I was."

The president nodded, showing no emotion. "That explains your poor impression of an attack dog these past months."

"That's bullshit. I've always done what you asked of me."

"And a lot more that I didn't ask for, it seems."

Palmer's eyes flashed. "You know what, Michael? I should have challenged your renomination; they goddamned sure wanted me to."

"Thanks for your admirable restraint."

"You can be a real sonofabitch," Palmer said. Angela shifted in her chair, looking like she wanted to hit him. "They wanted me to run because you alienated the entire party left. You belittled them."

"And you coddled them!" The president's voice began to rise. "You played them and turned them against me!"

"Now you're being paranoid."

The president's eyes lanced into Palmer like daggers. If they'd been back in the farmlands of northern California, Palmer would be eating dirt by now.

Like many of his predecessors, Michael Perez had come to 1600 Pennsylvania Avenue with great hopes for change. More than most, he'd genuinely sacrificed to narrow the partisan divide. But in the end, he'd been ripped to shreds by the political attack dogs in both parties.

"If you care about the future of the party," Palmer said, "you'll do what's best for the Congressional races. That has to be the focus now."

Here it comes. Perez flicked another speck of nonexistent dust, wishing it was his vice president.

"Resign," Palmer said, "and people will look to me as the top of the ticket." He said this as casually as someone ordering a cheeseburger and fries. "It's the only way to save a few swing seats."

"You want me to protect the party that turned its back on me?" Perez rose behind his desk, eyes glaring.

"It wasn't personal, Mr. President. It was just politics."

It's always personal, Perez thought. "So, then you *were* part of the decision two weeks ago to pull spending from my campaign and use it for the House races."

Palmer gazed back with indifference.

"Say it to my face at least."

"It was three weeks ago. Look, Michael, the best thing you can do is resign the top of the ticket. Beyond the House races, it'll take the wind out of Sanborn's sails right now. He's a much bigger long-term threat to the party than Overton will ever be."

For the good of the party. Michael pressed his fingertips hard on the desk surface, trying to contain his emotions. His reverence for the oval office had always helped him manage his temper, and he fought to ensure that today would be no exception.

"This meeting is over," Perez said quietly. "You can leave."

One side of the vice president's mouth curled into a sneer. "It's up to you, Michael. In a few days, you'll be an irrelevant footnote . . . I just thought you might want to use the time you have left for something other than getting your ass kicked." With that, Vice President Palmer turned on his heel and strode out the door.

Perez turned to look out the window as darkness enveloped the White House grounds.

"What next, sir?" Angela said.

"Palmer's always been a prick. But I think it's time I followed his advice."

CHAPTER 43

Six Days Until Election Day

THE NEXT MORNING AT NINE SHARP, President Perez strode into a full White House briefing room, trailed by a handful of aides and one very flustered-looking press secretary. Angela Dembe followed a moment later.

The press secretary leaned close. "What the hell is he going to say?"

"I have no idea," Angela told her.

"Good morning, everyone." The president smiled politely, gazing over the hushed room. "Thank you for coming on such short notice." A flutter of camera flashes briefly filled the air. "I have some things to say today to all of you here, and to the American people . . . Things I've wanted to say for some time now."

The gathered reporters edged collectively forward in their seats.

⌒

Just over a mile away in Speaker Overton's Congressional office, Grady O'Shea burst through the door without knocking, interrupting the Speaker's meeting with several colleagues from the Senate.

"Dammit," Overton announced with irritation. "I'm in the middle of something here. You may not have noticed but I still have a country to basically run."

"Perez is in the press room right now for an unscheduled announcement." O'Shea grabbed a remote and turned on the TV. "I have a bad feeling about this." The TV screen flicked to life, the president's image filling the screen.

"Unless we're bombing the shit out of someone," said Overton, "it doesn't much matter what he says at this point. And we're not, because I'd already know about it."

The President took a sip of water as a few more cameras clicked, and everyone waited for him to fill the growing silence. There was no teleprompter, and no notes. "I think it's fair to say that the time for campaign pretense is over. I took on the great responsibility of this office with the intention of healing the divides in this country. That was always my genuine hope. To each day make decisions that would move our great democratic experiment to a place our forefathers would approve of. In this regard, if I'm being honest with you and with myself, I have failed . . .

"And while I take full responsibility, I also believe this is a failure that was decades in the making. Governing this magnificent country of ours is complicated, to the point where doing it well is damned near impossible. Presidents aren't supposed to say that, but it's true. There was a time in government when complicated decisions for the greater good could be taken, because the leadership of both parties trusted each other enough to know that certain decisions were in the best interests of the country."

"The decisions I made during the TAP negotiations with China are just such an example; clearly in the best interests of the country, though for reasons that must remain confidential. Yet there are those who nonetheless chose to use that against me in this election. Now that's politics, and I signed up for that and fully accept my fate. But at a certain point, we need to step back from our political process and recognize the simple fact that something is broken."

Angela looked around and saw several mouths hanging open. Half the room wasn't even taking notes anymore; they were too shocked. She also noticed that Vice President Palmer had slipped into the back of the press room, looking like someone about to open a nicely wrapped gift.

"From the Oval Office to the halls of Congress, to the political arenas of our many cities and towns across America, it seems that when a politician dares to stray from ideology or cross the aisle to broker a solution to an important problem—including this horrendous and destructive shutdown—they are torn to pieces from every side. For four years, I've wrestled with my own party almost as much as the Republicans. And each year the parties draw further and further apart."

"Now you might say *"Well, Mr. President, you weren't as good a wrestler as you needed to be,"* and I'm fairly certain that's true. But the reason I come to you today is because I am certain that the current two-party monopoly, and I use those words deliberately, the two-party monopoly in which I have been an active participant is incapable of delivering the prosperity our forefathers envisioned, and which every American deserves."

"Here's the bottom line, folks. As a patriot, I feel called to make one final effort to move our great democratic experiment forward to a brighter future. It is an effort that I believe our forefathers would approve, and history will look upon favorably when I am gone. Effective immediately, I am terminating my campaign for re-election, and wholeheartedly endorsing the best candidate I can think of to set this great nation on a better path.

"I say to you now, Jack Sanborn for President. He has my vote, and I hope he has yours. Thank you, and may God bless America."

The moment of shocked silence lasted just long enough for Perez to pivot, leave the podium and get halfway out the door. The room exploded behind him. Vice-President Palmer's face turned ashen before he turned and stomped from the room.

～

In his office, a red-faced Clay Overton stood and hurled the large ceramic coffee mug he had been holding at the large TV screen. "Goddamned motherfucker!"

⌒

Angela remained motionless against the press room wall as aides flocked after the president, bouncing off one another. As several reporters gathered around her, she ignored their questions. Her mind was far away, remembering the last time she had felt such pride.

⌒

Jack, Jade, Lewis, Ethan and several staffers were gathered in the Club Room of the Carolina Inn. The meeting rooms and ballroom had been rented to serve as campaign headquarters for the final two weeks. Like everyone else, they tuned into the conference the moment someone told them about it.

"Oh my God," Jade said when Perez had left the podium. "What the hell just happened?"

"I can't believe he did that," Lewis breathed. "He's just . . . gone . . . out of the race."

Jack stood still; his heart pounding as he processed what had happened. Turning to Ethan, he saw the corners of his mouth twitch. "Wait, did you see this coming?"

Ethan shrugged. "I saw the growing possibility, but not the certainty."

"So, what does the math say now?" Jack replied.

Ethan blinked a few times, as if processing the information. He looked to Jack. "You just picked up the lead in twelve states and pulled even in seventeen to twenty more."

Jack felt a chill run through his body.

"What does that mean overall?" Jade asked.

"It means the probability differential is almost zero."

Jade shot him a confused look. "Which means?"

"We're tied."

⌒

Clay Overton looked at Grady O'Shea menacingly as he stood in front of the splattered, cracked TV screen. "I swear, if you say a word about Duverger's stupid fucking law, your ass is going to eat my shoe. Dammit!! I can't BELIEVE that coward Perez would do this! He's risking the whole system!! Everything!"

"I think that was his whole point," O'Shea replied blandly, producing an acid stare from Overton. "Time for Plan C, Mr. Speaker. Our eight-point lead probably just went to zero. If we're lucky."

"We can't rely on dumb luck to keep an imbecile from destroying everything we've worked for," Overton replied, smoldering. He moved to the window and stared out at the grey morning sky.

"So . . . is there a Plan C?" O'Shea asked. "We can triple down on the attack ads, but the data on those is looking pretty questionable."

"There's always a Plan C," Overton said, almost to himself. He watched people outside the Capitol building. Moving in all directions, going about their business. He wondered if any of them truly understood the stakes at this pivotal moment in history.

CHAPTER 44

Six Days Until Election Day

DEMARCO CONTI STOOD, bottle in hand, awaiting his turn at the register of one of DC's least-finest liquor establishments. After retreating from Overton's office nearly two days back, with nothing to show for his efforts but the pair of secondhand Allen Edmund shoes he'd bought for his time in that rarified air, the urge to drink was like a drumbeat in his head. By the time thirty-six hours had passed, several crash cymbals and a bass guitar had turned the racket into an ensemble.

Block after block passed as he wandered the streets, trying to suppress the painful truth that yet another opportunity to avenge Gracie had slipped away from him. Like so many other things in his miserable life.

He's going to call.

This was the mantra that had kept DeMarco from heading straight to the bottle after leaving Overton's office, and every hour since. He intended to be sharp when duty called, but duty had best get its ass in gear and call soon. While there was still some functioning remnant left to call.

As the hours ticked by, the mantra had slowly morphed from *He's going to call* to *Why hasn't he called* to *He's not calling, you stupid fucking idiot.*

DeMarco finally found himself standing in the short line at Marty's Discount Liquors, gripping a one-liter plastic bottle of Chinese vodka that cost a bit less than a fancy cup of coffee. Enough was enough. He wasn't even sure he'd head back to his dingy DC hotel room. A sheltered alleyway might be more fitting of the occasion. Something in his brain tried to tell him that the Sig in his holster and the liter of vodka in his hand were a bad combination, all things considered. But the warning went unheeded.

He stepped forward and placed the bottle on the counter with a thud. Before he could reach for his wallet, he felt the phone buzz in his jacket and answered it. "Yeah?"

"You sure you want to do that, Detective?" The voice was vaguely familiar.

"Nine-eighty, pal," called the oversized clerk from behind the glass that separated him from the clientele, such as it was.

"Do what?" DeMarco said.

"Buy that bottle of shitty vodka."

"Nine-eighty, dude. Let's go," said the clerk, in a hurry though DeMarco was last in line.

DeMarco looked around the store.

"I'm not inside," the voice on the phone told him.

DeMarco looked and saw Overton's bodyguard standing outside, looking in.

"Today, dude!" the clerk said.

"Fuck off," DeMarco told him, and turned away.

"Hey, you gotta put that back on the shelf, asswipe!"

Fortunately for the clerk, DeMarco ignored him and went outside. "What are you, my mother?" he said to Anton.

"I would have abandoned you at birth if I was," Anton told him. "Save me a trip out here looking for your sorry ass."

DeMarco contemplated pulling the Sig from its holster, but something about the man staring at him told him that wasn't the best idea. "What the fuck do you want?"

"Wrong question."

"Why don't you tell me the answer then?"

Anton gave no answer. Instead, he gave DeMarco a thin black card.

"What's this?"

"Everything you need to create your next opportunity."

"Yeah," DeMarco scoffed, "I read that in the fuckin' brochure."

"Say no then." Anton shrugged indifferently. "Be doing me a favor. I told him you were a waste of resources twice already."

"If that's your recruitment pitch, it needs work," DeMarco told him. Ten years ago, Anton's six inches and seventy pounds on him wouldn't have deterred DeMarco from taking him down. But that was ten years, a daughter, a marriage, two good lungs and a dismembered career ago.

DeMarco examined the card in the store's neon glow. It had no markings and felt heavier than it should have. He had no idea what was stored on it, but suspected that once he found out, there would be no going back.

Fuck it. What have I got to lose? He shoved the card in a pocket and looked up.

Anton was gone.

Chapter 45

Three Days Until Election Day

JACK AND JADE WALKED QUICKLY through the winding underground tunnels of Madison Square Garden, still feeling the electric energy of the twenty-thousand strong crowd that took in his speech. Four Secret Service agents flanked them as they made their way towards an exit.

A few days prior, Lewis had been reluctant to have Jack attend Cardinal Patrick O'Halloran's annual New York caucus. The event was a long-standing tradition for any aspiring presidential candidate, but Jack's lack of outward religious affiliation risked being on full display. With Overton also scheduled to make an appearance later in the program, the contrast risked raising concern among conservative voters.

Jack had made the decision to go ahead, banking that a shutdown country seemingly headed for ruin would outweigh any of the usual political lightning rods. Judging from the thunderous echo of applause that still seemed to follow them as they walked, his instincts had been correct.

"That was pretty good," Jade said.

"Pretty good?" Jack asked.

"Okay, it was good."

"You're sure it wasn't great though?"

"I don't do great."

"Well, maybe I do. I think it was great. Anyway . . . Nice work getting us to go first. Overton will try to paint me as the devil, but I don't think that'll be easy."

One of the Secret Service agents touched his earpiece and then turned to Jack. "Sir, The Speaker is in the building quite early for his speech and he's just around this next corner. Do you want to detour?"

"Detour? What for?"

"Well, sometimes candidates don't really want to . . . encounter each other."

"Fear of ideology infection, huh?" Jack quipped as they kept walking. "Don't worry about it."

"Not surprised he's early," Jade added, "he sees lateness as a sign of weakness." Now that Jack was fully aware of Jade's past connection to Overton, she didn't shy away from sharing the occasional insight.

"I guess being eight months late to end the government shutdown doesn't count," Jack noted.

They turned another corner and came to an intersecting hall that was blocked by several more agents. A hundred or so feet beyond them, the tall silhouette of Clay Overton leaned against the wall, a plume of smoke above him.

"Professor!" Overton called. He tossed the cigarette and started towards Jack. The blockade of agents parted, allowing the two men to approach.

"I'll meet you at the car," Jade announced, moving past Jack's agents and continuing down the hall. Jack couldn't blame her for avoiding the awkward moment.

"Mr. Speaker," Jack said, offering his hand. Overton looked genuinely surprised at the gesture and offered his hand in return.

"Sounds like you did alright in there," Overton said. "For an atheist."

"I have my spiritual beliefs," Jack corrected him, "so I'm pretty sure God and I are just fine."

"Oh. Given you've not said a word about your religious beliefs then, I just assumed. Beg your pardon."

"I'm sure you'll straighten all that out when it's your turn up there . . . But I feel I owe you a word of thanks."

"Oh, for what, Professor?"

"For Sarah's treatment. I understand you made sure it was FDA-approved so she wouldn't have to wait. That was awfully kind of you."

A faint smile tugged at Overton's lips. "You see, Professor, we politicians aren't all bad."

Jack resisted the urge to talk about widow bumps. "Not entirely. But you did try to hire my communications director, which feels a bit truer to political form."

"Well," Overton shrugged. "That one's pretty much done my bidding the past three years, so I guess I was accustomed to her . . . services."

"I'm aware," Jack replied.

"And that doesn't bother you? Her proven penchant for disloyalty?"

"Quite the opposite. Had she not experienced you up close, Mr. Speaker, I'm not sure she would have been quite so motivated to help me win this election." Jack saw the flash in Overton's eyes. He was indeed a hard man to read, but only two minutes into their polite conversation Jack's instinct told him one thing for certain: Clay Overton hated him.

"Professor, can I ask you a question?"

"Of course." Jack smiled, sensing that his confidence during their first encounter was beginning to get under Overton's skin.

"What in God's name do you think you're doing?"

"Are you looking for a general answer, or a specific one?"

"This little viral adventure of yours," Overton said, stepping close, "is incredibly dangerous, and will likely get people killed."

"You mean like the thousands who've already died because you wouldn't cut a deal to end this ridiculous shutdown?"

A vein in Overton's forehead bulged slightly. "Compromise is not what built this country, Professor. It's what almost prevented it from ever existing in the first place."

"The British left two hundred and fifty years ago," Jack said. "I think you and your musket ideology need to move on and figure out what it takes to serve the country we live in today."

"*You* presume to tell me how to govern," Overton said, his voice dropping an octave. "Is that it? Some nobody who pissed himself on national TV, and you think you have a better plan?"

"Any halfwit could come up with a better plan than what's been happening for most of the past year, Mr. Speaker. I myself have a one-point plan: put the two-party system out of business. Permanently."

"You're certifiable, you know that?" Overton asked. "You are also perhaps the greatest danger this country has ever faced."

"Coming from you, I'll take that as a compliment. But here's the thing—you made me . . . because without this shutdown, I'd still be teaching law. And you can put me right back in the classroom. All you have to do is call up Perez and end the shutdown. And *poof*, I'm gone. A political irrelevance."

This time Jack leaned closer, right in Overton's face. "But we both know you won't do that, don't we, Clay? Because this isn't about your country. This is about you. And that's the difference between us."

Overton's emotions were suddenly very easy to read. Rage. Fury. Hatred. For a moment, Jack thought Overton would deck him. But instead, he turned and walked away.

"Don't forget to vote," Jack called after him.

CHAPTER 46

Two Days Until Election Day

THE NEXT DAY, JACK RODE THE UNC HOSPITAL elevator up to Sarah's ICU floor. Special Agent Jonah Mullen stood beside him, eyes forward.

"You guys aren't much for chit-chat, are you?" Jack said.

"All focus on the job at hand, sir," Agent Mullen replied with a glance.

The elevator doors opened silently, revealing another agent. "Sir," he nodded. "Mrs. Sanborn's neurologist has asked for a word with you before you go in."

"Okay . . ." Jack replied, immediately concerned. He looked down the hall to see UNC's head neurologist coming towards him. Jack spoke first. "Is Sarah okay?"

"She's doing fine, Mr. Sanborn," she replied, but Jack immediately sensed there was more to the story. "I wanted to see you because I need to ask you something."

"Ask away," Jack said.

The doctor hesitated a moment. "Have you noticed anything . . . different about Sarah lately?"

"In what sense? I mean, with her still in the hospital it's a bit harder to judge what's normal."

"I get that," she nodded. "I was wondering more about her mental capacity."

"Well, you and your team are doing all the tests. Shouldn't you be telling me that?"

"Sorry. I should clarify. I don't mean any diminished mental capacity, I mean *enhanced*."

"In what way?"

"Improved cognition. Better long-term memory. A small sample of patients in the trial reported some rather significant improvements."

"I'm not sure I've noticed her remembering more than normal," Jack said, "but I can keep an eye out."

"How about her ability to process data?"

"Data," Jack repeated. *Odd choice of words.* "You mean equations, numbers, that kind of thing?"

"It could manifest that way, if the patient worked in numbers, I suppose, but what we've seen is more an ability to read situations and people, anticipate better, things like that."

"Sounds hard to watch for, but I'll let you know if I notice anything. Do these things indicate some kind of problem?"

"I wouldn't think so," the doctor replied, "but because this form of treatment is still so new, I'd like to play it cautiously here."

"Okay. Just tell me what that means."

"I'd like to put Sarah into light sedation for a few days. Her brain is still healing rapidly, and muting other stimuli will help it devote all resources to full recovery."

"Sounds a bit like being forced to stay in a dark room after a concussion," Jack said.

"I suppose that's not a bad analogy, though it's much more complicated than that."

"I assume light sedation is also okay for the baby?"

She nodded. "She'll be asleep, but barely. And pregnant women have surgeries too, Mr. Sanborn. It's fine."

"Have you discussed this with Sarah yet?"

She shook her head. "I was about to, but I heard you'd arrived, so I thought I'd catch you first." The doctor glanced at her watch. "I'll join you in a few minutes and we can all discuss it."

"Sounds good." Jack continued down the hall to Sarah's room. He didn't much care for the idea of putting Sarah back under so soon after she came to, but he wasn't inclined to go against the doctor's recommendations either.

Jack stopped in Sarah's doorway and was glad to find her awake and alone. She looked up at him. "Taking a break from the campaign trail?"

He smiled, stepped to her bedside and planted a soft kiss on her lips. "Just a short one," he replied. For someone still in the ICU, she looked damn good. "I think you have that pregnant glow already," he said.

"Yeah, or maybe that's the power of showering. You OK?"

"Sure, why?"

"Well, last night you were excited about having a virtual campaign day, but this morning you look worried."

Jack shook his head. "I'm fine. Virtual day is still on, so I'll be back and forth here."

"Something else on your mind then? About me, perhaps?"

How the hell does she know that? Jack immediately wondered if she might have heard his conversation with the neurologist, but they'd been too far away. Or maybe this was exactly what the doctor had meant about an enhanced ability to read people and situations. "The doctor says she wants to put you under light sedation."

"Light sedation. Sounds like my college days."

"Very funny," Jack replied, surprised at her lack of concern. "She says it's a precaution so your brain can dedicate itself to healing. Or something like that. I'm sure they'll come and talk about it in a minute."

"But you wanted to tell me first because you're nervous about it."

Jack wasn't sure if he was being hyper-aware, or she really seemed to be reading him like an open book. "Sarah," he began, "have you noticed anything different . . . since you woke up?"

"Like what?"

"I don't know. Brain processing stuff."

"Did the neurologist say there's a problem?"

Jack shook his head. "No. She said maybe the opposite." Sarah looked away, contemplating the question. "Does that make sense?" She turned her gaze back to him but remained silent. "Is there something you've noticed, Babe?"

"There was a moment," she finally replied, "it was strange. One of the nurses came into the room yesterday, and before she said anything I could tell that something was wrong."

"With you?"

"No . . . with her."

"You've always been pretty perceptive."

Sarah nodded. "Yeah, but in this case, when I asked and she told me what was wrong . . . It was like I already knew it."

They both sat in silence for a moment, contemplating. Sarah finally interrupted. "Did she say how long I'd be in sedation?"

"She said a couple of days."

Sarah frowned. "I'll miss election night."

"Maybe we should swap," Jack said. "You can wake me after the election."

"I think I'd rather be the sedated one, thanks."

CHAPTER 47

One Day Until Election Day

CLAY OVERTON BREATHED SLOWLY; his feet propped up on the mahogany desk that anchored his congressional office. He was finally alone, having had more than enough of his advisors panicking over the sudden evaporation of an eight-point lead. If it wasn't the day before the election, he would have fired every last useless one of them.

There's no room for panic on the battlefield. Improvise. Adapt. Overcome.

Overton's eyes scanned the four separate images displayed on the thin TV panel that had arisen from the far edge of his desk at the touch of a button. To most people, watching four news programs simultaneously would be anything but relaxing, but Clay Overton was not most people. In his business, information was weaponry, and you didn't stay on top in DC by doing one thing at a time. Each evening, weapons needed to be cleaned, oiled and fully reloaded. During his deployments as a marine, the nightly practice with his actual field weapons had helped him unwind. And while the weapons he used today were no longer the mechanical sort, they were no less deadly, as many in Washington had come to learn.

On this night, three of Overton's chosen newsfeeds were forced to co-exist on screen with an intrusion as he halfheartedly partook in a briefing about final sprint messaging for the campaign. Record SuperPac money meant it would be the largest two-day media buy in Meta history, blanketing all platforms, focused entirely on stoking fears of such rash inexperience finding itself in the seat of power.

Several prominent Democrat SuperPac donors and even the Russians were chipping in quietly behind the scenes, as the thought of an independent candidate posed a clear and present danger to their reliable channels of influence.

Overton nodded occasionally in the direction of the web conference in the bottom right of the screen. The RNC Chair was prattling on about poll-tested messaging that played any vote for Sanborn as a vote for the death of America's founding values of integrity and independent thinking. The more he went on, the less Overton understood what the hell he meant, but the movement to reclaim "independent" was less dim-witted than Overton had come to expect from the RNC Chair.

"Atta-boy Jimmy, confuse the shit out of them," he muttered. Confusion worked. Always had, even if it was confusion caused by others' incompetence.

Overton turned his attention to a pro-Sanborn newsfeed, highlighting his campaign activities over the past few weeks. He rarely learned anything new from this feed, but hatefully watching clips of a *fucking schoolteacher* he'd suddenly found himself neck-and-neck with, helped push the bile up the back of his throat. He knew that was a useful state of mind for battle.

"Any final comments, Mr. Speaker?" intruded the nasal voice of the overweight RNC Chair, snapping Overton's attention back to the live video conference in one corner of the screen.

"Yes," he replied, removing his feet from the desk and slowly leaning toward the webcam until his face nearly filled the bottom quadrant. "In twenty-four hours, all that will matter for decades to come is what each of you did in the final moments to bury this fucking bastard. Now go!"

With the flick of Overton's finger, the image in the bottom quadrant went black. At the same moment, there was a knock on the door. A chirp quickly followed as the lock released, signaling that the visitor was his bodyguard, Anton Reverdy; the only other person on earth who could open Overton's office door from the outside.

"Sir," he nodded as he stepped through the door and closed it behind him. "All is in place. Would you like to review the schedule?"

Overton looked up at the towering figure that had guarded him faithfully for close to twenty years. Anton had risked his life for him on more than one occasion and had been rewarded for his loyalty. "Has the schedule changed since we reviewed it this morning?"

"No."

"Is this you being overprotective?"

"This is me doing my job."

"Anton." Overton peered at him over his glasses. "Your job does not include assuming I cannot remember details we reviewed only hours ago." He could see Anton stiffen at the remark. "But thank you for the abundance of caution."

Anton gave a slight bow. "I'll leave you then." He turned on his heel and left, closing the door behind him.

Overton returned his gaze to the screens, all of which momentarily displayed images of Jack Sanborn on them. "Fucking schoolteacher," he muttered under his breath.

CHAPTER 48

Election Day

THE PACKAGE WAS EXACTLY where it was meant to be; nestled inside the spare blanket roll that had been carefully placed in the closet of room 303, in a precisely chosen Hampton Inn. Angel DaSilva turned it over in his wrinkled hands. The package was smaller than expected. This annoyed him greatly. Details and planning were everything in his line of work. Details either got you killed or saved your life. You obsessed over them, reviewing every element again and again, or you left something to chance and would eventually suffer the consequences.

He exhaled deeply and released the barbed ring of frustration that had been building behind his weary eyes, which were set deeply below a shock of cloud-white hair.

There were, of course, no published longevity statistics for his line of work, but you didn't need them to know it was rare for someone of his age to remain on the active list. And while he had slipped a few spots, he was still top tier. He chose the work rather than it choosing him.

He had always preferred low-profile assignments in the past. It minimized complications and, more importantly, minimized the risks. It made getting in and out easier, even if the assignment required the work to be up close and personal. That type of proximity was not often required, unless the security level demanded it. Angel had no desire to *feel it*. He'd never been one of those. The ego-types didn't last long; letting ego cloud one's judgment and accepting the riskier, higher-profile targets was a surefire path to a short-lived career. Angel's practice had been a long one, thanks to his ability to set ego aside. One of his handlers had referred to him as the *Angel of Death*, but Angel had spurned the label quickly. Angel was his given name, but to him it was just a name. He had others.

There was no room for morality either. He took assignments based on the play and the money, not on the mark. Mixing morality into the calculus was also apt to get you killed, just not by the same people. Eyes open. Head down. Work the details.

He did his best to stifle a cough, then inhaled deeply as he perched on the side of the neatly made bed. His muscular shoulders slumped a little more than usual, weighed down by a mix of fatigue and something more. Something which he had yet to accept but had nonetheless begun planning for meticulously. He was dying. In a profession where one accepted that one could die a hundred different ways, it seemed he was to die slowly. And painfully.

He removed a pale embroidered cloth from his pocket and dabbed his lips absently. There was no blood there, this time. The cloth was blotched pale pink and smelled sickly, even though it had been laundered so many times the smiling baby elephants stitched on it were barely discernible.

There was no doubt this would be his last one. But it would set her up for life, and that meant something. Having ended so many lives abruptly and without warning, the irony of his torpid demise presented itself as an awakening of sorts, but one with few outlets. All that remained was to leave something behind. For her.

Even if she never knew the money was from him, it was something, wasn't it? Yes, yes it was. She could be that much better off. And even the children she might have somewhere down the line. It didn't matter that no one but him would ever know.

He sat there a few minutes, on the clean bed with the few articles he needed for tomorrow laid out. The uniform, neatly pressed but not so new looking as to be noticeable. The schematics of the building.

The access badge with modified DNA chip to open the right doors. He squinted as he held it close, inspecting it once more in good light. Withdrawing a tissue, he wiped three tiny specs of blood from the back of the badge, silently admonishing himself for having missed them before. *Details either got you killed or saved your life.*

Satisfied, he put the ID card back on the bed and sighed. He returned to thinking about the daughter he had not seen in many years, wondering what his grandkids might look like if they ever came to be. He knew he would not live to see them, but the thought almost made him smile.

Angel shifted on the bed and opened the small grey package he'd retrieved from the wrapped blanket. The rectangular box wasn't much heavier than the air. He opened it carefully. His initial annoyance at the undersized package had shifted to intrigue at what was inside, mixed with anxiety at not using one of his familiar tools. It was necessary for the play, and he'd agreed to the extensive terms and instructions as detailed, but his brow furrowed at the thought of using a tool that was unproven, at least to him.

As expected, there were three inside. One for pre-testing prior and to then be destroyed. And two for the operation itself, one of which was purely back-up. The material had the texture of sharkskin but the pliability of a piece of treated leather. Angel lay the six-inch angular cut of alanine-spider silk material across his palm, watching it droop over the edges. He touched the thicker, ribbed end with his fingers and stifled a ripple of excitement before it could be felt anywhere in his body; emotions led to errors, and errors led to failure.

He would test one of the samples shortly by immersing it in water, as instructed, to transform the thin alanine spider silk material from a fabric easily hidden under clothing to a surface harder than steel. He was satisfied enough, however, to remove his encrypted phone and punch in the code word. It took four seconds for the reply to arrive, another seven for the separate text confirmation that half of the agreed-upon sum had been wired to his Swiss account.

He returned his attention to the articles on the bed, inspecting them again as his memory replayed the details of the job at hand.

Details . . . they either saved your life or got you killed.

It was a mantra that Angel had lived by for close to three decades of employment. The fact that the mantra now offered a certain irony on the final job of his career was not lost on Angel.

———

Sitting in his dingy DC hotel room, DeMarco Conti unzipped the black backpack he had retrieved earlier this morning from the specified bus station locker. He was alone, but instinctively looked around the room before unpacking its contents.

When he accepted the black card and its instructions from Overton's bodyguard three days back, his instincts pawed at him, telling him this wasn't a great idea. Three days on, his instincts had yet to change their opinion.

Fuck it. He emptied the backpack onto the bed. Instincts were one thing, but DeMarco was sober enough to recall that his instincts had been worth less than spit in either his personal or professional life. *So why listen to the fuckers now?* Especially when it related to what would probably be his last chance to avenge Gracie's death.

His thick fingers unfolded the uniform and laid it carefully on the bed, as if putting someone to rest. The ID badge that accompanied it had obviously used an old picture from the precinct files, but it looked close enough, as such things went. The building schematics looked clear enough; he could study those some more on the drive south. The nondescript burner phone looked a bit bulky but that was to be expected given its purpose. The contents of the small rectangular box, however, were what fascinated him. The three strips of thick gray material, ribbed at one end, looked like they could pass for a dozen different things. More than their appearance, however, the mere thought of being given what he assumed was government technology to carry out his mission, added a warming sense of gravitas to his quest.

DeMarco checked his watch. All on schedule. He would test the first sample in the bathroom sink, and then pack up so his self-driving rental car could take him to his destination. He'd never been to North Carolina before. Neither had Gracie. He found himself very much looking forward to the experience.

CHAPTER 49

Election Day

JACK AWOKE ON ELECTION DAY in the quiet of Sarah's hospital room. He stretched in the reclined hospital chair and pulled himself upright. He didn't feel as stiff as he expected after choosing to spend the night at Sarah's bedside instead of the small sleep quarters down the hall. *My body must be getting used to this abuse.*

He sat for a few minutes, just enjoying the sound of her breathing. The light sedation was doing its job, given that she didn't appear to have moved since the night before.

At the moment, Jack wanted to be nowhere else other than by Sarah's side. Perhaps, he thought, it was because election day had arrived. On the final day of the sprint for public office, candidates often hunkered down with family, eventually making their way to the polls hand in hand, all smiles for a final photo-op that would be carried on all networks. Jack's election day would have no such opportunity. *At least I slept in a little*, he thought, and glanced at his watch.

Jade had accurately predicted that the media would have a field day with Sarah's return to sedation. Jack's supporters were holding their breath, despite the newsfeed emphasizing that the sedation was merely precautionary. Detractors were accusing Jack of doing anything, even sedating his own wife, to curry advantage in the final hours of a tight race.

Jack knew he needed to get moving, but beyond being in Sarah's presence, he found himself enjoying the respite offered by the dimmed lights and solitude of her room. He finally stood, stretched and looked down at the woman who'd seen him through the darkest time in his life to date. She was with him again now; fearlessly supporting him in this improbable run, even if for the moment from a hospital bed.

He smiled and touched her hand. "There's no dress rehearsal, my love," he said, using the same phrase Sarah often used when she was about to make a leap. It was the same guiding phrase that she used when they decided to exit New York and move to North Carolina.

Jack heard footsteps. "Good morning, Professor."

He turned to see UNC's dedicated head neurologist in the doorway. "Good to see you," Jack said.

The doctor stepped into the room and spent a few moments taking in the data from the monitors by Sarah's bed. "It all looks good to me," she said.

"I might need to ask you for some light sedation too, after all this is over," Jack replied.

The neurologist gave him a smile. "I'm voting for you today, Professor."

"Well, that's one on the books at least. Thank you."

"But other than voting this morning, I will be here with Mrs. Sanborn. There's no cause for concern, but I plan to be here throughout the day."

"And you have my personal cell, yes?"

"I do."

"Can I ask you to give me frequent updates? Even just a text would help ease my mind."

'I will. Based on how she's doing, I'll start to lighten the sedation later this evening . . . so by tomorrow she should be up and around again."

"And doctor . . ."

"The baby will be fine as well, Mr. Sanborn."

Jack thanked her, planted a kiss on Sarah's cheek and made his way down the hall to the employee lounge, to shower and dress for the interesting day ahead.

The late morning atmosphere in the Club Room at the Carolina Inn had steadily ramped to a reverberating buzz. Half the room talked loudly into cell phones, while the remaining half spoke even more loudly to be heard among themselves. Lewis, Jade, Ethan, campaign director Leah and field director Patrick were all crammed into the plush, white-paneled conference room with a dozen other staffers, doing what they could in the final hours.

Patrick pulled the phone from his ear. "It's going to be raining all day in Pittsburgh!" he shouted at one of the other staffers. "We need to get volunteers with umbrellas to the polls. Pennsylvania is going to be down to the wire."

"Patrick," Leah answered back, "every state is going to be down to the wire."

Patrick shook his head dismissively and turned to the staffer. "Umbrellas, Pittsburgh, lots of 'em. Go."

"Umbrellas?" Jade asked, looking at Lewis.

"Rain suppresses voter turnout," Lewis answered, and surveyed the room like a general overseeing a battlefield.

"Democracy as long as we don't get wet," Jade said.

"Did we get the buses for the Tampa retirement homes?" Someone called out to the room. Another staffer on the phone answered by holding up four fingers.

"You know from a statistical point of view," Ethan said, "all this frantic activity will make no difference at all. You both know that, right?"

Lewis shot him a disapproving look. "Maybe you can pump up the troops with that awesome little pep talk a bit later."

"When is Jack supposed to get here?" Jade asked, looking at Lewis.

"He's going to vote first, so he should be here just after one . . . Or whenever he wants." Lewis knew his friend was never keen on keeping to a fixed schedule unless absolutely required. "It's going to be a long night," he said. "So, I hope he slept in."

Three black SUVs came to a stop in front of the Church of the Cross polling station, just on the edge of UNC's campus. Jack was in the middle SUV. As he looked out the window at the crowd, he realized they were close to the spot on Franklin Street where he had launched his campaign from the roof of a parked car.

Jack waited for agents from the other two SUVs to secure a clear entry path into the polling station so he could cast his ballot.

"Ready to exit the vehicle, sir?" *Every move carefully coordinated.*

"Ready enough."

Agent Mullen murmured into his sleeve as an agent opened the door. Jack stepped out and took in the crowd of several hundred and a huddle of reporters and TV cameras, all eager to capture the moment. He waved, smiled and made his way up the path toward the church entrance. He wished Sarah could be there with him.

"Professor Sanborn!" called one of the reporters. "How is Mrs. Sanborn?"

"Thank you for asking. She's good. Just a little light sedation. I think we should all be a little jealous of her, in fact."

The crowd laughed.

"Professor!" called a familiar voice.

Jack scanned the barricades and saw one of his Constitutional Law students smiling back at him. "Hello, Kristen." He stepped close and shook her hand. "How's that substitute teacher they got for me doing?"

"Boring, but I'll deal."

"Well, we'll see what happens today," Jack told her. "I may be back . . . or I may not."

"Not!"

"They're ready for you inside, sir." Agent Mullen said, which he knew was simple code for *'Let's get you in and out in one piece'*. Jack waved to the crowd and went inside for the surreal experience of casting a vote for himself as President of the United States.

Back in the Club Room at the Carolina Inn, Lewis paced furiously. "What the hell is wrong with these Texas exit polls?" he almost shouted. Jade, Ethan and the packed room of sleep-deprived staffers that were digesting the first wave of exit-poll data took little notice. "Does anyone—"

"It's only two o'clock, Lewis," Jade interrupted. "The polls have only been open for three hours out west."

"I'm not talking about the west, I'm talking about Texas! We're down by nine there and it was supposed to be a dead heat after all the press from the ballot ruling."

Jade could see the veins bulging on Lewis' neck. They looked like they were ready to pop.

"Forget Texas," Ethan announced. "It's lost."

"What?!" Lewis cried as he turned to face Ethan, "Barely anyone's voted yet!"

Ethan shrugged. "Doesn't matter. It was lost before today."

"But we were tied! The networks have been polling there for weeks!"

"They have their data, I have mine," Ethan said. "Believe who you want, but Texas is gone."

Lewis rubbed his forehead. "Jesus Christ, when were you going to tell me this?"

Ethan ignored the question. He was leaning over a large tablet displaying about as much data as any human eye could absorb. After a time, he leaned back and nodded. "Only California."

"What about it?" Lewis demanded.

"We're good everywhere else . . . California is all that matters."

"But good everywhere else? There's forty-eight other states, virtually all in play. How on earth can we be good?"

"In every scenario I can project," Ethan replied calmly, "we win enough of the four-hundred forty-three electoral votes left outside of Texas and California to be in a position to win."

"I'm guessing there's a catch to that," Jade said.

Ethan nodded. "The catch is, once Overton takes Texas, he'll be in the same position. So, California is the decider."

The entire room had fallen silent, everyone listening in on the conversation.

"But," Jade said, "that's got to be better for us. No Republican has won California since Reagan."

"Bush senior, actually, in eighty-eight," said Ethan. "Do you know when the last independent won California?"

Jade hesitated, almost afraid to say the word. "Never."

"Correct. Republicans are not the problem in California. Die-hard Democrats are. Too many of them are still voting for Perez despite the fact that he's pulled out."

"Seriously?" Jade said, stunned. "They didn't get the memo? Is that even legal? Voting for a candidate who's pulled out?"

Ethan shrugged and went back to studying his tablet. "He's still on the ballot there, and it's his home state, Palmer's still on the ballot too, so they have every legal right. Or they can write in Mickey Mouse if they want."

"They're betting on a horse with no jockey!" Lewis said, exasperated. "And we're up by five in California right now!"

"You won't be by dinnertime, according to my modeling."

"Wait," Jade said. "If it all goes as you think it will Ethan, but somehow Perez wins California—what happens then?"

"The House decides," Lewis said grimly.

"Really? Has that ever happened?"

"John Quincy Adams," Ethan replied. "If no one gets to two hundred and seventy, the House decides the President and the Senate decides the Vice-President."

"For which we have no one," Lewis added.

"Double-screwed," Jade noted.

"Yes," Ethan replied. "So, Lewis. You might want to focus on California with your umbrellas or buses or whatever sophisticated tool you think might help."

Jade was beginning to understand why Ethan had a reputation for being a recluse; making friends was clearly not his strong suit.

The Club Room door opened, and Jack stepped inside, followed by Agent Mullen. Jack had a phone pressed to his ear. "Thanks, Doc, appreciate the updates; keep 'em coming." He ended the call and pocketed the phone.

"You get hung up at the polling station?" Jade asked.

Jack smiled, knowing they had been hoping to see him a few hours earlier. "Nah, I know it's all coming down to California, so I figured why rush over." He winked at Ethan, then flashed a smirk at Lewis, who was not amused.

CHAPTER 50

Election Night

6:28PM

DEMARCO LOOKED STRAIGHT AHEAD, his hands needlessly holding the wheel of the self-driving car that had been rented with false credentials. He'd spent the first half of the journey down I-95 studying the relevant building blueprints until he felt he could walk the halls with his eyes closed. But by the time he crossed into North Carolina, the sky fading from burnt orange to violet, something in him craved a greater sense of control.

He wasn't about to disable the auto-drive; he'd barely driven in two years and the last thing he needed was to be pulled over for something stupid. Instead, he kept his hands lightly on the wheel, remembering Gracie's younger days when he managed to carve out some father/daughter "adventure" time. He'd grab a cheap rental car and they'd head out of the city for a night, maybe two. Once he knew they were in a safe enough area, left or right turns were decided by coin toss. Gracie would giggle each time she flipped the coin, enjoying the excitement of the unknown. He'd enjoyed teaching his only daughter that life could be an adventure, if you stopped and looked around once in a while.

She'd be in college by now.

His hands gripped the wheel a little tighter. He was tempted to step on the pedal but didn't; he was right on schedule.

7:01PM

Angel DaSilva was exceptional when it came to looking bored; that was how those in his line of work blended in. Drooping his shoulders and shuffling more than walking, he wore the visage of an older man still working a job out of pure necessity.

He felt his heart flutter for a moment as he passed through the millimeter-wave scanners and produced his ID for inspection. That type of physiological reaction in pivotal moments of his job was something he'd not experienced in a long time. He chalked it up to an aging body more than nerves.

"You're good," muttered the armed security guard at the service entrance, which had been modified for the occasion. Angel nodded, projecting a crafted expression of mild irritation at the extra fuss just to enable him to punch the clock at a job he'd rather not do at all. The security guard would likely forget all about him in a moment or two.

Angel made his way down the corridor, eyes forward, blending seamlessly into the flow of hallway traffic.

7:34PM

Clay Overton took the stairs up to his Congressional office two at a time. He had no desire to hurry, only to feel the blood moving faster through his veins during a day he'd been envisioning for decades. It was a destiny day, one that would make all the years of sacrifice worthwhile, even though the sacrifices were rarely his own.

He reached the top of the stairs and was met by another member of his security detail. Overton looked past the man and spotted an eager-looking Kyle Manning, the junior Republican Senator from Kentucky.

"Mr. Speaker!" Manning called out, opting not to approach as the remainder of Overton's protective detail closed the circle.

"It's all right, fellas," Overton said as he waved Manning over. He clasped the junior senator's hand between his own, making it all but disappear like a clam in a shell. "Are you ready for what's next, Kyle?"

"Eyes on the prize, Mr. Speaker."

"I think we're in for a great night," Overton replied, his face radiating like a small sun.

"And we've got both Houses ready if we need them," Kyle added with satisfaction.

"You mean if we don't win?" Overton replied, his eyes growing suddenly cold. "Is that what you mean, Senator?" He took a long moment to enjoy the confused expression on Kyle's dimpled face. The man suddenly looked like he wanted to throw himself down the stairs.

"I . . .. uh . . . Well, no . . ."

"It is good to have contingencies on the field of battle, though," Overton said when he felt the man had suffered long enough. He clapped Kyle on the shoulder. "We talked about that on the bridge before you kissed the pavement. Remember?"

Before Kyle could answer, Overton had released his grip and pushed past him, striding toward the office—where, to his thinking, the only real power in Washington had resided for the past nine years.

*****7:44PM*****

DeMarco let his hands move with the steering wheel as the auto-drive gently guided him to the off-ramp, leaving the interstate traffic behind. The sky was darker than ink, but he could see the piles of trash that lined the off-ramp like multicolored snowbanks. He briefly contemplated tapping the console to see the news, but he didn't give a shit about the election results, at least not in the conventional sense. He knew his destination, and that was all that mattered.

His car's headlights lit up a large roadside sign: Welcome to Chapel Hill, Home of the University of North Carolina Tar Heels, Eight-time NCAA Champions. DeMarco sniffed. He cared about basketball even less than elections, but nonetheless found himself humming softly as the car made its way toward the UNC campus.

8:20PM

"It's getting real now," Jade remarked as she, Jack, Lewis and Ethan stood and watched the wall of screens in the Carolina Inn Club Room. The top eight news networks were all on display. Each monitor projected some form of electoral college counter, tracking the candidates' progress toward the magical two-hundred-and-seventy number. Each one had the counter at fifty-four for Overton, twenty-one for Sanborn, and zero for the withdrawn Perez.

"Should I be worried?" Jack asked, looking to Ethan.

"So far it looks like Perez pulling out is helping Overton more than us," Lewis noted. "Vermont for Chrissakes! A Republican hasn't won there in eighty-four years! What the hell is that about?"

Ethan shrugged. "No need for worry at this point . . .about anything other than California. There will be a lot of smaller surprises tonight, and we'll get some red states no one would expect due to Perez backing out . . . But it's all within my modeling margins for the remaining forty-eight states."

"And our lead in Texas is dropping fast," Jack remarked. "As you predicted."

"I don't predict," Ethan replied, gazing down at his tablet, "I merely see."

Lewis rolled his eyes. "How about seeing some good news then?"

Ethan gave him a curious look, like a scientist studying the uncooperative subject of an experiment. "How about voter turnout is trending at double the last election?"

"That's more like it. More of that would be good."

"But it's still not as high as it needs to be. At least not yet."

"And he taketh away," Lewis replied. "I'll just sit over here." He moved to a corner chair and dropped himself in it.

Jack looked at Lewis, understanding his frustration after having poured so much effort into the Texas ballot challenge. "Texas or no Texas, it looks like we're in for a long night."

The California vote count flashed up on one of the monitors. President Perez was still maintaining a narrow home-state lead.

8:41PM

Clay Overton sat in his office, his feet propped up on the desk and his tie loosened. He sipped on a lowball of bourbon and did his best to tune out the chatter from O'Shea and the other staffers gathered in his paneled command post to watch the results roll in on a bank of monitors.

While he understood their enthusiasm mixed with anxiety, they'd done little, in his opinion, to merit such emotional attachment. They'd been enlisted over a period of a few months or, in O'Shea's case, just a few weeks. Whereas he himself had been working toward this moment for thirty years.

For a moment, he contemplated how it would feel to have a life partner to share this evening with, watching hand in hand as a lifetime of planning was rewarded. He took another sip of bourbon and blinked away the memory of his two miserably failed marriages. *Disloyal bitches.* Neither ex-wife had come close to meeting his expectations.

"How many states have been called?" said one of the staffers to no one in particular. Overton was not about to answer, having little patience for an imbecile with the apparent memory of a fruit fly.

"Eighteen," O'Shea replied, pulling a phone away from his ear. "And we're about to pull even in Texas."

Another staffer on his phone snapped his fingers and pointed at a screen. "Watch the CNN feed! They're about to call Georgia!" The chatter in the room fell away as everyone watched the CNN anchor puff up at being the first network to call yet another state.

—and we are ready to project that Clay Overton will take Georgia by three points over Jack Sanborn, with President Perez still garnering what looks to be his nightly average of about ten percent of the vote. That now gives Overton and the Republicans a strong early lead at seventy delegates to only twenty-four for the Sanborn campaign . . . There's still

a long way to go but Clay Overton certainly has to be pleased at the way things are looking right now . . .

The office erupted in cheers and fist pumps. Overton allowed himself a faint smile, his flat grey eyes revealing nothing.

*****9:09PM*****

DeMarco cracked his knuckles as the car guided itself into the UNC underground parking lot. He tapped the screen and accepted the auto-drive-recommended parking, between a Range Rover and a Porsche Cayenne. *Excellent choice.*

The instructions on the black card had been explicit: wipe down the interior and exterior contact points for the vehicle, which would soon be remotely disabled, with its memory erased. Three days with the black card and its instructions, however, had given DeMarco time to think.

She was his Gracie. He'd do this his way.

Besides, a little distraction for the local authorities couldn't be a bad thing. He pulled a flask from his backpack, screwed off the cap and sniffed the liquid. The smell was reminiscent of the worst alcohol he had ever consumed, and that was saying something. He was tempted to take a small sip. Instead, he opened the windows a crack, pulled a rag from his pocket and stuffed it halfway inside the bottle. He studied his creation for a moment, nodded, and pulled a Zippo lighter from a pocket. He lit the rag.

As the flames began to devour it, he gently lowered the flask to the passenger-side floor, then grabbed the backpack and stepped from the vehicle.

DeMarco's mind flashed back to the typical action-movie sequences he'd seen, with the hero walking casually away as something exploded behind him. He knew electric cars didn't explode like that, which was too bad, but he still felt good as he walked away unhurried, never once looking over his shoulder.

9:18PM

The wheels of the service trolley rolled silently over the hallway carpet of the Carolina Inn as Angel made his way toward one of the locations where his assignment was most likely to be completed. His dress, rhythm and forward posture gave him the appearance of a harmless elderly gentleman moving glacially through his dull-but-required tasks.

A large men's room with several private stalls presented itself along the way. He ambled to a stop as campaign volunteers flowed past in either direction. He left the trolley and stepped inside the marbled men's room. He was pleased to find it empty, especially of hotel staff, who might be tempted to get chatty. He was prepared for the possibility but preferred to avoid it.

He stepped inside the last stall and locked the door. He went still as he listened for any indication of movement in the men's room but heard only the gentle hum of the HVAC system. Satisfied, he reached into the end of his sleeve, just above the cuff. His fingers found the extra flap of material that guarded the alanine-spider silk tool stowed within, just above his wrist. He pulled, and the long cut of thick grey fabric slid from his sleeve and then drooped over his fingers.

He flushed the toilet with a wave of his other hand and waited for the water to still. His trained ears listened again for motion. Hearing none, he pulled a small adhesive strip from his pocket, peeled the backing and placed the strip over the toilet's motion sensor. He lowered his hand and the fabric gently into the toilet water. He could have opted for the sink, but that would increase the chance of someone seeing him, and he couldn't have that. *Details either saved your life, or got you killed.* And a little germy toilet water would not be the death of him tonight.

His fingers disappeared from view as chemical reactions were triggered and the water in the bowl shimmered and effervesced. His skin tingled, and he felt the object stiffen, just like the sample he had tested the night before. After thirty seconds, the water returned to normal.

Angel lifted the now hard-as-steel alanine blade from the water and wiped it dry with a cloth from his pocket. He ran his fingers across the blade and its ribbed handle, admiring the tool's deadly elegance, and it occurred to him that over the course of his long career, he had seldom, if ever, killed with a weapon of such beautiful simplicity. He supposed that was fitting, all things considered.

He slid the weapon back into his coat sleeve blade first, tucking it securely into a hidden fabric compartment. With the movement of only a finger when the time came, he could move the flap aside and gravity would drop the blade handle into his waiting grip.

Angel exited the stall and left the men's room quickly, for once, not bothering to wash his hands.

*****9:25PM*****

As DeMarco approached the building, he heard the distant sound of fire truck sirens. He knew that might or might not serve to draw attention away from where he was headed, but it felt good to do it nonetheless. Not much else in his life did, and that seemed justification enough.

He'd downed several long swigs of cough suppressant on his walk over from the parking garage, rationalizing that it wasn't a drink but for his own protection. He didn't need a coughing fit just now, from the feeble lungs that would soon fail him for good. As he approached the service door, he could feel the full effect of the cough medicine's pholcodine kicking in.

He stopped at the secure entrance, not bothering to look away from the camera over the door. None of that would matter soon enough. He held out an ID badge and tapped it on the scanner. There was a worrying pause, during which he wondered if the whole endeavor would fail right here, with armed men responding to a silent alert from a fucking door-scanner. But then the scanner *beeped* and the door unlocked, and he relaxed. For the moment. Because this was just the first of several obstacles to come.

Before he opened it, he gazed deliberately at the camera over the door, so it could get a good long look at him. He wanted people to know who he was, and why he was here. This was for Gracie.

*****9:37PM*****

Being a district attorney in New York had provided Jack with more than his fair share of adrenaline-charged moments in the courtroom. But those all paled in comparison to what he was feeling now, as election results and projections arrived at an ever-increasing pace.

"Why haven't they called Illinois yet?" Lewis all but shouted at the screens. "We're up by four there, dammit!" He pointed his finger at a staffer, who picked up a phone and started dialing. Jack wondered who he was calling, and to what effect.

"Missouri's gone," Jade announced as the screens flashed an image of a beaming Clay Overton, along with the ten electoral votes assigned to the "Show Me" state.

Before the anchors could weigh in on the Republicans taking Missouri, two separate networks displayed Jack's photo above outlines of Minnesota and Wisconsin. "They're calling them both for us!" Jack cried. "How many electoral votes is that again?"

"Twenty," Ethan replied calmly. "And I'm guessing they'll call Massachusetts next."

Jack shook his head as he took in the feverish activity around the room; most eyes were glued to either a screen or a tablet with almost everyone talking but to no one in particular. *I wish Sarah could see this*, Jack thought, and then second guessed that perhaps she wouldn't want the stress of it all after what she had been through.

"How's turnout in California looking?" Jade asked Ethan.

"The first-time voter surge keeps climbing, which is good for us and will open up a nice gap to Overton, but the Perez support is still above what I modeled . . . I don't like it."

Jack could feel the shift in Ethan's tone. He turned to Lewis. "If this goes to the House, what are our options?"

"Lose and lose," Lewis replied, looking up from his phone.

"Why don't we call the President?" Jade suggested.

"And say what? *I know you pulled out already, but can you please tell your people in California one more time?*"

"Yes, actually," Jade replied. "That's *exactly* what he should do. He didn't pull out only to have the House give this thing to Overton."

"It's a good idea," Jack interrupted. "See if you can get the President on the line, would you?"

"Um . . . looks like he's a little busy right now." She gestured toward a monitor, which showed the president stepping from the west portico of the White House. A group of reporters were waiting.

"Turn that up!" Lewis bellowed.

The room grew silent as everyone watched the president step to the podium. He held up a hand to silence a barrage of shouted questions, then adjusted the mic. "*Good evening. Just a very brief statement tonight to my fellow Americans, but in particular for the citizens of my treasured home state of California . . .*"

"I think I'm about to love this guy," Lewis said, and was promptly shushed by half the room.

"*While I am eternally grateful for the show of support many Californians have given me tonight, I now need to ask that for the final two hours of voting, anyone wishing to show me support, do so by casting your vote for Independent Jack Sanborn for President, and of course for Democrats in all House races. Doing anything else is simply playing with fire at this point. You will always have my loyalty as a native Californian, and my admiration, but it's time to secure the right outcome in this election, so we can begin the necessary reforms to our political system, which is clearly broken. Thank you, California, and may God bless every American.*"

With that, the President of the United States turned and strode back into the White House, ignoring the questions that erupted behind him.

"Yep," Lewis said, "I definitely love him."

"I can't believe he did that," Jack said, still staring at the screen. "Before we even thought of it."

"You might have a useful ally down the road there," Ethan suggested, "if the people can ever get past his deal with China."

Jack nodded, but before they could fully digest yet another patriotic act by the incumbent president, their excitement was doused with a bucket of cold water; the state of New Jersey and its fourteen electoral votes were being called for Overton.

"I'm now officially sick of seeing his face," Lewis announced.

"Way ahead of you there," Jade answered.

*****9:50PM*****

"Fuck Ronald Reagan and fuck Massachusetts," Overton declared to the gathering in his office. The state and its eleven electoral votes had just been called for Jack Sanborn. "The place is riddled with liberals anyway." Privately, he'd been intent on becoming the only Republican presidential candidate since Reagan to take the dark blue state. *And fuck the professor and that cowardly accomplice Perez, who threw in the towel. Asshole.*

"Our lead is down to twenty, sir," O'Shea said quietly. He was the only one in the room who dared speak the plain truth, even though none of it was news to Overton. "But they should call Florida any time now."

Overton inhaled deeply, concentrating and relaxing his body from within, as he would in the quiet hours between combat raids when in the Middle East. He closed his eyes. In the days leading up to the election, he'd gradually adjusted to the reality that a Reagan-like landslide was not in the cards, despite the great care taken in planning for this moment. *Reagan had Mondale. I get this freak show of an opponent and a bailing President tag-teaming my ass.* Deep down, Overton knew the battle would still be won, and that in war, the margin of victory was less important than the result. Even so, it was hard to see the race narrow.

He checked his watch and glanced up at his bodyguard, Anton. Their gazes gave away nothing, except to each other.

The returning chatter in the office fell silent as two more states were called: Florida and its thirty electoral votes for him, and Pennsylvania for Sanborn, with nineteen electoral votes.

Everyone froze, awaiting their master's appraisal.

"What a night," he said in a soothing tone, and tapped the desk with his fingers. "What a night to behold."

9:57PM

Being overlooked and dismissed in plain sight had been the only constant in Angel's life. That same constant was now his greatest advantage as he shuffled half-heartedly toward the east door of the Club Room, which was guarded by a single Secret Service agent.

Angel leaned on the service trolley, almost as if he needed it to keep himself upright. He said nothing to the agent, choosing to let his uniform, the trolley and a professional nod do his talking for him.

"Turn around, please," the Secret Service agent said blandly, scanning him with a wand. He took his time with the scanner, years of muscle memory guiding his slow, fluid movements.

Had the agent relied less on the latest technology and more on an old-fashioned pat-down, he'd have found the blade immediately. So much for modern technology. "You're good to go," he announced, pushing the door open for Angel, who felt certain the moment captured on security cameras would come back to haunt the agent.

Angel nodded and continued on his way. He appreciated the fact that the agent was well-mannered. Despite his many assignments, Angel had not yet been in such proximity to the storied agents of the United States Secret Service. It was a nice first for his tenured career—and a fitting last. He guided his trolley into the crowded Club Room and looked around until he found what he was looking for.

*****9:58PM*****

Jack stood in the crowded Club Room with his back to the wall of monitors, pressing a finger to one ear so he could hear his phone. "Thanks again, Doctor," he said as he ended another check-in with Sarah's neurologist. *Still resting peacefully, all is well.*

"Why haven't they called New York yet, or Ohio?" Jack said, his gaze returning to the screens that would soon reveal his future.

"You've been patient all night, Professor," Ethan told him. "Don't worry about New York or Ohio now."

"Yeah, okay, but if we think Overton's going to take Texas then we can't fall that far behind... Can we?"

"We're eighteen behind in the count," Ethan said. "And Washington state is coming up, which looks good for us. So, I suggest you focus your worries on—"

"California!" the entire room called out at once, all having absorbed Ethan's refrain that only one state mattered in the final balance.

Jack exhaled and looked around. "I think I'll stretch my legs. I'm starting to feel like a caged animal in here. Some outside air would be good."

Special Agent Mullen stepped toward him from his position near the room's west door. "Sir, I'm not sure a walk outside is a good idea without time to secure the route beforehand."

"Fine, let's hit the ballroom then," Jack replied.

"Still not ideal, sir."

"Agent Mullen, these are our people, they're eating with plastic forks in there and have been scanned up the wazoo. I couldn't even get a plastic knife to cut my own dinner. So pretty please, let's get out of this room for a bit."

Overhearing their conversation, Jade pushed back her chair to stand up, bumping into a porter who was passing behind her with a trolley. "Oh, I'm so sorry. I didn't see you there."

"My fault, Miss," Angel replied, bowing slightly to avoid prolonged eye contact. He silently collected another plate, working his way forward and again being left as he had been throughout life—noticed but quickly forgotten.

Jack moved towards the door. "Ready, Agent Mullen?" A sudden whoop made them both flinch as Lewis' voice filled the air. "Finally!! North Carolina!! We're getting close!"

Jack paused at the door and grinned at Lewis across the room. Having taken his home state, the delegate counter on every screen now showed Jack just two electoral votes behind Overton, with Texas, New York, Arizona, California and several others still up in the air. "Wanna take the temperature in the ballroom?" Jack asked Lewis.

"I'm good here," Lewis replied. He gestured to the screens. "Got all I need, and more."

"I'm coming," Jade announced. "You're not the only caged animal in here."

With that, Jack and Jade followed a reluctant Agent Mullen through the Club Room's west door. Those who remained took little notice of the silent porter, who now cleared plates a little faster than before.

10:03PM

A few minutes later, Jack, Jade and Agent Mullen entered the main Carolina Inn ballroom. Most of the volunteers present had been holed up for two weeks, toiling over phones and screens, doing everything possible to get voters to the polls with the right candidate in mind. Surveying the scene, Jack thought it looked like a human beehive. Constant noise and motion. On the far wall, several projection screens carried the top network news feeds.

"Professor!" someone called out. Jack turned to see one of his UNC law students. She waved and elbowed the person beside her, alerting them to Jack's unannounced entry. News of his presence spread like a chain reaction, and soon the whole room was clapping and cheering.

Jack smiled and waved, feeling a sense of awe and a little embarrassment at the high-volume reception. He turned to Jade. "This type of thing could really go to one's head."

"Yeah, I can help you with that," she told him.

"I bet. Kind of like the guy that Marcus Aurelius had follow him around, whispering in his ear, reminding him he was just a man."

"I can assure you my approach would be far less subtle."

Before the roar from the volunteers could fade, one of the big screens changed to show Jack's campaign photo over an outline of Washington state.

"We got the lead!" Jack's student shouted. The agents that flanked Jack kept their eyes on the jubilant crowd as the celebration edged a bit closer.

The lead was narrow with big states still to come, but it felt good to be out front for once.

Unnoticed by nearly all, an aging porter entered the ballroom, picked up a service tray and began making his way through the crowd.

*****10:11PM*****

Once DeMarco was past the service entrance, it took him less than seven minutes to activate the alanine blade in a men's room toilet and then find a wheeled trash can for cover. As outlined, he pushed it to the designated waiting spot outside a storage room door. He glanced at his watch. Almost time.

He reached into the breast pocket of his uniform and pulled out the burner phone he'd been given. It was surprisingly heavy in his hand. *Secret agent shit*, he thought to himself.

He thumbed the screen and sent the two-digit code to the pre-programmed number stored on the phone. Telling his handler that he was in position. Whoever was on the other end sent back another two-digit code, which meant *execute*.

DeMarco crossed the hallway, opened the storage room door and pushed the trash bin inside, pulling the door shut behind him. He took a deep breath. "For you, Gracie," he whispered. He punched in the final two-digit code to trigger the countdown and hit send. The phone screen went dark but for a small, sixty-second countdown. Satisfied, he leaned down and placed the device in the bottom of the trash bin.

He moved to the storeroom door and placed a hand on the doorknob. He steadied his breathing as he ran the count in his head, waiting for the next part.

10:12PM

DeMarco's mental countdown hadn't gotten down to thirty when he heard a loud bang somewhere far above him, and the storeroom lights went out. There was no light coming under the door, either. If the information on the card was correct, the whole building had lost power.

He opened the door and stepped into the darkened hallway. Dim emergency lighting flickered to life, alarms sounded, and confused voices filled the air.

"Phones are down too," someone said in the semi-darkness. Even with the emergency lighting, DeMarco could barely see well enough to navigate as he made his way around the corner, still counting down in his head. He did his best to look as confused as the rest of the staff who passed him on the way.

Ten seconds . . . five . . . three . . .

The sudden reports from the storeroom were slightly muffled, but easily loud enough to be heard by anyone nearby. It sounded exactly like gunshots. DeMarco had heard more than his share of gunfire, and the sound would have fooled him as well. And the "shots" kept coming, one after another.

He covered his head and stumbled forward, as if fleeing a shooter. A Secret Service agent came down the hall, weapon drawn. Staff were screaming in confusion as the shots continued to echo from somewhere.

"Where's the shooter?" he called out.

"Back there!" De Marco answered, never stopping. "Went into one of the rooms, I think!"

"How many?"

"Two!"

The young agent rushed past. DeMarco thought he seemed too young for the job. He also thought the agent's superiors would share his assessment soon.

DeMarco watched the agent round the corner and start down the next hall, leaving DeMarco free to make his final approach. He looked back down the darkened hall. It was now largely empty as the alarms continued their shrill chorus.

Almost there, Gracie.

10:14PM

Jack looked out across the ballroom. While he had watched presidential election results on TV many times before, Jack couldn't help but think of the cruelty. So much effort by so many volunteers would be quickly judged a huge success or a massive disappointment depending on what came down to just a couple of percentage points.

He could see some of the staff clinging to each other, literally bracing for more results. It reminded Jack of a three-point shot in basketball, except the shot seemed to agonizingly hang in the air for hours.

"You good?" Jade asked.

"What?"

"Are you good?"

"I'm fine." He looked at his watch. "I'm due for an update from Sarah's doctor though."

"I'm sure it's all good," Jade said. "They're probably caught up watching over there too."

Before Jack could reach for his phone, the big screens showed the image of Jack's face atop Michigan as the state's fifteen electoral votes were added to his lead. The room screeched and high-fived, but the celebration was cut short when Virginia and Ohio—and their combined thirty electoral votes—were narrowly called for Overton.

"Dammit!" Jade cursed, "I really thought we had Ohio."

Jack was down by sixteen now. The whole thing felt like a giant roller-coaster.

Jade eyed the Texas spread; Overton had opened up a two-point lead. "If we don't get New York, California won't matter when Overton takes Texas."

Agent Mullen leaned in close to speak into Jack's ear. "Lewis is asking if you're coming back to the Club Room. And for the record sir, I think that would be a good idea. He says you can address the troops later."

"We're fine here for a bit," Jack replied, "it reminds me of my college bar mosh pit days." He could see from the look on Agent Mullen's face that his humor wasn't welcome. "We'll be fine. These are our people. They're just a little excited."

The one occupant of the ballroom who did not look excited—the aging porter—continued to move forward in the dense crowd. He was less than eighty feet away.

10:15PM

DeMarco continued down the dim hallway, aiming for the last door on the left. The chair outside was empty, deserted by the Secret Service agent he'd seen earlier. DeMarco reached inside his sleeve, found the handle and pulled the alanine blade free.

The door was unlocked. He pushed it open, stepped inside and quickly closed it behind him. Two dim emergency lights provided the only illumination, enough to see there were no staff inside.

Just her.

"Hello, Mrs. Sanborn," he said softly.

He studied Sarah's face from a distance. She seemed sedated. Her hands were carefully folded, her smooth features peaceful, like a dozing Mona Lisa. She was beautiful.

So was Gracie.

He turned his focus to the task at hand. *An eye for an eye.* It didn't matter that someone else had orchestrated this moment, because it remained his opportunity to avenge Gracie's death. As a father. As a man. There could be no remedy for the pain he'd endured. His daughter had been left to be torn apart by wolves in suits, until she could bear it no longer. There had been no protection for her then. And now the only thing left was vengeance; the one responsible would feel the same pain that he'd felt, every day, for years on end.

The meticulous instructions on the black card had armed DeMarco and put him in the room, but as he pictured Jack's face, twisted and swollen by an anguish that would never leave, he had what he felt was the most poetically perfect idea of his life. To take her the same way Gracie had been taken.

He tucked the blade into a baggy pants pocket and removed his belt. He'd strangle every ounce of life out of her, just as Gracie had done in a courthouse storeroom, hanging herself instead of facing Elenestro's bastard lawyers one more time. It was perfect.

Eye for an eye.

He could feel his pulse rising, the thudding rhythm radiating down through hands that needed to get to work now. The seconds were ticking by, and that agent wouldn't stay gone forever.

DeMarco pulled the belt taut and stepped forward, the leather creaking in his grip. There were voices in the corridor.

Do it now.

He took a deep breath and extended the belt toward Sarah's throat.

"Hello, Detective Conti," Sarah said, her eyes flicking open. Her expression remained placid, with no hint of surprise or fear. "I know why you're here."

*****10:16PM*****

DeMarco blinked hard, momentarily paralyzed at being greeted by the woman he was there to kill. *How the hell did she know I was coming? How does she know my name?*

"Of course I remember you, Detective," she replied, as if reading his thoughts. "How could I not?"

"You don't know me," DeMarco said, hating the shake in his own voice.

"No, that's true. We don't exactly know each other. But I was in the courtroom during much of that trial. I saw how you supported your daughter."

"You can't even say her name." DeMarco's knuckles tightened around the belt.

Stop talking and do it, he told himself.

"Gracie. Such a beautiful name."

DeMarco's mouth went dry. He fought to control the thoughts suddenly exploding in his brain. "You knew I was coming?" he finally rasped.

Sarah shook her head, momentarily looking lost in thought. "No . . . no, I didn't know that, but . . ." She seemed to wrestle with a realization of some kind. "I remember it all. Everything."

"The fuck you do," DeMarco said, his voice like acid. "If you did, you'd know I'm not a detective anymore, thanks to your fucking husband." *Who deserves to feel the pain living inside of me.* He thought about pulling the knife from his pocket and plunging it down her throat.

"And you're here for revenge, for your daughter."

DeMarco stood frozen. Sarah's calmness, when she knew he was there to kill her, was something his mind refused to process. So, he just stared back at her, his expression making the truth plain.

Sarah nodded slowly. "I see."

Don't let her fuck with you.

He paced by the bed, his thoughts jumbled like a broken kaleidoscope. "I lost everything! EVERYTHING!" His mind raced. Things weren't going as planned. Things weren't going at all. *What the fuck is wrong with me?*

"I know," Sarah said. "And doing nothing would feel wrong."

"You need to shut your fucking mouth," DeMarco told her.

"We lost our daughter too. It was two months ago. Right here in this hospital."

"What are you talking about?"

"We lost our daughter at birth. I'm not saying it's the same, but I thought you should know."

"Your dead daughter has *nothing* to do with me!"

"Or yours with me, Detective. Can't you see that? You're in so much pain, it's pushing you over the edge . . . What would Gracie think of you now?"

"Don't you say her name," DeMarco warned, and stepped close.

Sarah's eyes were soft as she searched DeMarco's face. "What will she think of you five minutes from now?"

Goddamn her for making him think that.

"Is this how you honor her memory?"

DeMarco pulled the blade from his pocket and pressed the point to her throat. A little bead of blood formed at its tip. His breathing was labored. He felt like he was about to pass out.

"The truth is," Sarah continued, "this isn't about her at all. This is about you. There was no way you could have known. No way you could have stopped her. You need to stop blaming yourself."

"I don't blame myself. I blame your fucking husband."

"Yet here you are, your knife at my throat . . . Jack had a nervous breakdown that day. He still wakes up screaming, calling your daughter's name and wondering what he could have done differently. Just like you."

The blade wavered in DeMarco's hand, further piercing Sarah's skin.

"It's Elenestro's fault," she said calmly, "and he's already in hell."

DeMarco's arm suddenly felt very heavy, and his eyes blurred with tears. He could feel the hatred he carried receding. Diminishing. He jerked the blade back, as if surprised to find himself holding it, and dropped it on the bed. But where the hell could he go from here?

"You live your life, Detective, that's what's next."

"What?"

"That's all we can do for those we've lost. Live our lives in a way they'd be proud of."

DeMarco stared at her. It was like she read his mind. Part of him felt violated, like he'd somehow been tricked, or hacked. But a much larger part of him felt the welcome release of knowing that someone, somewhere, understood what he'd been going through. And if that someone had to be Jack Sanborn's wife, so be it.

The door opened suddenly, two of the hospital staff rushing in with flashlights. Sarah swept the bed sheet over the knife.

The first staff member looked at DeMarco. "Who the hell are you?"

The other looked to Sarah. "Mrs. Sanborn, are you all right? Ma'am, are you bleeding?"

She held a tissue to her throat. "Oh, that. I managed to cut myself, fumbling in the dark. Sorry. This is an old friend. We were just catching up on things as the lights went."

"Right," DeMarco added, wondering if anyone bought that line, given his staff uniform and unfamiliar face. He looked uncertainly to Sarah.

"Well," Sarah told him. "I know you have someplace to be. Don't forget what we talked about . . ."

DeMarco nodded awkwardly. He thought he felt the beginnings of a smile, but it had been so long he couldn't be sure. He left the room and made his way back down the hall, passing the Secret Service agent as he went. And as he left the hospital, he thought about where a life that honored Gracie might lead him, in the little time he had left.

CHAPTER 51

CLAY OVERTON SHIFTED in his office chair. His crowded office should have been abuzz with chatter after regaining the lead with the Virginia and Ohio wins, but instead an odd quiet had settled over the room. The Speaker sat quietly behind his desk, his eyes rarely leaving the screens other than to occasionally look at his watch. A half-dozen staffers were scattered around the office, watching their boss' cues carefully as Anton stood watchfully by the door.

O'Shea finally spoke up, his gaze still on the newsfeeds. "Perez's lead in California is down to half a point . . . I don't think he's going to hold on. His last-ditch message to tamp down his supporters might be working."

"Only a Democrat could win at losing," Overton replied, chuckling at his own joke, which visibly relaxed everyone in the room, except O'Shea.

"We're a point down in New York," O'Shea added, "Down in California by only a half-point . . . but as out of body as it feels . . . I'm pulling for Perez right now so this thing at least goes to the House."

"Arizona and Nevada?" one of the other staffers finally spoke up.

"Not enough if Sanborn takes New York as well as California," O'Shea replied, eyeing the white board on the other side of the office suspiciously.

Overton shot a disappointed look at him for giving the enemy the respect of using his proper name but said nothing.

Before Overton turned his attention back to the screen, he felt Anton's eyes on him. He glanced his way. Seeing his large hands folded in front of his waist instead of clasped behind him, Overton noted that Anton's index finger was positioned directly over the face of his wristwatch.

Almost time.

10:27PM

Angel had always been comfortable working in dense crowds, which made the Carolina Inn ballroom the perfect setting for him to complete his work. Sightlines were constantly shifting, and noise was a constant distraction for any protective detail, and he welcomed the combination.

He carried a small serving tray under his arm, continuing to look like someone harmful only to a stiff drink after their shift was over. He was now less than forty feet from his target. Soon, it would be too late to stop him.

He was jostled by attendees on both sides as he continued forward. The big screens scattered everywhere flashed suddenly and called New York for Sanborn. Hundreds of supporters seemed to leave their feet in unison. Angel used the momentary chaos to close the distance, glancing off several exuberant volunteers. He felt another body bump into him solidly. Then he felt a pair of hands press down. For an instant, he thought a Secret Service agent had made him. But when he turned, he saw a mousy, freckle-faced young volunteer.

"Sorry!!" she cried excitedly, "I almost fell . . . We're sooooo close!!" She continued to grip him tightly, as if trying to emphasize the point. His instinct was to remove the girl's clamped hands and move on. But before he could act on that thought, he had a better idea.

10:29PM

Clay Overton leaned back in his chair. He reached for the remote and turned the volume way up on one of the screens. The chatter from the staffers gathered around him fell to a hush, all of them assuming Overton knew something was about to break.

The truth was he just wanted to drown out their interminable noise.

The urgent voice of AGN's Chaaya Bandari cut off her panel of election experts and managed to draw Overton's attention.

. . . I'm sorry to interrupt you Judy, but the AGN election center is now ready to call Texas as well as Arizona for Senator Overton, which catapults him solidly back in front with two hundred and fifty-four electoral votes . . .

"Two-fifty-four," O'Shea repeated, fighting to pull his bulging frame from a club chair. "It's like a juicy steak you can smell but can't put a fork in."

"Which means what, exactly?" said one of the staffers.

"It means, you imbecile," O'Shea replied, "that we're so close . . . But without New York, we're stuck at two fifty-four."

"So, we either close the gap in California . . ." the staffer replied, glancing in Overton's direction.

"The proverbial photo finish," Overton announced. He rose and slipped on his jacket. Anton opened the door, and they left together.

*****10:31PM*****

Jack answered a video call from Sarah's doctor. It was her first call via video, which made him fear the worst—but the image that greeted him was Sarah's. "Babe, you're awake!" he said.

Sarah beamed back at him. "I can hardly hear you."

"I'm in the main ballroom," Jack said, "it's loud here. How do you feel?"

"I feel great."

"When did you wake up?"

"A few minutes ago. We had a bit of excitement here, but I'll tell you about it later. It's all good, my love."

Jack could sense something strange in her voice, but didn't want to probe mere moments after Sarah woke up. "Okay . . . great," he said.

"So, are we winning? What did I miss?"

"It's all down to California," Jack told her. "Which is exactly what Ethan predicted. It's gonna be tight."

"I can't believe this is happening," Sarah said. "Will you keep me on the phone with you?"

"Absolutely. Check out the scene here. It's intense." He flipped the phone around and held it up high so Sarah could share in the view.

As the anticipation in the room continued to build around Jack, the three agents kept their eye on the crowd that seemed to be closing in around them.

10:32PM

Angel had always been exceptional at switching off his emotions. *Emotions got you killed.* But now, in the final assignment of his career, he decided there was something poetic and beautiful about letting his long-neglected emotions seep in—for a very specific purpose.

A few moments of reflection on the choices he'd made in his life, and the daughter he'd effectively orphaned should be sufficient.

"Are you okay?" the mousey volunteer asked. "Why are you crying?"

Angel looked back at the young girl with a tenderness in his eyes. "I'm happy," he replied. "That this terribleness will all be over soon." And he meant every word of it.

"Me too," the girl said, still gripping his arms. "We're almost there!"

He nodded, knowing she'd misunderstood his meaning perfectly. Just as others, closer to the target, would likely also do. And what better final cover than being not just a harmless old porter—but a weepy, jubilant old porter who'd longed for a better America all his life.

This will be my finest work, he thought.

His face crinkled into a misty smile as he patted the girl's arm and moved past her. *Thank you, my dear.* Less than fifteen feet to go . . .

*****10:33PM*****

The Speaker gazed out the window of his armored limousine. Anton sat across from him as they made the eight-minute drive from the Capitol to the sprawling DC Convention Center. Overton couldn't remember seeing DC's streets so empty. Windows were boarded up, and heaps of garbage bags were piled at the curb. Even the small village of tents set up in Chinatown Park looked dormant. Usually, someone was burning something in there. He'd clean that up soon. That and everything else.

The limousine made its final turn onto Seventh Avenue and approached the Convention Center. The expected crowd of supporters and detractors waited by the barricaded entrance. Both sides sprang to life at Overton's approach, cheering or jeering in accordance with their political persuasions. Overton ignored them all.

The limo pulled to the curb. A Secret Service agent opened the door and Overton stepped out. He waved briefly to the crowd and joined waiting RNC Chair Jim Harper, a large man who never missed a photo-op.

"Look at you," Harper said, pumping Overton's hand for the cameras. "Always early."

"Look at you . . . Always fat," Overton replied as they smiled for the cameras.

"I don't know where we are, Mr. Speaker," Jim said, leaning close. "I expected New York, but losing Pennsylvania was a fucking gut punch we didn't need."

Overton knew that was code for *the RNC spent more in Pennsylvania than some countries' damned GDP; how the hell did you not win there?*

A loud scream spared him the need to respond. Overton looked back past the limo and saw a large figure in an oversized coat. He'd jumped the barricade and was sprinting straight toward him. Before he could close the distance two Secret Service agents tackled him to the ground. An instant later the three of them were blown to pieces by whatever the attacker had been wearing. Overton, Anton and Harper ducked down beside the armored limo, which shielded them from the blast. Body fragments rained down around them.

The next thing Overton knew, Anton was stuffing him back in the limo and climbing in after him, yelling at the driver to take off. Overton covered his ringing ears with shaky hands, flashing back to the roadside IED that took out his vehicle in Syria. He forced himself to take deep breaths. He dimly noticed a body roll up over the hood and ricochet off the windshield as the vehicle accelerated away.

*****10:34PM*****

Jack and Jade stood in the ballroom, watching Ethan and Lewis make their way toward them through the crowd. Sarah remained on the phone, taking in what she could of the electric scene.

"He still won't make a call on whether we'll win California," Lewis said when they arrived.

"Too close to say," Ethan replied. "Even my models have limits."

Jack looked back at Sarah on his phone to keep her updated. "Lewis and Ethan just got here."

The huge screens along the side wall suddenly showed the familiar outline of the state of California. The entire room fell silent as a newscaster spoke—

. . . We can now report that independent Jack Sanborn is projected to win California, making him the first independent since George Washington to be President of the United States!

The room erupted in wild cheers and applause. Jack felt an explosion of emotion that nearly lifted him off his feet.

"WE WON!!!" Lewis yelled, and grabbed Jack in a massive bear hug. "You fucking did it!!"

"Sarah!!" Jack yelled into the phone. "Oh my God, we did it!!"

"I can't believe it!" Sarah cried.

The whole room was jumping and screaming and tossing things

in the air. Thousands of red-white-and-blue balloons fell from the ceiling as booming music filled the space.

Jack looked down at the phone to see Sarah's beaming face, but had to put the phone to his ear to hear her. "I'm so proud of you, Jack! You did it!"

"I love you!" Jack told her.

Beside him, Agent Mullen had a finger pressed to his ear, trying to hear something coming over his earpiece. Something about Overton. "SAY AGAIN," he repeated as he spoke into his cuff microphone, the intensity of the noise overpowering a message about Speaker Overton. Given the noise, it would take Agent Mullen seven more seconds to hear the words in his earpiece clearly enough to act.

The outpouring of emotion from the crowd was unlike anything Jack had ever seen. It seemed everyone wanted to high-five or hug him, people he knew and mostly didn't, many with tears streaming down their faces. Jack just kept repeating "We did it!" as if he could hardly believe it himself.

"Mr. President," a gravelly voice said from behind.

Jack turned and looked into the teary eyes of an older Carolina Inn employee who'd also been swept up in the moment. His expression had a gentle but almost resigned quality, like he'd just been relieved of a lifelong burden. Jack was about to say something when the man seemed to stumble forward.

Jack reached out to catch him and felt a searing pain in his chest. He saw a flash of grey and red as something was pulled out of him. Before he could process that, three gunshots exploded beside him. Jack felt something spatter on his cheek that felt wet. Then everything went black.

10:35PM

Sarah jumped up from the hospital bed, screaming into the phone. *"Jack! JACK!"* His phone was on the floor, because all she could see were feet, legs, and glimpses of balloons.

The doctor rushed over and grabbed her arm. "Careful! You're still hooked to the IV."

"Turn up the TV!!" She grabbed the IV line that was plugged into her arm "And get this damned thing out of me."

A young Secret Service agent came in from the hallway. "Mrs. Sanborn, you need to stay calm."

"What just happened!? Tell me!" Her eyes pivoted wildly between the phone in her hand and the agent who was unsure how to respond, his own finger pressed to his ear as he listened for an update.

"I don't know any details yet, Mrs. Sanborn," the agent said.

The TV showed the ballroom in complete chaos. The words at the bottom of the screen froze Sarah's heart in her chest.

OVERTON/SANBORN DUAL ASSASSINATION ATTEMPTS
"Oh, my God."

CHAPTER 52

10:37PM

CLAY OVERTON MANAGED TO SIT upright as the limousine hurtled through the streets of DC, but the wrenching turns weren't doing much to quell the waves of nausea radiating through his body.

"Where are we going?" he finally asked, his breathing approaching normal. "Assuming we get there in one piece."

"GW hospital," Anton replied. "Side entrance," he added, speaking through the interior window where an agent behind the wheel was driving like his life depended on it. "And try not to kill us."

Overton's mind had cleared enough to recall that he hadn't been in a manually driven car in several years. He realized that was an odd thought. "No need to go there," he said. "I'm fine."

"Sir, we're *going* to the hospital," Anton said firmly. "You're bleeding."

Overton saw the blood on his hand, and wondered where it came from. He checked his shirt and pants for holes.

Anton pressed a finger to one ear, listening on his earpiece. He nodded but his face revealed nothing. After a moment he spoke loudly in the direction of the driver. "There's been an attempt on Sanborn as well."

"Copy that." the agent replied, not looking back.

As the car sped towards GW the two men in the back did not speak. After a moment, Overton pulled a handkerchief from his jacket pocket and slowly began to wipe the blood from the back of his hand.

10:39PM

Jonah Mullen had known since he was seventeen that he wanted to be a Secret Service agent. He graduated first in his class at Glynco, where Secret Service recruits trained, and had the Presidential Protection Division on his mind from day one. Four weeks ago, he was assigned to cover an emerging independent candidate who was suddenly polling high enough to be given Secret Service protection. It was an odd way to reach the life summit he'd strived towards for fifteen years, but he accepted the job with as much pride as if Jack Sanborn were POTUS himself.

Mullen didn't have time to contemplate the possibility that his PPD career may be the shortest in Secret Service history, but as his body continued to pump adrenaline the thought ricocheted around the recesses of his mind.

His reaction in the ballroom may have been a second or two slow, but his aim had certainly been true. The first two bullets had hit the assassin somewhere in the chest, the proverbial double tap almost instinctive, but the aging white-haired man inexplicably did not immediately fall. The third shot came a fraction later, traveling through a falling balloon and then spraying the elder man's brains into the air in a red plume that splattered anyone in proximity.

After plugging the wound and barreling through the ballroom crowd, Agent Mullen and two other agents practically sprinted down the main hallway, carrying an unconscious Jack Sanborn like a battering ram. The ambulance was waiting at the front door. Two Secret Service medics helped load Jack inside. Mullen climbed in after them.

Someone slammed the doors closed and the ambulance lurched forward, arcing sharply as it traversed the Inn's rounded front drive at impressive speed, its siren blaring.

Mullen watched the medics work as the ambulance raced towards the hospital.

"BP eighty over sixty. Pulse one-thirty."

"Looks like a single-entry wound, left side of chest at the anterior axillary line . . . Possible ventricle puncture."

"Respiration shallow . . . You seeing those neck veins?"

"Yeah, they look distended. Possible pericardial tamponade."

"What does that mean?" Mullen asked them, unable to sit passively.

"It means the knife probably hit his heart, causing the sac around it to fill with blood, which is why these veins in his neck are bulging as the blood flow starts to back up."

Mullen swallowed hard.

"We don't have time to get a drain going in here, but we got a probable haemopneumothorax as well." The paramedic shook his head.

"What's that?" Mullen asked again.

The paramedic replied calmly, not missing a beat as he stuck a needle in Jack's arm. "It means air and blood in the chest cavity from a punctured lung."

"BP sixty-five over forty," announced the second paramedic loudly.

"Make this thing fly!" the first paramedic shouted back at the agent behind the steering wheel.

"I am!" came the driver's reply just as Jonah felt his stomach fall as the ambulance crested a hill.

"Fly faster!" Jonah added.

10:41PM

Sarah stood to face the Secret Service agent blocking the door of her hospital room. She had just finished lacing up the trainers she had found in the closet along with one of her sweatsuits. "I'm not staying in this room—I'm going to Jack."

"Please, ma'am," the young agent said. "You're more secure here, and I'm sure Mr. Sanborn will be taken right into surgery. We can get updates from here."

"So, you know he's alive then." Sarah said as she stepped closer. "Has someone on that thing in your ear told you that?"

The agent shifted uncomfortably. "Uh, no, ma'am, I don't have a status at the moment."

Sarah stepped past him, bumping his shoulder. "Coming?"

The agent quickly followed her, mumbling into his cuff microphone as he walked quickly to keep up, breaking into a jog a moment later once Sarah did the same.

Once on the ground floor, Sarah followed the signs to the emergency room and arrived in time to spot Jack being wheeled in. Hospital staff tried to stop her from reaching him. "That's my husband!" she said.

Agent Mullen waved a hand at the hospital staff. "It's fine. She's clear."

Sarah pushed her way through to Jack's side. His eyes were closed, his face covered by an oxygen mask. His shirt had been cut open, and bloody bandages secured under his left arm. "I'm here, Babe, I'm right here!"

A doctor placed his hand on her arm. "Mrs. Sanborn, please. We need to get him to the OR right away."

Another doctor spoke as the gurney continued to move down the hallway. "Respiration thirty and shallow . . . we will need to intubate once we get him drained."

"What's the BP?"

"Sixty over forty . . . barely."

"Agent Mullen," Sarah said, "what happened?"

"He was stabbed in the chest Ma'am . . . I'm so—"

"Don't even say it," Sarah interrupted, her mind, despite the wave of panic that was engulfing her, beginning to grapple with the knowledge that there were three assassination attempts in one night, including her own. *No damned way that's random.*

A doctor intercepted Sarah as the gurney reached a set of steel doors. "This is as far as you go, Mrs. Sanborn. We'll keep the agents informed." He nodded at the young agent from Sarah's hospital room standing beside her.

"Please," Sarah said. "Don't let my husband die."

"We'll do our best," the doctor said, and vanished through the doors that were closing behind him.

Sarah leaned her hands and forehead against the closed doors and began to tremble. The magnetic locks deep within the heavy doors thunked loudly, causing her to flinch as the jarring sound ran through her like a rifle shot. Sarah then slipped down into a crouch, put her face in her hands and began to sob.

11:35PM

A few minutes later, Sarah sat numbly in a small private waiting room inside the UNC trauma wing, feeling utterly spent but trying to prepare herself for whatever came next. Agent Mullen sat in a chair across from her.

Sarah looked up as Lewis entered the room with Jade and Ethan. She stood to accept Lewis' embrace and buried her head in his shoulder. "My life doesn't work without him."

"I know . . . Have you heard anything from the doctors yet?"

"Not yet," she replied as she pulled back from him. "But they said every fifteen minutes."

"Agent Mullen," Lewis said, "what do we know about the guy?"

"DNA still being processed. Shouldn't be much longer . . . But with that type of weapon designed to get through screening, clearly, this guy was professional."

"Any connection with the attempt on Overton?" Jade asked.

Mullen shook his head. "Too soon to know."

"No, it isn't," Ethan announced. "The odds of these two attempts having no connection are infinitesimally small."

Mullen shot him a harsh look in reply.

Sarah contemplated informing the group about her unexpected visitor, but she held back for the moment. DeMarco Conti was no hired professional; of this she was certain, his motives were personal.

"Well, one thing for sure, agent," Lewis said, "You probably saved his life."

"I'm not sure I'd say that," Mullen replied.

"Three shots in heavy traffic, before he could stab a second time."

Mullen gazed at the floor, unable to accept praise while the man he'd pledged to protect was fighting for his life.

They all turned as a gowned trauma surgeon rounded the corner and joined them in the waiting room.

"He's stable right now, Mrs. Sanborn, but it's going to be a long procedure. The weapon did pierce the left ventricle and he's lost a lot of blood, but the major arteries don't appear to have been hit so . . . we have a good chance."

"You can survive being stabbed in the heart?" Jade asked, a look of surprise on her face.

The doctor nodded. "Heart punctures actually have a fifty-percent survival rate."

"Sixty-one percent," Ethan interrupted, prompting a sharp look from the doctor, "using the most recent data."

The doctor looked back at Sarah. "He also has a collapsed lung, but we're dealing with that. The heart wound is our greatest concern. We'll keep the updates coming as often as we can, Mrs. Sanborn."

"Thank you."

The surgeon departed as Agent Mullen put a finger to his ear and then murmured something over his mic in reply.

"Anything to report?" Lewis asked.

"President Perez just put the military on high alert."

"Was he targeted as well?" Jade asked.

"Not that we know of, but I guess POTUS doesn't believe in coincidences either."

11:40PM

Clay Overton stood in the GW hospital examination room, buttoning his white dress shirt. It was wrinkled and dirty, the collar flecked with someone else's blood. With one bandaged finger and a partially wrapped hand, the buttoning was slow going. Anton and O'Shea stood by the door.

"Need some help?" O'Shea asked.

"You can do my fly if you want," Overton replied.

O'Shea ignored that. "The lawyers are gearing up for battle," he said. They both knew that if the president-elect died before his vice president was confirmed by election or by both Houses outside of an election, then Overton—as Speaker of the House—was next in line for the Presidency.

It was considerably less evident what would happen if the president-elect survived but was incapacitated.

"Do you want to review their plans?" O'Shea asked.

"Premature, given our dear professor is still in surgery. But tell them I expect nothing less than perfection . . . In the meantime, let's go downstairs and make sure the world knows someone's still running this fucking country."

"Do you want to clean up first?"

Overton looked at his bloodstained shirt, and the bit of what he assumed was flesh or brain matter on his shoulder. "No. It's perfect."

*****11:45PM*****

Sarah nursed a coffee in the waiting room, her back to the muted TV. The others watched as the remaining states were called, if only to distract themselves until there was further news on Jack.

"How did we not win Hawaii?" Lewis muttered to himself.

Sarah looked at her watch. It had been less than fifteen minutes since the doctor had given the last update, but to her it felt like hours.

"I'm surprised it took his Dark Lordship so long," Lewis said as Overton appeared on the TV screen, approaching a podium in what looked like a hospital lobby. "He doesn't look too bad, considering he was almost blown up."

"Can we turn that up?" Sarah asked. Lewis cranked up the volume.

Reporters shouted questions at Overton, who held his arm close to his chest, showing off his bandaged hand. He paused a moment before speaking, which gave the cameras time to focus on his bloody shirt. His hair was slightly unkempt.

"Going for the Jackie O look," Jade noted coldly.

"Please," Sarah said, calling for silence.

"My fellow Americans," Overton began, as if he were president, *"great democracies invite great adversaries. And tonight, we have witnessed another attack on our very democracy, on its leaders, and on the principles for which we stand . . . But once more America continues unbowed. I stand here before you by the grace of the Lord and the great sacrifice of two incredibly brave Secret Service agents. My heart goes out to their families . . . And to Mrs. Sarah Sanborn and her husband Jack Sanborn . . ."*

"That's president-elect Sanborn to you, pal," Lewis said, only to be shushed by Sarah who had stepped closer to the screen. She seemed to be studying Overton closely.

"I would ask that all Americans pray for Jack Sanborn's full recovery from this vicious attack, and I pledge to all Americans now and to our allies, and especially to our enemies, that the perpetrators of these coordinated attacks on the very fabric of our nation will be swiftly brought to justice . . . Thank you and good night."

Overton turned and left the room, ignoring the chorus of questions that followed.

Lewis shook his head. "That prick never misses an opportunity."

"He missed a rather big one tonight," Ethan noted dryly.

"Lewis," Sarah said, "would you ask Mr. Overton if he'd come and see me, please?"

CHAPTER 53

*****6:55AM*****

EVERY TIME THROUGH THE NIGHT when a doctor entered the waiting room, Sarah could tell by looking at them what the message would be before the words were spoken. Not every detail, but the crux of the news to come, like an athlete who knows where the ball is about to go next.

Sarah was becoming convinced that her experimental treatment had somehow given her a kind of . . . hyperacuity, at least when it came to people's emotional state and her own recall. It was the same thing that allowed her to read DeMarco earlier—and probably saved her life.

Just after dawn, when the doctor returned, Sarah could tell it was good news. She didn't know how—his gait, his posture, *something*—but she knew. "He's going to make it," the doctor said, and offered a weary smile. Sarah hugged him. *"Thank you, thank you . . ."* She started sobbing, and the others came in for a group hug. Even Ethan, who leaned in awkwardly.

After a moment, the doctor continued. "The puncture in the left ventricle was much deeper than we thought. That's why the surgery was so long. But the repairs look like they're holding well."

"And his lung?" Sarah asked.

"Lung tissue heals quickly once the hole's closed and the lung's reinflated. I don't foresee any further problems there."

"Thank you again. When can I see him?"

"It'll be a while yet. They're moving him into ICU recovery now. He may be up for a short visit by late afternoon." He scanned the other faces in the room. "Just one, though."

*****7:30AM*****

Agent Mullen stepped inside the private ICU waiting room and closed the door. Sarah looked up at him from her chair. Lewis, Jade and Ethan were asleep. "Ma'am . . . Speaker Overton has arrived. He's down the hall in a private room."

"What's happening?" Lewis said, rubbing his eyes.

"My visitor has arrived," Sarah said, and stood up.

"I should go with you," Lewis said.

"I'd like to speak with him alone."

"You need to be careful," Lewis advised. "Don't let your guard down. And don't let the fact that he arranged for your treatment sway you."

Sarah nodded, more to herself than to anyone else. "Let's just say my guard is at full strength."

She and Mullen left the waiting room and made their way down the hall. Overton's room was easy to find; there were two Secret Service agents standing outside. "Looks like we're outnumbered," Sarah remarked as she and Agent Mullen closed the distance, "two of them . . . one of you."

"We can take 'em, ma'am," Mullen assured her.

The oldest agent said, "You can go in, Mrs. Sanborn." He then turned to Mullen, and his voice became considerably less friendly. "You can stay here."

Sarah instantly read the agents' silent judgment of Mullen for what had happened on his watch. She paused outside the doorway. "He saved my husband's life last night by taking down his assassin in a fraction of a second. An assassin someone else let into a supposedly secure building. Meanwhile, your protectee was probably saved by his limo." With that, she opened the door and stepped inside.

"Mrs. Sanborn." Overton extended his hand. Sarah took it as

gracefully as she could. "I just heard the news that your husband came through the surgery. Thank God for American medical care." He put on his best preacher smile and placed a second hand on top of hers. Sarah saw and smelled that he'd scrubbed up since last night's TV appearance, but the bandage and wrapped finger remained.

"Thank you, Mr. Overton," she replied, and moved to sit. Overton followed suit. "And thank you for coming to see me on such short notice. You've had a long night too. I'm glad you're okay."

"Thank you. But my night wasn't quite like yours. And please, call me Clay."

Sarah nodded, studied his face and contemplated his choice of words, taking in as much as she could. "It's good we can speak privately . . . Clay."

"Of course, and may I call you Sarah?"

"Not yet," Sarah said without a hint of discomfort. "We should talk first."

"A woman after my own heart: right to the point. If you called me here on your husband's behalf to get my concession, though, I have to tell you that I don't believe we're quite there yet." He leaned forward, eyes gleaming brightly, "But I will say your husband's campaign was clearly a message we must use to instill immediate reforms. And we will, but at this very moment my focus is on the safety and recovery of your husband and bringing justice to those behind these attacks."

"Of course it is, I understand that. But I didn't ask you here to talk about politics, Clay." Sarah's Mona Lisa smile emerged for a brief moment. *Nor did I ask you here to talk about the fact that my husband was just elected President, and you were not.*

"Oh." The Speaker shifted in his chair, revealing to Sarah his discomfort at not having a clear read on the situation. "How can I help, then? I understand you know that I provided some assistance to ensure your treatment was in place." He said this with the slightest of bows, which Sarah found an odd reveal. "But perhaps I can be of service in some other way as well . . ."

"You can be," Sarah replied, eyeing him evenly.

"By all means." Overton extended his palm in a sweeping motion. "Just say the word and it shall be done."

"Admit that all of this was you."

His features barely twitched, but she could see his mind was scrambling to interpret her statement. Watching him on the TV, delivering his speech after the attacks, the signals were there in every mannerism, every intonation. And she was *almost* certain she was right. But she needed to witness his reaction to being confronted in person, with no time to prepare or rehearse. It was the only way to be sure. And as she studied his face now, certain was exactly what she became.

"I'm sorry, Mrs. Sanborn, I'm not sure what you mean. If you're referring to your treatment, as I said—"

"Not just that, Clay. Everything . . . last night . . . I know it was you."

There was a flicker in his eyes that he tried to cover with a blink.

"You're obviously not well, Mrs. Sanborn. I'm sure this has all been a terrible shock to someone who's been through a lot already. I think we could all do with some rest."

"I'm sure you've covered your tracks well, Clay. But I can see the truth in your eyes, your face, in everything about you. That's why I asked you here, to see for myself. To be sure . . ."

Overton remained silent.

"Heightened perception is a side effect of the treatment you arranged for me. Or, I should say, my treatment that you arranged for your own benefit. Ironic, don't you think? You'd have been better off with the widower bump."

"I'm sorry," Overton said, rising slowly. "This is utter madness."

Sarah rose before him. "On behalf of everyone everywhere, thank you for finally noticing, Mr. Speaker."

Overton jerked a thumb at his chest. "I was almost killed as well, Mrs. Sanborn."

"Correct," Sarah replied coolly as she returned his stare, "you *almost* were. And I'm sure someone will be looking into that."

Overton thrust his chin in the air and stomped out the door, but there was no hiding the fear in his eyes.

10:40AM

Three hours later, Sarah stood at Jack's bedside. His eyes were closed and slightly sunken, his skin pale. She watched for a time as his chest rose and fell. As though she was seeing a photograph, her mind flashed back to their first night together, at her apartment in New York. They'd been dating for two months. She woke up the next morning and watched him sleep, wondering if he might be the one.

Watching him now, knowing his eyes might have closed forever, sent a warm flood of gratitude through her body.

You're still here. We're both still here.

"Aren't you supposed to be the one in the hospital?" Jack murmured quietly. He smiled faintly and cracked his eyes open.

Sarah's eyes welled up. She fought the urge to throw herself at him, and showered him with kisses instead. "I almost lost you," she said, and took his hand.

"I guess that makes us even then," Jack said.

She kissed him on the lips.

"No more hospitals after this," Jack said, squeezing her hand. "Not for a while, anyway."

"I'm with you there," Sarah said. "How do you feel?"

Jack shifted on the bed and winced. "Like someone who's been stabbed . . . I think. Who was it?"

"A professional, hired by someone else. Don't worry about that right now. You need to rest."

Jack played back the moment he was stabbed by someone who looked like a kindly grandfather. "Did he get away?"

"No. Agent Mullen killed him before he could stab you again."

"That was nice of him." He tried to remember the moment just before the attack, but drew a blank. His gaze flicked toward the window, and the sunlight streaming in. "What day is it?"

Sarah smiled. "Wednesday."

Jack's gaze snapped back to Sarah. "Wait . . . Did we . . . ?

She squeezed his hand. "Yeah, Babe," she said, voice breaking. "We won."

EPILOGUE—One Week Later

SARAH, LEWIS AND JADE STOOD in the hospital room, watching as Jack took his first bite of real food since the stabbing; Al's Burger Shack, one of his local favorites.

"It was a stabbing, not a heart attack," Lewis said, noticing Sarah's look of mild disapproval at the food choice. "And besides, it's the hospital food that'll kill you."

"All right," Jack said after downing his second bite. "My nurse-approved fifteen-minute workday starts now." He looked to the nurse in the corner with a smile. "Are you ready to time this?" She reached up and clicked an imaginary stopwatch with her thumb.

"It's a light list for today," Lewis said. "Just the VP thing." He pulled a file from his briefcase and slid it across the bed. "We're looking at January thirteenth for the referendum. We've gotten the candidate list down to five, but need to cut it to three, which we think is the right number of choices for the ballot."

"Down to five already," Jack said. "That was quick."

"Time is not our friend right now," Lewis told him. "I'm leaning toward Tabitha Kane."

"Former Arizona Senator?"

Lewis nodded. "I think tapping a DC heavyweight who left in disgust over the lack of reforms twenty years back sends an interesting message."

"She's not too old?" Jack asked.

"Are you too young?" Lewis asked. "There aren't a lot of young and departed DC reformers out there to pick from."

Jack looked at Jade. "Media reaction?"

"She was a Republican who turned independent, but didn't burn all her bridges in the process. So, she's not perfect, but also not a lightning rod for criticism. Definitely deserves to be on the list."

"Okay." Jack picked up the file. "Let me look at this for a day. What else?"

Lewis shook his head. "Like I said . . . light day today. Get some rest. We should have a list of cabinet options by tomorrow."

"That should be interesting," Jack said. "Especially Attorney General."

Lewis winced. "You're not thinking of pardoning Susan Pericote?"

"Maybe," Jack answered. "She'd be ready to come out guns blazing and unleash the Justice Department on the two-party monopoly."

"A lot of people will scream if you pardon her," Jade added.

"Tearing down the monopoly is the only reason anyone voted for me," Jack said. "And you know the House will fight an Attorney General nominee way harder than any other position. They know that person's main job will be to blow the duopoly wide open."

"So, she's the devil we all know, and could start on day one," Jade summarized.

"Exactly," Jack said. "No confirmation hearing required. And more importantly, I trust her. But we can talk all this tomorrow when we do the rest of the cabinet list."

"Guess that's about it for today then," Lewis said.

"One more thing before you two go," Sarah said, her tone serious. She looked to the nurse. "Could you leave us for five minutes, please?" The nurse nodded and left the room, closing the door behind her.

"What is it?" Jack asked.

She looked back at the group, and then her eyes came to rest on Jack. "I planned to tell *you* this first, but I kept putting it off."

"Are you okay?" Jack asked.

"I'm fine," Sarah said. She put a hand on her stomach. "And the baby's fine."

"Then what is it?"

"I can't prove it right now," Sarah said. "And it may be impossible to prove . . . But I know who tried to kill you."

THE END

Resources & How You
Can Make a Difference

WHEN I BEGAN WRITING *The Independent*, my only aim was to tell a great story. That all changed as I delved into the research phase of the project.

While I already knew it to be true, I was shocked by the extent to which the two major U.S. political parties have successfully restricted competition. There has been no single silver bullet. It has been the subtle work of decades that has built a large moat around the two-party system.

Moats, by design, are hard to cross. But with enough collective effort over time, the journey can be made.

Bottom line, the more we as citizens realize that the restricted political competition hurts us all, the more likely we are to get involved at a state level to support political reforms. The moat is not unassailable, and unlike medieval times, there need not be casualties in the process. It just takes persistence, patience, and time.

How, then, can we make a difference?

Supporting independent candidates for office is certainly one way to get involved, much like the support my protagonist Jack Sanborn received from an angry populace that mobilized quickly in vast numbers.

However, while it is not great fodder for a thriller, the real changes will come from election reform on a state-by-state level. Specifically, I suggest that anyone looking to support change look into the following initiatives and organizations (for more information, go to the Resources tab on my website, bradgoodwinauthor.com).

- Support advocacy and petition efforts for **non-partisan top four primaries** (helps ensure we get more centrist candidates to the ballot from the two parties, instead of the dark red and dark blue candidates that the hardcore political base tends to anoint in the current closed primary process).
- Support advocacy and petition efforts for **ranked choice voting** (helps ensure the candidate with the broadest appeal wins, and eliminates the "spoiler" argument that prevents many voters from voting for the candidate that truly represents their values. Look up Alaska ranked choice voting and you will see a great case study for change).
- Support advocacy and petition efforts for **non-partisan redistricting** (helps ensure seats in Congress are more often in play, instead of having districts so gerrymandered that there is no threat of an incumbent losing their seat).
- Look into the following organizations, all of which are making progress on the above means of voting reform: **RankTheVote, UniteAmerica, Divided We Fall, Common Cause, RepresentUS.**

The change can happen. It needs to happen. We can make it happen. Learn more at www.bradgoodwinauthor.com.

Acknowledgements

FOR THE PURPOSES OF PROVIDING a shortcut, and as an expression of thanks for providing added inspiration for this work of fiction, I enthusiastically refer you to the work of Katherine Gehl and Michael Porter, specifically their important essay *Why Competition in the Politics Industry is Failing America*. I came across their work when my story was nothing more than a rough outline. Their analysis both shocked me and compelled me to keep writing, even on the tough days when better words failed to emerge. While their work inspired me, any criticism to be levied after reading this novel is on me, not them.

Later in my writing process I discovered the foundational works of former Oklahoma Congressman Mickey Edwards, whose book *The Parties Versus the People* offers pragmatic solutions for political reform, as does former independent Senate candidate Greg Orman's insightful book, *A Declaration of Independents*. Added thanks to Lawrence Lessig for his educational and inspiring Ted Talk, "Lesterland", which I believe would spur even the most cynical among us into some form of action.

I would also like to thank Daniel Holt, Assistant Historian, US Senate Historical Office, for indulging and reacting to my hypothetical scenarios over and over. Again, any criticism of what may be considered constitutionally, politically or legally feasible in this work of fiction is on me and my own interpretations or presumptions of what could one day transpire, not on anyone else.

I will also confess, for the sake of brevity, there were instances when I chose to maneuver around a legal question instead of taking every single legal hurdle head on, thus over-extending the plotline (example: a large number of states currently require a VP candidate to be named in order to secure ballot access). I did my research, but if this or any other liberty taken disappointed any astute readers, my humble apologies. It is, after all, a work of futuristic fiction in which laws or their practical application can be subject to change.

Special thanks are required for the dedicated work of my editor, John Robert Marlow, who took me under his wing and sharpened my thinking and prose time and time and time again, always with patience, clarity and humor.

To my neighbor and fellow thriller writer, Mark Anthony Powers, who answered every single request for advice, no matter how mundane, thank you.

To Roy Lalonde and Anthony Buzzelli, both of whom stirred in me a greater reverence for stories well told, my thanks and gratitude.

To Sean Hayes and Monique Kavanagh, who took the time to listen and critique early drafts, so I was not reading aloud in an echo chamber, my humblest appreciation.

To my book designers, Adrijus Guscia amd Christy Day, and my publishing, web design, and book launch team, Martha Bullen, Jeremy Avenarius, Maggie McLaughlin, and Candice Jarrett, thank you. Without you, all is lost.

To the pioneers on my advance team (Beth, Shawn, Ted, Susan, Paula, Tanya, Clay, Rich, Chris, Jenn, Mike, Kelly, Sandra, Ruth, Sarah, Angela, Heather, Julie, Todd, and Olivia), you honor me with your time, support and wisdom. Thank you.

To Jonathan Harries, Eric Bishop, L.D. Beyer, Mikael Carlson and C.A. James, the gifts of your guidance and support have meant the world to me.

Lastly, words cannot express how grateful I am for the support and counsel of my wonderful partner, Marea. This project would never have happened without her endless encouragement; from the moment the idea was born on an interstate journey back to Chapel

Hill, to the thousand evenings I spent writing, re-writing and then re-writing again, to the endless readings she embraced with unconditional enthusiasm. Her belief in me never wavered . . . and made all the difference in the world. Thank you.

About the Author

BRAD GOODWIN is a globe-trotting marketing and general management executive with a lifelong passion for writing, storytelling, and well-crafted thrillers that keep the pages turning. *The Independent* is his debut novel, crafted in the quiet hours after his family went to sleep.

Brad grew up in the suburban sprawl of greater Toronto and studied economics and business at The University of Western Ontario. His 30-year international career in consumer goods has transplanted him from the shores of Milwaukee, Wisconsin to the rolling hills of Surrey, England. He now lives with his family among the loblolly pines of Chapel Hill, North Carolina.

When not working, writing, or spending time with family, Brad enjoys traveling, hiking, and eating anywhere new. His other life-long passions are learning to meditate without thinking of one of his characters and waiting for the Toronto Maple Leafs to win the Stanley Cup at least once during his lifetime.

To learn more or contact Brad, visit www.bradgoodwinauthor.com.

A Note from the Author

IF YOU'VE MADE IT THIS FAR, I'd like to express my heartfelt thanks for coming along on this political thriller ride. I hope that after you turn the final page, you will feel compelled to pause and contemplate what it would actually take to reform the US political system, and in particular how you, as a citizen, can play a role.

Motivating readers to action was not one of my aims as I began to craft this work of (hopefully entertaining) fiction. But, as the research hours piled up and sharpened my understanding of how the two-party duopoly has fortified itself, much to the detriment of everyday voters, my aim broadened.

If you enjoyed the book, please do me a kindness and leave a review on Amazon. It makes a real difference in the independent publishing world, and I do read every single one. Short or long, all reviews are gratefully received.

If you'd like to learn a bit more about Jack Sanborn and read the futuristic debate scene that was cut from the final manuscript, visit my website, www.bradgoodwinauthor.com. Please consider joining my mailing list and sharing your feedback on this book.

www.ingramcontent.com/pod-product-compliance
Lightning Source LLC
Chambersburg PA
CBHW071452140726
47997CB00005B/1691